A QUIVER OF MUSCLE, A CRY OF HATE

G'Kar felt something sharp press against his side. He looked down, saw the cold glitter of metal.

The Tuchanq was holding him at knifepoint.

The other Tuchanq came closer.

G'Kar remained as still as he could in the gently swaying car. He glanced sideways and up at the Tuchanq. "What do you want?"

The Tuchanq said loudly, "Revenge. You ravaged our planet, killed our people. You must die in return. All Narn must die. The Tuchanq will have revenge!"

G'Kar moved fast, slamming the harness upward into the chest of the Tuchanq in front of him. He leapt forward.

Too late. The knife slammed home into his side. . . .

D0695812

Look for

VOICES, BABYLON 5 BOOK #1
ACCUSATIONS, BABYLON 5 BOOK #2
BLOOD OATH, BABYLON 5 BOOK #3

in your local bookstore

BABYLON 5: CLARK'S LAW

Jim Mortimore

Based on the series by
J. Michael Straczynski

A Dell Book

Published by
Dell Publishing
a division of
Bantam Doubleday Dell Publishing Group, Inc.
1540 Broadway
New York, New York 10036

If you purchased this book without a cover you should be aware that this book is stolen property. It was reported as "unsold and destroyed" to the publisher and neither the author nor the publisher has received any payment for this "stripped book."

Based on the Warner Bros. television series *Babylon 5* created by J. Michael Straczynski. Copyright © 1994 by Warner Bros. Television.

Copyright © 1996 by Dell Publishing

All rights reserved. No part of this book may be reproduced or transmitted in any form or by any means, electronic or mechanical, including photocopying, recording, or by any information storage and retrieval system, without the written permission of the Publisher, except where permitted by law.

The trademark Dell® is registered in the U.S. Patent and Trademark Office.

ISBN: 0-440-22229-X

Printed in the United States of America

Published simultaneously in Canada

February 1996

10 9 8 7 6 5 4 3 2 1

OPM

For

Tim Keable
My last, best hope for a good story

And
Trees
All alone in the night?
Not if I have anything to say about it

And
Peter Darvill-Evans, Rebecca Levene, Kerri Sharp and
Andy Bodle
at Virgin Publishing.
For believing that where there's muck,
there's brass—
and sticking to it.
(The brass, that is—not the muck.)

In America, society's outrage over rising crime is such that few politicians can hope to win an election without declaring support for the death penalty.

From the UK Channel Four
television documentary
When the State Kills

I against my brother,
I and my brother against our cousin,
I, my brother and our cousin against the neighbours,
All of us against the foreigner.

—Bedouin proverb

CONTENTS

Prologue

Lies

How could he have known that with those three simple words he became responsible for the almost complete annihilation of the human race?

Earth Alliance President Luis Santiago
in his speech to the Senate
re Earth-Alien relations and the
inception of the Babylon Project, Earthdome, 2249

They came out of the immense gulf of space like ghosts, huge ships, more art than technology. By comparison the Earth ship DSEV *Amundsen* was little more than a clutch of battered tin boxes bolted rather haphazardly around a less than optimal frame. The alien ships were one-hundred-percent efficient. They were also utterly beautiful.

To Earthforce Captain Ellasai Ferdinand VI they were also utterly terrifying.

Even now, during the debriefing session in the amphitheaterlike Senate Chamber at Earthdome, as safe as it was possible to be anywhere in the Alliance, Ferdinand shuddered and sweated at the memory of them.

Efficient. Beautiful.

Deadly?

The truth was that as far as that particular facet of the alien ships was concerned, Ferdinand had no more idea than he had of what it might be like to hang glide naked from Olympus Mons. His experience of the alien ships extended no further than his first observation that they were the most efficient and beautiful artifacts he'd ever seen. It extended no further than this because in the first moments that the alien ships had appeared on his early warning systems and changed course, gun ports gaping ominously, to intercept the *Amundsen*, Ferdinand had ordered his gunnery officer to open fire with the full force of the most advanced weapons that Earthforce currently possessed.

Ferdinand had done something that all of his training and all his many years of experience had taught him he must never, ever do.

He had panicked.

The burst of plasma fire left the nearest alien ship drifting helplessly as Ferdinand spun the *Amundsen* about and initiated a jump-gate sequence. His last sight of the aliens, as the *Amundsen* vanished into the murky amber fog of hyperspace, was of the damaged ship erupting into a globe of light that for a brief moment burned as brightly as any sun.

The sight had left him sick and shaken. It had been many years since humanity's war with the Dilgar, and Ferdinand had only been peripherally involved with the fighting there. He was a man of peace, an explorer; his passion was to expand the limits of human knowledge and experience. He had never killed anyone in his life. The fact that he had made a mistake resulting in the destruction of a ship and the death of its entire crew, was nothing short of terrifying.

Ferdinand had retired to his quarters to consider his actions and had not left them until the *Amundsen* arrived in Earth orbit, three days later.

Now Ferdinand stood at attention in his dress uniform before a full assembly of the senate that served as both a debriefing panel and a review board.

"They're called *Minbari*." Vice President Santiago was a heavyset man whose worried expression and weary demeanor suggested he carried more than just excess physical weight. His voice was soft, yet in the stillness of the Senate Chamber it carried to every one of the hundred representatives of the nations of Earth and of the colonies. "We've received information about them from the Centauri Ambassador." Despite humanity's early fears that contact with a technologically advanced alien species would be damaging, the Centauri had proven to be no threat to human-kind. They had instead become a regular source of information and technology. "The fleet consisted of nine vessels. One was destroyed and several more disabled in the blast. The Minbari are a religious/warrior culture. The leader of their ruling council was aboard the ship that was destroyed."

Now Ferdinand understood why Santiago looked so worried. Downright scared would have been a better way of describing his expression. Ferdinand himself was beginning to feel more than a little fear as he scanned the rows of faces before him, from Pres-ident Jarrold on Santiago's left, through the full complement of representatives to the records clerk sitting before the huge semi-circular Narn bloodwood table which was the focal point of the Senate Chamber. With one exception the faces were expression-less. Only Santiago showed his feelings. Ferdinand had a sense of great machinery in motion, big wheels grinding exceedingly small. He swallowed hard. He was lying before these wheels in more senses than just one. One slip and it was his career that would be ground exceedingly small—perhaps even his life. Could starting a war be considered treason? The penalty for that was mindwipe—and that was if he was lucky. If not . . .

Ferdinand said nothing, merely licked a drop of sweat from his upper lip. For the moment silence seemed the most appropriate response.

The President stood. In the sunlight from the curved windows, her plain features were lit with dramatic harshness. When she spoke, her voice was as familiar to Ferdinand as that of his own mother. A rich contralto, the voice resonated in the council chamber. Ferdinand wondered that even with the new influx of alien technology, the broadcast system did not yet exist that could fully reproduce all the subtle nuances of that voice.

Santiago nodded. The Councillors remained silent. Only the soft pad of the court clerk working his terminal broke the silence.

The President spoke again. "What have our friends the Centauri told us of the Minbari?"

Santiago pursed his lips. "They are ancient. Powerful. Rich in culture and industry. Apparently they have never been known to bluff."

The President smiled then. "At the gaming table?"

"At anything, Madam President."

"I see. Including war?"

"That was the inference, ma'am, yes."

Another silence. The smile faded. Ferdinand felt the President's gaze on him and had another brief sensation of those big wheels grinding ever closer.

"Captain Ferdinand. You must understand that since the *Amundsen*'s flight recorder was wiped by the explosion of the Minbari vessel, your testimony and the testimony of your flight crew is our only means of determining the truth of this matter."

"I do."

"And it goes without saying that you understand that in this matter—that of the first contact between ourselves and such a powerful culture—the truth is of paramount importance?"

"I do."

"And that the future peaceful coexistence of two cultures may well rest on this truth?"

"I do."

"Very well, Captain Ferdinand. We have heard your report in every detail but one. So will you please confirm for the Senate the order in which the exchange of fire between yourselves and the Minbari fleet took place?"

"Madam, I will." For then and ever after Ferdinand felt his body shake with the truth of the matter. A truth that from then until the day he died only he and a handful of others would ever know. And with a breath of air that would never taste so sweet again, Captain Ellasai Ferdinand VI uttered the lie that would throw two great cultures into a holy war lasting half a decade and bring about the deaths of more than half a million living beings.

"They fired first."

We may never know why the Minbari surrendered. All we can know—and this is of paramount importance—is that to ensure the future of both races we must go forward from this day, not with fear and mistrust but with hope and joy. We must celebrate the differences between us as well as the similarities. We must speak to the future with mature hearts and voices. Because in the end it is the future which will judge us, and it will judge us by our actions here today.

—Earth Alliance President Santiago
in a public speech renewing his support
for the Babylon Project, shortly before
his death following the destruction
of Earth Force One near Io, 2258

Hey, Lou. You know, I'm feelin a little rough around the edges; maybe a touch of Mars-throat coming on. If it's okay with you I'll take Marge and the kids back to Amazonia Planitia and just sit this one out.

—Vice President Morgan Clark, shortly
before the death of President Santiago
following the destruction of
Earth Force One near Io, 2258. (*Attr.*)

The Senate Chamber in the central administration building at Earthdome had not changed much with the passing of nearly a generation. The ruddy bloodwood table had faded just a fraction under the onslaught of Earth's slightly fiercer sunlight, the carpets had been changed a couple of times, both times to an even more somber shade of dark brown, to match the table. Ex-President Luis Santiago's portrait had been added to the row of such portraits encircling the room.

It was midmorning. President of the Earth Alliance, Morgan Eugene Clark stood alone in the Senate Chamber, waiting for the Senate to assemble. He stood by the curved wall where a shield of glass paralleling the long table allowed an unobstructed view out over the parklands of the city once known as Geneva. The horizon was clearly visible, a line of snow-capped mountains glistening in the sunlight. The sky was the color of ice, a reflection of the most distant peaks. Nearer, the city spread out before him, a gleaming canvas of elegant verticals and efficient horizontals. Italian Portland stone gleamed softly in the sunlight, sweeping arches and Romanesque domes and galleries melding perfectly with shreds of glass and metal from which the daylight splintered in a mad chiaroscuro of light and shadow. And everywhere there was movement. Pedestrian movement. For no vehicles were allowed beneath the atmosphere shield. The reason for this was simple: Though no more beautiful a stone to build with existed than Italian Portland, it was a soft stone, subject to the whim of the weather; the erosion by acid rain brought on by carbon monoxide. With his background in architecture, none better than Clark knew that the whole of Earthdome was merely a symbol, a construct, a badge of office for Earthforce. In the long term the Capital City of the Earth Alliance was as ephemeral as a castle made of clouds.

Certainly if the Battle of the Line had not been successful, the Minbari war fleet would have reduced this city along with every other major population center on or under the Earth's surface to glimmering puddles of glass slag.

Shuddering at the thought of this beauty laid waste, Clark closed his eyes, allowing the sunlight that entered the Senate Chamber to play across his face. The light brought little warmth to his skin at this latitude, yet for Clark, the light was enough in and of itself. He screwed his eyes tighter, letting his mind seek out another moment of light, this one associated with death. The moment as Earth Force One sparkled like a Christmas tree ornament, its smooth hull dappled with explosions like sunlight upon a woodland pool. The engines detonated, the superstructure melted as the carousel section broke away like a discarded dish, only to be caught in the explosion itself moments later, to vanish in the expanding nimbus of light. There was no hope of escape for anyone aboard, including then-President Luis Santiago. In less time than it took to sip from a glass of wine, Earth Force One was reduced to a mess of loose trash orbiting before the sullen gaze of Io and the man they'd called "the last, best hope of Earth" was dead.

Clark opened his eyes. Now *he* was the last, best hope of Earth. He was going to make a damned sight better job of it than Luis Santiago had.

But there were going to be problems. He knew that. His ideas were radical. Subtle in their application, but radical. He had counted on a three-year term at least to get things moving—but the public had recovered remarkably quickly from the death of the much-favored Santiago. Less than a year into his term, already Clark was facing minor troubles. Some of the Senate had given voice to the opinion that Clark's policies were too hard-line, too insular. Clark knew where he stood with these men and women. They lacked his vision. His vision of peace through strength. Peace through unity. Peace through singularity. He wanted to be known as the man who brought lasting peace to the Alliance. He would do *absolutely anything* to accomplish that end. His drive and ambition were becoming known throughout the political world. Only last week at a reception he had overheard the representative for the Russian Consortium refer to him in a private aside to her husband as possessing the "straightforward, deadly elegance of a shark." Clark smiled inwardly. The image of a shark with his own somewhat fluffy eyebrows amused him greatly.

But Clark did not allow his amusement to distract him from the purpose of his meeting with the Senate. In the previous six months polls had been conducted; in some outlying areas his popularity seemed to be waning. The projections indicated he might have trouble holding office for a full term. He knew exactly what to do about that; he had historical precedents which dated as far back as Pericles' expansion and consolidation of the Athenian Empire in the Fifth Century B.C. Changes were coming. Big changes. But like all big things these would be built up to slowly. Give the public a chance to get used to them.

The voting populace hadn't changed since the days of Pericles. They were sheep; most would follow where he led. The method was simple: Provide sufficient political incentive to begin with and then allow social inertia to take over. Everything else was a downhill run.

That was what he was doing now: providing incentive. And what better incentive than consolidating humanity's hold over its own birthplace?

Clark nodded to himself. The Earth was running dry; its resources were almost exhausted. It could hardly support its human population, let alone the alien population already in residence in semi-uninhabitable regions such as Africa and India. Eighty-seven percent of all commercial technology and ninety-one percent of all food for the people of Earth now originated on the colony worlds. That was why places like Mars Colony, the settlements in the asteroid belt, the farms of Ganymede, and the ice mines of Europa were fighting tooth and nail for independence—and why it was inconceivable that their independence should ever be granted. Without them Earth was dead. If they gained independence and any sort of fair trade was established—Earth was dead. Earth could not compete in terms of finance or trade goods with any of the four other major alien governments. Earth simply had nothing. Nothing—except its hold over the colonies.

The future which so terrified Clark was one in which the birthplace of humanity became nothing more than a charity case for the wealthy alien governments. He could see it now: Be Kind to Humans Week. It was an unthinkable proposition for a species that currently ranked among the top five in power.

The irony was that although Earthforce was one of the largest military forces of the five major alien governments, it was also the most costly in terms of equipment and food to maintain. It was a tank without fuel, a nuclear submarine without the means to provide food for its crew. What Clark—and certain others— were coming to realize was that without significant political changes, Earthforce was a short-term item—terminally short-term. And without Earthforce—as it would be without the colonies—Earth was dead.

Pericles had been right. The only way for Earth to live was to kick out the parasites and consolidate. Consolidate and then expand properly. It was going to be a long struggle, and it might well be one he would not see finished. But Clark was prepared to start the process. In truth he could see no other way forward.

His motion to reinstate the death penalty for crimes other than treason was the first step; in moments he would discover how his proposal had fared when voted on by the Senate. In truth he was not too worried about the outcome; a couple of weeks of political horse-trading behind the scenes had allowed Clark to win one or two critical votes in the Senate. And since his proposal did not call for the creation of a new law but merely the reinterpretation of an existing one, it was unlikely to be declared unconstitutional by the Supreme Court. Even if the Senate was hung—a possibility—he knew how the deciding vote would be cast. Either way, the end of the next hour would see the inception of the first of many steps toward his vision of the future.

Clark watched as the Senate filed into the chamber, one by one taking their position along the curved bloodwood table.

When they were in position, Kobold, the Clerk of the Senate, announced their deliberations on Clark's proposed policy.

Watching them, Clark knew what was coming. He could read it in their faces as a child might read the graphics on a cheap home system. The expressions, the set of bodies, some relaxed, others tense. He could even tell who had voted for or against him.

In the end it would make no difference.

Kobold's words confirmed his supposition.

Even taking into account his political maneuvering, the Senate was hung, divided evenly, some for his proposal, some against. An even number remained neutral, unwilling to commit either for or against such an obviously hard-line policy.

Well, that was fine. Very fine indeed. Because as Clerk of the Senate, Kobold had the casting vote.

And Clark knew exactly what Kobold was going to say.

"Mr. President, I have the deciding vote. That vote will be cast for the speaker—assuming you can give both myself and the Senate a final assurance."

Clark was not surprised; he would indulge the Senate in their wish. The change in the law he had proposed would have wide-reaching implications; everyone knew that politics really was like the mythical dinosaur, slow to change, with most of its brain in its arse.

How Clark sometimes wished that he could just sweep away the old Senate, replace it with a new dynamic, fresh ideas, a group unafraid to draw from the past and look to the future, one that relished its position as a conduit for history.

With the help of his associates, that time might come sooner than anyone thought.

Kobold cleared his throat, a prelude to speaking.

Clark had expected conditions just as he had known the Senate would be hung on his idea. In fact he was luckier than he had hoped; there was only one condition. More of an assurance, really. He listened as Kobold spelled it out.

"Mr. President, in consideration of the proposed new wording of section one, paragraphs eleven through eighty-three, to wit, in incapsulation, the law as it relates to the reinstatement of the death penalty for the crime of premeditated murder, and after due consideration, the Senate require from you an assurance that the letter of this new law will not violate the spirit of it, which intent is to uphold and preserve the morals and standard of living of all who are subject to it. Further, and most important, we require an assurance from you that the law will be applied equally and fairly to all persons to whom it applies whether they be of human or alien birth."

And with utter sincerity, Earth President Morgan William Clark spoke the lie which was to result in the destruction of an entire species and have devastating consequences during the third great age of Mankind.

"I assure the Senate that reinstatement of the death penalty for the crime of murder will be applied to both humans and aliens with *complete and absolute equality*."

More than a century ago the Centauri came to us under the flag of friendship. We greeted them as brothers and they enslaved us. They put our world and our people to the sword. They demanded worship and sacrifice as would any gods; and as gods they have made us in their image. Now it is time to show how well we have learned the lesson the Centauri teach: it is time to take the war they started back to our new gods—and any race who would stand between us!

—Narn Leader J'Quoth'Tiel in his inaugural
speech following the successful revolt
against the Centauri and massacre
of the then administration,
Narn Homeworld, 2228

Narn Fleet Commander G'Kar listened to J'Tenniel's *Rhapsody in Red* as he ordered the release of plasma generators into the atmosphere of the planet Tuchanq.

The Rhapsody was peaceful music for a tranquil death.

If the Tuchanq only realized how merciful he was being, thought G'Kar as the sound of bloodwood flutes insinuated itself gently into his ear-slits. He could torture their males, enslave their females and pouchlings. He certainly would not be reprimanded for putting them all to the sword or the slaver's whip. But he was nobler than that. The Tuchanq were his adversaries and he would accord them respect due one to whom losing the fight was inevitable.

By omission the Centauri had taught all Narn the value of honor.

G'Kar had learned this lesson well at the hands of a Centauri master who took his pleasure in ways other than study of the aesthetic. G'Kar had killed his master shortly after that Centauri had hung G'Kar's father from the family prayer-tree as punishment for spilling the soup he had been serving at the dinner table. G'Kar's father had taken three days to die. G'Kar had joined the resistance and when the Centauri had finally been overthrown, had become a pilot in the Narn warfleet. Now G'Kar would implement for the seventh time the lessons he had learned so well at the hands of the Centauri.

He would kill all unessentials, preserving only that part of the Tuchanq culture necessary for the exploitation of the economy and ecology of this world; a world soon to become the latest acquisition of the expanding Narn Regime.

The second movement of the Rhapsody began with a fanfare and staccatto rythm of drums, before melting into a haunting melody stated on strings and reiterated by the flutes.

G'Kar smiled, swaying a thickly muscled arm in time with the music. How uplifting it was.

In time with the music, light bloomed in the atmosphere below G'Kar's command ship, bringing a brief day to the night hemisphere of the invaded world. G'Kar closed his eyes against the glare as he listened to the Rhapsody, hearing in the intricate exploration of its main theme a parallel to a vision his instruments pulled from the devastation below: dissolving buildings, screams choked as soon as formed by burning air, melting throats. Loved ones and strangers, males, females, and pouchlings alike; twisted, crumbling bodies blasted into vapor and left as nothing more than memories in the minds of those who would die immeasurably short moments later.

G'Kar's smile widened. The Tuchanq Capital City held ten billion people and a countless wealth of art and history. It made a perfect target, an example with which to subdue the outlying industrial centers, the planet's more valuable technological resources.

The light flared once more and died, in perfect time with the final reprise of the Rhapsody's main theme. The full orchestral ensemble descended by chromatic scales into silence, leaving the original bloodwood flute to restate the final form of the theme as the night hemisphere of Tuchanq became a sheet of darkness broken only by the palest flicker of distant starlight.

Two days later G'Kar set his ship down at the edge of a ten-mile-wide plain of black glass. The sun was rising across distant hills as he stepped from the loading ramp. Behind him heavy cargo ramps descended with terraforming machinery from the belly of the ship.

G'Kar walked to the edge of the ramp and stood there as the atmosphere heaved and buckled around him in the aftermath of the two-day-old explosion.

Before the ship was scattered movement. Survivors crawling among the charred landscape, they came as they came on all the planets G'Kar had conquered; the dying, the angry, the terrified; warriors, politicians, and civilians, victims alike, to beg for life. All now recognizing in the face of this single ship how helpless they were to affect their own destiny.

"People of Tuchanq"—G'Kar's voice was picked up by a gill microphone and his words were translated and amplified to storm-like proportions by the ship—"your Capital City—I believe it was called Lothaliar—has been destroyed by a plasma device of Centauri manufacture. You may have heard of the Centauri. They are a warlike culture whose aim is to enslave and rule. Allow me to introduce myself. My name is G'Kar. I am a representative of the Narn Regime: sworn enemy of the Centauri, who attacked my planet in the same cowardly way yours has been attacked.'' G'Kar paused to let the words sink in, words which rolled away to the distant hills like peals of thunder.

''Fortunately we Narn have driven the Centauri from your skies as we drove them from our own.''

G'Kar watched the growing crowd of people before him for a moment, gauging their reaction to his words. Then with a smile that would have broken the heart of any hardened warrior, he spoke the lie which was to condemn an entire culture to generations of misery, slavery, and death.

''We are the Narn. We are your friends. We come in peace to help you rebuild your world.''

Before the Narn came, no one was Landless since everyone inherited a stretch of their ancestor's Song and the stretch of country over which the Song passed. A citizen's verses were his title deeds to territory. With the coming of the Narn, the Songs were swamped by the sound of war and machinery. Land and Song became meaningless. Now the war is over, the machines are silent. There can be no more Land if the Song is dead. Therefore the Song must be sung again!

—From the introduction to the first public performance of "Song of Freedom" composed and conducted by Tuchanq Elder Stateswoman nuViel Roon following the Centauri occupation of the Narn Homeworld and the execution of the Narn administration, 2259.

You say there can be no more if the Song is dead. The truth is there can be more Song *if the* Land *is dead!*

—Unnamed member of the public attending the "Song of Freedom" performance, 2259.
(*Attr.*)

noMir Ru painted herself black to execute the Narn.

She did this for three reasons. Firstly for revenge: the sludge the Narn war machines poured into the rivers and oceans of Tuchanq was black. Secondly for ritual: the Narn had invaded her world by night—it seemed appropriate that they too should die by night.

The third reason was terror.

noMir Ru wanted the Narn to feel the same terror her people had felt over the last two generations. Blind, unreasoning terror as death struck in the night, taking family, friends, and loved ones into the cold cradle of Songless nevermore. noMir Ru was a silent killer, to Narn eyes a darkness upon indistinguishable darkness in the shadowed midnight of the prison.

Yes.

The Narn would know terror.

The first Narn died with surprise on his mottled face, a tired groan, and a pattering of arterial blood.

The second Narn gazed mesmerized at the glittering dagger hovering apparently unsupported in the darkness a hand's breadth from his face. The knife flashed twice. The Narn blinked and died.

She let the the third Narn scream before killing him, a bubbling mixture of fear and blood.

The mood in the prison began to change.

Panic. Fear. The smell of Narn blood.

The fourth Narn took longer to die because she deliberately missed the artery. She watched as he bled, tipped her head to one side to allow her spines to catch the full moment.

She hummed gently to herself.

The Narn whispered through bloody lips, ''Singing. The dark is singing.''

noMir Ru allowed her spine to collapse into the running position. On all fours she sniffed the air, angled her spines to catch the last nuances of the Narn's death.

By now the prison had taken up the dying Narn's words, a collective whisper from more than forty terrified Narn.

''Singing.''

"The dark is singing."

"The dark. The dark."

The whisper rose, became a gestalt scream of terror as she moved on, knife glittering in the darkness.

"The dark is coming! The dark! The dark!"

noMir Ru slipped through the prison, blood-spattered darkness on moon-shadowed night. One by one the Narn died. And when the voices were finally stilled the only sound left was her Song.

She sang her life. She sang her family land, now hers again, and she sang the new name the dying Narn had bestowed upon her.

And next morning, before the slaughter was discovered, she slipped through the newly proclaimed capital city of Ellaenn to the ocean where the single remaining Narn starship—a gargantuan commodities freighter larger than the Royal Palace—rode high in its watery berth.

Carrying her clothes in a plastic bag, she swam out to the hull and climbed aboard the freighter through a little-used organic waste vent port. Once inside she washed and then dressed, took her place among the diplomatic staff. They had drawn lots for the job of executioner. It had been Elder Stateswoman nuViel's instruction; no one was to know of her midnight foray—thus no guilt could be attributed or punishment assigned.

Later that day, in the Royal Park in the City of Ellaenn, noMir's voice lifted in song along with nuViel's. The Song of Freedom. When the crowd joined in you could hear them even above the rhythmic pulse of the freighter's station-keeping engines.

Two days later, thirty hours after a full honor guard had tipped the Narn into their own food reprocessors, colored and flavored and tinned the resulting organic mash, the rest of the diplomatic chorus came aboard the freighter, together with such pitiful supplies of fresh water as could be cobbled together from the secret hoards of the resistance.

The dead Narn came aboard as well. In self-heating tins.

With this action the Tuchanq had finally recognized a truth noMir herself had seen many months before. The Song was dead. The Land was dead. If the Tuchanq were ever to survive the death by starvation which the Narn had brought upon them, they must beg for help.

The people to whom they would turn were listed in the freighter's data banks, along with the name of their destination.

Babylon 5.

If their mission failed all Tuchanq would die.

Later, as the commodities freighter shouldered its way through the blood red fog of hyperspace, noMir petitioned Elder Stateswoman nuViel for permission to take the Song of the Narn she had killed.

When nuViel refused permission on religious grounds, she assumed the new Song anyway, naming both it and herself for a word spoken by the dying Narn. And although the fact that the name bore more resemblance to the Narn form than it did any Elder-sanctioned Tuchanq name made it technically both heresy and a lie, that meant nothing to her.

If the Land was to be saved, if the Song was ever to be sung again, then the old ways were going to have to change. She knew this for a fact.

Or her name wasn't *D'Arc*.

Part One

Among Shadows

December 12, 2259
Alpha Shift: Day

CHAPTER 1

If you go to Z'ha'dum you will die.

John Sheridan sighed, perched a bowl of steaming leek soup on top of a stack of paperwork that threatened to simultaneously cascade off all four sides of his desk, and leaned back in his chair. He shook his head, tried to find a place for his feet on the overcrowded desk, gave up when the wobbling stack of reports threatened to send his snack splashing into his lap.

Sheridan sighed again. He was a soldier. A leader of men. A man of action and decision. Until a year ago he had thought his destiny was irrevocably bound up with Earthforce, a moderately significant cog in the military machine.

That had all changed with his posting to Babylon 5.

They'd made him an administrator. A politician. They'd changed the rules. Clark had changed the rules. And Earthforce had let him.

Sheridan felt almost betrayed by this change of position. He'd been shuffled from pillar to post on one or two occasions in the past, but never so drastically. Never so far from home, from space. Babylon 5 was a city, one with all the disadvantages and none of the advantages of a planet-bound community. There had been times in the last year when Sheridan had been almost stir-crazy. There were too many walls. Too many rooms and corridors, hallways, chambers, parks, and gardens. Everything was too wide; there was too much headroom. The ground didn't move right. The gravity didn't fluctuate.

There were too many people.

Put on the spot, Sheridan would have to admit he was developing a distinct tendency toward agoraphobia.

And there were other things. Less obvious, more like . . . well, like Shadows, really.

If you go to Z'ha'dum you will die.

Babylon 5 was big; a space city five miles long anchored at

one of the trojan points between Epsilon Eridani 3, the planet
Euphrates and its small moon; in territory neutral to the five major interstellar governments. Built to cater for half a million in
an absolute pinch, the station's comfortable operating range
was somewhere in the two hundred- to two-hundred-and-fifty-
thousand range. A quarter of a million humans and aliens, living,
working, eating, breathing, sleeping, sweating together. For trade.
For commerce. For business. In the name of peace.

But somehow it never seemed to work that way.

Because with the idealism and the forward thinking came other
things, darker things. Homelessness. Sickness. Strikes. Rape.
Murder.

War.

The ethic of Babylon 5 was positive. But lately that wasn't
what he was seeing. What he was seeing was distrust, fear, anger;
more violence than ever before.

In some ways that was understandable. Of the average two-
hundred-and-fifty-thousand daily turnover about ninety-five percent was civilian. The civilian animal was, in Sheridan's
experience, notorious for overreacting, underplaying, hedging
bets, hiding the truth, ducking and diving and just plain lying at
every possible opportunity.

Then again, nobody was quite what they seemed here, including himself. General Hague had briefed him on a certain mission
shortly before his posting here. That mission had at first piqued
Sheridan's curiosity. Lately it had come to mean much more.
Nightwatch. The Star Chamber. The movers and shapers within
EarthGov. His job was to seek out their connections, their con-
tacts, find out how far the spider's web stretched. Monitor it if
possible; if possible stamp it out.

If you go to Z'ha'dum you will die.

Sheridan reached for his soup. It was still too hot. He got up,
stretched, yawned. He seemed to be so tired lately. Sticking his
pen behind his ear, he smoothed his uniform top and walked
around the desk to the office window.

The sky was green today, a healthy green unbleached by
clouds, divided only by the narrow tracks of the monorail, the

tiny gleaming beads of the core shuttles as they wandered busily back and forth.

Sheridan studied the view, for a moment considered opening the window, resisted the impulse. Even after a year aboard the station there was something disturbing about all that open space. Perhaps it was the Shadows.

If you go to Z'ha'dum you will die.

Sheridan's office was located at the top of the main administration block. From a height of three stories he could see the entire length of the carousel section. The Park. Trees and streams, the river, the parkland, the hedge maze, the Zen garden, the sports fields, the Rotunda, the Mosque. Twelve square miles of parkland wrapped into a hollow cylinder a mile and a half in diameter.

And under the ground? Twenty meters of dirt and rock followed by four levels of hydrobays, support systems, storage and silage units, water and oxygen reclamation units, chemical processors, farm equipment garages, and zoos. The zoos were for the worms and insects. Small animals and microbial life forms necessary to the ecology of the carousel and thus essential to all life on the station.

Sheridan smiled then. ''We've brought it all with us into space,'' he muttered to himself. ''Our hopes, our dreams, our art and literature, our faults and fears, our worms.''

If you go to Z'ha'dum you will die.

Sheridan studied his reflection in the window for a moment. Was he looking old? Was it any wonder if he was?

If you go to Z'ha'dum you will die.

Sheridan sighed, finally gave in to the memory.

It had been five months since Kosh had spoken the warning. Five months since Sheridan had learned his wife Anna, whom he had thought years dead, might still be alive. Five months since he had been told of the Shadows.

Since then his life had become a nightmare.

There were Shadows on Babylon 5. On his station. Invisible. Insidious. Calculating. Manipulating. They could be anywhere, watching, learning, reporting back to their force gathering on the Rim. They could be right here in this office now and he would never know it. And he could do nothing about them. Nothing.

Because Delenn said so. Because of a Minbari prophecy older than the Terran machine age. A prophecy which was, apparently, all too close to coming true.

Shadows.

Here. Now.

Sheridan felt his shoulders tighten against his uniform. Somehow he resisted the urge to swing around, study the room for the minutest clue, hope by his sudden movement to catch them by surprise. It was pointless. You never caught Shadows like that. Care and subtlety, caution. That was what Delenn advised. The hell with that. The Shadows had Anna—well, they *might* have Anna—well, he'd been *told* they might have Anna. But even a one in a thousand—a one in a *million* chance—was worth investigating. Kosh had told him he would die if he went to Z'ha'dum, but Sheridan loved Anna still and, like Ulysses before him, would attempt anything, dare anything for just one chance, however small, of *getting her back*. Kosh would help him. He'd promised. Well, he'd said he would help Sheridan understand himself, and that was as close to a promise of help as you got from a Vorlon.

Sheridan became aware his cheeks were aching. With an effort he unclenched his teeth. He blew out his cheeks and tried to regain control of himself. One moment's loss of concentration and look what it did to you.

Cold sweats.

A fit of the shakes a cargo loader couldn't damp down.

The office door bleeped politely.

"Come in." Sheridan shook his head, managed with an effort to cast off his dark mood.

The door slid back to reveal a woman of medium height dressed in Earthforce blue, who somehow contrived to appear a great deal taller than she actually was.

Sheridan turned. "Commander Ivanova. What can I do for you?" In the eight years since their first meeting on Io, Sheridan had almost never known Ivanova to move with anything less than a precise military bearing. It was ironic when you considered she was probably the most . . . *human* officer he'd ever met. And the most professional to boot.

"You wanted to brief me on the arrival of the Tuchanq delegation."

Sheridan nodded, felt his shoulders loosen. "That's right." He stayed by the window, unconsciously framing himself with the outside view. "The report's on my desk."

Ivanova shot an amused glance at the desk. "So's half the station manifest by the look of it."

Sheridan sighed. His life seemed to orbit around paper. Lots of paper. Reams in fact. There were duty logs. Personnel transfers. Equipment manifests. Cargo manifests. Inbound and outbound shipping authorizations. Repair chits. Requests for special cargo. Weight allowance checks. Diplomatic schedules. Diplomatic minutes. *Lots* of diplomatic minutes.

"Just between you and me, Commander, I suspect that one day very soon the entire station is going to pass the paper event horizon and vanish up its own behind."

Ivanova raised an eyebrow.

"In fact I'm not so sure that wasn't what happened to Babylon 4 when *it* vanished."

Ivanova made a curious and unique expression: half smile, half disapproving frown. It was an expression only she could get away with. Sheridan knew very well what had happened to Babylon 4; Ivanova knew it.

He moved his soup and reached for a report, handed it to Ivanova, put the soup back down on another teetering stack of paperwork.

Ivanova thumbed through the report quickly. "That's interesting. You don't often get quadrupeds on the station." More pages. "Hmm. They were annexed by the Narn, kicked them out when the Narn Homeworld fell to the Centauri . . . now they've got enough Narn heavy machinery to start a small war and no ecology."

Sheridan nodded thoughtfully. "No worms."

"Sorry?"

"No worms. No microbial life. No arable land or living ocean. No trees. No food. Just smog; black smog and acid rain. And eighteen billion citizens who'll be dead of starvation in very short order unless someone helps them."

"That someone being us?"

"Or one of the major governments."

Ivanova nodded. "Their ship—a captured Narn commodities freighter—arrived a few minutes ago. They're waiting for permission to come aboard."

"Better not keep them waiting, then."

"You're not coming with me?"

Sheridan glanced at his desk. "To be honest, it's very tempting. But no. I can't. I have an appointment to see Kosh in an hour."

Ivanova winked. "Another 'moment of perfect beauty'?"

"Another lesson in how to make the incomprehensible slightly less understandable, yes."

"My sympathies." Ivanova turned to leave. "If you need me just link in."

Sheridan nodded.

When the door shut behind Ivanova he sat once more at his desk. In front of him, a mountain of paperwork. In his head, a picture of Anna smiling.

If you go to Z'ha'dum you will die.

He reached for his soup.

It was cold.

CHAPTER 2

The Corps is your friend. Trust the Corps.

Ivanova left the administration block, took a personnel lift to the monorail, waited for the first core shuttle heading north.

North. South. Anywhere else in Earthforce, any other ship and it would be "for'ard" or "rear." Here on Babylon 5 the cubic capacity alone made a nonsense of the military-designations "bow" and "stern." In an irregularly shaped cylinder five miles long by a smidgeon under two in diameter it was north, south, spinward, retrograde, or "over there, mate!" along with a gesture which could include directions to a geographical position on the sky as well as the apparently level ground in your immediate vicinity. Ivanova didn't need to step closer to the tourist windows and check out the stunning view of the Park to know that only here in the shuttle terminal, three quarters of a mile "above" the "ground," did most spoken or gestured directions to anywhere inboard finally begin to make sense.

The shuttle was due soon; the platform was getting crowded. All were oxy-breathers except for a scattering of Cthulhin and one Exotic whose mirrorsteel *AE* Suit was covered in a layer of frost so thick that Ivanova couldn't read the environment designations. The Exotic was probably a Thrantallil, most probably the Ambassador or one of her attachés. When you breathed liquid metallic hydrogen at a pressure of eighteen atmospheres and tended to both explode and spontaneously combust when faced with an Earth-normal environment, only someone of ambassadorial status would really see the need to stray outside her quarters, let alone the alien sectors of the station.

The core shuttle pulled in then and the doors slid open. Ivanova set her feet carefully onto the Velcro floor strips and pulled herself into the practically zero-g shuttle. She settled onto one of the seats between a Drazi white-collar worker and a human sanitation engineer and strapped herself down, tuned out the multitude of squeaks, grunts, scrapings, and the odd musical bleep that passed for casual chat in the multispecies environment, and closed her eyes. It was a mile and a half north to Customs and Disembarkation—fifteen minutes by shuttle—in other words, time enough for a quick doze.

Drifting off, Ivanova felt her thoughts stray inevitably to Talia. Felt again her light touch, heard her whispered words. And something else; something more than the touch of bodies. The touch of minds—

She shook herself awake. This was no good. This was no good at all. These kind of thoughts just brought pain. Healing would come with time; until then it was best to simply put the pain aside.

Ivanova sighed, tried to get comfortable in the seat harness. Her head told her that displacing the pain was the worst route to healing, but her heart wasn't listening. She simply had too many years of denial weighing down on her to do anything else. Denial by her father of her mother's psi ability, denial by her family that her mother had been caged for years by drugs and ultimately forced to take her own life by those who called themselves her friends. And above all, far too many years of denial of her own latent ability as a telepath.

The Corps is mother. The Corps is father.

Ivanova clenched her jaw.

Screw the Corps.

She had a job to do.

Customs and Disembarkation was a hundred-meter-wide chamber running in a narrow strip around the rim of the service collar, the structure immediately south of the command and docking sphere, any approaching ship's first point of contact with the station proper.

In essential operation, Customs hadn't changed from the days of the good old-fashioned Concorde. A line of desks and clerks and slightly substandard computers, conveyer belts full of embarking or disembarking passengers, manual and automated luggage, a high level of background noise, a higher level of holographic advertising and the usual incomprehensible announcements, now as incomprehensible in Drazi and Pak'ma'ra as they had ever been in Spanish or Indian or Japanese. Efficiency and processing time through Customs hadn't changed at all in the last two-odd centuries. It still took exactly two minutes longer to process your claim than you needed to catch the first available core shuttle, and when you finally got to the terminal there was still just standing room only in the car.

The first sign that there might be trouble brewing came as Ivanova flashed her command ID and pushed through the Alternative Environment Suit Wide Loads Only terminal and entered the concourse. As she drew level with the terminal clerk's desk, the clerk—a hairless reptilian Cauralline—stopped her with a series of gentle glottal clicks. Ivanova waited impatiently for the translator attached to a belt circling the Cauralline's upper waist to process the clicks, an impossibly long fifteen seconds. When it came, the Cauralline's translated voice was in System

English with a dreadful German accent. "Commander Ivanova. The Tuchanq have arrived. Their processing is not going frictionlessly."

"Smoothly." Ivanova made the correction automatically. The translator software was state-of-the-art—but as with a lot of the technology inboard, the translator *hardware* was pretty much whatever old tatt EarthGov had been able to afford after the Babylon 4 fiasco.

The Cauralline blinked three of its six eyes impatiently. More clicks. A surprised grunt. More clicks. A fifteen-second wait, then, "That is what I said. Frictionlessly."

Ivanova uttered a humorless grunt. "No wonder the waiting time here is more than some species' life expectancy."

She waved away the clerk's further glottal exposition and strode purposefully into the ocean of passengers and their luggage, not so distracted by the clerk's attempt to communicate that she didn't notice when the occasional item of luggage actually had a slightly more purposeful and efficient look to its movement than did its owner.

The Tuchanq delegation had somehow managed to miss the Ambasadorial gate. They were smack in the middle of the concourse, surrounded by a crowd of curious onlookers. Well, that was understandable. This was the first time a delegation from Tuchanq had visited the station, and no one except the Narn had seen them before in the flesh.

Admitting to a certain curiosity herself, Ivanova pushed through the crowd.

Ivanova got her first sight of the Tuchanq—which should have been her second sign that trouble was brewing—by peering over the bandaged knee joint of a Throxtil decapod who, judging by the quantity of other minor dressings adorning his hugely muscled star–shaped body, had found the prevailing Earth standard one g, less than a fifth of that in which he had been born, somewhat awkward to adjust to.

She counted about twenty of the Tuchanq in a clearing ringed by curious onlookers. At least she *thought* there were about twenty. It was hard to tell because they were jumping up and down, weaving in between each other in a complicated pattern.

In, out, left, right, up, down. Sometimes as much as two meters off the ground at every leap. Sometimes they jumped on two limbs, sometimes on three or four. And when they jumped, they yelled. They jumped and yelled in rhythm.

And even in a universe whose basic operating principle seemed to be extreme physical diversity, they were *weird*.

For a start they seemed to be partly exoskeletal. Only partly. For another they seemed to be partly reptilian and partly mammalian—even partly avian; fur and scales and spines and feathers all bound up together in woven harnesses through which emerged a different number of limbs for each individual.

The Tuchanq jumped. They yelled. Then they began to sing.

Ivanova watched them, openmouthed.

In a wide circle around the Tuchanq the passengers watched, fascinated. The queues slowed and stopped moving toward the processing booths. The crowd got bigger. Some joined in with the chanting.

Ivanova found herself tapping a foot in time with the rhythm.

Beside her the Throxtil decapod bounced excitedly from one of its five pillarlike legs to the next. It *thrummed*; slightly off the beat and slightly off-key. The *thrumming* went up a semitone when the Throxtil inadvertently put its entire weight on its bandaged leg.

A furry Bremmaer scurried out from underfoot.

Ivanova followed Bremmaer's lead and moved sideways a couple of steps. That brought her into direct line of sight of the Tuchanq delegation.

Ivanova realized waiting for a quiet moment to speak was a nonstarter. Cranking up the volume on the translator she'd had G'Kar program for her, she bellowed in best drill sergeant manner, ''Allow me to introduce myself! I am Commander *Susan Ivanova*! As station administrator please allow me to *welcome you to Babylon 5*!''

Exactly fifteen seconds later an earsplitting series of growls and barks issued from the translator.

The Tuchanq stopped. As one being. They turned to face her.

And took off their skins.

Now that's an attention getter.

There was an eerie silence. Then a single shriek from the crowd that turned into laughter almost immediately. Ivanova blew out her cheeks and sighed. She now realized why the Tuchanq looked so strange. They were wearing costumes. Intricate constructions of fur and feathers, skin, scales, and bone.

Costumes.

Shorn of their costumes the Tuchanq looked superficially like humans. They were naked. The shortest was two and a half meters tall, rake thin, with elongated limbs and a short torso. Their faces were elongated too, thin, with no eyes. Instead they had mottled patches that wrapped around at least half of the circumference of their skulls. A ruff of spines in place of ears wrapped around the backs of their long necks. There were males and females in the delegation; so thin were they that only the obvious differences told them apart—and they weren't all that obvious. Their skin colors ranged from a brilliant canary yellow to a pale chocolate brown. In each case the skin of their palms and faces was lighter than at other parts of their bodies. As she watched several dropped onto all fours. As they did this their necks and shoulders seemed to stretch, bone and muscle altering configuration easily to adapt to a horizontal rather than a vertical weight distribution. Knees slid upward toward the belly, elbows pointed back toward the knees. Now Ivanova saw why, unlike human limbs, the Tuchanq arms and legs were the same length.

"Um . . . Welcome to Babylon 5," Ivanova said again, more quietly this time. Unfortunately she forgot to turn down the translator volume and so her softly spoken words came out rather like the howl of a timber wolf. A child in the crowd started to cry.

The nearest Tuchanq oriented to face Ivanova, her spines moving delicately around her head much like those of a sea urchin in water. "Thank you for taking the trouble to program your translator with our language. But we learned System English from the Narn. I think it would probably make a lot of sense to use that, don't you think, Commander Ivanova?" Her accent was flawless.

"I can go with that."

Initial surprise and curiosity fading, the crowd had already begun to disperse. The Throxtil decapod cruised away in a kind of

4:1 limp, cutting a path through the crowd toward the *Wide Load Only* gate.

The Tuchanq seemed to be studying Ivanova. As much as a creature without eyes could be said to study anything. "My name is nuViel Roon. I think I speak for all of us here when I say we are pleased to make your acquaintance."

Ivanova smiled. "Likewise. As I said, I am administrator here on Babylon 5. I would like to welcome you on behalf of the five major alien governments and the nonaligned worlds. If you wish I can show you to your quarters, help you get squared away, that sort of thing. Later we can arrange a preliminary hearing with Station Commander Sheridan and the advisory council to address your requests."

nuViel tipped her head slightly to the left, a movement Ivanova assumed meant affirmation. "Very kind, I'm sure." Her spines all tipped slowly to the left as well, then bounced back to their fan-shaped central position. "But first we must complete the ritual of arrival."

Ivanova shrugged. What had Sheridan said? Afford them every courtesy? "Please. Be my guest."

nuViel tipped her head again. "Thank you." She turned to face the rest of the delegation. Each reached into his or her costume and withdrew a thin, curved, wickedly sharp dagger.

Right at that moment Ivanova got her next indication of the trouble to come. It came far too late of course.

The Tuchanq formed a circle and dropped to all fours on the deck. Each placed the point of his or her knife against the side of his or her neck, approximately where the carotid artery would be in a human.

Aw hell, what is this?

"Uh—"

That was as far as Ivanova got before the Tuchanq, as one, pierced the skin of their throats with their knives.

Someone in the crowd of passengers screamed.

There was a rush of people away from the Tuchanq.

Blood that was too red for Ivanova's liking pattered onto the deck. She flinched, but the expected arterial sprays never came. A few more drops of blood pattered harmlessly onto the deck and ran together to form a small puddle. nuViel then began to smear the blood into patterns on the deck. Lines and circles and more lines and yet more circles.

Then they began to sing again. Quietly. Wordlessly. A whisper of sound in time with the rhythmic pattering of blood and scraping of nuViel's finger across the deck.

Ivanova stared at the Tuchanq delegation as they bled onto the ribbed decks of the Customs terminal. Oddly she felt not horror so much as an unlooked-for sense of awe and wonder. Adrenaline flushed her body. She felt invigorated, a sensation she had not experienced since her first encounter with an off-worlder more than a quarter of a century ago at the Russian Consortium's Second Centenary Independence celebration.

And all of a sudden she found herself smiling, felt a sense of *connection* she hadn't felt for years, as if she had an identity beyond that which she knew as herself, as if some part of her was capable of reaching out to other cultures and, if not identifying with them in a physiological way, then at least acknowledging that together, they and she, and all the other human and nonhuman races, were what made the universe such a . . . such a *real* place.

Ivanova came to with a little start when she realized that the whole of the Customs area had frozen in place for the second time. Queues of disembarking passengers all stared at the bleeding Tuchanq.

Nearby a human male was staring at the growing patterns of blood with undisguised horror while a Pak'ma'ra female was staring in the same direction with undisguised interest.

The man sucked in a nervous breath and backed away. The Pak'ma'ra wiggled her nasal cilia—the equivalent of licking her lips—in anticipation of what might, after a week or so's decomposition, turn out to be a good meal and tried to edge closer to the blood.

Get a grip, Susan. The Tuchanq may have touched you in a fundamental way but it doesn't change the fact that they're still bleeding all over the Customs terminal deck.

nuViel rose from a cross-legged position. ''Thank you, Susan. I may call you Susan?'' A single drop of blood ran from her throat. She mopped it up with a finger and then licked the finger with a tubelike tongue. "It is our custom to return something of ourselves to the Land in thanks for its nourishing us."

Ivanova nodded. "Right."

"I know technically we are not on Land, but"—nuViel made a gesture curiously like a shrug—"still we are already nourished simply by being allowed to breathe your air."

Ivanova licked her lips. "And the patterns?"

"That is our Journey. Our words were the Song of our Journey. From the moment of our birth on the planet of our birth, from nomadic warriors to civilized communities, through love and hate and joy, through birth and death and birth, to war and famine and despair, and beyond them to here. To this place of new life and new hope. To Babylon 5."

Ivanova found her mouth was dry. "Ritual." Around her the disturbed mutterings of the crowd faded, lost in the moment. Sheridan had once told her that Kosh had shown him *one moment of perfect beauty*. She was beginning to feel she may have just seen another.

nuViel tipped her spines in agreement. "All life is ritual."

And Ivanova knew then that nuViel was right. And she realized how what she had seen related to herself as part of the human race.

Ritual.

It all boiled down to that in the end.

It was midwife to our birth on the African plains; it kept us throughout our violent nomadic youth, from the cradle of civilization right through to this very moment she herself was part of. Now here we are, five thousand years and seventy-two light-years from those African plains, on the biggest single object ever constructed by humankind, and still ritual holds sway.

The ritual of acceptance.

Not everyone was capable of understanding its subtleties.

Some people, Ivanova realized, when a single voice lifted angrily from the crowd, were not even prepared to try.

"Don't you let those . . . those *things* come near my child!" A human voice. Female. A sentiment Ivanova might have shared five thousand years ago. Not now. Not here.

"They've got diseases!" Another voice. Another human. A man this time.

Ivanova turned to face the crowd.

Another voice cried, "We've all got diseases, mate. You've got more viruses in your gut than I've had hot dinners."

"Yeah, but they're terrestrial viruses."

"Come to think of it you've got more *gut* than I've had hot dinners."

"Come here and say that, slag-lover!"

"Aw, crawl back into your cave, why don't'cha."

"I *said* keep them *away* from my *Tommy!*"

"Asswipe!"

"Racist!"

Home Guard.

There was the sound of a punch. That was all it took. In moments a fistfight had started that threatened to spread through the crowd like a blight through hydroponics.

A yell went up from the crowd, part anger, part outrage.

They were going to kill each other!

A human fell into the ring of empty space around the Tuchanq, a Drazi at his throat. Ivanova stepped forward, wrenched the human away from the Drazi, dragged him to his feet.

"Thanks, sister, bloody scum are everywhere—"

Human in one hand, Drazi in the other, Ivanova brought her arms together with a frightening yell. Skulls cracked. Both antagonists went limp. Ivanova held both up at arm's length, human by the hair, Drazi by the skull crest. "*All right!*" she yelled at the top of her lungs. "*Anyone else want some more of the same?*"

Her voice had not the slightest effect on the crowd.

"Ah well. Can't say I didn't try."

Dropping both human and Drazi, Ivanova drew her PPG and fired a low-level blast over the heads of the fighters.

The crowd shut up almost immediately.

"Well? Anyone else got a view they'd like to air about human-alien relations?"

Faced with Ivanova's expression and her PPG the crowd revealed, predictably, no takers.

"All right then." Ivanova holstered her PPG and called security to cart away the unconscious human and Drazi. She turned to the Tuchanq, shrugged an apology.

Two security guards turned up at that point. "Commander. Are you okay?"

"I'm fine. Everything's under con—"

And that was when all hell broke loose.

A voice from the crowd shouted, "There's a Narn skull on that costume! They've killed a Narn! They're as bad as the Centauri!"

The Tuchanq turned as one, spines angling toward the voice.

"Murderers!" a Tuchanq yelled and sprang into the crowd. "Killers of the Land!"

Someone screamed. The Tuchanq howled. A Narn voice cried out in pain. There were more angry yells from other Narn in the crowd. About half the Tuchanq sprang into the crowd. In seconds they'd vanished from sight. The rest milled around in the little circle of space they'd made for themselves, smearing their own blood on the deck with their feet and erasing the record of their Journey.

Ivanova grabbed the security guards and charged through the crowd. She didn't have to force a way. The crowd parted before her, streaming away from the scene of the fight.

Eight or ten Tuchanq with knives. Five Narn armed with a bad attitude and not much else.

Someone was going to get hurt.

The Narns were thickly muscled and fierce, but they were built for stamina, not speed. The Tuchanq were all over them in seconds. Unable to fire for fear of injuring the Narn, Ivanova could only watch in horror as they were cut down. One of the security guards holstered his PPG and waded in with his shockstick. He put down one of the Tuchanq before the rest bore him down.

A Narn grabbed one of the Tuchanq, crushed her skull. A Tuchanq drove his knife into the Narn's back; he dropped with an agonized sigh.

Ivanova drew her PPG and set it to stun. She aimed at fighters—then lowered the weapon. If she fired now, even on a low setting, she might worsen the injuries of the downed guard. Holstering the PPG, she called to the other guard, "Call for backup!" She dove into the fight, grabbed the bleeding security guard, began to drag him clear. There was movement all around her, a blurred frieze of knives, snarling faces, retractable claws slashing, arcs of Narn blood splashing her uniform. A knife slashed her shoulder, drawing blood. A Narn fist crashed into the side of her head.

That's it. Now I'm really annoyed.

Dropping the guard, Ivanova staggered clear of the fight, drew her PPG, set it to its lowest setting, yelled as loud as she could to the remaining guard, "I've had it with this! Stun the lot of 'em!"

Two blasts of low-level plasma energy later it was all over bar mopping up the blood.

One Tuchanq was missing a handful of spines; three Narn were bleeding heavily from multiple wounds.

One of the Tuchanq was dead, skull crushed; a Narn died from blood loss while they were waiting for the medics.

Ivanova swore. What a bloody fiasco. Sheridan was going to have her butt for this. She examined the wound on her shoulder. Superficial. But the sleeve on her uniform was gone and that was going to take serious credits to fix. She swore again.

"Susan—*what have you done?*" nuViel was beside her, with the remaining members of the delegation, having finally pushed through the crowd. She was staring at the mass of stunned bodies, Narn and Tuchanq alike, the ripped-out spines, the blood. Her voice was pitched absurdly high. Surprise? No, more like outrage. Panic. Fear.

Ivanova whirled. "What the hell is it with you people? One war not enough for you? Look at that. One Tuchanq dead. One Narn dead." She struggled to remain calm. "Look at my sleeve!"

nuViel said nothing, merely stared, trembling, at the unconscious bodies.

"Well?"

A member of the Tuchanq delegation, a male slightly over three meters tall said, breathlessly, "A torturer can cut off my spines; allow me to breed and my child will be born with them. So with instinct!" He studied Ivanova closely, as if weighing up her ability to understand his answer. "We did not start the war."

Ivanova rubbed her eyes tiredly. Retied her hair. "I don't care if your old granny started the war! One more incident like this and *I'll* rip off your damn spines—and beat you to death with the wet ends. *Capisce*?" Without waiting for a reply Ivanova turned, caught sight of a familiar figure pushing urgently through the crowd, PPG drawn. "Hey, Garibaldi. Great timing as always."

Garibaldi studied the human and alien wreckage thoughtfully. "Jeez, Ivanova. Ever thought of entering the Mutai? You'd make someone a packet."

Ivanova stared at the security chief.

Garibaldi raised his hands apologetically. "Hey. No offense, right? Just my little joke."

She stared at him.

"Okay. I'm outta here." Garibaldi holstered his PPG and began to clear a way through the crowd for the arriving medics.

Ivanova sighed. At least she could still get the last word around here, even if she didn't actually get the last *word*.

It was a vain hope.

nuViel was still standing beside her, trembling as the medics tended the injured Tuchanq and Narn, then placed them gently on stretchers and carried them away. She tipped her spines toward Ivanova. "Are they dead?"

Ivanova sighed. "What do you take me for? Of course they're not dead. They're just stunned. They'll wake up in half an hour or so with a bit of a headache, but that's all."

nuViel tipped her spines to the right, and that was when Ivanova began to get a bad feeling. A feeling that the trouble had only just begun. "Susan, you don't understand. You have broken their Songs of Being. Driven them from their lives and homes and families. When the Tuchanq you have stunned awake, they will be *dead*."

Ivanova frowned. "What?"

"Dead." nuViel's spines shuddered in confusion. "In your terms . . . socially . . . dead." nuViel's spines settled as she found the right terms to explain her words. "They will have no sense of responsibility toward society."

"You mean insane?"

nuViel crouched onto all fours and began a keening song, breaking it only once to stare at Ivanova. "Violently insane! Psychotic!"

CHAPTER 3

G'Kar stared unblinkingly at Sheridan and tried not to sigh. That was something the humans did. Since Narn possessed both lungs and gills, none of his people should ever need to sigh. But like everything else they did these days, the Narn seemed to have unconsciously assimilated the gesture from some other species, thus losing another tiny piece of their own racial heritage. The thought made G'Kar frustrated and that in turn made him angry. He blinked again, wondered momentarily if that was another unconsciously assimilated gesture, then dismissed the thought angrily.

"Captain Sheridan, I wish to protest in the strongest manner." G'Kar made a tremendous effort to keep his voice calm. "One of my people—people as you know, for whom I am responsible—has been brutally killed. In public. In the Customs terminal. He was a refugee for J'Quan's sake! One to whom you offered sanctuary, if you have not forgotten."

"I haven't forgotten my promise, G'Kar."

"Then on behalf of my people I demand that reparation be made."

Sheridan sighed. "And what reparation would that be?"

"Well . . . several options have been discussed. After some deliberation I request that the Tuchanq be removed from the station and their request for help rejected."

Sheridan hesitated. G'Kar waited as the Captain tipped his head to one side, steepled his fingers, *sighed*. Rubbed his left eyebrow. Placed his arms on the desk and rubbed the forefinger and thumb of his left hand together. More gestures. The humans seemed to have an endless supply of them. Almost meaningless little bits of body language most Narn would find offensive if they could even configure their thickly muscled, heavily boned bodies to imitate them. Some part of G'Kar knew that he really ought to be study-ing these little gestures and signs with more diligence—he had heard others say that in some cases you could tell whether a human was lying or not simply by studying his skin moisture level. The truth was—and G'Kar was honest enough to own up to it, to himself at least—the truth was that for a Narn to whom the most subtle gesture for many years had been the thrust of a dagger into a Centauri belly, almost all alien body languages were just too subtle for him to interpret. G'Kar found the experience frustrating in the extreme—to be able to see that there was a whole subtext to most exchanges, even interspecies exchanges, but never to be able to divine its meaning. And to G'Kar frustra-tion was an enemy almost as deadly as the Centauri who had forced him to adopt for a second time the ways of war.

G'Kar stared at Sheridan.

He was *still* deliberating.

"Forgive my impatience, Captain, but I really must demand that you address this situation. It is of extrememe importance."

Sheridan spoke at last. "I know, G'Kar. And I'm sorry that one of your people has died." A hesitation, another thing the humans did which seemed finely calculated to allow them to avoid getting to the point. "And I understand the need for retri-bution." *Another* hesitation! "G'Kar, I consider us friends. Which makes it all the more difficult to say this to you."

Oh, get on with it!

"But . . . I cannot take any action in this matter which would threaten our negotiations with the Tuchanq."

G'Kar found himself spluttering angrily. It was something he did a lot around both humans and Centauri. "I don't understand! This station is neutral territory. You are here to keep the peace. You have given my people sanctuary. Now one of them has been murdered and you will do nothing! How can you take such a contradictory stance?"

Sheridan rose from his desk, licked his lips.

You'd have thought with all that moisture in their skin they'd have found a way of transferring some of it to their lips without the need to have to stop talking to do so.

"Well, Captain?"

"It's like this, G'Kar. The Tuchanq have come to us for help. Over the last twenty years the Narn military has both ruined the ecology of their planet with its heavy industry and been directly responsible for the deaths of a significant portion of the population."

G'Kar shuffled his feet—another human gesture—wondering how much Sheridan knew about the Regime's military actions on Tuchanq.

"I can see how the Tuchanq would feel"—a shrug—"well, *antagonistic* toward your people." Another *sigh*. "And yet according to Commander Ivanova's report and eyewitness accounts taken by Mr. Garibaldi, it was the Narn who started the fight."

G'Kar had been expecting this. "I too have accounts and reports," he said firmly. "And these reports say that the Tuchanq attacked first—and that their provocation was that a Narn observed there were Narn skulls attached to the Tuchanq clothing! Narn *skulls*!"

Sheridan rubbed his nose, began to pace. He looked at the floor, the window, anywhere but G'Kar.

G'Kar pressed home his advantage. "Not only that but I also hear that one of the Tuchanq—the one who actually killed the Narn—also murdered all forty members of the Narn administration on Tuchanq *after* a cease-fire between our worlds was declared. Does this not make her actions seem more like those of a murderer than someone who was defending herself from attack?"

Sheridan nodded. "G'Kar, you're manipulating the truth."

"The truth is a Narn has been murdered!"

"Killed, G'Kar. A Narn has been *killed*. We don't know that it was murder. In any case nuViel has assured me the incident will not be repeated."

"And you believe her?"

"G'Kar, until a month ago the Tuchanq were effectively slaves of the Narn. Their hostility is understandable. But, to answer your question, yes. I believe nuViel when she says there will be no more attacks. She has promised to keep the Tuchanq delegation away from the Narn population. And you can help matters by making sure your people don't go anywhere near the Tuchanq. If we all work together on this, keep them separate, there is no reason why we cannot work out a peaceful solution to the problem."

G'Kar felt a surge of anger and confusion. "Captain, let me make sure I understand you correctly. You intend to limit *my* people's freedom in order to prevent someone else's people from committing a crime?"

"G'Kar, it's a big station. There's room enough for everyone if we handle it right."

"But—"

"Look, G'Kar. The Tuchanq have come here asking for help. Why would they compromise that?"

G'Kar was about to make an angry reply when the door bleeped. Sheridan sighed, shrugged an apology. "Come in!"

The door opened. G'Kar cast an irritated look in its direction, then hissed with anger. *Mollari!*

Centauri Ambassador Londo Mollari stepped into the room, lacquered hair brushed defiantly upward, medals jangling arrogantly on his cloak of office. "Captain Sheridan." He beamed expansively. "Allow me to apologize for being a few minutes early for our appointment. I have come here to—" He stopped, seemed to notice G'Kar. "Captain? I am right about our appointment, am I not?"

Sheridan checked his link. "Yes, Ambassador. A couple of minutes either way aren't going to make a difference."

Mollari's eyes glittered. "Then may I ask what *Citizen* G'Kar is doing taking up valuable time allocated to the diplomatic staff?"

G'Kar found himself trembling with rage. Mollari! His arrogance bordered on the psychopathic. G'Kar said angrily, "I have come to Captain Sheridan to complain about an attack on my people, if it's any business of yours!"

Sheridan sighed. He began, "Londo, G'Kar, perhaps we could—"

But Mollari interjected with that oily smoothness of his, "You see, Captain. I told you they would be trouble if you gave them sanctuary. You would be better off surrendering the Narn population on Babylon 5 to the Centauri Republic for education and repatriation. It would save you so much . . . administrative trouble.'' Another pointed glance at G'Kar. ''And we would treat them very fairly, considering their crimes against us.''

G'Kar shook with rage. ''Fairly! Captain, if you were but to hear of the atrocities to which this . . . this *being* has been a party, you would be calling for *his* surrender and reeducation. They say they will protect our interests. The truth is that in their society *cattle* have more rights than Narn citizens!''

Mollari's eyes glittered angrily and his lips compressed to a thin line. He seemed about to respond when Sheridan cut through the anger with a question of his own.

''Just what is it you want, Ambassador Mollari?''

Mollari hesitated, cast a sideways glance at G'Kar. ''It is a diplomatic matter.''

Sheridan rubbed his eyebrow again. ''Just *tell me*, Ambassador! G'Kar is hardly able to go running with tall tales to his government, now, is he?''

''Very well, if you insist. I came here to arrange a meeting with the Tuchanq delegation.'' Another sideways glance at G'Kar. ''Considering their history I think we have a lot to discuss.''

Sheridan sighed with relief. ''Yes, well, you'll have to talk to Commander Ivanova about that. She's handling all ambassadorial duties for me at this time.''

Mollari nodded politely. ''Very well. I will do that. Thank you, Captain.'' Mollari turned to leave. At the open door he hesitated, turned back for a last look at G'Kar. He smiled thinly. ''A good cow is a better member of any society than the average Narn.''

That's it! Enough is enough!

Fists clenched, G'Kar moved toward Mollari, but the Centauri Ambassador was already gone, the door sliding shut in his place.

Anger unvented, G'Kar turned to Sheridan. ''How can you allow that! You see what he did? How he abuses his position and twists the truth to his own advantage? How can you allow such behavior?''

Sheridan raised his hands in what G'Kar took to be a placating gesture. "G'Kar. I know. Now calm down. You won't serve your people by letting Londo annoy you so easily."

G'Kar made a tremendous effort to regain control of his anger. "You are right." He walked to the office window, glanced out at the panoramic view. He finally got his anger under control and, turning away from the window, continued, "Captain Sheridan, I admit I do not have the Ambasadorial authority that I once did, but surely you must see that my request cannot go unfulfilled."

Sheridan threw up his hands. "G'Kar, your *request* is for the Tuchanq to be kicked off the station! If I do that where will they go? To whom will they turn for help? Who else has the technological resources to reengineer the ecology of an entire planet? If I do as you ask, not only will you have been responsible for genocide but I will have been a party to it." A pause, more pacing, more rubbing of the fingers, then *finally*, a direct look. "No. As I said, I'm sorry one of your people was killed. But I cannot and will not allow justice to be perverted for individual gain. Not for one dead Narn. Not for a *hundred* dead Narn. Are we clear on this?"

G'Kar nodded bitterly. "Very clear, Captain."

"And I want no further reprisals against the Tuchanq either, no personal attacks or vendettas from your people. Is that also clear?"

"Abundantly."

"Then I think our business is concluded." A pause. *Another* sigh. "G'Kar, for what it's worth, I really do sympathize with you on this one. Your people have been put through the wringer as it is, what with the war and"—he shot a look at the office door through which Mollari had exited—"well, everything. I understand how you must feel."

"Do you? I wonder."

"Look. If it's any consolation, you know that one of the Tuchanq died as well. nuViel has apologized and assured us the incident will not be repeated. I see no reason why we can't leave it at that for the time being."

"Then truly, you do *not* understand." G'Kar turned to leave, caught himself sighing as he did so.

I swear one day I'm going to turn into a damn human.

The office door hissed shut behind him, cutting off Sheridan and his sympathy behind a wall of blank steel.

CHAPTER 4

D'Arc jerked awake with a scream.

She was alone! Alone and dying in songless nevermore. Without even terror for company. Without friends, family, home, a sense of place, without even *herself.*

No. No. That wasn't true. It was fear that put those words into her. And if she had fear she wasn't alone. And if she wasn't alone . . .where was she?

What had happened?

She angled her spines, tasted the air; the human medics. She hummed the Journey, the Arrival. The Susan. Narn blood. Then fear, anger, violence, death!

Then what?

Nothing. No Song. No sense of self. *Nothing.*

And now she was here. Alone in this wilderness of strangers. Her Song of Being broken! *Alone!*

And then a voice.

"Hey, hey, calm down. Do you want to fall off the—oh hell, now you've done it. Larry, help me here, will you, her wound's bleeding again. We'll have to get her back on the gurney. I may have to sedate her." Words. Threat? Maybe. Fear? Anger? Don't know. No Song. No *Song.*

D'Arc crouched onto all fours, hands and feet scrabbling for purchase on the deck. Before her stood—she spread her spines, tasted the air—a *human.* Female. Frightened.

And beyond the human, D'Arc's own family. Unconscious! Dead!

"The Family." She spoke urgently, her voice laced with grief. "Their Songs are broken."

The human spoke again. "Sure, sure, calm down, okay? We have to get you back on this gurney."

"Their Songs are broken! They are mad! You must kill them; begin the Song of Birthing for their new lives."

"Larry, give me your translator, this one's busted. The junk they issue here. It's a wonder that anyone can understand anything. Now listen. My name is Mbotuni. Janice Mbotuni. I'm a doctor. I'm going to give you a sedative. It won't hurt but you will go to sleep for a while."

D'Arc shivered. Words without Song. Frightening. Threatening.

"Now don't get all uppity about it. I just want to help you."

D'Arc tasted the moving air as the human approached. Already on all fours, she crouched defensively, belly scraping the Land.

"Larry, give me the hypo."

Uncoiling her spine, D'Arc stood.

"Christ!"

The human fell backward. Sweat. Body movements rapid. Frightened. She was frightened. Poor human. Poor D'Arc. Frightened. Alone. *No Song*.

Alone and comfortless, D'Arc began to hum the only Song that remained to her: the Song of Journey.

"Larry, where the hell is Security?"

And another voice, a male: "Security? I think we've got a situation here. One of the Tuchanq is here. It's got a knife, took it out of some kind of abdominal pouch. It's singing. Just like before. And it's *big*."

D'Arc tasted the tension in the humans, read their fear and anger and *moved*. The humans fell back with a cry, but there were others in her way now. Others who didn't taste frightened. Who ran toward her, shouting; words without Song.

D'Arc moved again, the knife slashed, a human fell, blood spurting from a severed artery.

D'Arc sang her Journey, dropped to all fours, leapt over the humans, galloped naked through the steel and plastic of the Land.

The voices, the fear and anger faded behind her.

D'Arc moved as fast as she could through the station, wounded and starving as she was. A veil streaming backward from her head, her spines flipped this way and that, scanning the way ahead and behind, to each side, tasting the air, responding to scent and color and movement.

What was that? A *human*? A *Minbari*? Were they scared? A *Drazi*. A *Pak'ma'ra*? Were they a threat to her? How fast were they? A *Centauri*. A *Cauralline*. Were they chasing her? Not yet. It wasn't surprising.

The many different Peoples of this Land sang strangely.

Her feet and hands slapped against the deck, their light patter the sound of blood falling from an open throat to map the Land with Journey. The Song of Journey flowed out of her, connecting her to the deck, the station, the diverse life forms all around her. The Song flowed backward in time, through the Customs terminal to the disembarkation point, the commodities freighter, the jump gate, to her home, her family, her birth, and each link in the chain was forged with the blood of Narn. Of Narn, and now of human.

She sang louder; the Song of Journey swelled around her, evolving, defining her own place in this new Land to which it had brought her.

But something was wrong.

Her Song of Journey was not enough.

Her Song of Being was gone, silent, broken by the humans in the Customs terminal. The humans who had killed her.

Now she was alone. Alone and afraid. And with the fear came knowledge. To live she must begin a new Song of Being.

No.

She must *take* a new Song of Being from someone else.

Not from her own People. She needed a Song that would help her live here, in this new Land to which the Song of Journey had brought her.

She would begin the search immediately, before she became weakened with hunger. Her spines tasted thousands of beings within a quarter mile of her. Working, talking, loving, sweating. Thousands. They were like stars in the night sky. Alone, and yet all together. Their Songs were strange. But one of them, surely, would be right for her to take?

She wondered then if it was possible for these Peoples to share Songs.

No. That was impossible. Songs could only have one singer.

She would have to kill to take what she needed.

CHAPTER 5

When Londo Mollari left Captain Sheridan's quarters, he linked in to C&C and asked for an update on Commander Ivanova's position. He decided to meet her in person, make his request to see the Tuchanq delegation formally, face-to-face.

Mollari walked slowly through the Park toward the ground level monorail. As he walked his thoughts turned unasked to a familiar nightmare.

Two days.

They'd bombarded the Narn Homeworld with mass drivers for more than two days.

Children throwing rocks, that's all it had been. Just children throwing rocks onto anthills and watching them smash, watching the tiny beings come out to defend their homes against something that was impossible to defend against.

The rocks had been small asteroids dropped from orbit. The targets had been Narn cities. The tiny beings with no defense had been Narn men and Narn women and Narn children.

Civilians.

Eighty-nine million of them dead, half as many again wounded. Most dead in the time it took to draw a breath, not flattened but flashburned in the release of kinetic energy as a tonnage of rock equal to that of a small moon impacted with the atmosphere and surface of their world.

Mollari had been there when they died. In the comfort afforded him by the Royal Observer Ship he had eaten six perfectly prepared meals and taken fourteen hours of quality sleep while fifteen hundred miles beneath him great gouts of flame and smoke and dust rose to hide the sun and eighty-nine million Narn died.

Fifteen million dead for each meal he had eaten.

Twenty-three million more injured every time he awoke from sleep.

During the bombardment Mollari had thanked all the Gods that ever were for those great clouds of dust that hid the cities. Now he cursed them. For nothing real, nothing he'd actually seen could ever equal the scenes of devastation and destruction and pitiful agony that he saw in his mind every time he closed his eyes.

Mollari had made it possible for those Narn to die. He was the instrument of their death. He was responsible. It was his fault.

Sometimes he wished he could blame the whole thing on Morden and his associates, as he'd been able to do for the destruction of the Narn colonies in Quadrant Fourteen and Quadrant Thirty-seven.

Not this time. This time it had been different. All Morden had done was arrange for the destruction of the Narn fleet. The Centauri had taken on the might of an undefended planet and used weapons outlawed on all treaty worlds to reduce two centuries of civilization to rubble in as many days.

And they'd done it all by themselves.

"Bully for us!" Lord Refa exclaimed privately on hearing the news of the Narn surrender. "For creating a moment of glory to ring in the annals of history, the first step on the road back to power and fortune for the Centauri Republic. *Bully for us!*"

But Mollari remembered the words whispered to him by the dying Emperor on the day war had been declared. And he knew it was the first step on the road to damnation; and that he, Londo Mollari, was right up there at the head of the queue.

In this distracted manner Mollari wandered through the Park, onto the monorail, and eventually arrived at his destination: Sector Blue Seven, three degree spinward.

There was a crowd. Not often you got them on the station, not in Blue Sector anyway. It was the service sector after all, and there was generally little to see. Now there was a crowd.

Mollari inched carefully through. A space opened for him as if by magic. It was impossible to ignore both the space and the expressions on faces around him: the lips curled with disgust, the eyes turned away, the open hostility directed toward him. There was a lot of sympathy on the station toward the Narn situation, and that meant resentment of all things Centauri.

Ignoring the looks, Mollari kept edging forward until he could see through the crowd.

It didn't look good. A group of medics and gurneys, one over-turned. One of the medics was sitting on a gurney, wrapped in a blanket. Ivanova was there too. She seemed to be overseeing a second group. A number of aliens were strapped to the gurneys. They were thrashing and screaming hysterically. Another group of aliens, the same species, stood over them with . . . Mollari gaped. *With drawn daggers!*

No wonder the prisoners were struggling. They were going to be killed.

And Ivanova and the medics and the security contingent that was holding back the crowd seemed about to let them get away with murder!

Mollari tried to get closer, but the line of security guards blocked his view. He edged sideways, then stopped at the sound of a familiar voice.

"Looking rough, Londo. Guess you need some sleep."

"Mr. Garibaldi." Mollari attempted a smile but it fell flat. "How are you?"

"I'm fine. But I don't think you want to be coming through here. If you're on your way back to Green Sector you'd better try another route."

"Oh? And why is that, may I ask?"

"Alien trouble."

"I see. And would the aliens in question be the Tuchanq delegation?"

"Yeah."

"Then perhaps you could let me through."

"Well . . . I'm not so sure that's entirely appropriate right now."

"And why is that?"

"Because they're kinda . . . well, killing each other. At least that's what they're calling it. It's something to do with them being reborn."

Mollari studied Garibaldi closely. How much could he count on his fast-dissolving friendship with the human Warrant Officer? "Mr. Garibaldi, please. I ask to be permitted to come forward. I do it on my own cognizance." He spread his arms peacefully. "I can do no harm, now can I?"

"Well, that's a matter of opinion, Londo." Garibaldi did a quick take on the crowd nearby. "But if the looks on some of these faces are anything to go by, you'd be in trouble if I didn't let you through. Come on."

Garibaldi beckoned. Mollari followed him through the line of security guards.

Behind them a disturbance in the crowd seemed to merit attention. Someone was screaming to let the aliens kill each other. Home Guard. Garibaldi said, "Wait here," and turned away.

Mollari immediately walked close to the group of aliens and medics. He moved next to Ivanova. "Commander."

She half turned, gave a curt nod. "I'm rather busy, Ambassador."

"I can see. What exactly is happening here, if you don't mind me asking?"

Ivanova gave a little sigh, then shrugged. "It's no secret. The Tuchanq don't sleep. I stunned them. I broke their Songs of Being. Now they're insane."

"And this is why they're threatening their comrades with daggers?"

Ivanova shook her head, "Uh uh. No. They're the sane ones, the ones I didn't stun. They have to break the Song of Journey of the insane ones, or those individuals will be permanently psychotic."

"Fascinating."

"That's debatable. When both Songs are broken, nuViel—that's their Family Mother—will pronounce them dead and they

will begin new Songs of Being and Journey. As I understand it
they will be born again. Fully grown individuals with . . . well,
with all their life experience deleted. As if they were newborn
babies.''

"And they will no longer be insane?"

"Apparently not."

"Psychologists on both our worlds could learn something from
this technique, I feel."

Ivanova nodded curtly again. "Very possibly, Ambassador."

Mollari nodded, waited an appropriate few seconds, and began
again. "Commander, I've come to see you on the suggestion of
Captain Sheridan. I would very much appreciate it if you could
facilitate a meeting between myself and nuViel, on behalf of her
delegation. I wish to—"

Molari broke off suddenly as the Tuchanq began to sing.

"Commander, what are they doing now?"

"Singing. The Song of Birthing."

"Ah."

Molari lapsed into silence and watched as the Tuchanq in-
scribed their knives in the air over the writhing bodies of their
comrades. Then the knives descended and the inscriptions met the
flesh of the Tuchanq. The knives moved quickly, inscribing in
blood what seemed to Mollari almost to be maps on the pinioned
Tuchanq bodies.

Then with a final movement, the maps were slashed through
with a single line of blood.

By now the pinioned Tuchanq were screaming, but the singing
from the knife wielders was even louder. And somehow the two
seemed to merge, to meld into a whole that soared through the
decks until Mollari felt it must surely weave its way out into
space.

The medics stared openmouthed at the scene. One turned to
Ivanova. "Commander, they're killing each other! You can't allow this! At least let us get them to Medlab."

"There's no time." Ivanova signaled the medic to be quiet.
"You can see how violent they are. Their ceremony has to be
performed here and now."

The screams of the pinioned Tuchanq faded slowly as their

blood ran out of their chests and pooled on the gurneys. As the screams faded, so the Song sung by the others became muted, descended both in pitch and volume.

The singers slipped their daggers back into their pouches, descended slowly onto all fours. By the time they were fully crouched the pinioned Tuchanq were all unconscious through blood loss.

There was dead silence in the section.

Then a voice from the crowd yelled, "Goddamned aliens, let them kill themselves if that's what they want!"

Molari turned in time to see Garibaldi wade back into the crowd. There was the sound of a punch and the silence was complete again.

Blood began to patter off the gurneys.

At exactly the point Mollari was going to ask what was supposed to happen next, nuViel rose and approached Ivanova, then crouched until her face was level with the human's.

"Susan, the ceremony is complete. The Songs of Journey have been broken."

"What happens now? We can't leave half your delegation bleeding all over the deck."

nuViel tipped her spines to the left in agreement. "I would be very grateful for any help your medical staff could provide in treating our new Family. If they do not bleed to death they will awaken and begin new Songs, just as I have told you."

"Well, good." Ivanova heaved a sigh of relief. "Now there's just one problem."

nuViel straightened to her full two and a half meters. "The escaped one. D'Arc, she calls herself now. It means *killer*. She must be found and brought to us for the Song of Birthing."

"Security are already on it, but Babylon 5 is a big station. It's going to take them a while to find her."

"You must find her quickly, Susan. Don't forget she is insane, now. In your terms, psychotic. Her Song of Being is broken. She has no morals and no compunction. On our world she slaughtered more than forty Narn from the old administration. That was an execution, rigidly defined and sung by my Family. Now it is dif-

ferent. The urge to kill will undoubtedly surface again. This time
there will be no Song to stop her.''

Ivanova swore. ''I know, nuViel. We've already got a stationwide alert out for her.'' The sound of a punch and and a cry of
pain made her turn. ''Garibaldi! Quit punching that guy and get
over here. You've got a job to do.''

Mollari allowed himself to drift into the background of the
scene. He listened closely. nuViel's conversation had suddenly
opened up many interesting possibilities. So the Tuchanq needed
help, did they?

Well.

The Republic was always willing to help.

CHAPTER 6

B rian Grond paid through the nose for sex. He did this because
he liked unusual sex. Well. He wouldn't exactly have called it
that. As far as he was concerned his interests were simply a man-
ifestation of a perfectly normal and healthy urge. Others disagreed. Others had called it weird. Others had called *him* weird.
And worse things too. Pervert. Racist. Exploiter. Some even
called him a slag-lover. This last was certainly true, in a literal
sense if no other. But then, why shouldn't love (and its obvious
corollary, sex) be transmissible across frontiers? Across species
as well as races? Brian Grond saw himself not as a visionary, a
poet, a rule breaker, a pervert, a masochist, though he had been
described by some as all of these. Simply put, Brian Grond
thought of himself as a perfectly normal man with a perfectly
normal job and a perfectly normal family.

And a perfectly normal, healthy interest in sex.

With aliens.

Of course there were problems associated with his perfectly

normal, healthy urges. But nothing a good business head couldn't get around with a little application.

Hence the business trips to Babylon 5. Jacintha hated traveling; the kids were still at school at Syria Planum. So a twice yearly business trip to a city in space was the perfect place to (a) get away from his family duties so he could (b) work on his business presentations and (c) spend some of his hard-earned cash in a way he found both satisfying and rewarding.

"Oh don't get me wrong," he would say on the occasional times when the subject was raised by curious colleagues. "I love Jay and the kids. Would never leave them for anything. But . . . you know . . . humans just don't have what it takes. Never did, for that matter."

The responses were predictable; what the hell, you had to be broad-minded about these things. No point in sweeping it under the carpet. No one had been embarrassed about paying for sex since most of it had been legalized and unionized back in '21. The only reason he hadn't "fessed up" to Jacintha was that he knew she'd feel inadequate, and he loved her too much to upset her like that. No. It was best this way. This way she could spend his two lots of three weeks every year living her own life, getting on with her hobbies, seeing her girlfriends, generally doing whatever she liked with no comeback from him, while he could spend his spare time in those same six weeks lying next to, on or over, wrapped around or sometimes even through the bodies of a succession of exotic offworlders, blissfully aware of every little difference between them.

And all it cost him was a bit of money.

Well, all right, it was quite a lot of money actually, but it was worth it. And he could afford it. Business was on the up. Service contracts for business defense systems were normally far and few between. Now everyone seemed to want one. And have it serviced as regularly as they could afford. All this, of course, was good news for Brian Grond. With demand at a premium, it was a seller's market. Last year he had diversified the company, installed a sales section to dump new models into the market. In the last six months he had made so much money from selling systems and service contracts that he diversified again, added a research branch. Now he had a reputation for supplying not only excellent quality defense systems but innovative ones too. And he had recently opened up a new sales area: the home market. He was now selling passive defense systems which could recognize members of your family by their pheromones and let them pass while trapping an intruder via use of a harmless narcotic gas. Okay, there were a few glitches to work out yet. Recently he had offered a full refund on a system that had failed to recognize a homesteader's parrot and had gassed it. Unfortunately, the quantity of gas emitted was gauged for the body mass of a human intruder. The unfortunate homesteader had risen the next morning to a sickly smell and a decomposing parrot lying on his breakfast table.

But all things considered, Brian Grond was a happy man. Especially today. Today he was going to see Belladonna. Oh, Belladonna. With iridescent tentacles like jeweled snakeskin and suckers fit to make a man cry.

If a man could fall in love with a being shaped like a cross between a three-meter-wide starfish and a baby giraffe, then Brian Grond was smitten.

Belladonna had been the wildest, funniest, gentlest, most intelligent, sensitive, and sexually gifted of his many trysts.

And he had the data crystal to prove it.

He had the data crystal to prove it!

Brian Grond wished he could meet her a little closer to the core than Down Below, somewhere the gravity would allow him to perform some spectacular feat of jumping and heel clicking, with maybe a somersault thrown in for effect.

Oh, why couldn't more people see how wonderful this was?

And the best thing was that he had been able to sell a fair few home and personal defense systems to B5 staff during his stay here. That put up his profit and allowed a credit margin for a big blowout tomorrow, his last day on the station, and a trip around the marketplaces to buy a little extra-special something for Jacintha and the kids.

Grond found himself grinning. Not only had he been having the best sex of his life, he was also loaded as never before.

Oh life, thought Brian Grond, you are kind to me today.

He reached into his pocket and patted the data crystal fondly. Tonight he would add to its holographic record. It would be expensive, but again, worth it. He'd thought of some more interesting things for him and Belladonna to do together.

Grond looked around him as he walked. Three years he had been coming to Babylon 5, and Down Below had never lost its fascination. All right, it lacked a certain . . . *je ne sais quoi*, and it certainly wasn't the pristine habitat dome that Jacintha kept; nonetheless, for Grond, it held its fascinations. He certainly wasn't disturbed or made to feel guilty by the poverty and ill-health that was the mainstay of life Down Below. In his youth he had visited New Delhi, where the principal Indian culture had been supplanted by various sects of offworlders. India at night had been very much like Down Below was now.

The heat came from the heat exchangers and processors which fed down from the boulevards on the upper levels. The light came from whatever bulbs could be scrounged from topside. Occasionally starlight rose in narrow beams through portholes set in the floor. Once every twenty-four hours Epsilon Eridani shone through the portholes, but that light was diffused by distance and by grime on the crystal alloy panes. Even so it lit up Down Below in a series of radiating shafts, each moving as the station rotated, to send ovals of light gliding slowly across the walls, ceilings, the people the machinery, the service ducts and stalls.

The stalls, where you could buy everything from real jewelry to a real good time.

The lurkers could be dangerous, but if you kept your head down and didn't look anyone straight in the eye (or whatever passed for eyes) you would probably get by.

And the aliens.

The spine-tingling, heart-pumping adrenaline rush of humanoid and nonhumanoid alien life that lived, ate, fought, loved, and died here.

Down Below was a church. A shrine to the Unlike.

Grond came here to worship; the money he paid was an offering.

Tonight it would buy him Belladonna.

Grond made his way slowly past a line of moisture reclaimers

sucking condensation off a bulkhead wall. The reclaimers gurgled
noisily as they processed foul sludge into drinking water at various rates of efficiency. Three Narn and a squat, reptilian Ylinn
stood guard over them armed with spears made out of beaten and
sharpened conduiting. The Ylinn assessed Grond and promptly
ignored him. The Narn watched him suspiciously until the curve
of the hull carried him out of sight.

Five degrees retrograde a marketplace shuffled slowly around
the rim. The marketplace was vast, an amorphous mass of scent
and sound, a layering of tents and wheeled stalls, cloth, fabric,
and bric-a-brac that hid the curve of the hull from sight. Grond
passed happily into it, cast his eyes around for some trinket or
doodad, something one of the kids might like.

The marketplace opened to take him in and then closed around
him.

"Illustrate your body. Skin animations here. Holographic or
good old-fashioned 2D. A cred a centimeter. Three for anims."

"Fruit and sweetmeats. Only twenty-four hours old. Guaran-
teed only minimal bruising. Three microcreds per bunch."

"Used water reclaimer. Minor fixup. Eighty creds."

"Get your bamboo here. Genuine Terran bamboo! Hundred
and eighty creds per stem."

"Transxxxthxtll! Ddu cts stsnslators here! Hardware guar-
andgfsdgfbhhh! Only sixty flgkikt."

"Hey, man, you want stims? Reds. Blues. Any damn color you
like! Ten creds an' I'll even box 'em for ya. Another cred an'
I'll paint 'em too!"

"Eggs for sale! Three creds."

"Ytaxan pipeweed! Two creds."

"Sugar! Real sugar! Only sixty creds a pack!"

"Used software, minimal virus! Four microcreds per disk."

"Drinking water! Minimal virus! Two hundred creds per li-
ter!"

And clicks and squeaks and gutteral clucking and melodic
humming and a sound like a wind chime, and the gurgle of water
and the touch of vendors as they tried to stop him and sell
to him and all of it hyped out of the normal price range for his
benefit.

Grond smiled cautiously, nodded his thanks, allowed himself to be stiffed for a trinket here and there, a nest of speech-sensitive *gloppit* eggs for the kids, a holographic jigsaw for Jacintha. Microcredits. Small change.

The vendors smiled good-naturedly back, pestered him to the utter limit, allowed him to pass when it was obvious he wasn't in the market to buy, lost interest instantly when other customers came along.

Grond smiled to himself. The odd trinket. That was okay. Tomorrow was presents for the family day. Today he had better things to spend his money on.

The marketplace ended in a vertical shower of starlight rising through a wide grilled window. He smelled incense. Peach-colored smoke drifted through the columns of starlight.

He stood in the light, let it play on him while the marketplace drifted away spinward.

Beneath the light the rusty curve of Euphrates swung in an orbit that was old when Earth was born.

Beyond the light was Belladonna.

He moved forward, greeted by new sounds. New voices. Figures posing in cages of light.

"Hey, man, you want to do business?"

"You like my fur? It's silky, no?"

"Hey, nice tie. You can afford that, you can afford me!"

"What about it *hu*Man? You like males? Hermaphrodites? Children? Reptiles?"

And yips and barks and breathless sighs and distant squeals of pleasure or pain and a sound like a wind chime, and the rustle of cloth and the touch of fur and scales as they tried to stop him and sell themselves to him.

But he only wanted Belladonna.

She wasn't there.

Half a degree beyond the light, standing before a tent community illuminated only by flickering blue electric candles, a half-naked human male told him why. "Naw, man. Belladonna's legal. Takin' business from us. We move her on. You go too if you want it legal."

"Where did she go?" Grond felt disappointment gathering in

the pit of his stomach. Down Below was a cylinder three levels deep, three hundred and sixty degrees round, and three miles long. How was he going to find her?

"Who cares, man. Greener pastures." The man laughed. On Babylon 5 it was a bad joke and the man knew it.

Grond frowned. "I thought you were all legal these days."

The man laughed louder. "Some is, some ain't. Depends. Now you wanna do business or you gonna curve outta here an' stop wastin' my time?"

Grond tried to contain his disappointment. "Are you sure you can't tell me where she's gone? I've got money, you know. Hard currency, exchangeable, just the way you like it down here." He reached for his wallet but the man stopped him with a gesture.

"I see ya loaded, or I wouldn't be talkin' to ya. Now tell me what ya want an' pay up fer it or git."

"Well . . . if it's all the same to you, I think I'll try my luck elsewhere."

"Whatever." The man turned away, hesitated, turned back. "Just one thing, right? I like the look of ya. Got a dad your age. So this is free, right? Don't go flashin' that wallet around like it was a torch, right? Otherwise the only light you'll see is the light of heaven as they slit you from ass ta neck and take the clothes off yer back, and probably the skin off yer back too. I hear it makes fine lampshades. That's just a rumor though."

Grond shivered. "Is—is that really true?"

"Do I look like the kind who'd lie to ya? I may not be legal but I am a professional!"

"Yes. Yes of course you are." Grond shivered again. Maybe today would be a good time to go looking for family presents on the upper boulevards after all. "Thank you, Mr. . . . er . . . well, thank you very much. I'll bear that in mind."

"Yeah, well. You better." The man walked back down the line of tents and vanished into the peach-scented smoke and starlight.

Grond shivered. In something less than two minutes Down Below had lost about eight percent of its appeal. It was definitely time to go shopping.

Topside.

Avoiding the starlit cages and their tempting contents, Grond turned away to the north. And stopped suddenly.

An alien was standing directly in front of him, blocking his path. The alien was incredibly thin and tall, nearly three meters. A ruff of spines feathered out from—her? Yes, *her* skull. Some formed a shifting veil down her back, others stuck out in a fan around her head. Her skin was pale yellow, patterned with attractive brown streaks and splotches. She had no eyes.

She was naked.

Her spines angled to study Grond.

Grond craned his neck to meet the alien's "gaze."

The alien said: "You have cash."

Grond said cautiously. "Maybe."

"Not credit." The alien spoke as if to clear up any misunderstanding. "Cash."

"You've been listening to my conversation."

The alien tipped all her spines to the left. "Yes."

Grond was beginning to feel a little more at ease with this startling alien female. "What's your interest in my cash, anyway?"

"You need cash to intertwine your Song with others."

Grond laughed. "Well, I've never heard it put quite that way before."

The alien made a complex gesture with her hand, almost as if inscribing a map in the smoky air of Down Below. "I must continue the Song of Journey."

Grond nodded. He was beginning to understand. "Now, don't take this personally but I notice you haven't got any clothes on."

The alien tipped her spines again to the left. So far so good.

"You're naked and you need cash money and you need to travel. You're a working girl right? A *legal*, just like Belladonna. You're legal and they've moved you on just like they did her. You know where she'll be."

Again the spines tipped, this time to the right. *Who needs translators anyway?*

"Thought as much. So. Here's the deal. I'll give you cash, if you take me to Belladonna. That all right with you?"

The alien said, "I must continue the Song of Journey. I must take your Song of Being and continue the Song of Journey."

Grond smiled. "Exactly my thoughts. My . . . er . . . Song and your . . . Song. We'll go together. You lead and I'll follow. Cash on delivery, as they used to say."

To Grond's surprise the alien led him not south back into Down Below or spinward through the marketplace, but directly north, the way out of Down Below and back toward the legal sections of the station.

Odd. Still, Grond was not prepared to give up his night of joyful debauchery just yet.

After a while they reached the personnel lift by which Grond had come to Down Below.

And passed it.

Grond found himself following the alien up three levels on foot to a freight elevator. According to the specs stenciled on the outer walls, the elevator was designed to move cargo or heavy machinery such as shuttle cars or earth movers from the underground garages to various destinations from the Park through to the core monorail or the Cargo bays.

At first Grond was surprised by this, but the more he thought about it, the clearer it became. If Belladonna was legal, then it stood to reason she might have moved to better surroundings. And since she was probably the most exotic alien he had ever seen, it stood to reason she might actually prefer living in the lower gravity conditions near the core or in the alien sectors.

His mind settled, Grond happily followed the naked alien into the lift.

An overhead loading system was busy shuffling crates through the open doors of the elevator. Grond ducked as the last crate slid past overhead, slotted neatly into a racking system inside the elevator. Now there was only a few feet of floor space in which to crouch as the crates swung gently but massively above.

The doors clanged shut behind them.

The elevator accelerated upward.

One gravity. Two gravities.

Grond sat heavily on the deck. Beside him the alien crouched on all fours; her back and limbs seemed to alter subtly as her weight was distributed. Grond was impressed. Very supple. Very interesting. Distinct possibilities. Maybe he'd find her again later, after he'd seen Belladonna.

"What's your name?"

"D'Arc."

Grond nodded politely. "Pleased to meet you."

The alien's spines tipped also.

Above his head the crates creaked and swung on their racks, occasionally clunking solidly together as the elevator changed direction. Grond hoped their fastenings were secure. One loose crate at two gravities would flatten him. A flatbed autotrolley waited patiently to one side. A panel on the trolley's side warned the machine was under computer control, running a fixed program. Grond realized it would move automatically when the elevator doors opened and made a mental note not to get in its way.

He looked back at the alien, hunkered down until her belly was touching the floor, elbows and knees nearly meeting, both rising above the level of her back. She was big. Her head was still level with his chest. The light from the trolley's infopanel spilling gently onto her eyeless face and waving spines gave her the air of a pet that needed a good meal. Grond nodded to himself. It was a look some legals cultivated deliberately in an attempt to engender sympathy in their clients.

Grond watched the light patterns play across her skin for a moment, then caught himself frowning.

Something was . . . something was not quite . . .

He turned. Read the sign on the trolley again. *I thought so!* The trolley was in transit from the garages on deck three to Cargo Bay Seven.

What would Belladonna be doing in Cargo Bay Seven?

A sick feeling grew in the pit of his stomach.

—the only light you'll see is the light of heaven as they slit you from ass ta neck and take the clothes off yer back—

Grond found himself sweating, suddenly terrified.

—and probably the skin off yer back too—

The alien tipped her spines toward him.

—I hear it makes fine lampshades—

Grond reached in his pocket for his gun. Small enough to fit in the palm of his hand, Grond considered the standard issue PPG the best kind of personal defense system.

He couldn't find the PPG. His pockets were full of junk. The *gloppit* eggs. The jigsaw. The data crystal. His wallet.

Which pocket had he put the damn gun in?

The alien gave the impression of observing him closely. She didn't move. But Grond became aware the attractive brown mottling on her skin suddenly looked less like skin coloring than it did dried blood. Yes. Very much like dried blood.

There! He found the PPG. He took it out.

The lift lurched, slowed, and stopped.

Gravity vanished.

Suddenly nauseated, Grond found himself thrashing helplessly around in the narrow space between the doors and the nearest crate. It was as much as he could do to keep hold of the PPG.

Bracing herself against a crate, the alien stood. Her spines angled toward him, quivering eagerly.

The elevator doors clanked open.

Grond grabbed hold of a crate to steady himself and was immediately carried clear of the elevator into what looked like the air lock of a bulk cargo loader.

The air lock was ten meters long and already partially full of crates. Grond pulled himself to the far end of the lock as the transport system unloaded more crates one by one into the air lock. He stood up against a wide metal door. In all probability there were people on the other side of that door—the loader's crew—waiting to move the crates into the holds. The loader would then ferry them out-dock to the bulk freighters.

He shouted. "Hello? Anyone there? I'm stuck in here! Hello?"

No response. Of course not. The door was probably five or six centimeters thick.

Grond turned, tried to see back into the elevator. Was the alien still there? Had she come out? Had she really intended to attack him?

The crates clunked and thumped together as the transport system unloaded them one by one from the elevator.

From somewhere beyond a staggered wall of crates Grond heard the transport system withdraw and the elevator doors clank shut.

There was a pneumatic sigh and Grond felt his ears pop as the outer air lock door snugged home.

Grond sighed with relief. He'd made it clear of the lift. Clear of the alien. Roll on, tomorrow. The lads at the office will laugh their heads off when they hear about this little adventure.

He wedged himself against the inner air lock door and waited for it to cycle.

It stayed closed.

The loader *lurched*.

It was moving.

Grond banged on the door, bounced back from the reaction, fell with shoulder-bruising force against the nearest crate.

This wasn't good. He could end up anywhere. And you could bet it would cost him a whole packet to get a freighter Captain to return him to the station.

There were thumpings and clankings as the dock moorings unclamped from the loader. Then a deep silence broken only by a vibration that was transmitted through the deck and into his body via the crate he was clinging to. Grond imagined the loader's engines firing up, its thrusters edging it away from the dock and deeper into the loading bays, heading out-dock for the bulk freighters.

Grond rubbed his shoulder.

Oh boy. This wasn't good. Not good at all. He had an image to maintain. What was he to do now? Bang on the door like a lost kid until they let him in? Was that something a Company Exec would do? Mind you, was getting trapped in a cargo loader by a mad alien while looking for a six-legged prostitute something a Company Exec would do?

His thoughts were interrupted by a sound behind him.

He turned.

The alien! She was in the loader lock with him! Clinging to a crate not four meters away!

Grond felt his stomach lurch again, felt the fear punch back into him. Scrabbling in his pocket he pulled out the PPG again, struggled to turn himself so he could bring it to bear.

The alien *moved*. Reached into her stomach and—

Grond felt something thud into his chest.

*—knife that thing used a knife on me I'm stabbed I'm bleed-
ing—*

His fist clenched convulsively on the PPG, which discharged
wildly into the air. The bolt of energy pierced a crate, flickered
over the inner door and the control systems beside it. There was
a puff of smoke and a smell of burning from inside the crate.
Beside the inner lock door the control panel shorted with an elec-
trical fizzing sound. The door began to open.

Distantly Grond was aware of a calm voice telling him fire had
been detected in the air lock. There were some instructions about
doors and air pressure. Grond was, quite simply, far too terrified
to pay any attention.

Grond felt the PPG recharge, tried to bring it to bear on the
alien, but she wasn't there anymore. No. She was next to him
now, spines waving gently in the currents of air sweeping through
the lock. Grond struggled. Felt a wrenching sensation in his chest
and then another blow. No pain yet. Thank God, the wounds were
probably only superficial. He still had a chance.

The alien moved again. This time Grond couldn't follow the
movement because there was something in the way.

Bubbles of liquid. Red liquid. Floating in the air.

With a feeling of profound amazement Grond realized he was
staring at his own blood.

He felt hands at his chest, pulling, felt himself turned, his jacket
opened and claws scrabbled across his

*wallet, she's after my wallet, my cash, I knew I shouldn't have
tried to*

cry out but managed only a liquid gurgling. And it was hard
to breathe. There was something in his throat. Blood. There was
blood in his throat, and that was no good, because he would choke
on it and then he would die and the kids would never get their
gloppit eggs and Jacintha her jigsaw and he would never get to
see Belladonna again and she would never do all those delicious
things that made him cry out and gasp for air, and he was choking,
vomiting, as the pain finally hit him, jackknifed him over a crate
toward the opening air lock and someone was jabbing needles
into his *skin*, into his *ears* and his *eyes* and the pain spread
through his neck and chest and his limbs shook convulsively as

he tried to draw breath and he felt the PPG discharge again as he screamed with the pain—only there was no sound because the outer air lock was open too, it was *open* and there was no *air* and he struggled for *air* and there wasn't any and then there was only the pain, the awful *pain* and his body thrashing silently and droplets of his own blood vaporizing in front of his eyes and

blood that's my blood I don't want to look at it, at my blood I don't want to look at my own

CHAPTER 7

D r. Stephen Franklin awoke from a dream of death to the sound of his link buzzing insistantly on the back of his hand. He rolled over onto his back, grabbed at the covers to stop himself falling out of bed. "Yeah. Yeah. What is it?"

"Stephen! I've paged you three times now."

"That you, Mendez? What the hell time is it?"

"Time you got up. We've got what you might call a situation here."

Franklin sighed. "Get Mbotuni to handle it. I've only just got to sleep."

"Check the time. You've been asleep six hours."

Franklin jerked himself into a sitting position. "You're joking!"

"There's no time to joke. We've got a red flag in Cargo Bay 7B."

Franklin rubbed his eyes with the back of a hand. "7B? That's zero g. No atmosphere. Up in the superstructure."

"Yep."

"Aw hell." With an effort Franklin threw off the covers and clambered to his feet. He lurched into the bathroom, scrabbled for a bottle, slapped on a stim. Hesitated, slapped on another.

"Stephen? You still there?"

"Yeah. Sure. Just getting dressed." The stims hit and Franklin suddenly realized he *was* dressed. He'd slept in his clothes. He'd only been on shift for thirty hours. Surely he couldn't have been that tired. "Yeah, I'm here. Who called it in, Delvientos?"

"Bright boy. You taking stims?"

"No." Franklin leaned against the shower unit while the stims took hold of his head. "Okay, give it to me."

"Delvientos reports an accident in one of the auto loaders in transit through the docking bay. Lock malfunction. We got both hatches open, multiple loader-crew injuries, all minor, suit decomp . . . we got cargo crates all over the show, the big ones. One crush injury from that. The loader impacted with a dock crane and we got three dockworkers still trapped inside the crane, with decomp and crush injuries . . . we got at least one fatality, suit rupture, there's cargo all over the show—it's machinery, massive inertia stuff—and it's drifting. There's maybe half a dozen more people in the loader, no one seems to know for sure because it's still decompressing. Also there are reports of at least two John Does, one human, one alien, no suits, either stuck in the loader lock or drifting through the bay with the cargo. They're probably fatalities. That's it so far."

Franklin reached for his medical case, then abandoned it. A bunch of painkillers and some dopamine placebos would be worse than useless in this situation. "Get anyone you can with zero-g experience out to 7B. Get Jaline out of bed if you have to. Tell her to prep for suit surgery. And nurses, as many as you can get. And make sure they've all clocked time weightless. I don't want some nervous nellie who'll puke in his suit and give us a choke injury to worry about. Everyone else to run interference for you in Medlab One. Medlab Two gets all other casualties today. Got that?"

"No sweat."

"All right then. Get my trauma kit. I'll be in bay 7B personnel lock in fifteen minutes. Franklin out."

Quarter of an hour later Franklin floated fully suited outside the personnel lock and tried to ignore his own body odor while attempting to get his bearings.

Cargo Bay Seven was located in the zero-g superstructure rising above the rotating body of the station. Loaders ran from it out over the main part of the station and into free space whenever one of the really big transports had a shipment to pick up, or when, as now, the core was fully booked by other ships. The bay was rectangular in section, running lengthwise back along the station's "spine" directly "above" the main docking sphere. It was divided into sixteen smaller bays, four to each wall, designated "A" through "P." Each of these smaller bays had eight docks, two docks per wall, leaving a passage wide enough for two loaders to pass from one end to the other. Interior access to the bays was via cargo and personnel locks on the station-side walls. The whole complex was normally kept depressurized, open to space to facilitate the loading and unloading of cargo.

The main personnel access lock to bay 7B was situated on the station-side wall. From here, Franklin could see all the way along the bay toward the main channel which ran at right angles to the dock and led to space. There were cranes, loaders, abandoned cargos, figures in suits running service modules or working on repairs to the dock structures. Franklin tried to take it all in quickly. It wasn't the first time he'd been here but, as ever, the sheer scale of the place was overwhelming. He had to get his bearings fast; lives could depend on it.

He looked around for the damaged loader. It wasn't hard to spot. It was drifting slowly out-dock, partly hidden in a mess of tumbling crates, some of which had split to spill their contents into the bay, others of which had bounced off nearby dock structures and were currently spinning in all directions. A number of suited figures could be seen weaving in and out of the drifting cargo. As Franklin watched one of the figures narrowly avoided being hit by a spinning crate, which went on to impact against the station-side wall and burst open in a shower of broken machine parts and vaporizing packing grease.

Another group of suited figures clustered around the nearest dock crane, which also seemed to have sustained severe damage. It had, in fact, become separated from the dock and was now moving slowly toward the station-side wall. The glare of metal cutters reflected off the crane and the dock, the slowly spinning crates and their cargo of heavy machinery, the loader tumbling into the distance.

Franklin switched on his comm system. It was a mess of chatter.

"—no, forget that get them *all* out—"

"—*hell* is that cutter? I *said*—"

"—there with the other goddamn tools—"

"—out for that junction box!"

"—your goddamn head! Jesus, Mo, that was close!"

"—it tight, people, I said keep it—"

"—*hell* are the goddamn medics anyway—"

He switched to the emergency medical channel. "This is Dr. Stephen Franklin. I'm at the 7B personnel lock. Who's in charge around here?"

The radio crackled. "Dr. Franklin? Eddie Delvientos. Chief dock hand." A figure separated itself from the crowd surrounding the crane and approached. Franklin could see little puffs of vapor from a personal thruster as the figure sped toward him. Delvientos spoke and flew at the same time. "We got a bad one here, Doctor. We managed to get some of the suit decomp and crush injuries to the coordinator's office—that's it bolted to the wall twenty meters to your left—the rest are still out there." Franklin saw the figure gesture out-dock, toward the crane and the tumbling loader.

At that moment the inner lock cycled and the medical team arrived: Mendez and Jaline, half a dozen nurses and an anesthetist. All of them held medical equipment. Two nurses were carrying a stack of collapsible stretchers.

Delvientos arrived at exactly the same time as the medical team, reversing his thruster and settling gently beside Franklin.

Mendez stared out-dock, let her gaze travel from the tumbling cargo loader to the slowly moving crane. "That's the crane? Your riggers are in there?"

"Yep." Delvientos nodded inside his helmet.

"It's a goddamned mess. How the hell are we supposed to get to them?"

"I've got a team working on the crane, trying to cut a way through the wreckage to the trapped workers—but we've got a problem there too. The loader ruptured a fuel tank when it hit and we had a blowout. Zero pressure in the cargo bay meant that there was no fire but the moorings snapped. The crane is on the move. Its own systems are snafu and it's heading for the station-side wall of the cargo bay."

Mendez said, "So it'll get a little dented, so what?"

"You don't understand. That crane weighs eighty tons. It'll go through the wall like a plasma beam through packing grease. There are offices and equipment bays on the other side. All pressurized. We'll get a major decomp for sure."

Mendez swore.

Buzzing with the stims, Franklin felt his mind race ahead, assessing possibilities and options. "How long to impact?"

"Fifteen, maybe twenty minutes. We tried to lasso it and that slowed it a little, but then the cables snapped. Too much momentum, too little time."

Mendez leaned forward to get a better look at the crane. "Well, what damage will it do to the wall? For that matter what's on the other side of the wall?"

"Equipment bays, garages, that sort of thing. They're all evacuated for three levels in-dock. But it's the riggers trapped in the crane I'm worried about. I don't know if we can get them out in time. If the crane hits and they're still inside, they'll be crushed."

Franklin didn't bother to nod. "We can't do anything about the riggers in the crane until you've cut through to them. Dr. Jaline is the zero-g surgeon; she'll handle that side of things. Apparently you've got people still in the loader?"

Delvientos hesitated. "Man, I dunno. Look, this place is a mess, I jetted through more space in the last ten minutes than I have in the whole last month." He shrugged; the suit twitched. "One or two of the loader people managed to get into suits— they said there were people in the cargo lock. Sure, the crew numbers don't tally, but that don't mean they're inside the loader. They could be floating out *there*." Another gesture out-dock, to the drifting mess of crates and cargo. "If they're inside the loader, then they might be alive; some compartments may still have air— those that weren't damaged by impact with the crane—but your guess is as good as mine."

Franklin had heard enough. "All right. I see you've got personal thrusters here."

"Sure. AE-1s."

"I can run an AE. Get me a set. I'm going out to the loader."

"Look, Doctor, I got crews out there already—"

"And how many of them know how to treat decomp injuries or amputate a limb through a spacesuit without killing the patient? I haven't got time for an argument. I can handle myself in zero g. If I can't help when I get there I'll get the hell out of the way. Now are you going to get me that thruster set, or shall we just stand here and have a nice little chat while your people are dying?"

It took five minutes for Franklin to reach the debris surrounding the loader. By that time he was sweating. That was the stims. Hyping the metabolic system, collapsing time. It was why his sleep was terrible lately. Franklin knew the dangers accompanying overuse of stims. He could handle them. Sometimes it was the only way to get the work done. He turned up the suit dehumidifiers, tried to remember to stop grinding his teeth.

Together with two nurses he jetted carefully through the tumbling crates and drifting bits of machinery. He slipped between a crate and an exo-powerloader with defect stickers plastered all over the seat and console just before the two collided. The loader on its own weighed as much as a family transport. The crate burst open with the impact and more flying junk appeared. Evaporating grease sprayed over Franklin's visor. He wiped it clear. Something with multiple hydraulic rams nudged him firmly to one side. He slipped out from beside the machine as it smacked solidly into another crate and bounced away spinning slowly. A toolbox on its side burst, spraying him with a shower of small trash, fuses, bulbs, ceramic insulation plugs, some spanners, a pair of pliers. He ignored the stuff, sprayed gas from the thrusters, moved steadily through the junk toward the loader. The nurses followed.

Twenty meters from the loader he saw a pair of suited dockworkers. One was running interference for a second who was holding a body stuffed into the clear plastic of an emergency environment bag. The body was wearing blood-soaked civvies and no spacesuit.

One of the dockworkers waved to Franklin. "Hey, you a medic? You wanna see this boy here?"

Franklin jetted over. "He's been too long without a suit."

"But he's movin, man,"

"They do that. It's just fluid and air escaping from the body."

"Christ. We've been carrying him for God knows how long."

"Shall we dump him?"

"Someone else'll just waste time on him. Take him to the office and put him with the rest."

"Sure. Listen. Sorry to—"

"Forget it." Franklin switched frequencies. "Mendez? We found the first John Doe. Couple of dockers are bringing him in now."

"Check. What's his condition?"

"DOA."

Mendez sighed. "Okay."

Franklin said, "Jaline, how're you doing at the crane?"

"We're talking to the trapped riggers. Two are conscious. Minor crush injuries. One has got bad bleeding from the femoral artery. He's unconscious and his suit's filling up. I doubt he'll go the distance."

"The cutters?"

"Still going hell-for-leather. We've got about fifteen minutes until the crane hits. We're standing by."

"Keep me posted."

"Check."

By now Franklin had reached the loader. He signed off and grabbed the edge of the air lock. The hatchway was blocked by a crate wedged sideways in it. He positioned himself so he could see through the gap.

Something moved.

A piece of jigsaw hit his helmet visor.

Franklin moved his arm, batted aside the debris. The jigsaw drifted away into the loader air lock and then back, wafted past his helmet and out into the bay. Airflow. There was airflow here. He grabbed hold of the crate and pulled himself through the gap.

More trash. Machinery, bolts, nuts, a screwdriver, pieces of broken crate, hinges. Bits of jigsaw. A PPG. Was that a *gloppit* egg?

Franklin moved through the lock, pulling himself by the crates. The nurses followed.

He saw the alien as he pulled himself past yet another crate.

"Jimmy, D'Abo. We've got a live one here. Get me an oxy mask and an AE bag!"

The alien was wedged against the wall beside the inner air lock hatch. Franklin's eyes widened as he recognized the species. "Mendez! I'm about to bag our second John Doe. It's one of the Tuchanq."

"The runaway?"

"The very same. And she's alive. Unconscious but alive."

"That's a neat trick if you can do it."

"There's air venting from inside the loader—she must be breathing that."

"Why didn't it blast her out like the other guy?"

"She's stuck to the wall, somehow—ah. I see. Um. There's a PPG loose in here. Someone's shot her. Probably the other John Doe. Hit her arm. Her skin's welded to the wall."

"Lucky lady."

"That's one way of looking at it. She may lose the arm."

A crackle as someone else clicked into the emergency channel. "Franklin? Delvientos here. Listen. The loader's about to fetch up against number-three dock. We can't stop it. You don't want to be in there when that happens. You got about three minutes."

Franklin swore. Acknowledging Delvientos's warning, Franklin told the nurses to check the interior of the loader. They offered no argument, moved quickly through the lock.

Franklin looked more closely at the alien's arm and side. Could he ease the limb away and minimize physical trauma to the muscle and subcutaneous tissue, or was he going to have to cut?

The alien's arm—indeed her whole body—was a mass of bruises and decomp contusions. It was a miracle she was still alive at all. At least the oxy mask meant she was breathing a little more easily.

Franklin took hold of the alien's arm, pulled gently. The limb showed no inclination to come free from the wall. Franklin took

a scalpel from his trauma kit and began to explore the extent of
the skin damage.

"Two minutes, Doctor."

"Thank you, Mr. Delvientos."

Franklin told the nurses to get out. They appeared dragging a
bagged, semiconscious decomp victim. He wasn't bleeding too
badly; he might make it with a bit of luck.

"We found this one in the toilet."

"Lucky guy. Get him out of here."

Taking a firmer hold on the scalpel, Franklin began to slice
away the skin from the alien's arm and side, where it was fused
to the wall. Blood welled out of the wounds and vaporized.

"One minute."

"I hear you."

Too slow. He wasn't going to make it.

Abandoning finesse, Franklin wrenched the limb free of the
wall, slapped three or four medpacks over the long wound,
bagged the alien, and dragged her to the lock. He shoved her
outside and followed quickly, grabbing the body again and pushing himself away.

He didn't hear the loader crash into the dock but he turned as
a burst of flame, quickly extinguished as the loader's air was
consumed, briefly lit his suit and the surrounding debris.

More trash flew silently past.

Franklin oriented himself so his feet were toward the explosion.
An impact on his left foot wrenched his leg painfully and set him
spinning. Then the eager hands of dockworkers grabbed him and
the alien was carried away by nurses.

Almost immediately his radio crackled. "Stephen? We're
through into the crane." It was Jaline. "I've treated two of the
riggers for minor crush injuries. The nurses are bringing them out
now. The third is going to be a problem."

Franklin shivered, wished briefly he had another stim. "Give
it to me."

"The guy's leg is caught in the superstructure."

"Amputation?"

"Uh huh."

"Can you do it in time?"

"I think so."

"Be sure."

"I can do it. I could use some help though."

"I'll be right there."

By the time Franklin arrived at the crane, the top strut was frighteningly close to the dock wall. Maybe fifty meters. The whole thing was creeping along in eerie silence. He wouldn't like to guess how little time they had before impact. He jetted carefully toward the knot of suited medics and riggers, arriving as the second rigger was extricated from the tangle of wreckage surrounding the cabin and carried away by nurses. Attended by the remaining nurse, Jaline herself was half inside the cabin, suited legs sticking out, making an examination of the third patient. He tapped her on the foot and she wriggled carefully out.

"Anesthetic?" He asked the question tersely; there was no time for chitchat.

"Yeah. Three units gas through the suit breather. His vitals are about as steady as they can be. I need you inside to clamp the suit and direct the surgery. I can't see from here and I can't operate from there."

"No problem." Wasting no more breath on speech, Franklin pulled himself carefully through the narrow gap and into the cabin of the crane. The first thing he was aware of as he entered was the sound, the creaking and metallic popping of structural members as the crane moved slowly toward the wall. The sound was carried to him by direct contact between his suit and the crane itself, transmitted through the structure and then through the air in his suit to his ears. It was a frightening sound. The riggers had lived with that sound for nearly twenty minutes now—and that in itself was unusual in an environment where, if you heard a sound like this at all, it normally meant you had just seconds left to live.

Switching to the common channel, he asked Delvientos how long they had until impact.

The answer did nothing to cheer him. "Five minutes, probably less."

He twisted himself around so he was facing the rigger. He could see where the man's leg was trapped: it had vanished into the footwell in front of the control seats. The front of the cabin had been squashed in the impact, destroying the control systems and sending a tangle of metal to crush the man's shin and foot.

"In position."

He heard Jaline sigh above the noise of the crane. "You see the leg?"

"I see where it was. The suit is intact. Hand me the clamp."

A moment later he had assembled what looked like a half-meter-wide jubilee clip around the suit leg. He activated the hydraulic ram and the clip closed slowly over the upper leg. The suit ballooned momentarily, then collapsed as the clamp shrank until it was tight.

"Clamp in position. How long until impact?"

"Four minutes."

Now Jaline climbed partially back into the wreckage. Normally the cabin was big enough for three—now Franklin felt like a rat in a cage. He was just glad the rigger was unconscious.

"You got hold there?" she asked.

"Yep."

"I'm puncturing the suit below the clamp. Stand by to tighten the clamp when we lose internal pressure."

Using power shears, Jaline cut through the material of the suit. Franklin felt the pressure go immediately, squeezed the trigger of the hydraulic ram to tighten the clamp further. Blood spurted out of the cut Jaline was making, vaporizing in the zero pressure of the cabin.

Jaline stopped, called for suction, used a slender hose to suck away the blood from inside the suit leg. It took only seconds but even so Franklin had to wipe away a thin layer of sublimed blood from his visor.

He heard Delvientos say, "Jeez, where'd all that blood come from?"

Jaline's voice was as calm as her hands as they cut methodically through the suit. "The blood was in the suit already. He's been bleeding for a while. I think the fact his leg was so badly crushed actually saved his life. The wreckage had mostly pinched off the artery."

"Is he gonna be okay?"

"He is if I have anything to say about it."

Jaline handed back the suction hose and finished cutting away the suit leg. "Okay, I'm through. Give me a scalpel."

Franklin switched to the medical channel and said, "Make it quick. No points for neatness if we're smeared all over the dock wall."

"Right. Nurse, make that a heavy scalpel."

Switching channels again, Franklin asked Delvientos, "Time to impact?"

"Three minutes."

Franklin said, deadpan, "Dr. Jaline. I don't want to rush you, but I could really do with some breakfast, so if you could just hurry it along there I'd be more than grateful."

"Stephen, you're just no fun when you're on stims."

"Fine. Whatever. Just cut."

Another spurt of blood, smaller this time.

"Suction."

Globules of vaporizing blood vanished into the hose.

The scalpel glittered in the light from Jaline's helmet.

"Two minutes."

More cutting. Franklin felt his teeth grinding together. *Got to stop that.*

"Okay, I'm through the muscle. Give me a bone saw."

"One minute."

Switching back to the common frequency, Franklin said, "Everyone not directly involved with surgery move away from the crane. Now. Dr. Jaline and I will finish this. Move it, people! Nurse, give me that suction unit. Delvientos. Make sure my staff are clear of the crane."

"I heard that, Dr. Franklin."

Jaline said, "Suction. Thanks. Okay, Yeah, that's good. I can see now."

"How are we doing?"

"Goddamn riggers, what are their legs made out of anyway? Titanium? I'm gonna bill this guy for a new bone saw."

Delvientos said, "We're outta time!"

Jaline renewed her efforts.

Too late.

The first indication the crane had hit the wall was a metallic screeching sound transmitted to Franklin through his contact with the structure. The crane shook as, twenty meters away, the balance gantry crashed into the wall in slow motion. With an effort he ignored both noise and shaking.

"Jaline. Talk to me."

"Almost through. Almost . . ."

A sudden jerk. Movement all around. Steel rippled, girders bent, paint scraped away to hang in a lazy cloud of drifting particles.

The metal *screamed*.

And Jaline gave a cry. "Jesus! I've got a red light! My suit's punctured!"

Franklin grabbed the bone saw from her. "Get out. Now! Delvientos? Get the hell over here now with a suit repair kit and get Dr. Jaline out!"

A moment and she was gone, protesting. He ignored her voice. He reached into the footwell to get at the rigger's leg. At that moment the crane collapsed even more; the cabin buckled, finished the job for him by squeezing the leg in two as if it were paste pinched off from a tube of cream.

There was a trickle of blood, but the suit clamp held. The rigger moaned and wriggled, then lapsed back into unconsciousness. Franklin grabbed the rigger, tried to pull him clear. He came easily now, nothing to hold him back. He turned to the opening through which he'd entered the cabin.

It was gone, closed off by the collapse of the cabin.

They were trapped inside the crane.

He swore. Loudly.

The crane continued to impact with the wall. Metal bent and cracked. The cabin compressed even further. Then the ceiling split and the crane's central mast came down through the roof, between Franklin and the rigger, punched the floor out, continued on into the superstructure of the crane for several meters, then jammed tight.

Wasting no time on thought, Franklin pushed the rigger through the jagged hole and followed him through, just as the cabin itself smashed into the wall and was crushed flat.

Now he was in the central structure of the crane, actually inside the gantry. Still no way out but at least he could move away from the wall. Pushing the rigger ahead of him, wiping his visor free of blood every few meters, Franklin pulled himself along inside the crane. Cables tangled his limbs. Sweat misted the inside of the visor. Every time he touched steel, he heard the crane dying behind him, smashing continuously into the wall with a sound like a hundred metal foundries.

He pulled himself along hand over hand, vaguely aware of voices screaming in his ears, ignoring them because he knew he had to move or die, crushed as the part of the crane he was in hit the wall.

He gave the rigger in front another push. The suited figure didn't move. They'd reached the end of the crane; the winch house where all the heavy machinery was housed. He felt around past the rigger for a hatch. Couldn't find one.

Then he realized the winch house was moving. Toward him. Of course, it massed so much more than the superstructure, had more momentum. It wouldn't stop moving just because everything else had. He was going to be crushed flat between the winch house and the wall!

Grabbing the body, Franklin pushed himself back the way he had come. The length of girders was twisting, winding together. Metal screamed constantly. Blood trickled from the rigger's clamped leg, misted the space around his visor, made the girders slick beneath his gloved fingers. Franklin felt metal press against his back and legs, felt himself squashed into a fetal position by the winch house and the twisting girders.

Oh hell. This is not good. This is not good at all.

Franklin managed to gather the rigger against him and held on tight, as if the two of them together could stave off the inevitable.

It was useless, of course.

A girder clunked against his helmet. He heard the crane screaming as it died. A mass of cables hit the back of his knees.

He heard himself screaming. Not pain, that would come later. Defiance. A refusal to die. For all the good it would do him. At least he wasn't grinding his teeth anymore.

Helmeted figures pressed against the crane. Delvientos, Lopez.

Separated by less than a meter of buckling metal girders, yet as unreachable as Nurse Murchison's quarters. Visored faces stared at him, eyes wide. A gloved hand reached for him. He tried to reach back but couldn't move.

He saw mouths moving behind visors, heard vague snippets of noise. The scream of metal drowned everything.

A red light glimmered in his heads up display; one of the suit seals had given way. Air leak. Decompression.

The way this metal was shifting he wasn't going to be alive long enough to suffocate.

Then the pressure was gone. The central structure of the crane burst open like a squashed paper lantern. Franklin tried to pull himself toward the hole but already suited hands were there to drag both him and the rigger clear as the winch house smashed past where he had been and impacted with the tangled mess that was the rest of the crane and, in terrifying slow motion, punched both itself and the wreckage through the dock wall and into the station beyond.

The section blew out in a great gout of air and moisture and loose trash. But the area had been sealed off and the damage was contained. Only two sections depressurized. No lives were lost.

Fifteen minutes later, Franklin stood inside the personnel lock changing room with Mendez and stripped off his suit. His body ached from head to foot, and there were some decomp contusions around his left knee where the suit seal had given way. All in all his injuries were minor. A hot flush of energy from adrenaline, and from the stim tabs, made his skin come out in goose bumps.

He leaned against the metal wall of the changing room and tried to catch his breath. "You know, Mendez, the more I think about it, the more the idea of breakfast sounds like heaven."

Mendez studied him closely as she took off her own suit. "Looks to me like you already had breakfast, Stephen." She pinched her finger and thumb together to indicate something the size and shape of a medication tab. "On prescription. Know what I mean?" She wasn't smiling.

Franklin felt anger well up inside, controlled it with an effort. *For God's sake! How many would have died if he hadn't*—never mind. Forget it. Let it go.

He couldn't, not quite. "Look, Mendez, I know you're just doing your job, looking out for your patients." He stared at her. "Just don't make the mistake of thinking I'm one of them."

Angrily, he turned away from her and began to dress.

CHAPTER 8

John Sheridan felt the day was unraveling faster than he could tie it together. It was the Tuchanq. Technological help had seemed like such a simple request. Then the deaths started. Now here he was in Medlab looking at the result of death number three. Brian Grond. Businessman. Death by slow decompression.

Actually it wasn't quite as simple as that.

Together with Franklin and Garibaldi, Sheridan watched from the observation booth as Carla Mendez autopsied Grond's body, giving a running monologue as she did so.

"Subject is a forty-five-year-old human male. No deformities. Apparent cause of death was by slow decompression, that is to say suffocation. Face, neck, and hands show major bruising caused by blood loss through the capillary walls and the skin. Eyeballs show desiccation and full fluid loss. Blood loss from ears, nose, and mouth indicates possible internal trauma including but not limited to brain and lung hemorrhage. In addition there is medium-grade bruising to all parts of the body covered at the time by clothing."

As Lopez spoke she selected instruments from a nearby trolley, replacing new ones with those she had used. There wasn't much blood.

"Although death was caused by decompression suffocation there is one qualifying factor. I see two wounds in the upper chest region. Wounds are consistent with that of blows from a curved blade."

Sheridan and Garibaldi exchanged looks.

"I suspect my day just got a whole lot worse," Garibaldi muttered.

"*Your* day." Sheridan shook his head wearily.

They watched as the autopsy continued.

Beginning with a bone saw to divide the breastbone, Lopez worked in through the layers of the chest. Skin, subcutaneous tissue, muscle, all were reflected and clamped so that the extent of the two puncture wounds to the chest could be examined.

The wounds were deep.

"I'm no doc, Doc, but I'd say those were killing wounds, am I right?"

Franklin nodded to Garibaldi. "It's why I called you both down here." He frowned and then continued. 'Although we have no way of knowing what went on in that air lock, it looks very much to me as though the Tuchanq intended to murder Grond. The air lock blowout was simply an accident that complicated matters."

Sheridan frowned. "I don't get it. They come here asking for help. Then they attack the Narn. And now this."

Garibaldi glanced at Franklin. "You saw PPG damage in the air lock?"

Franklin nodded. "Even saw the PPG."

"Well then, it seems clear what happened. The Tuchanq rolled Grond for a reason we'll probably never know. Grond tried to defend himself. Hit the lock controls with a stray plasma bolt and bingo. One less operator in the business sector."

It wasn't good enough for Sheridan. "This whole situation is getting way out of control. Now, I reported the fight between the Tuchanq and the Narn to Earthdome and they seem content to let me handle matters. This new death is going to have to be reported, and it'll surely complicate matters. But how? Attempted murder? Actual murder? Self-defense? Death by misadventure? However it goes in the report it'll affect whether or not the Tuchanq get the help they need."

"Well. We do have a star witness." Garibaldi jerked a thumb at the intensive care unit where the Tuchanq was almost hidden behind banks of monitors and medical equipment. "But of course there's a problem."

"Isn't there always?" Sheridan looked at Franklin.

Franklin nodded. "The Tuchanq suffered decompression just as Grond did. She was lucky in that she managed to stay breathing long enough for us to bag her. But she wasn't one-hundred-percent lucky. We've been monitoring her since having treated her wounds. It seems very likely she has suffered major trauma to the brain."

Sheridan frowned. "You mean she's brain damaged?"

Franklin nodded. Anticipating Sheridan's next question, he added, "Right now she's in a coma. The extent of the damage won't become clear until she awakes, if she ever does. But if she awakes, it is my belief that the damage could be personality altering."

Aw hell.

"Also there will undoubtedly be some memory loss. Whether she'll have knowledge of the incident is problematic at best. But don't count on it."

"It's actually irrelevant what she remembers. The fact is she may have killed someone!" Sheridan sighed, apologized for his outburst. "When will you know for sure?"

"Whenever she wakes up and someone asks her."

"Helpful," muttered Garibaldi.

"Under the circumstances, I'm afraid it's the best I can do."

Sheridan thought for a moment. "We could have her scanned."

Garibaldi pursed his lips. "Lyta?"

Sheridan nodded.

Franklin said, "Lyta Alexander? I didn't know she was still in-station."

Garibaldi shrugged. "Now you do." He added to Sheridan, "Last I heard she was hiding out Down Below. She's been terrified of reprisals ever since she revealed Talia Winters was a Psi-Corps plant."

"Can you find her?"

Garibaldi removed one hand from his pocket long enough to rub his chin. "I can find a rainy day on the Moon."

Sheridan nodded. "All right then. That's one avenue of approach." He thought for a moment. "What else can we think of?"

Garibaldi scratched his head, and shrugged. "Not a whole hell of a lot, I'm afraid. Delvientos has dug the cargo loader black box out of the wreckage. But parts of the data have corrupted. Ronald down in communications is trying to reconstruct what he can of it now. I don't know how long it'll take but if it works we could have a full vid of the fight in the air lock . . . if there was a fight," he added. "What we do have are the personal effects removed from Grond's body—and those found floating among the wreckage."

"And they are?"

"Well. We got standard ID, which I've been able to verify. Brian Grond was a businessman, ran his own company. Business, Home, and Personal Defense Systems." Garibaldi shrugged. "Much good they did him."

"What else?"

"He had the standard bunch of junk in his pockets. Odd bits of paper. A paper notebook supplement to his link—it seems he was a bit old-fashioned like that. There were some odd bits of jigsaw. And a *gloppit* egg."

"A what?"

Garibaldi glanced at Franklin, who shook his head as if to say *Not now, Garibaldi!*

Garibaldi said, "It's nothing. A kid's trinket. It's not important. One thing was odd though. He had a credit chip."

"What's odd about that?"

"He had a wallet as well. With cash in it."

"Who uses cash nowadays?"

"Lurkers. He's been Down Below."

"That's hardly conclusive evidence. Perhaps he was a collector. You know, coin of the realm and all that."

Garibaldi shook his head. "He's been Down Below. And recently too."

"How do you know?"

Garibaldi held up a data crystal. "Found this on him."

"What is it?" Sheridan caught the data crystal as Garibaldi flipped it to him.

"It's . . . interesting."

Sheridan waited and Garibaldi continued. "Apparently Brian

Grond had a thing for sex with aliens. Hence his business trip here.''

Sheridan cast a quick look into the autopsy room at the body of Brian Grond. ''Interesting.'' He tossed the crystal into the air and caught it again.

Garibaldi frowned. ''It's not exactly one for the family album.''

''He had family?''

Garibaldi nodded. ''Wife and two kids. Syria Planum.''

''I'll need their address.'' Sheridan flipped the data crystal again and shook his head.

Garibaldi nodded, took the data crystal back from Sheridan, hefted it thoughtfully. ''Business sector. They'll be wanting receipts next.''

Franklin shrugged. ''It's legal. Why shouldn't it be tax deductible?''

Sheridan looked quickly from Garibaldi to Franklin and back again.

''What?'' Both Garibaldi and Franklin demanded defensively.

Sheridan frowned. ''I'll be in my office trying to work out what to tell Earthdome if either of you should come up with any other relevant information.''

Sheridan left Medlab without speaking. He had a report to make and next of kin to notify; he'd lay a month's wages to a fresh orange he was going to like neither response.

CHAPTER 9

The Corps is mother, the Corps is father.
Lyta Alexander snuggled deeper into the gloom of Down Below and tried to remember the voice, the voice that held her to this time and place. The voice. The music. The Song. Oh, it was lovely, the Song. As lovely as the voice of Down Below was

ugly. It had given her strength in times of need. It had given her hope and joy and purpose. It had kept her alive. It had changed her. Motivated her. Driven her. It had made her the woman she was.

But the voice was fading. Soon it would be gone. In a tiny corner of her mind Lyta Alexander wondered whether the strength and purpose the voice had given her would fade with it. She did not know the answer to that question. It was driven from her by need. The need to escape capture by the Psi-Corps.

Lyta Alexander was on the run. A fugitive from the Corps that had sheltered her and nurtured her, taught her to develop her skills as a telepath. Now they wanted her back. Not even dead. Just back. They wanted to open her mind up like a flower, extract the essence that was her experience and knowledge, the essential core that was Lyta Alexander.

They wanted to find out what she knew about the Vorlons.

About Ambassador Kosh.

She couldn't let them do that.

She *wouldn't* let them do it.

Allow that one moment of perfect beauty to be corrupted by Psi-Corps? She would rather die.

Lyta snuggled deeper into the gloom, tried to gather the darkness around her like a shroud. Her mind opened, setting traps and blocks, searching the darkness around her for a hunter's thoughts, prepared to deflect a search if she detected one or withdraw if the hunter was too powerful.

Lyta couldn't hear the sounds all around her, the rumble of machinery, the drip and clank of the moisture reclaimers, the hustling, the begging voices, the screams. Deaf from early childhood, she only knew the inner voices. The mind talk. Deaf, she could hear better than anyone alive.

The mind-voice of Down Below was ugly with pain and need.

The Corps is mother! The Corps is father! You're dead! You hear me, Alexander? You blew my cover—you're dead! Another voice bellowed into her mind. Talia Winters. Psi-Corps plant. Deep-level personality graft. Talia Winters was dead; the *old* Talia Winters was dead. And the new Talia Winters was back on

Mars with a mind loaded with classified information. Winters was safe and the Corps was hunting Alexander down like an animal.

Like an animal she had been forced to hide, move slowly, carefully, run when she had to. Sheridan had helped her by arranging passage for her on a Baltan Freighter headed out for the rim. All she had to do was to survive reprisals until the freighter docked and then she'd be gone for good.

But the Psi-Cops ship was coming; time was running out. One attempt had been made on her life already. She had no idea when another would come. Rejecting Sheridan's offer of sanctuary, she had retreated Down Below, where she hid like a cowed dog. Hid because it was the only way to stay alive and because she had to stay alive to reach Vorlon space. Even though she didn't know why.

She looked up suddenly, even though she saw nothing in the gloom. Dim starlight glimmered through a row of portholes. Faint beams shot laser straight through coiling smoke and dust. Distantly came the voice of Down Below, fear, pain, anger, hunger.

And something else.

A question.

How the hell am I going to find her in this mess of poverty and human scrap?

A familiar voice.

Garibaldi.

She reached out and touched him as he passed. He whirled, PPG at the ready. He was nervous as hell. He didn't like it down here. Didn't realize how . . . anonymous, how . . . *safe* it was.

"What the hell—Lyta? Is that you?"

She nodded.

"You look like shit."

"Has my ship docked?"

"There was a delay. You have time to do me a favor."

"A telepathic favor?"

"Yeah."

"There are other telepaths in-station."

"None that I trust."

She sighed. "Do I get to take a shower first?"

"I'd say that was mandatory."

She took the shower in Garibaldi's quarters, one of only two dozen on the station where hot water replaced sonic projectors. Afterward he took her to Medlab One, told her what he wanted on the way.

"So this Tuchanq, D'Arc, is unconscious, possibly brain damaged. You can't tell how badly so you want me to scan her."

"I know it's against the code but you can't say you haven't done it before."

"And look where it got me." She waited for a response but there was none. "You know, Garibaldi, every time I see you my life takes a turn for the worse."

Garibaldi shrugged, hands thrust deep into pockets. "What can I say? We live in interesting times."

They reached Medlab and he ushered her inside. She looked around. The complex was just as she remembered it: large, many roomed, with divisions sealing off isolation areas. Doctors, nurses, technicians, and orderlies moved efficiently about their jobs.

She bit her lip. Stopped herself turning and leaving right there. "People."

Garibaldi stared questioningly. "Yeah. We have them here. What about them?"

"Too many. You, me, Franklin, D'Arc. That's all. Or I'm out of here. Everyone else leaves."

Garibaldi looked at Franklin, who shook his head. He said, "Can't do it, Lyta. These people have jobs to do."

She nodded, turned to leave. "Thanks for the shower, Garibaldi. Let me know when my ship docks."

"No, wait!" Garibaldi muttered something to Franklin.

Lyta listened in to the thoughts behind the words, interrupted their conversation. "The iso-lab will be fine. The division is fireproof so no one could shoot through it." She nodded to herself. "It'll do fine."

She watched as D'Arc was transferred on a wheeled gurney to the main iso-lab. Franklin dismissed the orderlies, then beckoned her and Garibaldi inside.

She entered the iso-lab through the rotating air lock, shivering as she did so. The last time she had been here had been more than two years earlier to scan Ambassador Kosh as he lay dying after an attempt had been made to assassinate him. The moment she had spent in contact with Kosh had changed her life and very nearly ended the career of Geoffrey Sinclair, who had then been station Commander. Now there was another figure where Kosh had been, a lanky alien with a ruff of spines and a body which seemed to be one solid mass of decompression injuries.

According to Garibaldi, the alien had been on a ventilator. That wasn't the case now. Her chest rose and fell with a slow but sure rhythm. She was obviously in no danger of dying. Regaining consciousness, however, seemed to be a different matter entirely.

She stepped closer to the alien, glanced at Franklin and Garibaldi in turn. "What am I looking for?"

"Evidence." Garibaldi shrugged when she narrowed her eyes questioningly, passed the comment over to Franklin to answer in detail.

"I need to assess the level of personality change. This is determined by both the amount of brain damage and detectable memory loss. I'll need an accurate report of the way in which D'Arc perceives herself, whether there are any memories directly related to the murder, or to any time before the murder. Really, anything you think is relevent."

She pursed her lips. "You do realize nothing I find out will be admissible in court."

Garibaldi nodded. "I know. And I know that an uninvited scan is against a telepath's moral code as well. So don't think I'm not grateful. I'm hoping that when D'Arc regains consciousness we can confirm your findings with evidence that can be presented in a court of law."

"And if she doesn't regain consciousness?"

Garibaldi shrugged, thrust his hands deep into his pockets. "Then the problem kinda goes away. Permanently."

She nodded impatiently. "All right. The quicker we get started the quicker I can get out of here."

She moved closer to D'Arc, closed her eyes. She opened her mind to the alien, felt for points of contact. She wondered what she might find. She'd once been anchor for a TP who'd scanned a killer's mind. Even peripherally the experience had been terrifying. And this time there was no anchor to bring her back if she lost herself. She wondered if either Garibaldi or Franklin had any inkling of just how much it cost her to scan under these conditions. Probably none at all.

She shook her head. Why the hell was she doing this anyway? She could get killed. Or worse.

She had a momentary flashback—a memory of her second and last meeting with Kosh. The last time she had seen him outside his encounter suit. His voice had been strong then, churning in her like a choir, an orchestra of light.

There is one more thing you must do before you leave this place.

She nodded inwardly.

For you, Kosh. Not for them, not even for me. I'll do it for you.

She reached out to the mind of a killer, searched for the voice, the fear, the pain, the anger, the hunger to kill, the images of death, the blood, the terror.

And found nothing.

No voice. No memory. No self. No Song.

No death.

She broke contact, hardly needed to make an effort to do so. She centered herself, shut down her receptors, put the blocks back up again. When she opened her eyes, both Franklin and Garibaldi were staring curiously at her.

She took a breath, licked her lips. Shook her head. "She's like a newborn child," she answered Franklin's unspoken question. "No memory, no experience, no nothing. I can find no trace, conscious or subconscious, of any intention to murder."

Franklin pursed his lips. "Are you sure?"

She sighed impatiently. "Doctor, if someone questioned your professional competence what would your response be?"

Franklin grinned self-deprecatingly. "I'd probably tell them to go to hell."

She said nothing. Franklin got the point.

"Well, I'm glad that's settled. Garibaldi, perhaps you could take me back—" She stopped. Something . . . something was . . .

Singing of death.

She whirled. Beyond the transparent dividing wall the main area of Medlab was filled with figures. Aliens, tall like D'Arc, spines waving gently, stirred by currents of air and by their own movements. Ivanova was with them.

Alexander felt her breath catch in her throat. Her head was pounding. *Here* was the fear she had sought! *Here* was the anger, the intention to kill!

The leading alien had approached the entrance to the iso-lab. The lock cycled and she entered. She reached into her pouch and withdrew a dagger.

Alexander felt the world reduced to chaos around her, felt her head pound with the Songs of death. She grabbed Garibaldi, swung him around to face the aliens. "They're going to murder her! They're here to murder D'Arc!" She pointed at Ivanova, who had just entered the iso-lab. "And she's going to let them!"

She saw Ivanova stare at her, eyes narrowed. *Fear. Surprise. She's scared of me. She's* angry *with me.*

No. She's *amused.*

Garibaldi rubbed his chin. He laughed softly. Alexander heard the laughter in her mind and suddenly realized that she'd made a mistake. She sighed with relief.

The aliens weren't going to hurt D'Arc.

They were just going to kill her.

After that she'd be fine.

She sighed again, felt a chuckle force itself out.

Aliens.

At least it wasn't her problem anymore.

She glanced quickly at Garibaldi. He didn't need to be telepathic to get the message. "Come on. I'll take you back Down Below."

As she followed him out of Medlab, she heard Franklin say, "Ivanova, I want to know what this female is doing in my iso-lab and what the hell she intends to do with that dagger and I want to know *right now!*"

Alexander shot a quick glance at Ivanova as she left the iso-lab. Ivanova pointedly ignored her. Alexander shrugged, followed Garibaldi out of medlab and back Down Below.

She smiled as she walked back into the darkness. *His* voice was coming back. The Song was coming back. She hadn't lost it after all. Now there was nothing between her and the Vorlons. Nothing but a few hundred light-years of empty space. And she knew how to deal with that.

CHAPTER 10

Sheridan took the Gold Channel transmission from Senator Sho Lin in his quarters. He had a moment to study the Senator as the transmission locked in. What he saw didn't exactly set his mind at ease. Though well into his sixties, Sho Lin normally gave the impression of energetic youthfulness, optimism. Not so today. As the transmission decrypted Sheridan could see that he looked careworn, exhausted. In short, he presented the aspect of a man whose age had caught up with him at long last, and with terrible cost.

Typically, Sho Lin wasted no time getting to the point. "Captain Sheridan, the President has asked me to inform you personally of a change in the law that affects your situation there on Babylon 5."

Sheridan frowned. "Go on, Senator."

"The reinstatement of the death penalty for the crime of murder was officially ratified earlier this morning at a full meeting of the Senate. It will be announced to the public at a news conference later today."

Sheridan began to feel a bad case of indigestion coming on. "I'm not sure I understand. The death penalty is the ultimate punishment, normally considered only for treason. Have you evidence of treason on Babylon 5?"

Sho Lin shook his head impatiently. "You misunderstand. Treason is not the issue here. The issue is murder. The murder of a terrestrial citizen by a member of an alien delegation."

"You mean the Tuchanq?"

"I do. Here at EarthGov your report on the situation has reached the highest levels."

Sheridan nodded agreement. "And I was advised to use my own judgment in the situation."

"Which situation has now changed, as you very well know."

"Senator, I—"

To Sheridan's surprise and annoyance, Sho Lin cut him off. "Captain Sheridan, do not misunderstand me. While the matter concerned only the Tuchanq and the Narn, your jurisdiction was clear. Now a human has been killed. I should say *murdered*. The new law is very specific under such circumstances. The alien in question must be brought to trial and punished for her crime."

"Are you telling me that D'Arc is to be executed under the terms of the new law?"

Sho Lin nodded. "The directive comes from the office of the President himself."

Sheridan pinched the bridge of his nose, wished he could put the transmission on hold long enough to slap on an antacid. "Senator, I'm not sure you are aware of the full circumstances here. If I might—"

"Your report was very thorough, Captain. Believe me, all aspects of this case have been considered."

"With respect, Senator, I must disagree. As you can see if you study the appended medical report, D'Arc has suffered brain damage. Her personality has been drastically altered, bringing the responsibility and culpability for any crime prior to her injury into question. And there's the larger picture to consider. The Tuchanq have come here to ask for help. If the President was aware of these facts I'm sure he would not have considered—"

Once again Sho Lin cut Sheridan off in mid-speech. "I assure you, Captain, that all aspects of this case have been considered. *In full.*"

Sheridan held his temper in check with an effort. "Senator, please hear me out. D'Arc has no memory of the murder, no memory of her previous life. Her mental functions have been reduced by over eighty percent. She's like a child. Medically speaking, D'Arc can no longer be considered the same being who committed murder. Even setting aside the wider considerations I have already mentioned, it would be immoral for her to be punished as such.''

Sho Lin sighed impatiently. ''Regrettably that is a judgment you are not empowered to make.''

Sheridan held back his anger with an effort. ''Senator, it seems to me that EarthGov is determined to make an example of D'Arc simply to illustrate a change in the law. Is that in fact the truth?''

Sho Lin's anger was plain. ''Captain Sheridan, you overstep the bounds of your authority! I am sure I do not need to remind you of your responsibility to EarthGov, let alone your obligations as an officer of Earthforce.''

Sheridan pursed his lips angrily. ''No, Senator. That's something you don't have to do.''

''Then the matter is settled. The trial will take place at the earliest opportunity. If necessary the execution will follow immediately thereafter.''

Sheridan frowned. ''You mean here on Babylon 5?''

''Of course.''

Sheridan felt his hands clench in frustration. This whole business was going from bad to worse. ''There is neither precedent nor structure here to carry out the President's instructions. The Tuchanq have ambassadorial status and as such cannot be tried by a civilian judge.''

''Not so, Captain. Diplomatic immunity can be revoked by Presidential order under the terms of the new death penalty. After all, if that were not the case how could the law be applied fairly to all?''

Sheridan's indigestion was burning a hole in his gut. ''Let me make sure I understand you correctly. You are asking me—as Commander of Babylon 5—to pass judgment in this case. To effectively sentence someone to death?''

''Considering the importance of the matter, it could hardly be assigned to anyone else.''

Sheridan shook his head. If it wasn't so serious the situation would be laughable. ''Senator, I request permission to speak to the President directly on this matter.''

Sho Lin shook his head. ''Not possible, I'm afraid. The President is currently unavailable." Sheridan was about to protest when Sho Lin continued, "The man who held the position of State Executioner during the War Years has been reinstated. He is scheduled to arrive at Babylon 5 within the hour. You will see to it that his arrangements for the trial and execution are carried out in full."

Sheridan could hold in his anger no longer. "I must protest. This whole situation is proceeding without due consideration for basic human rights and with a regard for the law that borders on . . . on the ludicrous!"

"*Captain!*" Sho Lin cut Sheridan off. "Let me emphasize: this matter is not under discussion. It is not a request. It is a Presidential directive." A pause. "As I have said before, I needn't remind you of the consequences to your career if you fail to comply."

Sheridan controlled his anger. "No, Senator," he repeated bitterly.

Sho Lin hesitated, seemed about to speak, paused again, sighed. "Captain Sheridan, all I can say is this: If this case proceeds according to the law to an acceptable conclusion, then both Babylon 5 and you personally will have been granted an instrumental role in the creation of a better future for the people of Earth." Another pause. "I'm sorry but there really is no other alternative."

The transmission ended.

Sheridan sat heavily at his desk. He got up. He paced. He thought of Anna. He went to the window. He stared out at the Park, the saplings which might one day grow into trees, given the chance.

Why wasn't I just born a worm?

He realized he'd spoken out loud when a voice behind him said, "You are late." The voice was musical, laced with harmonics; it hung trembling in the air like the scent of orange blossom.

He turned.

Kosh.

"I'm sorry. I've missed my lesson."

"No."

Sheridan frowned. "I don't understand."

"That is your second mistake."

Sheridan stared at Kosh, at the encounter suit, mottled amber and brown, shot through with a rainbow glimmer, colors G'Kar would find appealing. He had stopped wondering long ago what was inside that encounter suit. He knew: It was hope, rage, terror, wonder. A Song whose lyrics seemed accurately to reflect his life at this point in time. And suddenly he knew. He knew he couldn't keep it all in anymore. He wasn't built for this. Not for this. He was a soldier. A moderately important cog in a big machine. If he tried to keep the truth in anymore, he would simply burst.

He licked his lips. "Kosh. Things are happening. I have no control over them. Um . . ." He took a deep breath and plunged ahead. "I'm *scared*."

"Fear is a mirror."

Sheridan blinked. Whatever he had expected it hadn't been that. *Fear is a mirror?* What kind of horse-hockey was that? He began to speak again, angrily this time, but Kosh had already turned away. The Vorlon glided from the office and although the warmth and strength of his voice lingered for a moment, Sheridan felt more alone than he had since first hearing of Anna's death. No, not alone, not quite.

There was still the fear, the anger.

And the Shadows.

Part Two

Hunting Shadows

December 12, 2259
Alpha Shift: Night

CHAPTER 1

Jacintha Grond shuffled slowly closer to the Customs terminal. Her head was whirling with a confused mixture of emotions. Half her adult life had been dominated by Brian Grond. Now he was gone and all it left her was more problems. More questions.

To one born on Mars, movement was an effort here. Her breath came only with a struggle, the air was so thick. And her legs and back already ached with the increase of gravity to Earth-normal.

She rummaged in her bag for her passport and Customs documents. Paperwork. Everything was paperwork. All rules and regulations. She hated them. Hated them. Brian loved them of course. Most of the Terrans working Marsdome seemed to as well. Perhaps such a love of red tape was endemic to those born on Earth. She smiled. The thought appealed, though Brian would never have found it funny.

The smile faded. Brian was dead. She was here to collect his body.

When the message from Syria Planum administration had arrived informing her of Brian's death aboard Babylon 5, her overriding feeling had been one of surprise. Not fear. Not pain. Surprise—and the tiniest hint of relief.

The feelings were confusing. Her husband of six years was dead. The father of her children was dead. Shouldn't she feel upset? Ravaged by his loss? Enraged and shocked?

Before she could answer these questions she became aware of a voice approaching. "Here. Ted, she's over here. Come on!" The voice was human, female, slightly aggressive. *Pushy.*

Jacintha turned when the voice stopped beside her, found herself face-to-face with a woman in her early middle age with a cute bob and a determined light in her otherwise too-friendly eyes. The woman beckoned and a man approached carrying a video recorder. He aimed the recorder at her face and began to line up a shot.

Jacintha blinked, felt the Christmassy glitz of the Customs terminal begin to drain away.

The woman said, "Jacintha Grond? It is Jacintha, isn't it? DeBora Devereau, Channel 57 news. I presume you are here to collect your husband's body for transport to Mars and burial?"

Jacintha nodded. "That's right I—"

Devereau nodded sympathetically. "I understand the restraining order EarthGov has placed on the body must be particularly distressing."

Jacintha blinked. "I beg your pardon?" Her stomach rumbled. How long had it been since she had last eaten? Twelve hours? More?

"You mean you don't know that EarthGov have restricted the movement of your husband's body to aid the autopsy and provide direct evidence, if required, for the trial?"

Jacintha felt the crowd surging around her slow and then come to a stop. Eyes regarded her almost . . . hungrily. "Trial? What trial? What are you talking about? My husband died. I'm here to bring his body back for burial."

"So no one from EarthGov or the B5 administration has spoken to you about this?"

"No. Brian has to be buried. I paid for my own flight here. No one said I couldn't come. No one said anything in fact."

"And how do you feel about the fact that information regarding your husband's death and his . . . proclivities in-station . . . has been withheld from you? Do you think it was accidental or deliberate? Do you think it could have any bearing on the newest change in terrestrial law—that pertaining to the death penalty?"

Devereau pressed insistently closer and Jacintha found herself backing nervously away. What was all this? Brian was dead. That was all she knew. What were these other things? The death penalty? Proclivities . . . ? What proclivities?

Had he been up to his old tricks again?

Jacintha felt her face fold into a scowl. An old anger surged inside her. She felt the last of her sense of wonder slip away, to be replaced by a set of very familiar feelings: emotional numbness, anger, betrayal. "You mean did I know Brian had been sleeping around? Yes. I knew that."

Devereau almost leapt with delight. "So what you're saying is that you knew your husband was renting sacktime with the legals here. How do you feel about that, Jacintha? What is it like to know your husband is enjoying sex with aliens?"

Jacintha felt her anger intensify. The crowd seemed to press in around her with stifling intensity. The video camera seemed just centimeters away from her face. Devereau pressed closer with her microphone, using her body language to demand answers to her questions.

More members of the press arrived, different networks who'd noticed Devereau's attention focused on her and had come to investigate.

She was assaulted with questions.

"How do you feel about Brian's death?"

"What will you do if they won't release his body?"

"Have you considered the political ramifications?"

"Why do you think Brian was screwing aliens?"

"What was he like in bed?"

The anger flared suddenly. Who were these people? They weren't people. They were animals, a pack of animals crying out for blood, her blood, her feelings.

"Please—I've just arrived. I can't think. My husband's dead. I don't know anything. Why don't you speak to the administration?"

It did no good. The questions rained endlessly around her.

"Did your husband do this often?"

"How did you feel when you first found out?"

"What was his favorite position?"

"Have you told the children yet?"

And suddenly she could take no more. It was too much. Tears came in a flood and then she was barging her way out of the line. Hands grabbed at her, demands to look at this camera or that camera, a barrage of questions that she heard only as the sound of thunder, of a desert sandstorm ripping at the habitation dome. She almost dropped her bag, struck out when someone came too close, ignored the cry of pain as the reporter—she thought it was Devereau—fell backward, lost herself in the crowd of aliens crowding the Customs terminal. Her legs and back ached horribly.

It was too much. She had come here for Brian and now it would be on the news and the kids would see it, see her, crying, and why couldn't they leave her alone because it was all just too—

A hand took her arm then. A polite but firm voice spoke directly to her. "Mrs. Grond? I'm from Station Security. I'm sorry about this. I'll get you through the terminal. If you'll come with me, please."

She went with the officer. But her anger didn't fade as the crowd parted to let her through. It was as if the space the security officer created around her didn't exist.

The press couldn't follow—but their questions could.

And as the questions assaulted her so her anger grew.

CHAPTER 2

Arranging the meeting with the Tuchanq delegation had not been a problem. Ambassador Mollari had assigned the task to his aide, and Vir had done a magnificent job.

Now here they all were, himself, Vir, nuViel, her Chorus, all in the same room, one of the conference rooms that were available for use subject to the usual booking fee. Mollari smiled inwardly when he remembered a particular occasion in the past when his propensity for gambling had left his Government's funds insufficient to book the room. That had been embarrassing. But no more. Now his credit was unlimited. As far as his Government was concerned he could do no wrong. Mollari was learning to like the feeling. There were balances of course, but weren't there in everything? Mollari's first and foremost loyalty was to the Republic. His vision was of a glorious hand stretching out from star to star, people to people, uniting systems and galaxies in a universal peace. All right, there might be a few minor scuffles on the way, but ultimately what was that compared to the grand design? Would the future remember the Narn, the Dilgar, the Pak'ma'ra? He thought not. Their stars were dim compared to the potential glory of the Republic.

Londo Mollari wanted only one thing before he felt the fingers of an aged G'Kar at his throat, and that was nothing more than to hand more of those stars to his people. More of those worlds.

Worlds such as Tuchanq.

What of their resources? The Narn war machinery abandoned there? What could be accomplished on Tuchanq to benefit his Government?

Mollari became aware that Ivanova and Vir were both staring at him. nuViel was speaking. Oh yes. That was right. Now what had she been saying? Something about getting to know a representative of the Republic at last.

He mumbled a polite nothing, smiled ingenuously.

nuViel responded almost as he had expected. A tip of the spines, a leaning closer, as if to pay closer attention. Mollari felt a thrill slip along his pouched tentacles. The predictability of it all was more satisfying than a rigged deck in a game of poker.

Well, almost.

nuViel said, "I have waited a long time to meet a representative of your Government. If only to redress the lie the Narn told us about you."

Mollari winked at Vir, put on his most agreeable voice. "Ah yes, the Narn. An honorable race." Mollari placed an ironic emphasis on the word *honorable*. "One so honorable they used Centauri weaponry to subdue your planet and then blamed the Republic for crimes they committed themselves."

nuViel's spines fluttered in agitation. "They are our bane; destroyers of the Land."

"I have seen other worlds to whom the Narn have offered their hand in friendship." Mollari sighed, shook his head. "A terrible waste. Whole cultures perverted to the cause of war." He shivered. "Still, that is more than enough talk of the Narn. We are all aware of the atrocities they committed while governing your world. I, on the other hand, am here as duly appointed representative of the Republic, with a genuine offer of friendship. Of help for your people." A hesitation. "Of help for the Land."

nuViel tipped her spines interestedly toward Mollari. "Go on, Ambassador."

"I have been authorized to offer the help of my people. We can provide terraforming equipment, ecologists, and engineers to run it. We can make the Land live again."

nuViel hummed quietly to herself. "And what would the Republic require in exchange for this service? I warn you, we are by no means a wealthy culture."

Mollari shrugged, beamed expansively. "Why would we want anything in exchange? We are all friends here. Intelligence is the province of maturity. We can help you, so we will. And . . . just between you and me, nuViel, I have had words with my Government—I am well connected there, as I expect you know—anyway, I have been able to extract an additional promise from the Emperor." A pause for effect. "We are prepared to place a small peacekeeping force on your moon. In order to demonstrate our . . . *friendship*, should the Narn or anyone else feel that they can . . . *take advantage* of our friends." Peripherally, Mollari was aware that both Ivanova and Vir were keeping their faces carefully blank. Good. It seemed professional behavior was finally beginning to count for something around here. He beamed even more expansively at nuViel, widened the look to take in her Chorus. "Now what could be fairer than that?"

nuViel considered. Her spines tipped toward the other members of the delegation, including, Mollari noticed, those who until very recently had been pronounced insane.

nuViel angled her spines back toward him. "Your offer is generous, and we thank you. However, the humans and the Minbari have also offered us help. They have imposed no conditions upon us."

"nuViel, we ask for no conditions." Mollari pursed his lips. "The Narn destroyed the Land, brought starvation upon its People. When the old and the infirm died, they were put into machines and reprocessed as food for the remaining population."

nuViel shuddered. Excellent. His words were hitting home.

"I am sure I do not need to remind you of this. The Narn are your enemies, as they are ours. Is not the enemy of my enemy my friend? We of the Republic are your friends. We can make your world green again. Feed you again. We can remove the machines from your world, take them away to be broken and destroyed, or put to more profitable use. We can give you back the Land that once was yours.''

nuViel consulted again with her Chorus. "Ambassador, there is much merit in what you say. But we must consider fully all aspects of the help you offer. For while it is true that you have made no aggressive moves toward our people, it was the Republic who used illegal weapons to subdue the Narn homeworld.''

Mollari's eyes narrowed. Ivanova was smiling thinly. Vir maintained a neutral expression.

Mollari allowed a hint of righteous anger to enter his voice. "We took what steps we could to defend ourselves against the Narn aggressors. In subduing the Narn homeworld, we were responsible for freeing Tuchanq.''

"I understand this. It may be that from evil good may come. As I said. We must consider all of our options.''

nuViel tipped her spines to the left, rose along with her delegation. The meeting was at an end. Ivanova cast a bright look at Mollari as she followed the delegation from the room. Too bright. Mollari frowned. The Tuchanq weren't going to accept his offer. The Emperor would not be pleased if that eventuality came to pass. And though the effects of that anger might be slow in coming, Mollari knew too well on whom the eventual punishment would fall.

He thought quickly. "Vir. Please be so kind as to find Mr. Morden for me and inform him I need to speak with him in my quarters. Urgently.''

Vir's expression was unreadable. Still, Mollari had an inkling of what his aide might be thinking. No matter. Let them hate him, let them all hate him. He would submit for approval only to posterity. Let the future judge him. He knew what the verdict would be.

Londo Mollari left the room with a faint smile playing gently about his lips.

World to world, race to race, star system to star system.

The future beckoned.

CHAPTER 3

Sheridan met Jacintha Grond at the entrance to his office, ushered her inside with a word of greeting, studied her as he followed her inside.

Mars born, she was tall. Thin. Attractive in a harsh way. Her prominent features sagged slightly under the earth-normal gravity prevalent in-station. Her face was calm but the set of her body revealed the emotional toll the last twenty-four hours must have taken on her. Sheridan felt every sympathy. He introduced himself and offered his hand. Her grip was surprisingly strong.

He showed her to a comfortable seat facing the office picture window. "Can I get you anything? A drink? Have you eaten?" Sheridan thought carefully about what to say to her. Under normal circumstances her husband's body would have been shipped home for burial on Mars.

These weren't normal circumstances.

He wondered how much of the truth it would be fair to tell her; probably quite a lot more than he was going to tell her. He offered a slight smile which she did not return.

"Captain Sheridan, I have come here for my husband's body. I do not want anything to eat or drink. I find the gravity here exhausting. The trip was almost prohibitively expensive. My flight back is booked for sixteen hours from now. When I return I will have to arrange the dispensation of my husband's business. So if you will be kind enough to take me to Medlab, I would like to see Brian once more before he is taken aboard the liner."

Her voice was calm, emotionless. Sheridan knew that was sometimes the case. Relatives would be unable to express emotion until actually seeing the deceased. Jacintha Grond had probably been unable to acknowledge her husband was truly dead. After all, the last time she had seen him he was alive, probably excited to be off, worried about what to pack, telling Jacintha he would miss her and the kids, promising them presents. Oh yes. He understood her need to see her husband. But shipping him home was going to be a whole different problem.

"Mrs. Grond I can arrange with Dr. Franklin for you to see your husband's body. But . . ." He hesitated. "I am afraid you won't be able to take the body back home with you just yet."

Jacintha blinked. "I don't understand."

Sheridan took the seat beside her. "How much do you know about your husband's death?"

Jacintha licked her lips, half closed her eyes, remembering. "I made him promise to take a holiday when he got back. A month away together on a rent-and-roll along the Valley Marineris. He didn't want to. I knew that. To be honest, I was glad he was going away. Things were strained between us. He was Earth-born; I'm third-generation Martian. The gravity is . . . well, it's a problem. And there were . . . other things. Other problems. We'd been married six years, most of them bad. It wasn't going to last. Now he's dead." Jacintha shifted her gaze from the window to Sheridan. "What do I know about his death? Only that I am not surprised by how little I miss him." She sighed. "I think perhaps I'll have that drink you offered. Scotch if you have it."

Sheridan pulled a dusty bottle from a glass cabinet. "Rank doth have its privileges. I managed to get this shipped out from a family in the Highlands."

She did not respond to his small talk, took the drink neat, swallowed it in one gulp. She held the empty glass in one hand, turning it endlessly with her long fingers and watching daylight from the window pass through it to form splintered patterns on the gray carpet. A moment of silence, then, "You said I couldn't take Brian home with me."

Sheridan nodded. "That's right."

"Why?"

"Mrs. Grond, your husband was murdered by a member of an alien delegation currently petitioning for help to restore their planetary ecology. As you can imagine, this complicates matters."

"I see."

Sheridan watched Jacintha closely. Was she sitting up a little straighter? Was that intense look on her face simply due to the struggle against Earth-normal gravity and air density? Impossible. She was in shock. Who wouldn't be? Struggling to understand. To comprehend how planetary politics could stop her from burying her husband and mourning his death.

Once again she surprised him.

"There will of course be a trial. The Tuchanq in question will be charged with murder. The change in the death penalty makes it inevitable." A hesitation. "Brian's body has to remain here as physical evidence of the crime. In case the trial becomes . . . complicated."

Sheridan blinked in surprise. "That's right."

He felt her gaze harden as she answered his unspoken question. "I found out about it almost the moment I arrived in-station. From a reporter who wanted to interview me."

"The press." Sheridan sighed, remembering his own experience with the press almost exactly four months before. "Mrs. Grond, I am so sorry that you were subjected to—"

She cut him off with a bitter gesture. "That's perfectly all right, Captain. I couldn't get the information I wanted from Babylon 5 via Mars Colony Administration. Ms. Devereau was the first person who seemed to know the facts surrounding my husband's death."

Sheridan considered. "Did you give her an interview?"

Jacintha smiled thinly. "I think you could say I gave her something she'll remember for a while."

"So . . . if you spoke to Channel 57 then I presume you know about the . . . other details of the case?"

"That my husband was . . . what's the phrase? 'Renting sacktime with aliens?' Yes. I've known for some time. He never realized, of course. That was the other problem I mentioned."

Sheridan studied Jacintha closely. So far she seemed capable of casually defeating any expectations he might have had of her. If this was to work out the way he hoped, it seemed sensible to make no more assumptions. "Forgive me but you seem—"

"Cold? Somewhat distant? Do you blame me? I fell out of love with my husband a long time ago. When you find out your husband is having sex with aliens, it sheds a whole new light on why an Earther might have wanted to marry a Mars-born in the first place.''

Sheridan found himself thinking back to his own marriage to Anna. He'd wanted a traditional wedding. She insisted on holding the ceremony in the ruins of Anara VII the year a planetary alignment had lit up the night sky with a double ring system, six planets and fifteen moons. Said she got a *good vibe* from the place. A sense of history, of reaching out across space . . . a sense that by declaring their own love amidst what remained of this alien civilization they were declaring more than just a love of each other but a greater love, that of the human race which they represented for other worlds and cultures, and beyond that to . . . well, *everything*, was the word Anna had used in her marriage vows. He'd smiled then, gone along with her somewhat altruistic view of the universe, for a few days even found it inspiring himself. They'd both been a lot younger then, of course. Over the years Anna had grown out of her youthful impulsiveness and into the methodical scientist he loved more now that she was gone than ever.

''Oh yes.'' Sheridan nodded. ''I think I can understand your feelings.''

Jacintha put down her glass. ''Captain Sheridan. As head of the administration here on Babylon 5, I hold you responsible not only for Brian's death, but the suppression of the facts surrounding his death, the desecration of his body by an autopsy I did not authorize, and now the refusal to release his body for burial.''

Sheridan stood, tried to keep his voice calm despite the frustration he felt. ''That's unfair. The death of your husband is a pivotal event in the upcoming trial. The reason you weren't informed about the facts surrounding the death is that we've only just found out the truth ourselves.'' Sheridan sighed as he found himself on the defensive. He wanted to scream out the truth, force her to hear it and accept it: *The case goes deeper than you might think. The change in the law regarding the death penalty is a political expediency. Your husband's death is being used by the Senate as a lever to secure the office of a racist President!*

He could say nothing, of course.

"The press seemed to know all about it." Her voice was bitter.
*Of course they do, it was probably leaked to them by someone
on the Senate!*

"It's their prerogative to know."

Jacintha stood, anger blooming across her angular face. "Have
you any idea at all how condescending that is?"

Sheridan spread his hands, wished he could teleport off-station
for about the next million years. "I'm sorry, I didn't intend that—"

"I'm sure you didn't. Now listen to me, Captain. I don't care
about politics and I don't care whether some alien culture can or
cannot take care of their own planetary environment. My husband
is dead. I want him home for burial and I am going to take him
home. On the ship in which I booked passage. In sixteen hours.
Do you understand?"

Sheridan sighed again. "I simply can't let you do that. This is
a precedent-setting case under a wide-ranging change in the law.
The Senate have been very specific about their requirements as
has the President."

"He's Earth's President. Not Mars's." Jacintha bit off her
words, stood, trembling angrily. She seemed about to scream, to
race across the room despite the high gravity and strike out at
him in her rage. She did neither. Instead she was silent for quite
a while before speaking again. "I assume I am free to talk to the
press about this? Or have you the power to detain me as well?"

"Of course not." Sheridan raised his hands in a placatory gesture. "Mrs. Grond, I had hoped that wouldn't be—"

"I'm sure you did," she cut him off. "Well, now it is necessary. And I shall make sure both your part and that of the Senate
in this matter is very clear to Ms. Devereau and her news team."

Jacintha turned to leave the office.

Sheridan let her go.

After the door had closed behind her he took the bottle of
Scotch and a glass to his desk and sat down. He poured himself
a drink. Only the second in as many months. He wondered what
DeBora Devereau would say if she could see him now, bottle in
hand, drinking to relieve the stress of his office.

The anger began then.

He had only done what he had to do, what he had been forced

by the Senate to do. He wondered if Jacintha Grond would see it that way—afterward. If she would understand the part he had forced her to play in this political charade. How he had used her.

Probably not.

The guilt began then, swamping the anger.

Sheridan reached for his drink.

CHAPTER 4

Franklin entered his office, dimmed the lights, sat at his desk. He cradled his head on his hands. Thought about taking another stim. He reached for the bottle, put it back in the drawer unopened. *Too much of a good thing.*

He was beginning to get the sweats again. The tabs were wearing off. He knew all the signs. Headache. Irritability. A pounding in his ears as his blood pressure compensated for the drug being sweated out of his system.

He blinked. Even with the lights dimmed it was too bright. There were too many shadows, too much contrast. Stephen Franklin suddenly felt he was in the grainy world of an old black and white photograph, a prisoner in a single two-dimensional slice of time. He felt compressed. Crushed. Like the riggers in the crane. Felt everything was bearing down on him, squashing him into his own little life, his own little time and place.

Oh yeah—that was the other symptom of stim abuse: depression.

Franklin dimmed the lights even more, wondered if he dared take an upper to compensate for the stim withdrawal. Just the one would do it. Just while he was on duty. As soon as the dockers had been treated he'd clock out, go to his quarters, whack a little Mendelssohn on the quad, and just crash. Ten or twelve hours of natural sleep should set him to rights. Then a healthy breakfast, roughage and fruit juice, balanced vitamins, all the amino acids and proteins five thousand years of human evolution hadn't managed to obviate the need for yet.

Yeah. That'd do it. Sleep. Sleep and breakfast. Just what the doctor ordered.

Except for the dreams.

The dreams of death; dreams in which an entire race was obliterated.

Dreams of Lazarenn.

Six years. Six years they'd known each other. How could the silly old coot have been so stupid? He was a *doctor*! Yet he'd let the disease that decimated his people run its course until it was out of control, and even as it claimed his own life, Lazarenn would not acknowledge it; the Markab social programming was simply too good.

When Lazarenn died, only Franklin and his staff had stood between the Markab and their death as a species. He had found a cure—too late to save the Markab.

The operation was a success, but the patient died.

He had failed.

He shuddered. Crap. This was all crap. Learn and go forward. The vaccine existed; his work had not been entirely for nothing. The disease had been able to jump species. Now future outbreaks could be contained. Learn. And go forward.

For now there were the dockers.

He stood up, shook himself awake. The dockers needed treatment. He was needed. He reached for the stims.

The door bleeped.

He licked his lips, put the bottle back in his desk drawer for a second time. "Come in."

The door opened to reveal a cloaked figure. Human. Or humanoid. "Lights." The room brightened and Franklin saw the visitor was a human male dressed in the robes of an EarthGov official. "Can I help you?"

The figure came in. "I hope so." His voice was firm but gentle. It was the voice of a professional. A doctor's voice.

Franklin studied the visitor. "Come in. Take a seat. Get you some coffee?"

The man shook his head. "No thank you, Dr. Franklin. I have come here to talk. To ask for your help." He shrugged. "Possibly to ask for your blessing."

Franklin stood, swayed slightly, gripped the desk for support. "I don't understand."

"Then I'll explain." The man stepped forward. Franklin looked closely at his face. Mid-fifties. Laughter lines. A youthful face despite its obvious age. The face of a teacher or . . . somehow, Franklin couldn't get the idea out of his head his visitor might be a doctor. "I have been sent by EarthGov." He offered a wallet. "My ID."

Franklin examined the ID. It seemed genuine enough. One curiosity: No name was given. "I see you have Gold Level clearance. Shouldn't you be talking to Captain Sheridan?"

The man shook his head. "It's you I need to see."

"Well then, why don't you just go ahead and tell me why?"

The man nodded. "I need to use the *life-giver* machine."

Franklin sat heavily. "How did you know about that? I've only had it a year. I've told no one about—" He shook his head. "Why?" He knew the answer even before the man spoke. "No, don't bother to answer that. You've come to kill D'Arc, haven't you? You're the damn Executioner. That was why there was no name on your ID." Franklin licked his lips, felt a surge of anger. "My God, the fools. Didn't they read my report? Didn't *you* read my report?"

"Yes."

"Then even the summary should have—"

The man held out his hands in a placating gesture. "I understood your report in full."

Curiously, Franklin felt no surprise. "I thought you were a doctor."

"This is true."

"And yet you can do this? Wipe someone out? Kill them in cold blood?"

"Oh yes."

Franklin stood again, bouyed upward on a rush of adrenaline and rage. "My God, man. You're a doctor. Doesn't the Hippocratic oath mean anything to you? D'Arc is not a criminal. She's brain-dead. She's a different person now. A child. She cannot bear responsibility for her actions. Executing her is immoral!''

"Execution is mandatory. The President has sanctioned it. The public need it." A sigh. "Dr. Franklin, in every state, in every period of history there has been a place for state-sanctioned execution. It is a punishment and a social ritual. It gives the public a sense of place, helps them to define themselves. It is a comfort—and it is very necessary. Some might say that the root cause of all social ills in the last century could be attributed to a lack of capital punishment."

"What?" Franklin was dumbfounded, outraged. "What kind of justification is that? You're saying that reintroducing the death sentence for murder will improve the quality of people's lives? Is that what you're saying? That's a load of—''

The visitor frowned, interrupted, "I don't have to debate the issue with you, Dr. Franklin. I am allowed no opinion on the matter one way or another. I am simply here to do a job. I have the authorization to take what I need to do that job."

"The hell you do!" Franklin activated his link. "Franklin to Security, I have an intruder in my—''

The visitor closed one hand over Franklin's, deactivated his link. Franklin jerked his hand away. "Don't you touch me!"

"I am an Executioner. I touch everyone."

Franklin blinked.

The visitor continued, "Capital punishment rules have existed for more than six thousand years. The Babylonian King Hammurabi drew up the first recorded version. He rejected barbarity, stabilized society. He made capital punishment a public spectacle and ritual in order to demonstrate the power the State had over those who would attack it."

"D'Arc has not threatened the 'State'! She killed a businessman—and even that hasn't been conclusively proven."

The visitor ignored Franklin, continued, "In the past, D'Arc's execution would have become a celebration for life. With your help, and the use of the *life-giver*, that will now be true literally as well as philosophically."

Franklin shuddered. "What next? A public procession? Fruit

throwing? Why not put it on ISN? Broadcast it prime-time to the worlds of the Alliance! That'll really deter the proles, won't it?''

The visitor sighed. "I'm sorry you feel that way, Doctor. I know you have the *life-giver*. I know you took it from the woman Laura Rosen and I know you used it to save the life of Warrant Officer Michael Garibaldi just under a year ago. By Presidential Order the machine is now to be reinstated in its original capacity, as the state-sanctioned method of execution." The man caught and held Franklin's eyes. "You must agree. It's more civilized than a hangman's noose or spacing."

"Agree? Like hell I'll agree. And there's no way you're going to use that machine to take someone's life. I'd rather destroy it."

The man sighed again. "I had hoped you wouldn't say that." He activated his own link. "Security? You can come in now."

As Franklin watched, amazed, Garibaldi and two guards entered his office. "What the hell? What is this? Garibaldi? What's going on here?"

"I'm sorry, Doc. I don't like this any more than you do. But he's in charge of the execution. I gotta do what he says." Garibaldi shrugged. "And what he says is, hand over the machine."

Franklin spluttered, felt himself sweating, wished he'd had time to swallow another stim.

Garibaldi turned to the man from EarthGov. "I'll get the machine. You wait here." He beckoned Franklin out of the office. Dazed, Franklin followed.

"Garibaldi, what the hell are you doing? You know he's going to use that machine to kill D'Arc?"

Garibaldi sighed, removed one hand from his pockets long enough to rub his chin. He leaned closer to Franklin and said quietly, "Look, Doc. I said you had to give him a machine. I didn't say which machine."

"But he'll know what it looks like. He knows everything else."

"Nope." Garibaldi sniffed. "He only knows what was in the report."

Franklin stared at Garibaldi. "How do you know?"

Garibaldi pursed his lips, said quietly, " 'Who watches the watchmen?' Coupla shifts ago I got wind of some black market information sales via channels no one knew I was monitoring. I couldn't pull the transmission because that would tip the receiver off that his source had been rumbled. But I could tweak it a little. Limit the damage.''

Franklin stared at Garibaldi with a mixture of surprise and outrage. ''Why didn't you tell me? How did you know where to look for the information?''

Garibaldi tucked his hands back into his pockets. ''Call me suspicious. Call me naughty,'' he said with obvious and deliberate vagueness. ''The point is we can fob him off with something. Sheesh, look at all this gear you've got in Medlab. If it was me I wouldn't be able to tell if I'd been given a lethal device or my old gran's sewing machine.'' Garibaldi raised his eyebrows and grinned. ''Think of it as a kinda mechanical placebo. Know what I'm saying?''

Franklin frowned. ''I'm beginning to get the picture.''

Garibaldi nodded. ''Good.'' He jerked a thumb back toward Franklin's office. ''Now, the man with no name in there tells me he'll be visiting the Mosque to pray for guidance after he has the machine. So we'd better not keep him waiting, had we?''

''Whatever.'' Franklin looked around for something that might fool someone who lacked intimate knowledge of the specific alien technology in question. He ought to have the components here to fake up a pretty lifelike substitute for the truth.

He was beginning to think he might even enjoy it.

CHAPTER 5

Sheridan found Delenn in the Stone Garden, meditating. She seemed to be doing that a lot lately. He briefly wondered why but the thought was pushed aside by more urgent matters.

''Captain Sheridan.'' She rose, moved toward him on quiet feet, slight, apparently delicate, yet possessed of a strength most would be surprised to find immutable. Strength, intelligence . . . and something else, something Sheridan had difficulty admitting to himself existed in women since the apparent death of his wife aboard the *Icarus*.

Delenn was beautiful.

Her exterior skull structure only added to her exotic beauty.

The fact that she was a Minbari, one of the race who had come within a heartbeat of wiping out humanity, simply muddled Sheridan's feelings even further.

"John." Her voice was quiet, yet he knew it would command attention even in the most crowded of situations. He found it soothing, like a cool hand upon his brow. "How may I be of help to you?"

"Delenn. I've been handed a political hot potato by EarthGov." Sheridan shook his head, laughed ironically. "Hot? It's scalding."

"Go on."

"Senator Sho Lin has given me a directive from the President to try and execute a member of the Tuchanq delegation for the crime of premeditated murder." Sheridan rubbed his eyes tiredly. "They want to make an example of her. But I don't think they realize what might be at stake here. The existence of a planetary culture rests in the balance. And there is the moral consideration of executing someone for a crime that she can no longer be considered to have committed."

Sheridan watched Delenn for a reaction. He expected sympathy, understanding at the very least. He got nothing. Had she missed the point?

He continued, "It's all so obvious; they're not even making an attempt to rationalize it. Through me the President can be seen to be implementing a crackdown on crime, thus reinforcing his own position while at the same time gaining more support for his policies regarding human-alien relations. And if it all goes to the wall, well, it'll only be John Sheridan in the line of fire. There's nothing clever about it. And nothing I can do to avoid it."

Sheridan stared hard at Delenn, willed her to understand. "I feel . . . *railroaded* by this whole situation. None of it is my doing and none of it is right. The President is valuing his agenda way above the truth and the little people are all getting caught in the political crossfire.''

Delenn was silent. She probably knew what he was about to ask.

''Ambassador, your people co-founded Babylon 5. I appeal to you as their representative to help me. Use your influence with the Minbari government to make the Senate see reason. You can go through higher channels than I can. Together we can beat this thing—and maybe save an entire race from extinction.''

Sheridan was held by Delenn's gaze. And he suddenly knew what her reply would be, suddenly realized just how far he had been railroaded by his own government.

''They've got to you, haven't they?'' His question was rhetorical. ''Asked you to help support the law by upholding their decision. That's why you came here, isn't it? Who did you speak to? Sho Lin? Kobold?''

Delenn lowered her eyes briefly. ''Senator Voudreau spoke directly to me on behalf of President Clark.'' She hesitated, ''You have to understand. My influence is not what it was. Because of my postchrysalis state my government would in all likelihood pay my request no heed. If I supported you in defiance of your own President, the Gray Council would be just as likely to override me and support his decision to execute D'Arc. We do not execute our own kind, but here the council would be blameless, while showing your people to be barbaric, which some might like.''

Sheridan frowned, felt his anger returning along with his indigestion. ''That's just great, Delenn. I thought I could count on you. I thought we were friends.''

''I fear that politics and friendship are worlds apart.''

''So . . . what? We'll applaud madly when the Executioner for the State administers D'Arc's lethal injection and then have a party afterward to celebrate the enhanced safety of the public at large, is that it?''

Delenn said nothing, plainly embarrassed by his outburst.

Sheridan turned away, embarrassed himself by his lack of control over his anger.

After another moment's silence, Delenn turned to leave. ''I'm sorry. I think it would be better if I were to—''

Sheridan turned quickly. "No, Ambassador. I'm the one who should apologize. I was way out of line. This problem is mine. I have no business foisting it off onto you."

Delenn looked back at Sheridan. "I did not only come here to discuss this situation. But perhaps now it not an appropriate time to ask if you would care to dine with me this evening."

Sheridan felt a rush of emotions, chiefly confusion. The last time he had dined with Delenn it had been an experience and a half. "Dinner. Um. I'd love to, you know that. But . . ." He shrugged his shoulders. "Delenn, I enjoy your company very much and I look forward to our time together. But it wouldn't be fair to either of us if our thoughts were on D'Arc. Would it?"

Delenn nodded, seemed about to speak, then fell silent. She turned to leave and this time he didn't stop her. At the entrance to the garden she turned and said, "I understand." The door closed behind her with a pneumatic wheeze only slightly softer than her voice.

He was left with only her words for comfort.

They were no comfort at all.

CHAPTER 6

G'Kar stared out of the window of the core shuttle, three quarters of a mile to the ground. Who would have thought it was merely the landscaped interior of an irregular cylinder revolving in space? It looked so real. So much like the surface of a real planet.

A real planet like . . . well, like Tuchanq, for example.

The last world he had bombed into submission.

The last world whose people he had enslaved.

Abruptly G'Kar took his eyes away from the view, concentrated on the interior of the shuttle car. Soft plastic, muted lighting, chromed safety bars. G'Kar could warp one of those bars in his fist with almost no effort. He sighed. It was so easy to be strong, to fight and kill. So much harder to be at peace, to live in hope for the future.

Harder still to live without hope at all.

There were some three thousand Narn still in-station, either claiming sanctuary or having been granted refugee status. Despite a plea from Station Commander Sheridan not to escalate the tension, the Narn had formed into a loose resistance movement. Isolated from their planet they might be, but powerless they were not. Currently more than three quarters of the Narn population held jobs in-station, both white- and blue-collar jobs. That was Sheridan's doing, J'Quan bless his pouchlings. When Mollari demanded the repatriation of all Narn—a fancy term meaning no more nor less than their return to abject slavery within the Centauri Republic—Sheridan had spearheaded the refusal to comply. And he had won his case too. Although G'Kar had lost his powers of Ambassador at large, he had gained something equally valuable to his people. The friendship of Sheridan, Garibaldi, Delenn, and the others. Their friendship—and their unspoken help. All that Sheridan had asked in return was that G'Kar use his influence over his people to maintain the peace in-station—a peace that was brittle at the best of times, threatening to explode into violence at the slightest provocation. Still, G'Kar had kept his promise. So far there had been only minor incidents of violence toward the Centauri population—none of which had been traceable back to the Narn. And that was good enough for G'Kar.

The shuttle car stopped at one of the embarkation points and a number of other passengers came aboard, including one human in diplomatic robes who took the seat next to G'Kar.

G'Kar studied the human for a moment. He seemed a little overawed by the view from the windows. G'Kar nodded to him. "An impressive view, is it not?"

The human nodded. He didn't seem to want to speak.

"Is this your first time in-station?"

"Yes." The man's voice was curt. He really didn't want to talk.

Nodding acknowledgment, G'Kar left the human alone, let his mind drift back once again to the reason for his meeting with the leaders of the underground. Rumors had been heard of a Narn warship—the last to remain intact after the war—apparently lost or hiding somewhere in hyperspace. If the ship existed and could be contacted—well, that might tip the odds a little in favor of some reprisals against the enemy.

G'Kar didn't really have a lot to smile about these days, but he ventured a smile now. A smile in anticipation of Centauri death.

The core shuttle pulled into another station and more passengers came aboard. G'Kar glanced at them absently, then hissed quietly with annoyance.

Four of them were Tuchanq.

Too tall by far for the human-standard low-g restraints, the Tuchanq held on to the chromed safety bars, swaying back and forth with the motion of the car.

They stared at him.

He stared back, felt himself become even more angry. But the anger was tempered with guilt. For G'Kar was honest enough, with himself at least, to recognize that what the Narn had done to the Tuchanq—what *he* had done to them—was only marginally different from what the Centauri had done to the Narn.

But no. The similarity was a passing one only. The Narn were benevolent rulers compared to the Republic. *Everyone* was benevolent compared to the Republic.

G'Kar looked back at the Tuchanq.

They moved closer.

G'Kar said nothing, felt for his harness release, touched the control that unlocked the safety bars restraining his shoulders.

Other passengers in the car picked up on the tension. One by one their conversations lapsed into silence.

One of the Tuchanq leaned over the human sitting next to G'Kar. He got up, moved away. There were no other seats so he stood beside the double doors and clung to a safety strap.

The Tuchanq scrunched down into the seat next to G'Kar. G'Kar felt something sharp press against his side. He looked down, saw the cold glitter of metal.

The Tuchanq was holding him at knifepoint.

The other Tuchanq came closer.

G'Kar remained as still as he could in the gently swaying car. He glanced sideways and up at the Tuchanq. "What do you want?"

The Tuchanq said loudly, "Revenge. You ravaged our planet, killed our people. You must die in return. All Narn must die. The Tuchanq will have revenge!"

G'Kar moved fast, slamming the harness upward into the chest of the Tuchanq in front of him. He leapt forward.

Too late.

A quiver of muscle, a cry of hate. The knife slammed home into his side.

The scream that was torn from his lips was as much due to embarrassment as pain. He had been caught out. He was a warrior and he had been caught out. Never assume there is safety in neutral territory! Never!

Pain ran along his side; he felt skin and tunic tear as he wrenched himself away from the Tuchanq. The car had erupted into movement and sound: screams, all manner of translated chatterings, barks, and squeals. Three dozen individuals got up as one and ran to the farthest point of the car, pressed in a huddle beneath the rear window. One human threw a punch aimed at the second Tuchanq's head. The punch seemed to connect but the Tuchanq ignored it, whirled, slammed her knife into his chest, thrust him backward with contemptuous ease. He sagged to the floor, groaning, blood pumping from what looked to be a terminal wound.

G'Kar made use of the moment. Swung a fist himself. He may not have been the fastest of movers, but he was strong. The blow should have crushed the Tuchanq's throat like a paper lantern.

The blow never landed.

G'Kar blinked.

He was sure he had—

The third Tuchanq closed in. G'Kar twisted clumsily away from his dagger, which tore a hole in the tunic covering his thigh. He felt the knife sink in, screamed as it scraped against the bone. He fell, pain flooding his mind. He wasn't going to die here. Not here, not like this. There was too much left to do. Too much! Die now and Mollari would laugh at his funeral. No. No! *No*!

G'Kar scrambled upright, grabbed the nearest passenger for

support, nearly fell again when the being—a Cauralline—pressed herself even farther back into the mass of stunned passengers.

The Tuchanq ran forward, spines rigid, knives at the ready.

G'Kar glanced past them out of the forward window, then did the only thing he could do. He pulled the emergency handle beside the doors.

They slid open, admitting a blast of thin, cold air.

The car continued, entering a support pylon; increased pressure drove a blast of air into the car. Passengers reeled, grabbed seats, restraints, each other for support.

G'Kar felt the blast of air rock his body. He was ready for it because he had seen the pylon approaching. He braced himself against the shock and when the Tuchanq reeled helplessly he leapt. Crashing heavily into the nearest Tuchanq, G'Kar smashed a fist into his chest as they both reeled sideways into the wall and bounced back toward the doors. The Tuchanq fell with a cry, blood flooding from his body. G'Kar grabbed the knife, plunged it into the alien, withdrew the weapon, and hurled it clumsily at the next nearest aggressor.

The knife missed, clattered harmlessly against the end window.

The reaction to his throwing the knife bounced G'Kar against the door frame and back into the body of the car. The Tuchanq wasn't so lucky. He slid right out of the doors, fell against the wall of the pylon tunnel, was whipped abruptly back along the five-centimeter gap between the tunnel and the car. A single scream, the cracking of bones and the Tuchanq was gone. The mashed body smeared across the outside of the windows, punching the glass out in a rush of blood.

The remaining Tuchanq scrambled to their feet, knives poised. Backs to the forward-facing window, they leapt toward G'Kar.

He didn't move.

The car emerged from the pylon.

The air pressure inside the car fell abruptly as it equalized with that outside the pylon tunnel. It only took a moment, but that was enough. Carried forward by their own momentum, the Tuchanq were caught with no means of anchoring themselves. They were swept toward the door. One managed to grab a passenger, who flailed for support. Other passengers reached for them but it was too late. Tuchanq and passenger were sucked out of the doors, began the three-quarters-of-a-mile fall to the ground.

G'Kar grabbed hold of the nearest seat harness, hung on tightly, tried to decide whether the scream he could hear was that of the falling figures or simply the wind.

Someone hit the door control; they hissed shut.

Blood drenched his side and leg.

His breath came in short, agonized bursts.

Stunned, the passengers made a kind of collective sigh, part fear, part relief. Someone began to cry.

G'Kar let the minimal gravity take him, sagged to the floor. His blood followed more slowly. He sucked in a breath, winced as pain shot through his side.

He checked his link.

The entire incident had taken place in less than a minute.

Ignoring the pain in his side and leg, he pulled himself across to the remaining Tuchanq. The alien wasn't moving. G'Kar reached for his neck to check for a pulse.

His hand slipped through the flesh as if it were mist.

G'Kar jerked back in shock. No wonder most of his blows had not connected properly. This wasn't a Tuchanq at all.

It was someone wearing a Changeling Net!

G'Kar groped for the real body inside the illusion, ran his hands along the bloody chest, touched the control mechanism and deactivated it.

The body rippled, blurred—and *changed*.

In seconds there was a human lying in place of the Tuchanq he had seen. A human dressed in old, soiled clothes and the mesh of the Net. A human who moaned with pain and stirred briefly before lapsing back into unconsciousness.

A lurker.

G'Kar allowed himself to relax. He activated the link. ''Security? This is Ambass—this is Citizen G'Kar. I'm in the core shuttle. I wish to report an attempt on my life.''

Only after he had given all the details and been assured that a team of medics would meet him at the next embarkation point did G'Kar allow himself the luxury of wondering who would want to kill him—and why?

CHAPTER 7

"We found the first body pulped against the south side of the Mosque." Garibaldi raised his eyebrows, gave an ironic twitch of his lips. "Adds a whole new meaning to the saying 'Nearer my God to thee,' doesn't it?"

Seated at the desk in his office, Sheridan steepled his fingers, shook his head. "And the others?"

Garibaldi cocked his head to one side, a tiny movement equivalent to a shrug. "There were four. G'Kar killed one, another managed to get himself smeared all over the inside of pylon three, the other landed on the baseball pitch." Garibaldi licked his lips. "We just got the Drazi Green and Purple teams organized too, as an alternative to them killing each other once a year. Now this one comes hurtling outta the sky, totals the autopitcher, buckets of blood, and suddenly the Drazi are starting to think an annual homicidal rage is a neat thing after all."

Sheridan sighed. "And G'Kar?"

"Doc Franklin fixed him up good as new. Well, all but. I expect he'll limp for a bit, but then a good limp never hurt anyone."

"And that's your full report?"

Garibaldi pursed his lips, thrust his hands deeper into his pockets. "Nope. Two things. Both of which you're gonna like about as much as a shower full of slugs."

"Tell me."

"First thing: G'Kar reported being attacked by members of the Tuchanq."

"Oh not again!"

"Mm, but that's not all. You see—they weren't really Tuchanq at all. They were lurkers. Humans actually. What remained of their ID suggested they might have affiliations with the Home Guard."

"Aw hell."

"It gets better. G'Kar says he was attacked by humans disguised with Changeling Nets to resemble Tuchanq. Witnesses confirm this. Problem is—there weren't any Nets. Not on the bodies, not near the bodies, not within a hundred meters of the bodies; I checked. No debris either. But we did find one on the body in the core shuttle.''

Sheridan frowned thoughtfully. ''Changeling Nets can alter someone's appearance, but they can't just vanish into thin air.''

''I know. Now hold your hat for this: One of my men thought he saw a movement in the body that landed in the baseball pitch. He said it looked to him like the body was lying on top of something. But then the body just sagged. He got a glimpse of something glowing underneath—but when he went digging there was nothing that could have supported the body—nothing under there but the dead guy's shadow.''

Sheridan licked his lips.

Shadows.

''So the implication is that in this instance when the user died, the Net self-destructed. Which would mean whoever is responsible for the killings is really serious about not being found out,'' Sheridan said.

Garibaldi nodded.

''What else?''

''Second thing: this.'' Garibaldi dug into his pocket, produced a plastic evidence bag. He opened the bag, dumped a bloodstained ID onto Sheridan's desk. ''One of the bodies was that of the man EarthGov sent here to execute D'Arc.''

''Oh *hell*.'' Sheridan studied the ID, turned it over in his hands. Portrait of a killer. Portrait of a dead man. ''This situation is getting way out of hand.''

Garibaldi nodded. ''You said it. The President wants D'Arc executed for a murder she can't be held responsible for, and the body count's now up to eight, one of whom was the Executioner.''

Sheridan sighed. ''This is crazy. We have to stop this thing now.''

Garibaldi agreed. ''Guess I shouldn't have booked that day off after all.''

''The situation needs to be investigated.''

"Right. We'll need to know who brought the Changeling Nets in-station and who hired the lurkers to kill G'Kar." Garibaldi thought for a moment. "I think it's time to have a chat with the one person in-station who knows something about everything."

"n'Grath?"

"None other."

"That'll mean a trip to the alien sector."

"It'll also mean a mountainous peak in my expenses graph for this week."

Sheridan smiled thinly. "Keep me posted, all right?"

"You got it." Garibaldi left Sheridan's office.

When the Warrant Officer was gone, Sheridan logged on to the comm net, began to encode a report to send to Earthdome.

Ten minutes later the Gold Channel message was heading for Earth at multiples of the speed of light and Sheridan was reaching for a bottle of headache tabs.

CHAPTER 8

Hands thrust deeply into pockets, Garibaldi mooched away from the admin block to the Green Sector monorail station and took a car heading for the Zocolo.

Ten minutes later he was ensconced in a booth in an out-of-the-way bar frequented only by himself and a half dozen furry Bremmaer, nursing a tall glass of ice water, chasing the lemon with a cocktail stick, and trying to decide how best to proceed with his investigation.

Another monorail car sighed past overhead as he thought. Getting in contact with n'Grath was problematic at the best of times. It would take time to set up a meet. Garibaldi activated his link and contacted security control, told Allen to set the wheels in motion. Allen began a scan of red sector and told Garibaldi he'd call him back when he'd located n'Grath.

Garibaldi cut the link and sipped his water. There were days when he longed for the silken burn of a good bourbon in his gut. Most days he could shut out the thought. Today looked like it was going to be one of those days when trying to forget the past was harder than usual. Setting aside both his drink and his intro-spection, he activated his link again. "Garibaldi to Ivanova."

"Ivanova. I'm tired, I'm off duty, and I'm halfway through a cheese and spinach and peanut loaf. This had better be good."

Garibaldi grinned. "I've been thinking about the Tuchanq—and this whole D'Arc situation. I need to talk over a few things. Can you meet me?"

A sigh. "Why don't you join me for dinner?"

"Cheese and spinach and peanut loaf?" Garibaldi smacked his lips appreciatively. "Sounds great. See you in ten."

Susan Ivanova's quarters were in officers' country, which, to-gether with the ambassadorial sector, was built into the northern-most wall of the carousel. When Ivanova let him in Garibaldi made straight for the picture window and stared out over the park from a height of four stories. Framing the left side of the window, he could see the distant curve of the playing fields nestling at the foot of one of the core shuttle pylons. The pylon appeared hori-zontal from this view. Directly overhead, beyond the core mono-rail, diverted sunlight glinted off the dull dome roof of the Mosque.

Ivanova joined him at the window carrying two plates of food. "Penny for them?"

"I scraped a guy off the Mosque wall today." Garibaldi ac-cepted his plate of food with a murmur of thanks.

"Yeah, I heard about that. Messy."

Garibaldi nodded. "For him and me both. Still. It'll teach him to go after G'Kar armed with just a knife." He tucked away a forkful of cheese and spinach and peanut loaf. "Mmm. This is good. You make this yourself?"

"Uh-huh." Ivanova nodded. "Got the recipe off the net."

"And I thought that was only good for spying on people."

She grinned. "Garibaldi, you're paranoid."

"It's in the job description."

"Talking about the job—what was it you wanted to know about the Tuchanq?"

Garibaldi carried his food across to the dining table. "Well. It's like this. Captain Sheridan wants to avoid a diplomatic incident. Especially since he feels D'Arc cannot be held morally responsible for murder."

Ivanova nodded. "And I agree with him, don't you?"

Garibaldi frowned. "It's not as simple as that for me. I'm an officer of the law. And I believe in that law. If D'Arc is guilty, she should be punished."

Ivanova put down her fork. "Are you trying to tell me you think D'Arc should be executed?"

Garibaldi pursed his lips. "If she's found guilty—and if it's what the law demands. Yeah. I guess so."

Ivanova seemed taken aback. "Michael. This doesn't seem like you. What about the moral issues? If D'Arc is brain-dead, surely she's been punished already?"

Garibaldi sighed. "Susan that's . . ." He struggled to find the right words to express what he thought. "That's a great philosophy. But I deal in reality. It's my job, it's who I am. I mean . . . what's the point in having laws if you don't abide by them?"

Ivanova frowned. "Well, at the very least you must admit that the mere existence of execution as a punishment devalues human life."

Garibaldi thought about that one. "I'd say it means the exact opposite. Look at it this way: By carrying out an execution, we're saying that we value life *so much* we're gonna use the ultimate punishment against anyone who commits murder."

Ivanova uttered a short, humorous laugh. "I . . ." She stopped, began again. "That's . . ." She shook her head. "Never mind." She began to eat again. A moment later she added, "Eat your food. It'll get cold."

Garibaldi shoveled a forkful of loaf into his mouth. The food seemed to have lost its flavor. Ivanova was staring at the table. What had begun as a straightforward conversation had somehow turned into a rather disturbing examination of his own morals and beliefs.

He lifted another forkful to his lips, forced himself to chew.
The silence dragged on.

Eventually he sighed, put down his fork. "Look, Susan. People, they're all different. Politics. Religion. It's different for everyone. But we're friends, right? We can agree that we both want justice for the guilty, protection for the innocent. That's gotta be true, otherwise why would we even be here?"

It was an apology, but she ignored it, instead lowered her fork to her plate and looked up angrily from her food. "How can you say that? Now you're twisting the truth and playing on our friendship to get me to agree! There's a word for that. It's blackmail. Emotional blackmail. And I won't—"

How the hell did we get from an apology to this?

"Hang on a minute. I only meant—"

"Of course you did. But never mind. You just keep thinking might is right and justice is on the side of the innocent. We wouldn't want to disillusion you now, would we?"

Garibaldi felt his anger rise. "Don't be stupid. That's not you talking, it's some prolife propagandist with more literary skill than common sense!"

Ivanova's face suddenly lost all expression, a sure sign of extreme annoyance. "Garibaldi, I can't believe you just said that! Don't you believe in the basic right of an individual to happiness and justice?"

"Not when they get them at the cost of someone else's life I don't, no."

Ivanova began to say something, bit off her comment, stared silently at the table.

Garibaldi struggled to control his anger. "Look. Susan. All I meant to say was—"

He was interrupted as his link bleeped. "Garibaldi. Go."

"Chief? Allen here. I've set up that meeting you wanted with n'Grath. He'll be in Red One in an hour; he'll meet you at the Dilgar Memorial in the Hanging Garden."

"Check." Garibaldi thanked Allen and cut the link. He looked at Ivanova. She was managing to eat and ignore him at the same time. "Look. I was about to say I'm—"

Once again she interrupted. "It's all right, Michael. You don't have to explain, and you certainly don't have to apologize. It's your politics and your opinion. Now if you don't mind, I'd rather not talk about it.'' A momentary silence, then, ''I don't know what's going on around here lately. Ever since the Tuchanq arrived, things have been . . .'' She sighed. ''Getting way out of control.''

Garibaldi hesitated, then, ''Yeah well . . . like I said . . . I'm sorry.''

''Sure.'' Ivanova began to clear up the plates.

Garibaldi rose. ''Do you want some help with those?''

''No. I'm fine.''

A moment. ''Um . . . guess I'll be going then.''

''You don't have to do that.''

''I got a case to work.''

''Well . . . okay.''

''Thanks for dinner.''

''Sure.''

''Catch ya on the flip side.''

''You do that.''

Garibaldi left Ivanova's quarters feeling unsettled and depressed. She was right. Just lately the whole damned shabang was going to hell in a handbasket.

Abruptly Garibaldi shook his head. *The hell with this. You said it yourself: You've got a case to work. So work it.*

Sure.

CHAPTER 9

Alone in the observation gallery which curved through two degrees of hull directly beneath the Docking Sphere, Vir Cotto sat cross-legged on the transparent floor and watched the stars move in gentle arcs beyond his knees. The lights in the gallery were kept deliberately dim; Vir felt he was sitting cross-legged in space. Once every fifteen minutes or so the rust-colored globe of Euphrates would move past the port, its single moon glimmering palely when the planet itself was not in view.

Located at the Ellfive point between planet and moon, Babylon 5 was caught between a rock and a hard place, surrounded by the darkest night imaginable. It was a position Vir could identify with. He shuffled sideways, eased the pressure on his knees, moved his robes of office so that he could get a wider view of the stars.

Secrets.

He was surrounded by them: his family's secrets, his government's secrets, Londo Mollari's secrets.

Vir hated them all.

He hated what his life had come to represent. He was Centauri. Shouldn't he be proud of that? Londo was Centauri and *he* was proud. Then again Londo was flawed. Vir knew that well. Too well. He'd seen what his mentor was capable of, how far he had fallen in his reach for glory.

As a race, the Centauri were old, decrepit. Though powerful, their power was that of something old, senile . . . Vir searched for the right analogy. A soldier. That was it. An old soldier, mind gone, clinging to memories of past glories while holding a fully charged weapon in palsied hands. A soldier with ultimate power and no honor. A soldier whose overriding aim was to recover what he had lost—and who would pay any price to do so.

The Republic was prepared to pay that price. A price that included their own corruption, a price that included the death of innocents . . . indeed the death of *innocence*.

The Narn for example. Civilians. Children. All gone. Those that remained were humbled, enslaved by the Republic for a second time in as many centuries.

No.

Vir Cotto was Centauri and he was *not* proud.

He turned at a sound beside him in the gallery.

G'Kar.

The Narn glanced at Vir, said nothing.

Vir scrambled quickly to his feet. He hadn't had occasion to see G'Kar since . . . well, since that time in the lift a month or so ago, when he'd tried to express his sympathy for the ex-ambassador's plight, and that of his people. The Narn looked older now, his skin rougher, the dark patches upon his skull ringed with the pale orange hallmark of stress. His lips were compressed to their usual thin line.

Vir forced himself to meet G'Kar's gaze. The Narn's eyes were a penetrating scarlet, shot through with gold flecks. Obsessed eyes. Eyes that had seen atrocities Vir could only be scared of imagining.

G'Kar held Vir's gaze for a moment longer, then turned away. The lighting on his face changed to a brilliant amber as Euphrates swung into view. G'Kar spared the planet a glance, then looked back at Vir. "Euphrates is very beautiful today."

Vir nodded, unable to think of a response.

G'Kar continued, "Every culture has a concept of Heaven. Somewhere better to go when all is lost. J'Quan tells us Heaven for the Narn is gold. Euphrates looks very much like Heaven to me today."

Vir nodded quickly.

G'Kar shrugged, a massive gesture. "Of course that may just have something to do with the fact that it hasn't had all of its major population centers bombed into radioactive slag."

Vir swallowed nervously. Everyone knew the Narn were not exactly tolerant of the Centauri here in-station. What if the ex-ambassador took it into his head to—

"Is it true?" Normally deep and sepulchral, today, Vir realized, G'Kar's voice held a roughness and a liquid gurgle that spoke of injury. For the first time Vir became aware that G'Kar's posture was slightly hunched, as if he were in pain.

"I don't understand. Is what true? That the Republic bombed your cities? I told you already how I feel about—"

G'Kar held up a massive hand to silence Vir, then pulled aside his tunic to reveal a set of bandages enshrouding his chest. "Is it true that I was attacked by lurkers—humans in the pay of your mentor, Londo Mollari?"

Vir cleared his throat—another nervous gesture. Sometimes his life was nothing but nervous gestures. "I . . . I'm afraid I don't know what you're talking about. I heard, of course, that you were attacked, and I'm . . . well, I'm glad to see that you are still alive, obviously, but—''

G'Kar sighed impatiently.

Vir rushed on, ''Of course, you could always ask Ambassador Mollari himself.''

''And do you think he would give me an honest response?''

Vir swallowed again, elected not to reply.

G'Kar pursed his lips at Vir's silence. ''Of course not. Londo Mollari will not speak to me. I am afraid he no longer recognizes me as an equal.'' A bitter silence, then, ''Or sometimes, I think, as a life form of any significance at all.''

Vir bit his lip, blew out his cheeks. This was so unfair! Couldn't Londo *see* what he was *doing*? The problem was, of course, that Vir could well imagine G'Kar's accusations to be true. Hiring someone to attack a private citizen was outrageous behavior, but no more outrageous than anything else Londo had done in his reach for glory on behalf of the Republic.

Vir tried to find the words to express his sympathy and yet make G'Kar understand the limited extent of both his knowledge and his influence. What came out was a kind of nervous gurgle.

G'Kar twisted his muscular face into a frown. ''Vir, as Mr. Garibaldi says, I have no evidence. I am not demanding anything. I am asking for help.'' A pause. Red eyes held Vir's unwaveringly. ''A little over a month ago you expressed sympathy for my plight. If you were not lying then you will help me now.''

Vir felt himself shaking. ''I can't . . . um . . . I can't help you.'' More words came in a rush. ''Not because I won't help you, G'Kar, or because I don't sympathize, you have to believe that, but because I simply don't know!''

There was a long silence. Despite himself, Vir could simply find no words to fill it.

G'Kar seemed to shrink inwardly. In such a massive being it was a pathetic sight.

''I should have expected no less from a *Centauri*.''

Abruptly he turned and left the gallery.

Vir stood quite still, shivering as the hatch sealed behind the Narn. He licked his lips. G'Kar was right. He was useless. He had no courage; no destiny that wasn't bound up inextricably with that of Londo Mollari and Morden.

Vir watched the gold bulk of Euphrates glide out of view, let his eyes adjust to the prevailing starlight. He wished he could just leave all this behind, go home. Get married to some doxy and just forget about Londo Mollari and G'Kar and the terror, guilt, and shame that he felt every time he thought of either.

Impossible, of course.

Because G'Kar would continue his own investigations. Vir knew enough to realize that at least was true. Knew also word of the investigation would inevitably find its way back to Londo via other channels. Then Londo would find out about his own conversation with G'Kar. And no matter what the truth was, Londo would believe the worst of Vir.

And Vir knew then that if he was not to compromise his own self-appointed position as Londo's whispered conscience, he must betray G'Kar's confidence himself. He must warn Londo that G'Kar was becoming suspicious—and that he had been talking to Garibaldi.

As Vir considered his options, which were really no options at all, the silver arc of the Euphrates moon slipped into view. Its brilliant light cast shadows upward along his body and onto his face.

In that moment Vir began to understand exactly what real responsibility was. In that moment he had just the tiniest inkling of how Londo must feel about his relationship with Morden. With the understanding came a self-knowledge that was both hateful and terrifying in its honesty.

Vir wondered if Londo hated himself as much as Vir was coming to hate him.

CHAPTER 10

The chapel was simple in construction: a cube-shaped annex to Medlab, three meters on a side. Its walls were draped with dark cloth. Rows of pews took up most of the room.

Brian Grond lay on a raised dais in front of the seats. He was covered from ankles to neck in a white shroud.

Jacintha Grond stood in the narrow space between the seats and the dais. She breathed deeply, shudderingly, feeling her nerves fray a little further. If Sheridan could have seen her now, she thought, he would be surprised. Surprised that the cold, aloof, faintly arrogant woman he had spoken with could stand here trembling, on the edge of tears, before the body of a man she did not love.

There were probably a lot of things about her that would surprise Sheridan. He was an officer, an administrator. A red-tape man. Oh, he came across as sympathetic enough, but what did he really know about it? He was probably married to some GROPO-groupie, some stay-at-home who was happy to bring up the kids and forget any chance of a life of her own.

Jacintha dismissed these self-indulgent thoughts by looking around the chapel. An odd name for a room containing nothing of any greater religious significance than a few old curtains. Then again, she supposed, if they had tried to place icons from even just the major religions in here there would be no room for visitors—or the deceased for that matter.

The deceased.

Brian.

Jacintha licked her lips and—finally—lowered her eyes to the shrouded body, the face. His face. Brian's face.

He was not as she remembered him.

He was pale. The skin was bruised. There were contusions on the cheeks, a cut above the eyebrow. Brian was a big man. Well, wide, anyway. In life he had been given to sudden movements, dramatic if somewhat clumsy. Now he seemed somehow shrunken, as if death had robbed him of more than just his life, as if it had somehow managed to . . . to *dull* his presence even in her memories of him. As if it had taken the full color stereo image she had of him in her mind and reduced it to a flat, black and white copy, grainy and insubstantial.

Or had *she* done that by not loving him?

It didn't matter. What did was the fact that Brian was gone. When he was buried her life would be her own again.

She sighed, settled wearily into one of the pews, sighed again as the ache in her legs and back subsided a little, then felt guilty at the sense of relief. Brian hadn't had any relief. How had he felt? Had he known that he was going to die? Had he had time for a last thought? What had been his last sensations? Feelings.

How could she ever know? How could she ever even presume to try to understand?

Tears came then. She rested her head in her hands and surrendered to the feelings cascading through her, all sense of time and self washed away in a confusing torrent of emotions, until eventually there were no more tears, just a confused, vaguely uncomfortable emptiness that seemed desperately to cry out for something, some emotion to fill it.

There was nothing. She was empty. Drained.

When the sound of pews creaking told her there was someone beside her, she looked up. A figure was sitting in the front row, an arm's length away from Brian. A human, dark skinned, wearing doctor's whites.

"You must be Dr. Franklin."

He nodded, glanced from Brian to her and back again. "It sounds morbid, I know, but . . . you can touch the body. If you want. Sometimes it helps. To let go."

"Doctor, I haven't 'touched' my husband for nearly three years." Despite her grief and confusion, Jacintha found herself giggling, wondered briefly what Franklin must think of her, then instantly dismissed the thought from her mind, the smile from her face. "Believe me, letting go isn't a problem."

Franklin shrugged. "Whatever's right for you."

She nodded agreement. "What's right is for me to take Brian home and bury him."

Franklin sat perfectly still, said nothing. She felt something from him though. Irritation? Embarrassment? Surely not . . . shame?

"I'm . . . uh . . . I'm afraid I can't let you do that."

Another flash of anger. "So the choice is yours, is it?"

Now it was Franklin's turn to utter a humorless laugh. "If it was up to me, you could leave on the next flight." A hesitation. "The directive comes from EarthGov."

"I understand. They pay your salary. You have to do as you're told." Where had that bitterness in her voice come from? Did she really care whether Brian's burial was delayed a few hours or days? Did it really matter in the long term? Or at all for that matter?

Yes. It mattered to her.

She just couldn't say *why*.

Franklin nodded. "I'm sorry you feel that way. You should know it isn't like that. Both Captain Sheridan and myself have—"

'—every sympathy. Yes. I know. He said that too."

She watched his eyes then, saw into his head. Saw his doubt about her strength. Saw herself as he saw her: confused, upset, impressionable, shocked, lonely. The image angered her, made her even more determined to let no one else make assumptions about her, her state of mind, ever again.

Starting right now.

"Doctor, I told Captain Sheridan and now I'm telling you. I have a flight booked in fifteen hours. My husband and I will be on that flight. Or half the galaxy will know via the public broadcast networks why not."

Franklin sighed, seemed about to speak. She didn't wait to hear what he had to say. She simply rose and left the chapel, too upset to discuss the matter further.

CHAPTER 11

Vir found Londo in the Dark Star, probably one of the busiest of the Zocolo bars. The Dark Star was owned and run by Taan Churok, an old Drazi with a penchant for ancient pop music and fistfights, one of many entrepreneurs who had seen the advantage in obtaining a license to open twenty-four hours per day in order to catch business from workers from all three duty shifts.

The bar was just this side of legal, had been known to teeter on the edge occasionally. Taan Churok, the owner, was rumored to have been a winner of the Mutai in his younger days. Vir had personally found this claim dubious until the day when a pair of Morellians had stomped in high as a ComSat on salted wheat crackers and demanded free time on the gaming tables. Taan Churok had granted them three free spins each in the name of a quiet life, but had drawn the line when the Morellians had demanded free time backstage with the dancers.

Taan Churok had told them they were getting no free anything, with anyone, backstage, onstage, or anywhere else for that matter, unless it was free directions to the exit. The Morellians hadn't liked that. They'd told Churok the only thing more out of date than his morals was his music. Vir had quietly sidled toward the exit himself at this point, only to be overtaken by a bloody Morellian dragging his semiconscious friend as fast as he could on only three legs away from a glowering Churok.

From that time on Vir had come to take both the owner of the Dark Star and his taste in music a little more seriously.

Vir stood in the entrance to the Dark Star and studied the crowd of Centauri and aliens drinking, shouting, watching the dancers, gambling. Two-hundred-and-fifty-year-old human rock music was a solid wall in the smoky air, battering at Vir and plucking at his clothes with such frantic energy that he was surprised the noise dampeners were able to stop it getting out into the Zocolo.

Vir forced his way through the crowd. All around him people

of various species shouted, clicked, barked, and whistled to each other above the music. Vir passed a Deneth triplet giving each other the eye, scrambled underneath the arched segmented coils of a Ynaborian Sinning—dangerous because her eyes were squeezed tightly shut and each of her fifty-kilo segments seemed to have picked up the rhythm of a different subbeat of the music—and finally stepped over a drunken Froon collapsed across the hugely muscular fifth leg of a Throxtil. The Throxtil was so engrossed in a tactile conversation with a blind Cauralline that it simply hadn't noticed the snoring Froon wrapped snugly around its leg. Vir hoped the Froon came to before the Throxtil decided to sit down.

Vir moved on through the crowd. He'd expected to find Londo at the gaming tables, a simpering female on each arm, a trio of dice in one eager hand, a large drink clutched firmly in the other.

Not today; today Londo was doing the other thing he did well.

He was propping up the bar.

Vir watched him from the ramp leading down from the Zocolo. He looked so alone. His back was hunched defensively, his eyes were downcast, his whole demeanor seemed heavy with sadness. He stirred his drink absently, fished out some kind of sweetmeat, popped it into his mouth, chewed as absently as he had stirred.

He sipped his drink.

Even the half-naked Centauri dancers seemed unable to hold his attention for longer than a few seconds.

Vir felt unlooked-for empathy. Sitting there, quiet, alone in the crowd, Londo reminded him very much of himself.

He shook his head, put aside the maudlin thoughts. He pushed through the crowd toward his mentor, took the next seat. It didn't escape his notice that no one was sitting too close to Londo, and it was obvious that it hadn't escaped Londo's notice either. He looked up as Vir sat, a mixture of surprise and pleasure at the thought of company. His face fell when he saw who it was.

"Vir. It's only you."

Vir ordered drinks for them both. "It's still early. I thought you would have been talking to the Tuchanq delegation."

"They are still considering the Republic's offer."

The barman placed a drink in front of each of them. Londo

lifted his immediately to his lips. "You have completed your work for the day, Vir?"

Vir shook his head. "I have found something out which, I am afraid to say, distresses me greatly."

Londo uttered a short, humorless laugh. "Look at all these happy smiling people around you, Vir. Do you think they would be here if they were truly happy elsewhere? Everyone is distressed about something. Do you not think I would understand that? I am one of these people after all."

Vir sighed inwardly. Since the appearance of Morden instation, Londo had become increasingly withdrawn. Since the war had ended he had suffered terrible mood swings. Elation and depression. Incredible highs followed by desperate lows. And Vir had been drawn into those mood swings with Londo, at times admiring the Ambassador, at other times pitying him, at still others laughing uproariously at some bit of outrageousness as the old and altogether too rarely glimpsed Londo Mollari shone through the darkness that his life had in recent months become.

Vir licked his lips. "Forgive my saying so, Ambassador, but . . . just lately you seem . . . well, a little down."

Londo downed half his drink. "Don't you worry, Vir. It's a passing phase."

"Perhaps it would pass more quickly if you saw Dr. Franklin, asked him for a prescription . . . perhaps something to help you sleep . . . ?"

"No!" Londo answered quickly. Too quickly. "The only medication I need is right here in the bar." Londo finished his drink and ordered another. "So," he added as he waited for the drink to arrive. "What brings you to my little drunken aerie, this fine and glorious day?"

Vir shook his head, somehow unable to bring himself to confront Londo with G'Kar's accusation.

Londo pointed a finger at him. "Vir, let me give you a bit of friendly advice. If you want to become an Ambassador in your own right, there is one thing you must learn. Never, ever let them see you hesitate."

Vir shook his head, uttered his own version of Londo's humorless laugh. "I was merely attempting to protect your feelings, Ambassador."

Londo sat up straighter on his bar stool, slopping his drink over his robes as he did so. "And that's another thing you must learn, Vir. When to go for the throat. The art of politics is when to strike, when to hold back."

Vir nodded. Londo was very drunk. Perhaps he'd speak to him later. He got up to leave, felt Londo's hand on his arm holding him back.

"So tell me, Vir. Here we are, both of us together in an informal situation. and I am four-fifths drunk. So you tell me. Is this a time to go for the throat? Or is it a time to hold back, consider the situation, listen, and learn?"

Vir frowned. "Ambassador, I don't understand what—"

"My dear Vir, of course you don't!" Londo interrupted in a slurred voice, spreading his hands and slopping his drink as he did so. "That is why I am the Ambassador and you are the attaché!" Mollari beamed expansively, took another slug of his drink, turned his attention away from Vir toward a Centauri dancer performing on a raised stage on the other side of the room.

That was when Vir began to get angry. "All right, Ambassador, if that's the way you want it. I had thought to mention something which has come to my attention, but seeing as how you are obviously—"

"Obviously nothing, Vir!" Londo interrupted again. "Just get on with it, will you?"

Vir tried to control his anger. "I have spoken with G'Kar. He accuses you of trying to have him killed. Is this in fact true?"

Mollari blinked, then abruptly laughed out loud. "Why, Vir, I think you may actually have learned when the time is right to go for the throat after all!"

Vir felt his hands clench uselessly by his sides. "*Is it true*?"

Londo took a deep breath, finished his drink and ordered another. Vir wasn't halfway through his first drink yet; Londo was already on his third since Vir had joined him. He stared at Vir, a direct stare, eyes too wide, too bright. Not for the first time Vir had an impression of what it might be like to make an enemy of him.

"Vir, let me tell you something. We sit here together and you see an old drunken Centauri. One with delusions of grandeur, perhaps. One whose control over his gambling and drinking is slipping; oh just a little, but slipping nonetheless. You see a fat old Centauri with his mind locked in the past while his ambition reaches past his abilities into the future. Well, let me tell you something, Vir. My vision is not unique. If you were any sort of Centauri yourself you would share that vision. A vision of the Republic as it could be. As it will be. And let me tell you, Vir, anything I can do to make that vision happen, I will do. Knowingly, willingly, with joy."

Vir felt sick. His mouth worked silently as, for the second time in as many hours, the right words simply would not come.

"Nothing to say, Vir? Well? Is it time to go for the throat? Or time to hold back? Why don't you tell me, Vir? Show me what you've learned in your time here with me."

Vir found himself shaking. The music in the bar was deafening, smashing into his head. Human music. It seemed to be everywhere these days.

"Ambassador . . ."

"Yes?" Amusement. Indulgence.

"Londo . . ."

"*Yes?*" Irritation now. And impatience.

"Did you do it? Did you have G'Kar attacked? Did you try to have him killed?"

And Londo laughed, loud and long. "Oh, no, Vir, no, no, no. It seems I was wrong about you. That was the wrong time to go for the throat. You should have waited, listened, learned. Perhaps offered me another drink. Loosened me up even further. I'm sorry, Vir. You were wrong. But never mind. At least you've learned that there is still much to learn. I tell you what: Let me buy you another drink to commiserate." Londo waved drunkenly at the barman.

Vir said quietly, slowly, "Do you remember when my family tried to have me removed from office, taken back to Centauri Prime? You helped me then. Threatened to leave if I was made to leave. You said I was indispensable to you. I thought we could trust each other. I thought we were friends."

Londo sniffed, drank deeply from the freshened glass. Avoiding Vir's gaze, he stared at the bar top. "This new Republic is no place to form friendships, Vir," he said eventually. His voice was barely audible above the music.

Vir could control his anger no longer. "Is that more political advice? Or your self-pity speaking?" He got up to leave. "Perhaps it's the drink speaking?" He stared at Londo very hard, willing him to understand. "Then again perhaps it's not you at all. Perhaps it's *someone else* talking."

Londo lifted his eyes to regard Vir with something akin to surprise.

"In any case, I'm both afraid and ashamed to say that you're right." Vir pushed through the crowd and left the bar.

He had some serious thinking to do.

CHAPTER 12

Garibaldi stopped by Security Control to pick up an old bag of cash he kept lying around for bribes, briefed Allen quickly on his itinerary, then jumped onto a personnel lift that shot him up toward the core of Blue Sector. From there he donned an AE suit and moved south until he came to the first of the entrances to the alien sector.

Red Sector, as it was officially known, was essentially a huge cylinder within a cylinder built around the station core. Like the carousel it rotated—but faster than the main station in order to provide the extremes of gravity heavy planet dwellers found comfortable at its outer rim. The cylinder was separated from the main station infrastructure by a double hull. Access was through air locks situated radially around the core.

The idea was you stepped through one air lock, crossed a short stretch of curved deck, stepped across the interface where the floor changed speed, gained a little weight (not too much here at the core), and then entered the alien sector through another air lock.

Garibaldi stepped with special care across this floor interface between sections. There was an old story about a guy who'd owed big money in the casinos whose feet had been hyperglued to adjacent pieces of floor moving at different speeds. It had taken twenty minutes for his leg to be torn off. He'd been saved . . . but the medics had to chase him halfway around the core to stanch the bleeding.

He'd heard people bust a gut over that one for an hour, improbable as it was.

Garibaldi stepped carefully across the interface, cycled the lock that let him into the Hanging Garden. Running the length of Red Sector, the Hanging Garden was a long cylinder wrapped around the station core. Curved glass panels set into inner and outer walls gave visual access to both the core shuttles and the business and habitation cylinders located further out toward the rim. The cylinder's atmosphere was mainly methane-ammonia, the second most commonly occurring atmosphere besides the oxygen-nitrogen variations. The Hanging Garden got its name from various-sized spheres of soil that were floating at different distances from the core, supported on thick chains that were anchored to both inner and outer walls. Growths of phosphorescent alien vegetation ranging from bush- to tree-size clustered in lumps around these tethered balls of soil, their fronds spreading out in slowly waving masses. The bright globes of vegetation receded into the distance until their color was leached away by the foggy atmosphere. Aliens and humans seeking an alternative place of recreation to the earth-normal Park glided through this environment, their AE suit lights winking through the fog like clouds of glowing pollen caught in shafts of sunlight.

Garibaldi activated his thruster set and moved into the fog. He had arranged to meet n'Grath at the Dilgar War Memorial, located halfway along the chamber.

n'Grath was Trakallan, a methane-breathing insectoid whose natural home was the upper middle atmosphere of one of the gas giants orbiting Beta Lyrae. Nobody seemed to know when n'Grath had actually come aboard the station. He seemed always to have been here. But if you wanted something, n'Grath could get it. Hardware, software, secrets, chocolate. Anything was up for grabs. If you had the money.

A Changeling Net would cost a lot of money. Four of the things would damn near bankrupt anything less than a medium-size government. That didn't leave many possible buyers. n'Grath would know who.

There was a problem, of course.

When Garibaldi reached the War Memorial it was to find n'Grath dying.

The Trakallan was loosely tethered by one mandible to a patch of vegetation some meters away from the Memorial. The other three mandibles were waving feebly in an attempt to attract help.

He was bleeding to death from a PPG wound in his thorax.

Garibaldi chinned his helmet commswitch and linked into the med channel. "Garibaldi. Got a medical emergency in Red One. It's n'Grath. PPG wound to the thorax. We're by the Dilgar Memorial. You better get here fast. There's a lot of blood."

He looked quickly around. The attack had only just taken place. The edges of the wound were still hot. Not only that but a crowd had only just begun to gather. The attacker was here. Somewhere close.

n'Grath began to struggle. Garibaldi tried to hold him still. Was he convulsing? Having a heart attack?

No. He was trying to talk.

n'Grath scraped his mandibles together; his translator, miraculously undamaged, waited fifteen seconds and then faithfully reproduced the scraping noises as system English with a thick German accent. "Garibaldi . . . someone . . . kill me . . . "

"Did you get a look at them?"

" . . . Centauri . . . "

"Why did they do this?"

" . . . don't . . . "

Garibaldi thought fast while trying to keep pressure on n'Grath's wound. The alien was not exactly without influence in-station. Anyone who wanted him fried would have to be prepared to deal with the consequences. "Listen, n'Grath. I need information. Do you know who hired some lurkers to kill the ex-Narn Ambassador G'Kar?"

"...Centauri..."

"Yeah, yeah. That's who tried to kill you. I need to know—"

"...no...Centauri...hired..."

Garibaldi smiled grimly. "The Centauri hired the lurkers?"

"...yes..."

"The same Centauri who tried to kill you?"

"...yes..."

"And Changeling Nets? Did you supply them?"

"...don't..."

Garibaldi swore. If n'Grath didn't know of any Changeling Nets, then there weren't any in-station to know about. So where did that leave him?

"n'Grath. Do you know who attacked you? Do you have a name?"

n'Grath scraped his mandibles together. The translator hummed and clicked. "...wouldn't give...found out anyway..."

At that moment the medics arrived. The doctor—a human—cut into Garibaldi's frequency. "We'll take over now, thank you. Nurse E'Lin, get an IV line here—large bore. And stand by to ventilate. With all this epidermal damage his remaining spiracles will be hard pushed to supply enough methane to his body. He could go into respiratory arrest at any time."

n'Grath was still struggling with Garibaldi's question. "...name...Askari..."

The doctor said, "Mr. Garibaldi, if you please. We have a job to do here."

Garibaldi muttered an apology, moved aside to allow the medics access to n'Grath. As human doctor and Narn nurse began to work, n'Grath scraped his mandibles weakly together again.

"...no opportunity to...bargain...double the cost... for..."

Garibaldi moved closer, said, "Don't you worry. Walk out of Medlab in one piece and I'll pay you three times what this info is worth."

"Garibaldi...you're...full of..." n'Grath scraped his mandibles again but the translator just produced nonsense sounds.

Garibaldi allowed himself to drift slowly away from n'Grath. He drew his PPG. There was a slim chance the assassin was nearby, waiting to see if his attempt on n'Grath's life had been successful. He placed a call to security for backup, then moved away from the medics, thinking hard as the drifting figures slowly receded into the fog. So. Someone had tried to kill n'Grath. That meant they knew someone would try to find out who hired the lurkers. That meant they'd know about him being here now. If that was the case they'd probably try to kill him next.

A sudden movement caught his eye. A glint of light on metal. A gun barrel.

He kicked the thruster pack into high gear and—

—that was when the plasma bolt burned into his AE suit and smashed him into the glowing canopy of a nearby globe of vegetation and

the suit my suit's ruptured my faceplate's cracked I'm breathing methane I'm burning my face I'm burning up I'm gonna puke I'm gonna die and my face it's burning my face and chest and

hands took him and held him and jerked him free of the clinging foliage and then a bright light burned into his eyes and a vaguely familiar voice was calling for help on the med channel and for a long time that was all he remembered.

CHAPTER 13

G'Kar dimmed the light in his quarters to a ruddy ochre glow, walked painfully to the bloodstone altar he'd brought with him to Babylon 5 from Homeworld. He lit the black ceremonial candles, let incense drift into the air in pungent clouds. It was too painful to bow before the altar so he pulled a low stool forward and sat on that instead.

He studied the Book of J'Quan laid on the stone table before him. The answers to everything could be found in the Book, if one looked hard enough.

G'Kar had been looking for answers almost since the day of his arrival in-station.

All he had found so far were more questions.

Take tonight for example. It had been just six hours since he lay bleeding in the core shuttle. News had already reached him of Garibaldi's investigation. Now more information had arrived, brought by E'Lin, a Red Sector nurse who also happened to be part of the Underground. More news of Garibaldi's investigation. Evidence. A name.

The name of the Centauri who had hired the lurkers to kill him. Askari.

With the knowledge had come a question: What should he do with the name now that he had it?

The investigation had proven dangerous for Garibaldi—someone had tried to kill him. No doubt the same person who had tried to kill n'Grath. The same person who had hired the lurkers to kill him.

G'Kar touched the Book, ran his thick fingers as gently as he could across the clumsy bindings. The Book was old, had been in his wife's family for generations. That was the tradition: to pass the Book from mother to daughter down through the years from the past into the future. J'Ntiel had given him the Book when his appointment to the Babylon 5 Advisory Council had been ratified. The Book had not been a permanent gift, rather a loan, a responsibility he knew would be passed to his firstborn daughter. At the time, G'Kar had not known how to respond to the honor his wife bestowed upon him except to reiterate in action how much he loved her. Now his world was dead, and probably J'Ntiel with it, and G'Kar had very little hope that he would ever hear the cries of pouchlings, much less of a daughter.

Not knowing hurt the most. Not knowing if J'Ntiel was alive or dead. Because he couldn't pray for her soul. Not yet. In case she was still alive.

G'Kar inhaled the incense, felt his head reel. Dr. Franklin would probably have advised against use of ritual incense so soon after medication. To *Q'Uarthonn* with Franklin. And all of the humans for that matter. And the Minbari with their damned spiritual pacifism. Everyone!

Especially the Centauri.

He breathed more deeply. Considered which passage of the Book to study for the answer to his dilemma.

He opened the Book, flipped the thick pages, became more impatient as no solution presented itself. Eventually, as the candles began to burn low, G'Kar realized the truth. The Book had never held answers. The only answers were to be found within himself. The Book was not even really a guide.

Just an emotional prop.

A tool.

As, say . . . a dagger was a tool.

G'Kar snuffed out the candles, and in the pungent darkness he reached for the only other object on the altar. The bloodwood case containing his ceremonial dagger.

He opened the case, removed the elements of the dagger; the blade, the hooks, the stone handle, the leather bindings.

With each part his feelings grew more intense. Love, fear, frustration, anger.

As he assembled the dagger and bound the parts tightly together, so his emotions fused into a terrible rage; an utter, overwhelming need for revenge against those who had taken his world and his family and any possibility of a future that he might once have had.

Dagger assembled, G'Kar lurched stiffly to his feet. He swallowed two of Franklin's painkillers—normal tabs were unable to penetrate his skin—and leaned against the stone wall while they took hold.

Then quietly, very quietly for such a huge being, G'Kar left his quarters.

He found the Centauri, as he had been told he would, an hour later at a window party in the Park.

Light for the Park came in through the hull via three sun ports spaced equally around its circumference and running almost all of its length. The ports were a mile long, rectangular, subdivided by mirrors into transparent sections through which Euphrates sun shone as the station brought it into view. The sunlight, not only essential for the growth of the vegetation in the Park but also for the psychological well-being of those who lived and worked in-station, was directed via the mirrors onto strips of land, so the Carousel was divided into three daylight areas and three nighttime areas. In truth atmospheric propagation ensured that the ambient lighting in even the darkest areas was really only the equivalent of a cloudy evening. But the psychological effect prevailed.

The Centauri in question had booked ground space in one of the paved observation galleries which ran along the edges of the windows. Bordered by low bushes, the galleries were positioned beneath ground level but well above the curved surface of the window itself, five levels below. The galleries were walled with redbrick, contained ornamental bushes and lovers' seats. Generally they provided privacy for those taking recreation time in the Park. The galleries were particularly popular at "night," when the view through the window could be spectacular. Access to the galleries was by stone steps cut into turf ramps which descended from ground level. Now G'Kar peered through a juniper bush and over the lip of the window, down the ramped half level to the gallery. About a dozen Centauri were there, sitting on prayer mats, standing around chatting, or gazing over the wall and out of the window into space.

G'Kar glanced quickly over several tables loaded with fast-disappearing drinks and sweetmeats, and concluded that the party must be nearing its end.

Good. He wouldn't have long to wait.

G'Kar looked around until he spotted the Centauri in question.

Askari was a young, arrogant example of his species if G'Kar had ever seen one. He was leaning on the gallery, posing unconsciously as he glanced casually down and out into space via the sun mirrors. Like the rest of the party, the Centauri wore sunglasses. G'Kar was glad he couldn't see his eyes. That pleasure would come later.

G'Kar settled himself down on a stone bench close to the edge of the window, overlooking the gallery. The ritual incense pulsed in his blood, in his brain. His wounds pulsed in his chest, his side, his thigh.

An hour went by.

The party began to break up.

G'Kar waited, meditating on the question that would soon be answered.

The mirrors shifted in the windows; across the Park day and night switched places.

G'Kar found himself plunged into a gloomy twilight. The gloom deepened as he strolled as casually as his wounds allowed toward the gallery. He found Askari leaning against the railing, staring down into the window and out across the depths of space. The Euphrates moon hung as a silver arc in the window. Askari was looking at it as he finished his drink.

He was alone.

G'Kar spared a moment to wonder why he had remained here when all of his fellow Centauri had gone. Was he staring out into space and considering his destiny? His place in the future? G'Kar would show him his place in the future.

He padded silently up behind Askari.

The Centauri sipped his drink.

G'Kar drew his dagger—

—Askari turned—

—and G'Kar plunged the dagger into his chest.

The Centauri blinked, gasped. He tried to scream; G'Kar's hand over his mouth stifled all noise. He began to struggle. He dropped the drink, which spun away into the window and shattered, spilling broken glass and thick red wine across the silver arc of the Euphrates moon.

G'Kar eased Askari down onto the concrete and shuffled sideways with him until they were both in the shadow of a large juniper bush which hung over the lip of the gallery. He jerked in G'Kar's arms.

"If you struggle the knife will merely penetrate your body more deeply."

Askari became still. His eyes, wide open with fear, stared up at G'Kar unblinkingly.

G'Kar gave a little sigh, settled himself more comfortably on the concrete beside the Centauri.

"Do you know," G'Kar began conversationally, "I have per-

sonally taken the lives of more than twenty-five Centauri since
my father's death.''

The Centauri said nothing. His eyes flickered frantically from
side to side though. Seeking help. G'Kar smiled. There would be
no help. Not here. Not now.

G'Kar studied the bleeding Centauri thoughtfully. ''When I
was a child I used to imagine what it was like to be a killer, a
murderer. I never could. Of course that was then.'' He smiled.
''Since then I have become intimately aware of the Centauri
anatomy. Where the killing blows should land. How deep to
cut, whether to use the edge or the point, whether to . . . wiggle
it about a bit before pulling it out.'' The smile widened. ''The
blow has penetrated your heart's outer ventricle. At the moment
blood is pumping into your chest cavity. You may have noticed
a dizzy feeling. That's due to blood loss. At this time the blow
is not fatal. But you only have a few moments at the most before lack of oxygen to the brain ensures that your life, should
you retain it, will be nothing more than that of a vegetable.
Now . . . '' G'Kar helped the Centauri sit upright, carefully removed his link and held it up before his pain-filled eyes. ''I am
going to ask you a question. If you answer me honestly I will
call the medics and tell them where you are. A word of warning: Hesitation will only bring unconsciousness that much
closer. And if you are unconscious you cannot answer the question, do you see?''

The Centauri began to cry.

G'Kar studied the tears thoughtfully, saw mirrored in them the
tears of a Narn adolescent who had watched his father die by
Centauri hands.

A moment, then G'Kar said, ''Here is my question: Who ordered you to hire lurkers to kill me?''

Askari blinked. His pupils were contracting. Consciousness was
receding fast.

''Do you understand the question?''

Askari nodded.

''Do you have an answer for me?''

Again the Centauri nodded.

G'Kar said, ''I am going to remove my hand from your mouth
now.''

Askari gasped, sucked in a huge breath, then grunted with pain as his chest moved.

"Well? I am waiting."

"Mollari. It was . . . Londo Mollari that ordered me to have you killed. He gave me . . . Changeling Nets . . . he said . . . he said . . . please . . . help me . . . call the . . . medics . . . please . . . "

G'Kar licked his lips. He handed Askari his link back. "Hold this for me, would you?" He lifted the Centauri, felt tears against his neck as he walked him to the railing overlooking the window.

Askari was fumbling with the link, couldn't quite make it work. "You said you . . . you would . . . "

G'Kar frowned. "Yes, I did, didn't I? Ah well. Compared to murder lying is a minor sin, don't you think?' Taking hold of his dagger, he pulled it from Askari's chest. The Centauri sighed as fresh blood bubbled from his chest and mouth. He dropped the link, which clattered over the edge and fell five levels into the window. "Please . . . I have a family . . . "

"I'm sure you do."

And G'Kar picked Askari up and heaved him over the railing.

He watched as the Centauri fell five levels to crash against the glass-steel window and eclipse the silver Euphrates moon with a Rorschach pattern of blood.

G'Kar looked down at the body for an indeterminate time. He tried to take satisfaction from the Centauri's death. He tried to tell himself it was a tiny thing compared to the atrocities the Centauri had committed against his people, his family.

It didn't surprise him in the slightest when he merely felt sickened by his own violence.

He turned away, cleaned his knife on one of the Centauri prayer mats, placed it back in his pouch. He climbed the ramped half a level back up to the Park. Saplings whispered in the dim gloom of night. Distantly, people talked, worked, loved. Life went on.

G'Kar wondered how long it would be before lurkers ventured out onto the window via the maintenance access Down Below and took away the body. They would rob the Centauri of his clothes and trinkets to sell at market, probably dump the body itself into the moisture reclaimers. In another week a quarter of a million people would probably have consumed a few molecules of the being who had tried to have him killed.

G'Kar was able to take no comfort from that thought either. Not from any misplaced sense of morals, but simply because he knew the job wasn't finished yet.

There was still Londo Mollari to reckon with.

And then of course, there would be his own ritual suicide to consider.

But that was for later.

For now, there was just the incense sparking in his brain and the pain of his wounds to tell him he was still alive, that he wasn't the one who had died.

That and the thought of *revenge*.

CHAPTER 14

When Jacintha left the chapel and Medlab, she found herself unsure which way to go. The problem was, she didn't know what she wanted to do. But then again was that any wonder? She'd come here to get Brian, take him home and bury him. That was simple enough, wasn't it?

Not for the Babylon 5 administration, it seemed.

Jacintha supposed she would have to think about renting a room, calling home to tell Janna, her neighbor, she was going to be longer than they'd thought and would she mind looking after the kids for another day?

And would she mind making sure they didn't watch the news broadcasts?

Her mind made up, Jacintha began to walk toward the Blue

Sector monorail terminal. She turned a corner—and walked into a demonstration. The corridor was filled with humans and aliens carrying banners and chanting. Writing on the banners proclaimed:

Protect Innocence!
Save the Tuchanq!
Love the Alien!
Free D'Arc!

She stopped short. In that moment she was swept up in the group and tumbled along a number of corridors into the Blue Sector Plaza. With more space the press of people around her eased slightly, but only slightly. The demonstration was drawing a crowd.

Jacintha tried to get her bearings, turned, attempted to walk out of the demonstration and through the crowd into a space clear of people. Signs indicating the way to the monorail terminal caught her attention. If she could reach that—

Before she took more than a dozen steps she was confronted by a young woman. The woman thrust a plastic badge into her hands. The badge reiterated the slogans painted on the signs and chants.

"Love the alien, save the Tuchanq," the girl chanted, whirled away into the crowd.

Jacintha struggled to get her bearings, struggled even harder to get her feelings under control. Save the Tuchanq? It was a Tuchanq who had killed Brian. Who had *murdered* Brian. This D'Arc about whom the demonstrators were chanting.

Jacintha felt herself jostled with increasing violence as more people joined the growing crowd of prolife protestors.

And suddenly it wasn't just her body being assaulted by the noise, the banners, the chanting; it was her mind as well. Because until now she hadn't had much time or inclination to think about the conditions surrounding Brian's death. He was gone. That really was what mattered. Now she was not so sure anymore. Now the circumstances surrounding his death seemed very important indeed.

Another demonstrator thrust a fistful of scrappily printed literature into her hand. "Save D'Arc, protect innocence!" the man chanted.

Jacintha felt her confusion grow into rage. She grabbed the man by his lapels, shook him as hard as she could. "Save D'Arc? She killed my husband!"

But the man had broken away without hearing her words. She caught a glimpse of a disgusted expression splashed across his face before the crowd hid him from view: horror, pity. He thought she disagreed with his ideals. Thought she was a racist. A Home Guard.

Jacintha finally managed to push her way clear of the crowd. She realized she was crying again when a woman slung her arm around her shoulders and comforted her. "I know you're upset. We're all upset. It's a political fiasco. We won't stand for it. Come with us to Blue One and picket Security Control. They've got D'Arc in a cell there. We'll show the administration that the people have a conscience even if EarthGov doesn't. We'll show them we won't stand for this kind of immoral behavior toward an intelligent being."

Jacintha shook off both arm and words, ran as fast as she could under the earth-normal gravity toward the monorail terminal. Her chest ached; her back and legs were in agony. She had to stop. Just stop and rest. Just for a moment.

No. She had to go on. She had to see for herself the being who had killed Brian, who had fundamentally reshaped her life.

She had to see D'Arc.

No matter what it cost her.

CHAPTER 15

G'Kar stood outside the door to Londo Mollari's quarters, wondered how two years of striving for peace had managed to bring him to this moment of violence; how a century and a half of freedom from the tyrant's reign had somehow brought his people back to slavery again.

He shivered.

The humans would say he was back to square one.

That wasn't quite true. Now he had purpose. That and the dagger; he could feel its weight against his waist, cold, comforting. A tool with which he would define both the following few moments and afterward, his life, his future.

Fresh bandages wrapped his chest and thigh beneath clean clothes. He had removed the old, bloodstained ones before he left the Park, replacing them with others he had carried with him in a small kit bag. The bloodstained clothes were now shredded, dumped into the recycler in his quarters. That would cost him an extra ten credits for power usage. this week—but then again he could afford it now.

Very soon he would have no need of affording anything ever again.

G'Kar banged on the door to Londo Mollari's quarters. There was no reply. He banged again, more loudly this time.

Mollari's voice echoed irritably from within. "Whoever it is— go away. I've got a hangover. I want to be in pain by myself."

G'Kar allowed himself a thin smile. "Mollari. It is G'Kar."

Long silence.

G'Kar drew himself up to his full height and said, "I have come here to negotiate the terms of the surrender of the Narn population on Babylon 5."

Another long silence.

The door slid open.

G'Kar entered.

The door closed behind him.

G'Kar found himself looking around Mollari's quarters, the opulence, the vanities, the expensive luxuries. All unnecessary, now.

Mollari emerged from the bathroom wearing a sleeping robe. His eyes were puffed, rheumy, his hair bedraggled. He had obviously been fast asleep only a few minutes before.

Mollari waited for G'Kar to speak.

"It has been many months since we have talked with anything like civil tongues," G'Kar said quietly. "So I would be grateful if . . . " Then he stopped. He was here to kill someone. Not conduct pleasantries with them. And anyway—standing here, staring at Mollari—all he felt was rage. This being had been responsible for the decimation of his homeworld. He was a despot, a tyrant in the making. To such a being civil words would have no meaning—and in any case the time for words had long since passed.

Mollari adjusted his robe, waited for him to continue.

G'Kar said nothing, felt Mollari's eyes on him. Did he suspect? The Ambassador may be a sop but he was nothing if not observant.

G'Kar cast his eyes submissively toward the rich carpet. How much had that carpet cost Mollari to ship in-station? The cost of medical treatment for ten Narn casualties? Twenty? And the commission of his portrait hanging upon one wall: artists' time was valuable; that portrait might have bought the lives of a hundred Narn.

Mollari said impatiently, "You said you're here to discuss terms. Discuss them."

G'Kar felt himself growing angry. The arrogance of the man! To even consider discussing the enslavement of G'Kar's people while still dressed in his pajamas.

G'Kar lowered his eyes even further. Mollari must believe him implicitly. "Can we not at least have one drink together before we negotiate terms?"

Mollari considered. "Victor to vanquished?" He pursed his lips, rubbed sleep from his eyes, thoughtfully preened his crest of hair. Eventually he nodded. "It would be only . . . civilized." He half turned away from G'Kar to walk toward the kitchen area. "I will prepare—'' Mollari stopped then, as if suddenly aware of the position he was in.

Too late.

G'Kar pulled the dagger from his pouch, lurched painfully across the intervening space, and slammed the dagger up to its hilt in Mollari's back.

Mollari let out an agonized wail and sank to his knees. G'Kar pulled the knife free. Mollari's hands arched back toward the wound as blood soaked into his robes. On all fours, he managed to turn to face G'Kar. His eyes were bright with a terrible rage. ''You . . . you . . . ''

G'Kar smiled. ''Now you understand. Your greed and arrogance have laid you at my feet.''

Mollari struggled to speak. Blood bubbled from his lips instead. He collapsed into a sitting position, shaking violently with shock, making choking noises, trying to suck air into his ruined lungs.

G'Kar stood over him, asked softly, ''Do you know why I hate you so much?''

Mollari gurgled, eyes wide with pain and rage . . . and now fear.

G'Kar explained it to him. ''I have lain awake at night for months trying to work it out. At first I got nowhere. We were so different, you see. You the bloody tyrant, myself the innocent victim. I could never understand what would drive an intelligent species such as the Centauri to invade an agrarian world like Narn. But then, slowly, with your help, I began to see the truth.''

G'Kar held Mollari's shoulder, pushed the dagger firmly into his chest, twisted it, pulled it out again sharply.

Mollari let out an agonized squeal.

G'Kar released the Ambassador, and he slumped onto his side. His head slammed into the floor, sending strings of spittle and blood to stain his expensive carpet.

G'Kar said, ''Today I killed a Centauri in cold blood. Stabbed him in the back. Without honor. Without fair warning. Does this sound in any way familiar, Ambassador?''

Another choking gurgle.

''No? Substitute for a dagger four lurker assassins disguised as Tuchanq and see if it becomes any clearer then.''

Mollari's eyes widened. Surprise? Shock? Probably both.

"You see, Ambassador, the lowly Narn has intelligence after all." G'Kar kneeled beside Mollari, showed him the dagger with his own blood smeared along the blade, said bitterly, "I hate you because I'm like you. We are the same. And you have made us that way."

G'Kar lowered his face close to Mollari's, inhaled deeply. "Let me taste your last breath, Ambassador. Let me taste the fear, the anger—the injustice, the *humiliation* of being stabbed in the back." He paused, smiled. "Let us share one last moment together: *victor* to *vanquished*."

G'Kar looked into Mollari's eyes, pushed the dagger back into his chest. Mollari jerked backward with a cry. Blood welled from the new wound, soaked into his robes.

G'Kar bent even closer, listened for the last sound Mollari would make, the rattling sigh in his throat as death finally claimed him.

Instead he heard a faint bleep.

Mollari whipered " . . . Vir . . . "

G'Kar looked down the length of Mollari's body. Something was moving at his waist. Quickly he wrenched aside the robe, snarled angrily. The tentacles. He'd forgotten Mollari's *tentacles*. One of them held the Ambassador's link, peeled off the back of his hand. It was active.

" . . . *Vir!* . . . "

How long had the link been active?

G'Kar wrenched at the knife buried in Mollari's chest. It moved an inch and then jammed between his ribs. G'Kar rocked the dagger. It wouldn't come free.

There was a soft sigh of noise from floor level.

Mollari was *laughing*.

G'Kar stood, scrambled backward away from the dying Ambassador, pressed his back to the door.

Mollari spoke, though how he summoned the strength to form words, G'Kar was unable to imagine. " . . . not . . . die . . . yet . . ." A gurgle, then, " . . . together . . . die together . . . years from . . ." The words turned into laughter, as if Mollari had shared a joke he knew G'Kar could not possibly understand. A moment, then his laughter bubbled away into silence.

Behind G'Kar the door opened as his elbow hit the control. The corridor beyond was empty. For how long?

G'Kar stumbled from the room into the corridor beyond, his head whirling. *Not die yet? Die together? Years from—?* What was that supposed to mean? Damn Mollari! Even in death the Centauri mocked him.

No matter. Mollari was dying; that much was obvious. Revenge was his after all.

G'Kar jumped as the door closed behind him, sealing off Mollari's dying whimper. He hurried away from the Ambassadorial section. He couldn't afford to be discovered yet. There was still one death to arrange.

His own.

CHAPTER 16

Garibaldi jerked awake with a cry—at least he tried to cry out. His throat wouldn't work properly.

He became aware of a figure at his side. "Hey, there, take it easy. You've been unconscious for nearly three hours."

Franklin.

He was in Medlab.

But the plasma bolt—the ruptured faceplate—

He began to struggle again.

There was the sting of a needle as Franklin administered an injection. "Garibaldi, you're more trouble than you're worth. Calm down or I'll put you out again."

Garibaldi struggled to get his throat working. "You and whose army?"

Franklin did not smile. "Drink this. It'll take the edge off that pain in your throat."

Garibaldi allowed himself to be helped into a sitting position, took the cup and swallowed the contents. "What happened? I was shot. I should be dead."

"The AE suit absorbed a lot of the blast. You've got some ammonia burns because the suit was breached. That's what the pain in your throat is. Basically. You're lucky to be alive."

"I don't get it. I remember getting tangled up in the trees, the mask coming off . . . Doc, I was a goner. How did I survive?"

Franklin indicated a figure sitting beyond a glass wall in the ward visitors' area. "Guy over there pulled you out, took you to the medics treating n'Grath—who, before you ask, is going to be fine after a few weeks' regen therapy. Which is what you really ought to have on that throat."

"Want to see him." Despite Franklin's protests Garibaldi levered himself out of bed, managed the feat by sheer willpower. He stood in pajamas and bare feet on the cold floor, tottered weakly across to the visitors' area. Franklin sighed, went with him in case he fell.

He reached the visitors' area. The figure had his back to Garibaldi, attention apparently absorbed by a magazine.

Garibaldi began without preamble, "Hey, I guess I owe you a big favor for saving my life—"

He broke off as the figure turned.

That *smile*.

It was Morden.

He stood, nodded to Garibaldi, left the ward without a backward glance.

Garibaldi shivered.

Franklin helped him back to bed.

"Where's my link? Got to speak to Sheridan."

"I'll tell him you're awake."

Garibaldi nodded, sank into the bed. He sighed. Franklin was right, he shouldn't have moved. His throat was killing him. And his chest. And his face. And his back.

Garibaldi let his head fall back onto the pillow, closed his eyes. Morden. The guy from the Icarus that Sheridan had made such a

brouhaha over only a couple of months ago. Morden had been
trouble then; Garibaldi had no reason to suppose he'd be any
different now. So what was the guy doing running around Red
Sector and saving his life?

Garibaldi's thoughts were interrupted by a low humming noise.
And a sound like someone breathing. "Hey, Doc, back already?
I guess you just couldn't keep away, right?"

He opened his eyes.

Not Franklin.

Kosh.

"Obligation is a hangman's noose."

The Vorlon's translator produced the words almost as music.
Then, while Garibaldi was trying to frame a suitable reply, he
simply turned and glided out of the ward.

Garibaldi watched him go and shivered. Suddenly it seemed
very cold in the ward. Very cold indeed.

CHAPTER 17

Blood.

  Great Maker, how could there be so much blood?

Vir stared down at Londo Mollari's body and saw in its huddled, pathetic, blood-soaked form a vision of the future.

So clear.

Humans. Minbari. Narn. Centauri. Everything gone. Just blood
and memories and radioactive wastelands where planets had once
been vibrant with life.

The process had already started with the Narn Homeworld.

The future was coming.

Vir knelt beside his mentor. The carpet squelched as his knees
touched it. He was kneeling in Londo's blood.

Londo gurgled softly. Still alive. For how long?

A moment passed. The stench was foul. Vir expected to want
to be sick—was surprised when the feeling never came. He studied the body dispassionately. What would Londo say if he were
Vir now?

There's a time to go for the throat.

Acting Ambassador.

Short-term powers; Vir was realistic enough to know his tem-
porary position as full Ambassador would never be ratified by the
Republic. But short-term powers; what could be accomplished
here and now with short-term powers?

Some good?

Maybe.

If Londo died.

A bubbling sigh. '' . . . Vir . . . '' A tiny movement.

Vir saw the knife then, and everything changed.

A Narn ceremonial blade.

G'Kar's dagger.

Vir felt his world lurch suddenly.

His fault. This was all his fault. If he hadn't been put off by
Londo's drunken aggression, if he'd made sure he was safely back
in his quarters, if he'd realized for one moment that there was a
real danger associated with G'Kar, then . . .

Londo would not be lying here. Bleeding. Dying.

And the choice that lay before him would not exist.

Because Vir really did sympathize with G'Kar, his people. Because the Centauri were evil. Because Morden cast shadows over
all he touched, and right now both Londo and himself were as
far into darkness as it was possible to go and still have minds of
their own left to acknowledge their guilt.

Vir's mind skittered over the implication of the dagger in Londo's chest. That G'Kar had used it was obvious—but why had
he left it here to incriminate himself?

What if he hadn't used it? What if someone else had left it
here to incriminate him?

Vir put out a trembling hand and touched the dagger.

The hilt was warm, had accepted the heat of Londo's body,
was bleeding it out of him, and with it his life.

Londo jerked reflexively at his touch, let out a bubbling sigh of pain.

Vir let go the dagger. If he removed the blade now the wound would be worsened. If he didn't G'Kar would be implicated in what surely must amount to murder.

Vir activated his link. "Vir to Medlab. I have a medical emergency in Ambassador Mollari's quarters. The Ambassador has been stabbed and is bleeding to death. Please send help immediately."

Without waiting for acknowledgment from Medlab, Vir grasped the dagger. Pulled it. Mollari jerked, cried out weakly. The blade would not come free. Licking his lips, Vir twisted it, finally yanked it free with a scrape of metal against bone and a rush of fresh blood.

Mollari jerked, cried out again.

Unwilling to admit his motivations even to himself, Vir managed to hide the dagger in his robes just moments before the medics arrived.

CHAPTER 18

Sheridan sighed as the door to his quarters bleeped. He had hoped for a short rest; it seemed such was not to be. "Come in."

It was Ivanova.

And nuViel.

The Tuchanq was not happy. "Captain Sheridan. The Susan has told me of the situation. She has told me that D'Arc is to be tried and executed for murder. Is this true?"

Sheridan clambered stiffly to his feet, feeling as if he'd spent three straight hours in front of the baseball autopitcher.

"You have to understand. There has been a change in the law which—"

"—law which doesn't affect the Tuchanq!"

"This is arguable."

"We are not the ones arguing."

Me neither, sister!

Sheridan licked his lips. "Look. Politically my hands are tied. Morally I agree with you. Executing someone who cannot be considered culpable for a crime she may not even have committed is a moral outrage. But I'm under orders from the President."

"The same President to whom, through you, we are appealing for help."

Sheridan rubbed his eyes and nodded helplessly. "That's right."

nuViel said bitterly, "We thought the Narn were bad. At least their motivation was within our comprehension. Yours is truly alien. I don't know if we will ever be able to understand it."

Sheridan held out his hands, palms uppermost, in a beseeching gesture. "nuViel, please. I'm not done with this thing yet."

Sheridan caught Ivanova's eye. Her look said it all.

Don't count on it.

nuViel angled her spines to study him. "Captain Sheridan, the Susan speaks highly of your abilities and your trustworthiness. As our first meeting in this Land I trust *her* judgment in this. But understand me: your own moral considerations are irrelevant. D'Arc has undergone the ceremony of birthing. You say she is not responsible for her crime. I say the person who committed that crime is dead. D'Arc is a *totally different person.* If you execute her you will be guilty of murder yourselves. We will be forced to withdraw our request of your government, and from your supporters the Minbari, and turn to the Centauri for help."

Sheridan spread his hands, felt like screaming, *This is ridiculous! I agree with you!* Instead he said more calmly, "Believe me, nuViel. Nobody is going to be executed while I'm in charge of Babylon 5."

nuViel tipped her spines to the left, hesitated. She began to speak, but stopped when the link bleeped for attention.

He answered. "Sheridan. Go."

The face of the communications duty officer blinked onto the screen. "I have an incoming call for you, sir. Gold Channel. Ultraviolet priority. It's Senator Sho Lin."

Sheridan rubbed his forefingers and thumbs together. No matter what Sho Lin said he was in for an argument.

"Put him on."

But the screen flashed up the words: *INCOMING MESSAGE RECORDED.*

The message was short, to the point. "Captain Sheridan, your report of the accidental death of the Executioner for the State has been received. The Senate has reviewed the facts and has judged the matter of D'Arc's guilt or innocence unsuitable to be tried in civil court. As highest-ranking Earthforce officer in-station you have been appointed to preside over a military trial. I am authorized to inform you that you are hearby appointed Executioner for the State pro tem. By direct Presidential Order it is now your personal responsibility to sit in judgment at the trial and, if necessary, carry out the punishment of the alleged murderer D'Arc. As of this time you are now acting for the Senate as judge, jury, and executioner in this matter."

The transmission ended.

Sheridan turned to face nuViel. He began to speak, found he couldn't.

nuViel said, "It seems my trust was misplaced after all." She hesitated. "Perhaps it would be better if we asked for help from the Centauri Republic."

nuViel turned and left the room.

Ivanova stayed behind, her expression shocked. Sheridan waved her after nuViel. As soon as he was alone he reached for the scotch still on his desk. Reached for it . . . poured it . . . then tipped it back into the bottle and put it away, this time in the drinks cabinet, where it belonged.

Some solutions were too easy.

He had to think.

God, he had to *think*.

Part Three

Becoming Shadows

December 13, 2259
Alpha Shift: Day

CHAPTER 1

Jacintha rode the monorail to Blue One, followed floor markings to Security Control. There she identified herself to a tall man with kind eyes set into a tired face, who introduced himself as Deputy Chief Allen. He took her to an office off the main administration room. The office was dimly lit by a couple of dozen monitors, some of which were situated on the glass surface of the large desk which dominated the center of the room.

Allen gestured for her to take a seat, then sat himself, behind the desk. "What can I do for you, Mrs. Grond?" Allen was polite, his voice showing neither sympathy nor any judgment of her. She was grateful for that at least.

"I understand you have the alien who murdered my husband here."

Allen nodded cautiously. "She came out of her coma some hours ago. It seemed more sensible under the circumstances. Medlab isn't exactly what you'd call the most secure area in-station."

She nodded impatiently. "Whatever. I want to see her. Talk to her."

Allen rocked backward in his chair, considered her words. "Why?"

She bit her lip. Shrugged. "I . . . You'll probably think me very stupid. The truth is, I don't know. I just got caught up in a demonstration. Apparently a lot of people want to see my husband's killer get away with her crime. I want to know why."

Allen studied her closely.

A moment of quiet, broken only by the faint audio feeds from the various monitors.

Allen nodded thoughtfully. "I can't let you into the cell. I can show you D'Arc on a monitor. Will that do?"

"If it's all you can do."

Allen glanced narrowly at her then.

Had he expected an argument? A flood of tears and anger directed at D'Arc? If that was the case he was going to be surprised.

Allen switched channels on a monitor. The picture resolved to show the alien crouched in her cell. Like a terran dog she was curled into a ball, back arched, arms and legs drawn inward. Her ruff of spines fanned slowly across her neck and around her head. She appeared to be sleeping. Sleeping and dreaming. Like a dog, she jerked occasionally. Jacintha watched her for a few moments, trying to work out how she felt about this alien who had changed her life. As before, when looking at Brian's body, the overwhelming sensation was one of confusion.

After a few moments D'Arc uncoiled her limbs and Jacintha realized she had not been asleep after all. Allen told the camera to zoom in. D'Arc scrambled to all fours, shuffled to one side; the camera picked up a pattern on the floor. The pattern was a random swirl of lines and arcs. The patterns shone, as if freshly painted, except that was impossible because there was nothing there to paint with—

Jacintha glanced at D'Arc and suddenly recoiled. A wound on the alien's throat leaked slow blood.

She had painted the patterns *in her own blood*.

Jacintha glanced at Allen. "Is that normal?"

Allen shrugged.

Jacintha was about to push for more details when, on the screen, D'Arc suddenly threw back her head and howled. Even through the monitor's imperfect reproduction Jacintha could hear the pain and loss in the alien's voice. The howl rose in pitch and stretched out into a terrible scream, almost one of physical pain.

Surely that sound couldn't be made by an intelligent being?

D'Arc began to move then, suddenly leapt sideways, began to run around the cell. Round and round, faster and faster, howling and squealing, leaping at the walls, scratching and scrabbling, muscles bunched, back rippling with muscle and tendon, leaping to howl at the monitor, to smash the wall with her body again and again until, exhausted, bruised, she flopped to the deck, crawled back to her pattern of blood, curled up around it and became still except for an intermittent, dreamlike jerk.

Her howls faded to a faint whine.

D'Arc's posture reminded Jacintha of that of her youngest child curled up in bed with a hot water bottle or teddy bear, huddled up with a familiar toy against the cold Martian night. D'Arc shivered; Jacintha felt herself shiver in sympathy.

Phone the kids. They'll be scared to death, what with me rushing off like this.

"I thought the Tuchanq were an intelligent species?"

"There was an accident. D'Arc suffered brain damage in an air lock blowout during . . . the attack."

"I see." Should she feel triumphant at that? Be pleased that some kind of punishment had already been exacted on Brian's killer?

She felt nothing. Was that due to shock? Indifference? Where was the rage? The guilt? She lowered her head, waited for the tears to come again, felt nothing.

Nothing.

Thanking Allen, she left Security Control.

In the corridor she stopped, aware once again that she had no real plans. Nowhere to go, nothing left to do. Fourteen hours remained until her flight was due to leave. What was she going to do in the meantime? Was there any reason why she should make good on her threat to speak to the Press? Was there any reason why she shouldn't?

Oh the hell with this line of crap.

She would rent a room. Phone the kids. The hell with the expense. It would be a comfort for them. Hell, it would be a comfort for her.

Yes.

Room. Then kids.

Worry about introverted questions later. Much later.

Mind made up, Jacintha walked to the monorail and took a car heading toward New Arrivals and Accommodation Assignment.

CHAPTER 2

Sheridan stared through the glass wall of the observation room into Medlab, where Dr. Franklin and his staff were operating on the comatose form of Londo Mollari. Sheridan shook his head wearily. What the hell was going on? The Tuchanq, D'Arc, the deaths of Grond and the Executioner, all these were bad enough. Now Ambassador Mollari had been stabbed—in his own quarters. It was as though a collective madness was running rampant throughout the station.

A madness stemming from D'Arc.

With Sheridan in the observation gallery was Vir Cotto. The Centauri attaché hovered nervously, his hands clasping and unclasping across his expansive belly. Sheridan glanced sideways at Vir, wondered what he was thinking.

Sheridan smiled at Vir; the Centauri's face crumpled into a hesitant half smile, before resuming its worried expression. Sheridan frowned. Vir wasn't much more than a kid really. To walk into Londo's quarters and see the Ambassador just lying there in a pool of blood . . . without a doubt it would be a traumatic experience.

"Do you think he'll be—" Vir broke off before completing his sentence. Sheridan wasn't surprised. It was obvious from the frantic activity within the theater that Londo's chances weren't good.

Sheridan shook his head. "I don't know, Vir."

Vir nodded. "The Republic will have to be told about the attack."

Sheridan pursed his lips. "Yes. When will you do it?"

Vir shrugged. "I would have to make the call from my quarters. Privacy, you understand. If I go now to tell them and he . . . you know . . . and I'm not here . . . well . . ."

Sheridan nodded sympathetically. "I understand. It will take the Republic several hours to get a ship here; I don't suppose a few minutes either way will make much difference."

Vir nodded. The movement was a little too fast, a little too desperate. "No. No, Captain, I'm sure you're right. I don't suppose that they will."

Vir turned his attention back to the operating theater then and watched in silence for a few more minutes, before turning away and taking one of the seats normally occupied by medical students under Franklin's tutelage. He put his head in his hands, sucked in a deep breath. Apart from that he was silent for a long time.

Sheridan looked back into the theater, at the masked and gowned surgeons, nurses, an anesthetist, all working with dizzying speed around the open body of Londo Mollari. Scalpels flashed with laser light, monitors twinkled. A nurse mopped sweat from Franklin's brow; another handed him a fresh scalpel, took the bloody one from him and laid it in a tray full of other such used instruments. A moment and then the scalpel was replaced again. Sheridan saw Franklin's mouth working behind the mask; a nurse stepped forward with a suction hose. Clamps followed, then sutures. All this carried out in deathly silence on the other side of the gallery wall. Sheridan momentarily considered turning up the sound to get a better idea of how surgery was proceeding but then cast a sideways look at Vir, trembling, head in hands, and decided it would probably not be a good idea.

Sheridan sighed. He knew he should really be talking to the Tuchanq, not watching the operation. There was nothing he could do here, after all. He'd left Ivanova on her own to deal with the alien delegation throughout the whole crisis and that was hardly behavior befitting the ranking officer in-station. Still, she was their first point of contact and, as such, their requested liaison. And he knew she was more than capable of dealing with any . . . *tension* that might arise within the delegation. Still, it seemed hardly fair to either the Tuchanq or to Ivanova to have her ask them on his behalf to wait while one of their number was tried and possibly executed.

Yet even if he did see them in person, what real good would it do? He'd still be telling them the same old story.

A footstep nearby told him someone else had come into the

gallery. He turned. It was Garibaldi. The Warrant Officer was wearing pajamas. A bruise spread high across one cheekbone. His face and hands looked red and sore.

Sheridan said, "Michael. Shouldn't you be in bed?"

"Nah." Garibaldi attempted to shove his hands in his pockets—then realized the pajamas didn't have any pockets. "Snuck out while Franklin was treating Londo." He frowned. "Bad business."

Sheridan nodded. "How are you feeling now?"

Garibaldi shook his head and frowned, then winced as his cheek moved. "I was in the alien sector. I got shot. Every damn Christmas it's the same. I'm beginning to think Santa Claus has got it in for me." He made a concise report, relating his visit to n'Grath, the discovery that the Centauri had hired the lurkers who had attacked G'Kar.

"Typical." Sheridan frowned. "So the one person we could get more information from—Londo—has been attacked himself."

Garibaldi managed a painful smile. "Knowing Londo, I wouldn't be surprised if he stabbed himself just to keep from answering certain awkward questions."

Sheridan thought sometimes Garibaldi's humor was just a little too black. "I'd be surprised if the two attacks are unconnected."

Garibaldi nodded. "Knowing Londo and G'Kar, I wouldn't be surprised if they attacked each other."

Sheridan thought about this. "It's an attractive theory. Londo attacks G'Kar through intermediaries. G'Kar finds out about it and strikes back in revenge. It holds water."

"But why would Londo want to kill G'Kar in the first place?"

Sheridan raised his hands. "Right now, your guess is as good as mine. Great, isn't it? What with the Tuchanq thing going to trial half the station seems to be at each other's throat."

"Yeah, well, here's another bit of good news for you." Garibaldi coughed, rubbed his throat. "Got a little visit from Ronnie in Communications while I was laid up. He's managed to clean up the data from the loader's black box."

Sheridan sighed with relief. "At last. Some real information."

"Yeah. And it doesn't look good for D'Arc. According to the

vid record she stabbed him all right. From where I was watching it sure looked to me as if she wanted to kill him.''

"There's no possibility of it being tampered with?''

Garibaldi shook his head, winced. ''Nah. Ronnie's a good man. He knows CGI. If he says it's straight, it's straight.''

Sheridan absorbed all this information with mixed feelings. He shook his head. ''You know what this means, don't you?''

Garibaldi nodded. ''D'Arc will go on trial for murder. The evidence will condemn her—''

"—and I'll have to find her guilty and execute her.'' Sheridan gritted his teeth. ''Damn. Michael, damn it all, why did EarthGov have to pick *now* to illustrate a point of law?''

Garibaldi shook his head sympathetically. ''I know, I know . . . but hoping for a change in the law now is wishing for the moon. You've got to face it: The Senate's got you by the short and curlies.''

"I know, and I don't like it.''

Garibaldi shrugged. ''Yeah, well, anyway—it looks like Doc Franklin's gonna be a while in there. If you don't need me for anything else for a bit, I'm going to go and get dressed. Then I guess you'll want me to look into this attack on Londo.''

Sheridan nodded. ''I'm sorry, Michael. I know it's been a long day already. But when the Centauri find out what's happened they're going to want answers and they're going to want them fast. If anyone here can supply those answers, you can.''

Garibaldi nodded, turned to leave. At that moment Franklin left the theater and came out into the observation gallery. He nodded to Vir and Sheridan as he pulled off his mask and smock. His gaze lingered on Garibaldi, but before he could say anything Vir leapt up from his seat and moved quickly across the gallery.

"Doctor? Doctor can you tell us how bad it is . . . will Ambassador Mollari . . . '' Vir seemed to gather his strength for the question. ''Will he live?''

Franklin sighed, led Vir toward Sheridan and Garibaldi. ''What you have to understand here is that Londo was badly injured. He suffered knife wounds to his chest and back. Two of those wounds punctured vital organs. Both liver and spleen have been irreparably damaged. He has a cracked rib and the outer wall of his heart was torn.''

Vir gasped.

"Now the heart damage was superficial, luckily. I was able to repair it. The rib was standard stuff, no bother. But the other organs . . . well. I did all I could; in the end the damage was simply too great.'' Franklin shrugged. "Maybe if whoever attacked him hadn't pulled out the knife I'd have been able to . . . well. That doesn't matter now.''

Sheridan glanced at Vir. He was pale, shaking. Was it any wonder? There was a catch in his voice as he spoke.

"I don't understand . . . are you . . . are you saying Londo's going to die?''

Garibaldi added, "Yeah, Doc—if that's the case why all the activity in there?'' He jerked a thumb at the theater, where surgeons were still working on Mollari.

Franklin nodded. "Well, it's not quite so cut and dried. At the moment the damage is terminal. Too much damage, too much blood loss, not enough time before brain death occurs, lack of donor organs—''

Vir looked up. "Organs? I can have donor organs brought from Centauri Prime within . . . within hours.''

"It's too long, Vir. We just can't keep him alive that long.''

Vir's face crumpled again.

"But, as I said, there is a chance.''

Sheridan said gently, "Go on.''

"Well. We could use the *life giver*. The alien machine which I used to save your life, Mr. Garibaldi.''

Sheridan studied Franklin's face. "What's the catch?''

Franklin hesitated. "To save Mollari would take a vast amount of life energy. It would cost the donor his own life.''

Sheridan saw what was coming. "But if you could use many different donors, each sacrificing a small portion of his own life energy . . . ''

Franklin nodded. "Then Ambassador Mollari could be saved, yes. But the thing is, it would take more than a dozen volunteers to safely provide the life energy required.''

Sheridan considered. "In that case you had better start looking for volunteers."

Franklin looked directly at Vir. The Centauri looked away. "I would offer my services, of course, but . . . I expect the Republic will declare me Acting Ambassador until an envoy is sent from Centauri Prime."

Sheridan said, "That may be true. But surely you can talk to the Centauri population in-station? See if any of them would be willing to help?"

Vir nodded. "Of course I can do that. I'll organize it right away."

As he turned to leave, Franklin said, "We're going to put Londo in a cryotube. Lowering his body temperature drastically will reduce the chances of brain damage and enable us to keep him alive longer." Franklin shrugged. "But that's just delaying the inevitable. We need those donors. And we need them quickly."

"I understand, Doctor. And thank you." Vir hurried from the gallery.

"I'd better get back; they'll be needing me soon to help prepare the *life giver*." Franklin nodded to Sheridan and Garibaldi and left the gallery.

Garibaldi began to follow him out, but Sheridan stopped him. "Garibaldi. Hold on."

"Sure. What's up?"

Sheridan took a small device from his pocket and activated it. He saw that Garibaldi recognized the device as being the surveillance jammer General Hague had left with them last time he'd visited the station. The time Sheridan had let Garibaldi, Franklin, and Ivanova in on his secret: General Hague's investigation of the Government, and of the conspiracy surrounding Luis Santiago's death.

Garibaldi nodded at the device. "I take it this is is about EarthGov?"

Sheridan nodded. "I didn't want to say anything while Vir was in the room. But while you've been unconscious I've been doing some digging of my own. General Hague was helpful. I've found out the reason behind the President's decision to make an example out of D'Arc. Clark is running way behind in the polls. Senator Crane is taking advantage of this lapse of public confidence to make another bid for the office of President. Clark is going to resign and call for a vote of confidence—after a public display in which he can be seen to be cracking down on crime.''

Garibaldi nodded. ''I'm with you. And we're the display. Or rather D'Arc is.'' His face twisted with disgust. ''Clark is using us to get himself back into power.''

''That's right. He's hoping such a display will heighten public confidence enough for the people to vote him back into office.''

''That's . . . '' Garibaldi searched for the most damning word.

''Politics.'' Sheridan finished for him.

''Yeah, right. So what happens now that the evidence proves D'Arc is guilty of murder?''

Sheridan sighed. ''There'll be a trial. The evidence will be presented. If I find D'Arc guilty of murder, then the law is very clear on the matter. The Senate will demand an execution and they'll be within their rights to do so. And I'll have to carry it out.''

Garibaldi's face crumpled into a look of sympathy. ''Oh man. Now I know why I never bucked for Command.''

Sheridan found himself irritated by Garibaldi's remark. ''It's no laughing matter.''

''Yeah, sure. Sorry.''

Sheridan nodded an apology himself. He switched off the jammer, shoved it back into his pocket. ''Look. You'd better start working on how to handle security for the trial and . . . afterward. The Senate want the press in on all of it. They want a televised trial, special programs, the works.''

Garibaldi looked shocked. ''You're joking. Even leaving the Home Guard out of things it'll be a three-ring circus. We'll have riots from arse-end to Blue Sector.''

''I know. And it's down to you to ensure the public safety during the whole sorry mess.''

''And all this on top of trying to find out who attacked Londo.''

Sheridan frowned. Something Garibaldi said made him . . . no. Not something Garibaldi had said. Something *Vir* had said—or rather something he *hadn't* said.

"Michael—about this Londo business. You might want to start by talking with Vir."

"Oh?"

"It might be nothing, but in all the time he and I were here watching the medics operate, he never requested an investigation to discover who carried out the attack." Sheridan hesitated, visualized Vir's behavior over the last hour. "It was as if he never even thought of it. Or thought one was unnecessary . . . " Sheridan shrugged. "Of course it might just have been that the shock of finding Londo drove all other thoughts from his mind."

Garibaldi narrowed his eyes thoughtfully. "It's a possibility. I'll have someone look into it."

"Thanks."

"No problem."

"Right. Well, I suppose I'd better get back to—" Sheridan broke off as his link bleeped. "Sheridan."

"Deitrich, C&C, Captain. "We're just had a report that maintenance workers in Brown Seven found the body of a dead Centauri. He's been stabbed, sir. Murdered."

Sheridan covered his link, glanced at Garibaldi. "I haven't even had breakfast yet. What else could go wrong?" Uncovering his link, Sheridan continued, "I'll get Mr. Garibaldi to look into it. Is that all?"

"I'm afraid not, sir." Deitrich's voice held a note of apology. "We've got problems with the press. One DeBora Devereau from Channel 57 News is asking to conduct interviews with all senior staff."

Sheridan sighed. "As if we don't have enough to worry about. Please inform Ms. Devereau that she can speak with the most important staff in-station immediately. And then direct her to the life support techs in Blue Twenty-nine. Sheridan out."

Garibaldi grinned his agreement. "If the sewage engineers aren't the most important people in-station, I don't know who is."

Sheridan stared hopelessly at Garibaldi. "I swear, there are days when I wish I had never . . . " He shook his head wearily. "Never mind."

CHAPTER 3

G'Kar was alive. Every movement, every breath, every tiny sensation he experienced told him this.

He very much did not want to be alive.

He wanted to be dead.

He wanted to be with his family.

There was a problem.

The dagger. The blade he'd left in Mollari's body. He could not commit ritual suicide without it.

G'Kar paced. He sighed. He shuffled. He did all the things the humans did. He sat, banged his fists against the bloodstone altar, then put his head in his hands, then got up and did the whole thing over again.

No dagger. No death. No *dagger*.

He couldn't die. It was so stupid. He couldn't die.

This is ridiculous!

He walked stiffly to a closet, withdrew his holster and sidearm, took the gun from the holster, put the barrel against his temple.

Now. Do it now before you lose your nerve!

G'Kar hesitated. He seemed to hear Mollari laughing at him.

Not die yet. Die together. Years from now.

Mollari had been laughing. At him. Laughing.

Why?

G'Kar put the gun back in the holster, put that back in the cupboard. He walked stiffly back into the prayer room and sat awkwardly before the altar. He pressed a thick hand against the mass of bandages covering his chest, felt his heart thumping solidly underneath as it had all his life, pumping blood around his body and into his brain. The motion was firm, decisive; no confusion there.

Tonight he had acted according to his heart. Tonight he had killed a sworn enemy. He had pushed a blade into Mollari's body and bled his life out onto his own carpet. He should be celebrating. One more Centauri dead; one more beyond the reach of their pathetic collective "future glory." He felt no remorse at the job; slaughtering animals would hold more guilt.

So why this confusion?

Why the fear?

Was the fear that of discovery? Of how he might be perceived by others? Of what might happen to him?

Was the confusion derived from the fact that even now some part of his mind was telling him peace was possible, even essential?

G'Kar asked these questions and more, directed them to the altar in High Narn, the ancient Tongue of J'Quan. He listened in his room for many hours, but there was no response. He studied the holy texts but found no comfort in their fables and half truths. He lit bowls of ritual incense but, enraptured, knew only the evils of past and future, both of which cast deep shadows across the present.

And when the candles had burned low and the texts had been closed, when the incense had faded, dimming the fire of rapture in his mind, then G'Kar knew that he was truly alone. Alone with his questions, his wondering, his despair. Alone in the night.

The door bleeped.

"Who is it?" Was that his voice? Slurred with lack of sleep and incense?

"Sheridan."

G'Kar nodded to himself. So. They had found the knife. Found it and come for him. So be it. The decisions, the questions, the need for answers and the desperate fear of shadows, all had been taken from him.

Thank J'Quan.

He opened the door.

Sheridan nodded and came in, eyes watering with the remains of the incense in the air. "G'Kar, I—" Sheridan coughed, wiped his eyes, began again. "I could always come back."

G'Kar waved Sheridan into the room. "No, Captain, that will not be necessary. My rituals are completed for the evening."

Sheridan nodded, drew a breath. "Well then, I have some news which I thought you might want to know."

"Indeed?"

Oh just get on with it. Arrest me, condemn me, just get it over with!

"There has been an attack on Ambassador Mollari."

Sheridan waited for a response; G'Kar was simply too weary to give him one.

"You don't seem surprised."

"I'm not. The Centauri have many enemies."

Sheridan frowned. "Someone stabbed him three times: twice in the chest, once in the back. He's in Medlab now. Doc Franklin doesn't hold out much hope. I thought you might want to . . . well . . . look. I know what he's done to your people, but you have worked together here and I thought . . . I thought you might want to see him before . . . well, before he dies."

"That was a kind thought, Captain." The words came out automatically, a platitude and he could see Sheridan knew it. The truth was he was confused all over again. Evidently Sheridan had not come here to arrest him or accuse him. In fact he seemed completely ignorant of the truth. Then again, perhaps J'Quan had denied him a ritual death for a reason: perhaps Sheridan's arrival here had prompted the answer he had been seeking. He thought for a moment before speaking further.

"Captain Sheridan, let me tell you something about Londo Mollari. Something you may not know. Earlier today he hired some lurkers—humans—supplied them with Changeling Nets with which to disguise their appearance and told them to kill me."

Sheridan frowned. "I didn't know you were so well informed of Mr. Garibaldi's investigation," he said pointedly.

G'Kar avoided the implied question by asking one of his own. "You did not ask why Mollari should attempt to have me killed."

Sheridan seemed to consider pursuing his previous line of inquiry, hesitated, then said, "You're going to tell me though, aren't you?"

G'Kar considered. It *must* be deliberate. "Think about it. I am killed, apparently by members of the Tuchanq, who have every reason to hate me. Since I am Narn and could technically be considered subject to the Centauri Republic, they would have every right to 'protect Narn interests,' and incidentally, their own, by annexing Tuchanq. They would cite the Narn invasion of Tuchanq as ample reason for aggression on their part, in the process gaining possession of all the Narn heavy weapons systems and construction factories situated on Tuchanq that were abandoned at the conclusion of the war.'' G'Kar studied Sheridan's reaction; the human wasn't slow. He was getting it very clearly. ''Clever, isn't it? Even more clever when you realize Mollari would have the added satisfaction of knowing my death was the instrument by which the Republic expanded its frontiers to include one more innocent system.''

Sheridan seemed to think about this. ''You do realize that you just made yourself a prime suspect for this attack, G'Kar?''

G'Kar shrugged, felt the bandages tighten painfully about his chest. ''Myself and more than three thousand other Narn.''

Sheridan considered, nodded thoughtfully. ''The shape of the wounds inflicted on Ambassador Mollari match that of a Narn ceremonial dagger.'' He hesitated. ''May I see your dagger, G'Kar?''

G'Kar studied Sheridan closely. ''Are you accusing me, Captain?''

Sheridan sighed. ''G'Kar, sooner or later someone is going to come asking these questions. Would you rather it be the Centauri?''

G'Kar shook his head, took his dress uniform dagger from its place beside the uniform in his cupboard. He offered the dagger hilt first to Sheridan.

Sheridan studied the blade for a moment, refused to take it. No wonder; it was twice the size of any wound the ceremonial dagger could have made. Then again, Sheridan could not know this was not G'Kar's ceremonial dagger, could he?

Or could he?

He was certainly studying the blade closely enough.

''I notice the bindings are missing.''

Startled, G'Kar almost dropped the blade. ''Er . . . yes . . . they are replaced regularly. I had discarded the old set of bindings before the war . . . Now of course . . . there can be no new ones shipped from Homeworld.''

Sheridan nodded. "I see."

I'm sure you do.

G'Kar offered the blade again. "Please. Make a closer examination."

"Thank you, that won't be necessary." Sheridan turned to leave and G'Kar put the dagger back into its sheath, resting both on the nearby altar.

G'Kar studied the human thoughtfully. So much had changed about the man since he had pledged his personal effort to helping G'Kar win back his Homeworld. And what *had* happened to the dagger he had left buried to its hilt in Mollari's chest? Had Sheridan hidden it? Had he come here simply to fulfill a duty, to—what was the phrase—*tick boxes* for the administration?

How much did he really know about the attack on Mollari?

"Captain."

Sheridan turned.

"I just wanted to say . . . thank you."

Did Sheridan's eyes narrow suspiciously? It was so hard to tell with humans.

G'Kar continued quickly, "For informing me of Mollari's . . . plight."

Sheridan seemed to relax. "I take it I can tell Dr. Franklin to expect you in Medlab then?"

G'Kar considered. "Yes. Of course."

"Then I'll be going." At the door Sheridan turned, and it was as if he could see right through G'Kar, right through him to the core of his being. "One thing, Ambassador: Londo Mollari is dying. I consider us friends, G'Kar, and I stand by the promise I made to help you win back your world. But make no mistake: If there was evidence you had committed a murder I would have no choice under current law but to arrest you and put you on trial. And . . . well, you'll find out soon enough what that would mean."

Without waiting for a reply, Sheridan left. As the door closed quietly behind him, G'Kar found himself shaking. Sheridan had just delivered a warning.

But if he hadn't found the dagger, who had? And what would that someone do with it?

When would G'Kar have to pay the price for his revenge against Mollari, and how great would that price be?

More questions to which G'Kar had no answers. And, lacking answers, he returned to the altar, lit more candles, burned more incense, inhaling deeply until his mind sparked with a familiar and welcome chemical fire.

The incense tasted of the past, of his father, slowly strangling on the family prayer-tree as birds pecked at his still-living flesh; and it tasted of the future, of evil gathering unimaginable distances away, approaching, casting its shadow back in time across the present moment, a shadow that G'Kar sometimes wondered if only he could see.

A shadow that was cast across them all.

CHAPTER 4

Vir stared at the Narn ceremonial dagger. Such a simple tool, a blade, yet when wielded with intent it could shape power and personal destinies.

Vir cleaned the blade slowly, trying to understand fully the implications the use of this particular weapon had already had upon his own power and destiny.

The message to Centauri Prime had gone about as well as could be expected. Lord Refa had confirmed a ship would be sent and would arrive within ten hours. Until then Vir had the powers of acting Ambassador. The last thing Refa had said to Vir before ending transmission had apparently been in the nature of friendly advice.

"This is a heavy mantle for one so young to wear. My advice

is . . . to avoid making complex decisions until the new envoy arrives.''

Refa had smiled reassuringly when he'd said that, one Centauri to another, one politician to another. But Vir knew Refa. He understood the truth behind the words. And the truth was simply this: Refa didn't want Vir to upset the status quo by exercising any of the powers he now officially possessed.

If for *any complex decisions* you substituted the phrase *any decisions at all,* you would have an accurate summation of the meaning behind Refa's apparently friendly advice.

Vir had closed down his end of the communications link and spent the next twenty minutes in thoughtful contemplation of the Narn dagger and the implications it held.

Now he looked at the dagger and wondered if it would not perhaps be sensible to allow Mollari to die.

The answer to that must be *no.*

The humans had a saying: *Better the devil you know.* Londo had his own slight variation on that theme: *Better the devil who owes you a favor.* Now Vir could understand the distinction. If Vir became responsible for saving Londo, then the Ambassador would be in debt to him. And that debt could be used to good advantage at some point in the future. Perhaps it would even allow Vir to reverse Londo's decision to ally himself with Morden and his associates.

His mind made up, Vir placed a number of calls to various places in-station, requesting representatives of the Centauri population to visit him in the Ambassadorial suite immediately.

He concealed the dagger just as the first arrived.

Twenty minutes later they had assembled, the dozen or so key members of the Centauri population in-station.

Vir had them sit and explained the situation to them, made the request for volunteers.

Even before he finished, Vir began to get a bad feeling; the delegation was restless, fidgety. They allowed him to finish more out of politeness than any real interest.

Almost before the last words left Vir's lips one of the delegation was standing. Kantell. A man hardly known for his support of others.

"Acting Ambassador. Vir. The news of this unfortunate affair has already reached elements of the Centauri population. A request for help was not unanticipated. Unfortunately . . . what you ask cannot be."

Vir clasped his hands together. "I don't understand."

"The situation has been discussed. I am sorry to say that the Centauri are unable to provide the help you seek."

Vir tried to contain his surprise, his frustration. "Are there none among you who would spare just a little of their life energy to help save the Ambassador? I have been assured the process is quite painless."

Kantell smiled, overbright, overgenerous. "It is not the fear of pain which prevents us from helping you, Vir. It is simply that . . . there are none among us who wish to be seen as too close to Ambassador Mollari. It is known that he has . . . acquaintances . . . and . . . well, let's just say that there are some among us who believe that these acquaintances may have been responsible for the attack on the Ambassador's life."

Vir had a sudden image of himself kneeling in a pool of blood, pulling the dagger from the Londo's chest and hiding it.

Kantell continued, "I think you will find that fear of those acquaintances will prevent any Centauri in-station from helping him."

Vir felt anger rise to swamp the guilt. *You mean you want Londo to die in the hopes that you might be able to befriend his acquaintances and reap the power they bring for yourselves!* He said nothing, however; such an accusation would be dangerous for someone in his position. Instead he tried to control his anger, scanned the eyes of the Centauri before him. As one they were carefully neutral, lacking in sympathy or understanding.

"How many of you took advantage of the Ambassador's generosity during the last year? Aldan, you requested a political favor to improve the position of your family as I recall. You, Fentin, were outcast until Mollari spoke on your behalf to the Council." Vir felt his voice strengthen, bolstered by his anger. "All of you were quick enough to ask the Ambassador for favors that none other than he could grant. Yet now when his life lies in the balance, none of you will help!"

Vir waited. Some of the eyes were cast downward in shame or embarrassment. For the most part they remained stony, emotionless.

Vir felt his anger turn to disgust. "Go, all of you. And be thankful that I am not the vengeful man that some in my position could be!"

When the delegation had gone, Vir sat behind Londo's desk and placed his head in his hands. He felt like jumping up and down, screaming with rage, frustration. *The ungrateful curs. May they and all their family and their friends and their family's friends die without rank and—*

His link bleeped.

Vir jumped at the unexpected sound, realized how tense he had become, had the first inkling of the true responsibility of office.

It was Franklin. "Vir. Have you made any progress finding some volunteer donors?"

Vir blinked, glad the doctor couldn't see his face. "I am working on the problem, Doctor. How is the Ambassador?"

"Not good." A pause. "Vir, I didn't think finding volunteers was going to be a 'problem.' "

"Neither did I, Doctor. I hope to have news soon. Vir out."

He cut the link. He looked around the suite, searching for some inspiration. The Centauri in-station wouldn't help. Refa and the new envoy were half a day away. That left Vir *holding the ball*, as the humans said.

What was he to do? Roam the hallways begging help from total strangers? If the Centauri wouldn't help, what hope could there be that the general population would?

Vir activated his link. "Acting Ambassador Vir to Ambassador Delenn."

A moment, then a male voice answered, "This is Lennier, Vir. Ambassador Delenn is unavailable right now. May I help?"

"It is a matter of some urgency, Lennier. Life and death, in fact."

"Then you will find the Ambassador in the Stone Garden in the Park."

"Thank you, Lennier."

"You are welcome."

Vir gathered himself together, rose to leave the suite. At that moment the door bleeped.

"Come in."

It was Garibaldi. Vir nodded a hurried welcome. "Mr. Garibaldi. What can I do for you? I'm in rather a rush, so if you could make it quick, I'd be grateful."

Vir felt Garibaldi's gaze on him, noticed for the first time the Warrant Officer's weary demeanor. Was his face a shade redder than normal? With humans it was so hard to tell.

"Finding the robes of office a little heavy, Vir?"

Vir uttered a companionable laugh which he felt afterward probably came out more distraught than friendly.

Garibaldi came into the suite and the door closed behind him. "Vir, I know you've got a lot of work to do. But I have to ask you something."

Vir sat down behind the desk, sighed. "Ask away then."

"What do you know about the attack on Londo Mollari?" Garibaldi's unwavering eyes held him.

Vir felt the weight of the dagger in his pouch, concealed within his robes. "I . . . don't know what you mean."

Garibaldi frowned thoughtfully. "You found the body. You haven't filed a report yet."

"I was waiting to be contacted by security. That is the way things are done, isn't it?"

Garibaldi shrugged, jammed his hands into his pockets. "Consider yourself contacted."

Vir pursed his lips. "Well. It's like I told Captain Sheridan. I'd been working. I went to the Ambassador's quarters to check on some information and . . . and there he was. Lying there. I thought he was dead."

"And that's it?"

Vir shrugged. "I called Medlab immediately. What else do you want to know?"

"Did you see anyone leaving the Ambassador's quarters? Anything else suspicious?"

"No." Vir hesitated; the dagger seemed to be increasing in weight inside his robes. "Not a thing."

Garibaldi sighed. "Ah well. Perhaps when you're ready you can come to Security Control and file a full report."

Vir nodded eagerly. "Of course, Mr. Garibaldi. I'll be sure and do that. Now if you'll please excuse me, I really do have pressing business."

"Still looking for volunteers?"

Vir nodded, found himself suddenly able to return the Warrant Officer's frank gaze. "Mr. Garibaldi . . . you and Londo were friends, were you not? Perhaps you would consider—"

Garibaldi shuffled uncomfortably. "Look, Vir. Don't think I don't appreciate Londo's position. I . . . " A long pause. What was Garibaldi thinking? "Look, Vir, it's like this. Londo and I haven't really been getting along so well lately, what with his involvement in the war and everything, and well . . . " Another hesitation. Garibaldi's face smoothed into a familiar neutral expression. "Look. I'm just too busy right now. I have a major investigation on my hands just trying to find out who attacked him. You understand."

Vir nodded. "Of course." He wondered how much of his bitterness showed in his voice. Not that it mattered. Not to Garibaldi anyway.

After Garibaldi left, Vir sat at the desk for a few more moments, trying to regain his composure. Vir had heard it said that Garibaldi was a good friend and a dangerous enemy. Vir was beginning to understand the truth of those words.

He got up then, left the suite in search of Delenn.

He found her, as Lennier had said he would, in the Stone Garden.

She looked up as he approached. "Vir. I was meditating on the forthcoming trial."

Vir nodded politely; inwardly he was screaming with impatience at the niceties. "It is an important matter, Ambassador. And worthy of some thought." He hesitated. "I don't wish to interrupt, but . . . "

Delenn smiled. "Please join me."

Vir sat beside her on one of the many benches which encircled the expanse of neatly plowed sand and precisely positioned stones. He felt the Minhari's gaze on him as he sat. Unlike Garibaldi or Kantell, no hint of judgment in the gaze. No condemnation, no accusation. Merely patience and acceptance and a joyful curiosity.

Vir made no pretense of understanding the significance or importance of the Stone Garden; he nonetheless had the sudden and absolute conviction that Delenn was perfectly within her element here.

He looked at her, studied the ridges of bone emerging from the skin of her head, saw the way in which her still-novel growth of human hair was arranged around it in the most attractive manner.

Delenn smiled gently. "You have come to ask for my help."

Vir uttered a humorless laugh. "Is there anyone on this station who doesn't know more about my business than I do?"

Delenn's smile widened, then smoothed into an attentive expression. "Ask your question, Vir."

"Ambassador Mollari is dying in sickbay. No one else will help by volunteering even a little of their life energy so that he may live. Will you?"

Delenn appeared to consider. For a moment Vir caught the briefest flicker of emotion on her face. Was it anger? Fear? Triumph? Whatever it was, it was gone so fast that later he would question whether he had really seen it at all.

Delenn turned away from Vir, looked back across the Stone Garden. Beyond the far edge a couple were walking arm in arm. Beyond them the landscape curved upward past the monorail terminal until the colors of the fields muted and blurred and turned into the sky.

A gentle wind blew across the garden; thermal currents from daylight to nighttime areas ensured that a gentle wind always blew in the Park.

When Delenn spoke, her voice was gentle as the wind, but her words were uncompromising. "Vir. I take it you are unaware of the Minbari belief that the soul is sacred and must not be compromised."

Vir blinked. "I am not asking that you donate your soul, Ambassador."

"I know that, Vir. But for us Minbari, the soul and the life force that you refer to are one and the same thing. If I were to offer even a portion of my life energy to save Londo, then my soul would be compromised. And I cannot allow that to happen under any circumstances.''

Vir nodded. ''A religious conviction. I understand. But what about others of your people in-station? Surely they will help?''

Delenn considered. Her expression was almost unreadable. Vir got the feeling he was missing some subtlety. Or that Delenn was deliberately holding information back, inventing an excuse or obscuring the truth in some way.

Her voice was quiet and very serious when she eventually spoke. ''Of course, you may talk to whom you wish. But I fear you will be disappointed. No Minbari will volunteer to help you. Your time would be better spent asking someone else.''

Vir nodded. ''I understand, Ambassador.'' He hesitated, went on bitterly. ''It seems your much-vaunted interest in helping others has been exaggerated.''

Delenn's lips compressed to a thin line. ''I am sorry you feel that way, Vir.''

''I'm sorry that I have to feel that way, Ambassador.'' Vir fell silent. Somehow his words left him feeling as if he had been unfair to Delenn. Well, maybe he had, but he had a life to save, a job to do. If bitterness and unfairness got the job done, then so be it.

Vir got up then and left Delenn with her sand and her stones and her hidden truths.

On the way out of the garden he almost walked into Ambassador Kosh, gliding silently in the direction from which Vir had come.

Vir stared at the Vorlon, or rather at the Vorlon's encounter suit. Abruptly he said, ''Uh. excuse me, Ambassador Kosh?''

Kosh stopped, swiveled so the suit was facing Vir.

Waited silently.

Vir blinked. ''Uh . . . Actually, it was nothing, Ambassador. Please. Don't let me keep you from your business.''

Without acknowledging Vir's words in any way, Kosh turned and resumed his movement away from Vir. He hadn't said one word during the entire exchange—but still Vir shivered. What was that human saying? *Someone's just walked over my grave*?

Vir shivered, hurried away.

CHAPTER 5

Renting a room turned out to be quite affordable after all. Brian might be dead, but his credit was still good.

The room was small, containing little more furniture than a bed, a chair, and a link terminal. A small bar held kitchenware and appliances. A smaller cubicle contained the bedroom and bathroom facilities.

Once in the room, Jacintha wasted no time but dialed immediately into the station comm net and opened a line to Mars. She spent a few minutes updating Janna on her situation, then asked to speak to the kids.

Jacy came to the screen. At five she was two years older than her brother, thin, normally bubbling over with raucous energy. Today it was obvious she was subdued, though excited to see her mother.

"Hello, Jacy. Where's Robbie?"

"Mum! He's asleep. Janna said not to wake him up. Janna said you were on Bab'lon 5! Is Daddy there?"

Jacintha felt her heart melt. She hadn't told either of the kids yet why she had left. Time enough for that when she got back. "No hons, he's . . . he's working."

"Did he get me a *gloppit* egg?"

Jacintha bit her lip. "I don't know, honey. I'll ask him."

"Okay."

"Now listen, Jacy. I just called to make sure you were being good and not giving Janna any trouble."

"We're not."

"I'm glad to hear it. Jacy, I have to go now, because this call is very expensive."

"More expensive than a *gloppit* egg?"

"Yes, lots more. But I'll be home tomorrow. Look after your brother for me, okay?"

A long silence.

"Jacy?"

"I will."

Jacintha began to get a cold feeling in her stomach. "Honey? Are you okay?"

Jacy bit her lip, said nothing.

"Jacy, darling. Tell Mummy what's wrong. Janna hasn't had to smack you, has she?"

Jacy, blinked, seemed to be on the point of tears. Quite suddenly, she shouted, "You *said* Daddy had a *gloppit* egg. You *said* that, Mummy, but *how* can Daddy have got me a *gloppit* egg? *How* can he do that when *the man on the stereo said Daddy's dead*?"

Jacintha felt her heart lurch.

"Honey, I . . . Daddy is . . . ' She felt her own face crumple, tears falling, a mirror to Jacy's. "Where did you hear that?"

"On the news. While Janna was putting Rob to bed. I know I wasn't supposed to but . . . "

"It's okay, honey. That's okay, I'm not cross."

Oh dear Lord, they need me. They need me now and I'm seventy-two light-years away.

"Now, Jacy, I want you to listen very carefully. It's true that Daddy has had an accident. I'll be back tomorrow to explain everything. In the meantime I want you to take care of your brother for me. And I want this to be our secret. Do you understand? I don't want you to tell Robbie."

"You don't want me to tell him about Daddy?"

"No, honey. Can you do that for me? Keep a secret?"

"Yes."

"Okay then. Now be good for me, okay?"

"Yes."

"Good. Can you get Janna again for me?"

"Yes."

When Janna realized what had happened she was appalled. "Jay, I'm so sorry, I didn't have a clue she could operate the stereo tank without the remote."

"She's a smart kid."

"I know. Oh, Jay, what are you going to do? What do you want me to do?"

"Just . . . keep them under control until I get back. I'll be home tomorrow on the *D'Alembert*. I'll tell them then, myself, properly."

Janna nodded, seemed about to burst into tears herself.

Jacintha said good-bye and cut the link.

The images of her daughter's accusing, tear-streaked face remained imprinted on her mind long after she had flung herself on the bed and surrendered to an uneasy, dream-filled sleep.

CHAPTER 6

Franklin was waiting for Sheridan when he returned to his office after leaving G'Kar. The doctor did not look happy.

"Is there a problem?"

"You could say that. Between the two of us, Vir and I have approached representatives of just about every species in-station. No one will volunteer even the least little bit of their life energy to save Londo."

Sheridan sighed inwardly. *How did I guess you were going to say that?*

Franklin went on. "I don't know what it is. Some refuse on religious grounds, others give no reason. You want my opinion? I think they're all scared."

"Of the procedure?"

"No. Of Londo. I don't know if it's escaped your notice lately, but it sure hasn't escaped mine. Londo seems unpopular with far more than just the Narn. Even the Centauri population seem somehow . . . scared of him. His own people!"

Sheridan steepled his fingers. "I am told the Centauri envoy will not arrive for another six hours yet."

"That's too late, of course."

"So. What can we do about it?"

Franklin rubbed his chin, leaned forward. "You're the ranking military officer here. If you *asked* for volunteers from among your staff—well . . . they wouldn't have any choice, would they? And it's not as if the procedure would harm them . . . "

Sheridan stood. "I can't do that, Doctor, and you know it. Sure I'm the captain here. But if I give someone a direct order to donate life energy, I'm not better than . . . "

President Clark.

' . . . any dictator in history. In any case. How would you enforce such an instruction? And how would I justify the order morally?"

Franklin uttered a short, humorless laugh. "You're worried about morals? There's a man's life at stake. Now I know he's not the most popular person in-station right now, but he is a person nonetheless. It's within your power to save him by ordering volunteers forward. Will you do it?"

Sheridan didn't hesitate. "No." He held up a hand to stem the anticipated outburst. "But I can authorize a stationwide appeal. There are a quarter million people in-station. We only need a dozen."

Franklin's lips thinned angrily. "And how long do you think it will take for the message to disseminate among the population, for any potential volunteers to present themselves?"

The question was rhetorical and Sheridan knew it. "It's the best I can do, Doctor."

Franklin said angrily, "It's not the best you can do. It's just the best you can do without compromising your image of yourself."

Sheridan opened his mouth to respond angrily, then stopped. Was Franklin right?

"Doctor . . . " He began an apology, aborted the attempt before it had even begun. "I suggest you prepare a data crystal for broadcast."

Franklin reached into his pocket and brought out a data crystal. He placed it on the desk between them. "Your appeal."

Without another word, Franklin turned and left the office.

CHAPTER 7

Garibaldi got his first inkling of the violence to come shortly after leaving Vir in the Centauri Ambassadorial Suite.

As he was crossing the Green Sector Plaza heading for the monorail terminal, he was accosted by a group of humans and aliens, several dozen in all. They were waving prolife banners and chanting.

One of the group pressed a plastic badge into his hands. "Love the alien, Citizen. Come to the trial. Be part of the voice of the people." A smile and the girl was gone, whirled away by the mad rush of demonstrators.

Garibaldi glanced at the badge. It was cheap, a home-stamped thing of plain gray plastic with words written on its surface in scrappy handwriting.

Love the alien!
Justice for all—not some!
Save the Tuchanq!
Free D'Arc!

Garibaldi stared at the words with some bemusement. Wherever the human race went, there went the crackpots, the misguided idiots with more money than sense and a misplaced sense of ideals. Sure, D'Arc should be saved—if she was innocent. But the evidence didn't look that way to Garibaldi. He sighed, shook his head, slipped the badge into his pocket, resumed his walk toward the monorail terminal.

What was amazing was not so much that there were groups prepared to go to any lengths, however misguided, to protect the interests of aliens simply because they *were* aliens but that the news of D'Arc's guilt and impending trial had hit the streets so damn *quickly*—

His thoughts were interrupted by screams from behind.

He turned. Across the plaza the group of prolifers had run into a smaller but considerably more vicious group made up of humans only.

"*What are you playing at?*"

"*Earth for Humans!*"

"*Let the Slags burn!*"

Home Guard.

With a muttered curse, Garibaldi activated his link, called in the incident to Control, and ran back toward the group.

By the time he got there blows had been exchanged. The girl who had given him the badge was on the deck bleeding from a head wound. The rest were going at it as if they were practicing for the Mutai.

Garibaldi drew his PPG and fired a warning blast into the air.

"Now listen up! You got thirty seconds to disperse before I arrest the lot of you!"

"*They started it!*"

"*Damn slag-lovers!*"

"*What do you know about love anyway?*"

And it started all over again. Punches were thrown, the prolife signs were torn down and trampled underfoot.

A lump of plastic looped out of the melee. Garibaldi ducked, glimpsed the words *Protect Innocence*! as it sailed overhead.

This was dumb. Someone was going to get seriously hurt—probably himself. Time to take the bull by the horns.

Garibaldi scanned the group, isolated the main protagonists, waded in. He took more punches than he gave, but when he emerged from the group it was to leave two deeply unconscious humans, one from each camp, lying in his wake.

The rest calmed down then.

Garibaldi dusted his hands, looked around for the backup he had called for. Found himself face-to-face with a minicam operator and a barrage of questions.

"Mr. Garibaldi, isn't it? DeBora Devereau, Channel 57 News. With the trial of D'Arc set for less than an hour from now, and violence, such as that we have just witnessed, on the increase, what are your plans for keeping the peace? Do they include more

violence of the kind you have just demonstrated? Mr. Garibaldi,
for the record, just how does it feel to use violence to subdue a
fellow human being?''

Garibaldi raised his hands to ward off the camera and questions. ''Whoa. Someone let the animals out of the zoo.''

''Mr. Garibaldi, would you care to expand that comment for
Channel 57 viewers?''

Garibaldi gathered his wits and took stock. Facing him were a
news team. And an irritatingly attractive female reporter. She was
staring intently at him, a hand mike thrust almost into his face.
''Mr. Garibaldi, is there any truth to the rumor that D'Arc's trial
has been fixed? That her guilt is already predetermined and the
verdict reached? Mr. Garibaldi, once again, would you care to
tell our viewers what it feels like to subdue a fellow human being
by violence?''

Garibaldi struggled to hold his temper in check. He jerked a
thumb over his shoulder to where the remains of the mini-riot
were being mopped up by security. ''Don't you believe in freedom of speech?''

''Yes, but—''

''That guy was a racist. I disagreed with his politics. Call it a
discussion.''

Devereau's laugh held not a teaspoonful of humor. ''Mr. Garibaldi, that's hardly the point. You hit that man in the face—
twice. I have it on vid. Now what is your comment on that?''

By now Garibaldi had recovered his breath. And his wits. He
glanced at Devereau again and laughed. ''By the look of that
black eye you ought to be asking someone else that question, not
me.''

Devereau's lips compressed to an angry line. She turned to face
the camera, blocking its view of Garibaldi. ''That was Warrant
Officer Michael Garibaldi, Chief of Security on Babylon 5 and
one of the members of staff I have been trying repeatedly to meet
with for several hours. Now we know why he is so often unavailable for comment.''

She turned and threw a nasty grin at Garibaldi. ''Thanks,
champ.'' She turned away again and Garibaldi heard her saying

to her cameraman, "Are you sure CGI can erase the bruise before we go on air? God, I'll kill Jacintha Grond if I have to do another voice-over—"

Garibaldi wiped a hand across his face. It came away bloody. And somehow his collar had gotten ripped half off.

Turning away, he began to disperse the crowd which had gathered around the incident. For the most part the people he told to move on took one look at his bloody face and did just that. When the crowd was dispersed and the last of the prolifers and Home Guard were being tagged for a night in the cells, Garibaldi began to think about moving on himself.

That was when he became aware that Devereau was still talking. The man she was talking to looked familiar.

It was Morden.

He was smiling, perfect eye-candy. Devereau was hanging on every word that came out of his mouth.

"So tell me, Mr. . . . Morden, is it? As a member of the public, a man in the street, as it were, what do you feel about the events here today? Do you feel a kinship with your fellow humans in the Home Guard? Or are you prolife?"

Morden produced a bemused expression. A little smile. As if he was surprised to find himself on the receiving end of so pointed a question. "I suppose I would have to say that all life is important in some way." He nodded to himself. "Yes. That's what I believe. Life is important. If you know what to do with it."

Devereau grinned. "Amazing. Okay, Ted, cut it there. Mr. Morden. Thank you. I wish everyone was as quoteable as you."

Morden spread his hands and smiled warmly. "Off the record, Ms. Devereau—surely that's not all you want?"

Devereau laughed. "Off the record, you may be right. This violence-versus-morality angle is kids' stuff. I did my political potty training on it. What do I want? I want big news. Prime-time news. Give me wars and violence and injustice and suffering, and let me bring the truth to the people. That's what I want." She stopped then, suddenly aware she might be going a little overboard. "Off the record, that is." She smiled.

Morden nodded but did not return the smile this time. "Thank you.'' He turned away, leaving Devereau to stare after him with a brief, puzzled expression before shaking her head and turning to her cameraman. ''Okay, Ted, shoot some of these smashed-up signs and then we'll call it a wrap.''

Devereau and the cameraman moved slowly away, getting interesting angles on the cleanup squad bagging the debris of the fight.

Morden walked unhurriedly toward Garibaldi.

Garibaldi met his eyes and shivered.

That guy creeps me out.

''Mr. Garibaldi.'' Morden nodded. His eyes were cold, flat, belied the warmth of his smile. ''And what do you think of the violence here?''

Garibaldi felt compelled to answer, if only because the man had saved his life the previous night. ''I'm prolife, if that's what you mean. Assuming the accused is innocent, of course.''

''Of course.'' Morden nodded thoughtfully. ''Take your friend Londo Mollari, for instance.''

What was this?

''Londo? What about him?''

''Well, I've heard he's dying. You were friends, weren't you? You could save him.'' Morden hesitated. ''Call it a favor returned.''

Garibaldi stared at Morden. ''Now just wait a minute. It would take a dozen people to save Londo.''

''Or just one. One who was prepared to sacrifice himself for his friend.''

Garibaldi uttered a short laugh. ''You are out of your mind.''

Morden said nothing.

Garibaldi felt compelled to add, ''I'd die.''

Still Morden said nothing.

Obligation is a hangman's noose.

Garibaldi felt the blood drain out of his face.

Morden shrugged suddenly. ''Then I'll consider the debt yet to be repaid.'' He smiled. ''Join me on the monorail?''

Garibaldi shook his head slowly, wondering as much at the

sudden wave of guilt which washed over him as he did about Morden's outrageous suggestion. "Thanks. I think I'll walk off these bruises."

Morden nodded, turned away, resumed his unhurried pace toward the terminal.

Garibaldi watched him for a moment, then turned and walked in the opposite direction. His link bleeped as he did so. "Garibaldi. Go."

"Sheridan here. We need to talk."

"I heard that. Be with you in ten."

Garibaldi cut the link. As he did so his foot crunched down on the sign that had been thrown at him earlier. *Protect innocence!* proclaimed the blood-smeared words. He stumbled over the sign, realized the Channel 57 cameraman was recording him, recovered his balance, and moved on.

CHAPTER 8

G'Kar stood in Medlab, stared down at Londo Mollari's body cocooned in the medical cryotube, saw in the pale skin stretched tightly across brow and cheekbones the face of his dying father. Granted the skin was a different color, the shape of the skull and the presence of hair totally alien; what linked the two in G'Kar's mind was the ever-present shadow of death that hovered nearby. In both cases death was inevitable. No donors had yet come forward to help Mollari, even though Dr. Franklin's appeal was being broadcast to newspoints and public vids stationwide almost constantly. The appeal was running alongside the announcement of D'Arc's trial, set for half an hour from now, hoping to gain sympathy from the prolifers who might be watching.

G'Kar knew the truth. No one would volunteer to help Mollari. Not even prolifers. The Centauri had dug his own grave with selfishness and greed, was doomed as surely as if G'Kar's blade had pierced his heart with the first blow.

With that thought, G'Kar remembered the dagger. Remembered the blood, the rasp of steel on bone. Mollari's dying cry as he had fallen, bleeding, to his knees.

What had he done? J'Quan, what had he done? To kill with honor, in combat or war, this was acceptable. To strike from behind, then to torture, to prolong the agony—and twice in one day. This was unpardonable.

G'Kar was damned. Only ritual suicide would balance the scales—and that was impossible.

Because the dagger was still missing.

He felt a presence beside him. Franklin, or some nurse checking on Mollari's vital signs. They would go away eventually.

He waited. The figure remained. He turned.

It was Vir.

The Centauri was staring at Londo's face with an unreadable expression.

G'Kar followed his gaze. Tried to ignore the presence at his side. Couldn't. Vir was Centauri. Betrayer of covenents. Invader of his world. Killer of his people. Killer of his family.

Suddenly unable to stand the presence—even the smell of the Centauri beside him, G'Kar turned to leave. Vir looked at him then and he stopped. He met Vir's gaze, found it as unreadable as ever.

"Do you know, Vir," he said slowly, precisely. "Someone once asked me what I wanted. I said I wanted the entire Centauri race reduced to ashes. 'And after that?' he asked. And do you know what? I didn't know. I hadn't looked that far ahead."

Vir shuffled nervously from foot to foot, clutching his hands together as if holding something out of sight beneath his robes.

"Now I am looking that far ahead—and there's nothing to see. No future at all. Because there's nothing left to have a future. Just the ruins of civilizations, the burned-out husks of planets where life once teemed in all its many forms." He stared at Vir, caught the Centauri's gaze with his own, willing him to understand. "I have seen the future and it holds nothing. Nothing but shadows of things that might have been."

A moment of silence in which the life-support systems surrounding Mollari clicked and hummed quietly to themselves.

G'Kar continued quietly, wearily, "Who to blame? That's the question. Once I was sure. Not anymore."

G'Kar turned away from Vir and Mollari. Began to walk toward the entrance to Medlab.

"G'Kar, please wait." Vir's voice trembled. Guilt? Fear? He was right to be afraid of G'Kar. *I could crush his skull with my bare hands. End his life in a moment. But what good would it do*? It was a question G'Kar had never asked himself before. A question he could not even begin to answer.

G'Kar looked at Vir again. Saw sympathy in the Centauri's expression. Sympathy in his weary eyes. Sympathy in his very submissive stillness.

"I don't need it!" G'Kar's shout had the medical staff peering in his direction. A moment, a shrug of apology. Let them all think he was referring to the tragedy of Mollari's death. Vir knew what he meant. The knowledge was there in his eyes. In his expression. The understanding.

I don't need your sympathy.

Vir nodded.

I know.

He moved then. Took something from beneath his robes. A slim shape wrapped in a Centauri religious cloth. He offered the parcel to G'Kar.

"I said I was sorry."

As G'Kar took the parcel, Vir turned to leave Medlab.

Feeling the first stirrings of an emotion he would have been hard pressed to describe, G'Kar unfolded one end of the cloth.

The emotion was fear. The emotion was guilt. The emotion was horror.

Vir had given him back his own ceremonial dagger.

The very blade with which he had taken Mollari's life.

Not Sheridan or Garibaldi.

Vir.

He imagined Vir finding the dagger, pulling it from his dying master's body, hiding it from sight before the medics arrived to treat Mollari for his injuries. Imagined the horror on his face, the thoughts running through his head as he had cleaned the dagger, wrapped it, walked through the corridors to bring it here. To give it back.

G'Kar quickly rewrapped the dagger and slipped it beneath his robes. He stared at Mollari again, let his eyes wander across the pale skin, the wasted flesh.

Even in death the thrice-damned Centauri reach out to torture me.

Vir had saved G'Kar. What would he want in exchange?

Whatever it was, it was unimportant.

Nothing mattered anymore.

G'Kar chuckled, drawing curious looks from the medical staff. He ignored them. How could they know the ironic truth?

G'Kar stared at the still figure and nodded acknowledgment which the dying Ambassador would never see.

It would no doubt amuse Mollari greatly to know that in attempting to protect G'Kar from discovery, Vir had merely made it possible for him to perform the ritual suicide his belief now demanded of him.

CHAPTER 9

Jacintha Grond watched the trial of D'Arc from the public gallery of the People's Court in Blue Twelve.

She had never been in a courtroom before. Even the public gallery was a surprise. For a start everything was made of wood—well, plastic shaped and finished to look like wood. Secondly, the gallery was packed. This in itself was no surprise bearing in mind the contentiousness of the case. What was a surprise was that the mass of human and alien figures—some hundred or so in all, she supposed, that were squashed into the gallery—were so quiet you could have heard a slow leak in a pressure dome.

Beyond the gallery the court was filling with people. The Clerk of the Court sat in front of the Bench, his back to the Judge's chair. Facing the Clerk, with their backs to the dock and the public gallery, were the lawyers for the Defense and Prosecution, together with their assistants and witnesses. One whole row of seats to the right of the court was filled with members of the Tuchanq delegation. A woman in Earthforce blue wearing the rank of Commander sat beside them.

There was no jury; its dismissal had been a requirement for a military trial.

The Judge's chair was, as yet, empty. The Judge would be the last person to enter court—after the defendant had been called to the dock.

Members of the press stood with cameras and recorders, in a line that stretched around the courtroom, between the front of the public gallery and the stairwell through which D'Arc—the defendant—would be called. Some of them were recording images of the evidence. This was laid out in plain view on a table beside the court bailiff. It consisted of the black box recording of the time immediately prior to the murder, Brian's PPG, his wallet—opened to show a credit chip and a large roll of cash—and the murder weapon itself, D'Arc's dagger.

All these items were bagged in clear plastic. Spots of dried blood could still be seen on them.

Jacintha shivered. Perhaps coming here had not been such a good idea after all. She thought about leaving, but the way was now blocked by several more members of the public who had come to watch the trial.

Putting aside her uncertainty with an effort, Jacintha looked around for a seat in the public gallery. There were no spaces. She found a place at the back of the gallery to stand. Already her back was beginning to ache again.

What was she doing here? Did she really care what happened to D'Arc?

She had found herself pondering these questions more and more intensely in the last few hours. She still had no answers.

She had tried to arrange another meeting with Sheridan, to find out exactly when she would be able to move her husband's body. He had been constantly unavailable. Despite repeated requests, the administration had provided her with no information whatsoever. It was as if, as far as they were concerned, both she and Brian had simply ceased to exist—or be important anyway.

Unable to stay in her room after awaking there from a troubled sleep, Jacintha had spent the last few hours visiting the public areas of the station and trying to find something interesting going on in which to involve herself—in between watching the bulletins as they were broadcast on the public vids.

Several hours had passed in this manner. Babylon 5 was big—but it wasn't so big you could wander around it for more than a couple of hours before running into an area listed as off limits to the civilian population. And after a while even the Park became boring. There was only so long you could watch a mech-driver laying irrigation pipes or a tennis tournament or a park-keeper polishing the granite blocks of the War Memorial.

Jacintha was not sure when her desire to actually go to the trial, as opposed to watching the broadcast, was born. She suspected it was while wandering the hedge maze . . . mind and body in a kind of leafy-green sensory deprivation. Nothing to worry about or think of other than the hedge, her route, and the occasional other maze-goer.

Yes. It must have been then that she really began to examine the implications of Brian's death, then that she began to deal with the shock and consider the options available to her. It was the thought that there *were* options available to her that brought her mind inevitably to the subject of her husband's killer. The Tuchanq: D'Arc.

Because the alien's actions had changed her life. There was no doubt in Jacintha's mind about that.

And suddenly, but with a growing curiosity, Jacintha began to wonder about D'Arc's motivations. Her reasons. What was it that had driven her to kill?

That was when Jacintha had found a seat in Green Sector Plaza,

one stop from the Stone Garden, and began watching the public
broadcasts dealing with the preparations for the trial. It was here
that she had watched the preliminary hearing in which Sheridan
had been named Judge. It was here, also, when the young man
with the intense expression and a clipboard had come up to her
and asked her to sign a petition to "Free D'Arc."

Jacintha had stared for a long time at that clipboard—the plain
sheet of white paper half covered with signatures. Had stared at
it for so long, in fact, that the young man was on the point of
moving away from her with an impatient look when she took the
offered pen and quickly scribbled her name at the bottom of the
list.

That was the moment in which she realized how she felt about
D'Arc. And somewhere during the hours she spent watching the
bulletins in Green Sector Plaza, the decision to actually attend the
trial—until now only a faint possibility in her subconscious
mind—crystallized into a firm decision.

At that moment the Clerk of the Court called for the defendant
to be brought in. Jacintha felt herself jostled from one side as
more people crowded into the public gallery. She became aware
that humans and aliens all around her were suddenly pushing
forward toward the front of the gallery. A collective sigh encircled
the gallery as D'Arc was led, in restraints, into the courtroom.

The Clerk of the Court bade everyone rise, then called for the
Judge.

Sheridan entered and sat in the Judge's chair.

In the ensuing quiet, the Clerk read aloud from a prepared
statement.

"In the case of Earth versus D'Arc of the Tuchanq the following charges are presented before this court: One, that the defendant did, on the afternoon of the twelfth day of December of the
year 2259, willfully attack with intent to murder the civilian businessman Brian Grond. Two, that in so doing the defendant was
responsible for loss of life and injury to Earthforce personnel then
working in the cargo bays. Three, that in so doing the defendant
was responsible for damages to Earthforce property and private
cargo amounting to one point eight million standard credits."

Pushing aside the pain in her back and legs, the tired fuzziness of her mind, Jacintha tried to concentrate on the proceedings in the courtroom. She stood up straighter in her position against the back wall of the gallery, so as to get the clearest possible view of D'Arc.

The Tuchanq was shuffling uneasily in the dock, her spines tipping this way and that, tasting the air. She seemed nervous, confused. She whined constantly, occasionally gave a little bark. Her back seemed strained, as if she was trying to crouch onto all fours, as she had when Jacintha had watched her on the security monitor some hours earlier. The restraints prevented this movement.

The lawyer for the Prosecution rose and made his opening statement, to the effect that he represented EarthGov and that he would show the defendant guilty of premeditated murder.

The lawyer for the Defense followed this speech with one of equal precision and politeness in which, she said, she would demonstrate the exact opposite.

There being no witnesses to the actual murder, the Prosecution produced as his first piece of evidence the black box recording of the time immediately prior to the murder.

The lights were dimmed in the courtroom and the recording began to play. Jacintha found herself watching, from a point near the ceiling of the loader's air lock, as Brian entered along with several crates of cargo.

"You will note that the inner lock door is sealed at this point. No other persons are in the chamber. Until D'Arc enters, that is."

And Jacintha watched as D'Arc entered the air lock. Brian was at the innermost end of the lock and couldn't see the alien. Jacintha felt her stomach lurch. Found herself mouthing a warning. It was no good, of course. Brian could no more hear her voice than her children could, seventy-two light-years away on Mars.

D'Arc crept forward, moving around the crates toward Brian. He still hadn't seen her. Jacintha felt herself sweat. She clenched her fists, felt her nails bite into her palms. Why didn't he move? Surely he could see something, hear something—

Then he did move, alerted by a sound perhaps, or a movement seen from the corner of his eye.

Too late.

D'Arc was on him. The dagger plunged into his chest, once,

twice. Jacintha felt her breath catch in her throat. She let out a little moan, a mirror to Brian's grunt of surprise and pain. Beside her a Drazi turned and stared at her. She made an effort to un-clench her hands, to relax her breathing. To her surprise it took her only a moment to accomplish this.

She returned her eyes to the record, saw then that Brian had a gun in his hand—the same PPG that currently lay bagged on the evidence table next to the court bailiff. There was no blood on it yet, of course.

The record unfolded. Brian struggled, D'Arc moved in close, the gun discharged, the figures separated in a cloud of debris. Money, bits of jigsaw, a *gloppit* egg all drifted in a cloud around Brian. And blood. He was bleeding into the air. A crimson mist formed around him. Then D'Arc moved again, the gun discharged again, and static obscured the picture.

The Prosecution halted the recording and brought up the lights.

Jacintha let out a breath she had not realized she'd been hold-ing.

The Prosecution said, "At this point the recording ends. It is my contention that the second PPG discharge, which destroyed the lock sensors and allowed both doors to cycle open, also de-stroyed the link between the camera and the recorder." The Pros-ecution had the recording rewound to a still frame of D'Arc stabbing Brian. The frame was ghostly, overlaid by reflections from the courtroom lights. Jacintha found herself staring at a faint reflection of the public gallery in the screen, saw herself in min-iature mapped over the image of her dying husband.

The Prosecution continued, "Although the victim's autopsy de-termined that decompression injuries contributed toward his death, it is clear that the killing wounds were in fact those inflicted with the dagger you saw, by D'Arc herself."

The Prosecution sat.

Sheridan nodded. "Does the Defense have anything to say in response to this evidence?"

The Defense lawyer rose. "Your Honor, I simply wish to re-iterate that, at the time the record stops, Brian Grond was, in fact, still alive." She sat.

"So noted." Sheridan nodded. "The Prosecution may proceed."

The Prosecution stood. "Although there are no material witnesses to the actual murder, I would like to call on a relevant testimony. The Prosecution calls nuViel Roon to the stand."

A whisper of surprise swept the court. It was clear this development was unexpected, to say the least.

As Jacintha watched, the leader of the Tuchanq delegation rose somewhat uneasily from her place on the benches. She glanced at the woman in Earthforce blue seated beside her. The woman looked serious but nodded.

The Tuchanq took the stand and was sworn in.

The Prosecution began by asking, "Would you please state your name and position for the record."

"My name is nuViel Roon. I am Elder Stateswoman for the Tuchanq."

The Prosecution asked, "You are responsible for the Tuchanq? You are their leader?"

The Tuchanq's spines trembled almost nervously. "That is correct."

"I see. And are you familiar with the defendant?"

"I am. It is D'Arc, formerly known to us as—"

"Thank you, Ms. Roon. As an associate of yours, you have known D'Arc for . . . what, months? Years?"

"Several years. The Song of her Family and my own have been—"

"Yes, thank you. So. Having known the defendent for years, you must have known her when she carried out the cold-blooded murder of more than forty Narn executives in the then administration of your planet?"

Jacintha bit her lip. D'Arc had killed *how many* Narn?

nuViel trembled. Her fingers, clasped on the podium in front of her, clenched hard enough to mark the plastic. "With respect, Your Honor, I wish to point out that a state of war existed between—"

The Prosecution interrupted, held up a hand. "Please confine yourself to answering the question. Did you know the defendant when the murders in question were committed?"

"Yes, but—"

"And as such you could testify that the murders were in fact committed by the defendant?"

"Yes, but she was acting under—"

"Thank you. A simple yes or no will suffice."

nuViel's spines rippled in agitation. "Yes."

"And that the murders were carefully and deliberately planned, and executed without compunction or any trace of mercy?"

"Your Honor, I would like to—"

Sheridan tapped the gavel lightly. "I must ask you to confine yourself to answering the question."

nuViel stood up straighter. "Yes."

"In other words the defendant has shown on over forty separate occasions that she is fully capable of the crime of premediated murder?"

"Objection." The Defense rose. "Prosecution is leading the witness."

"Sustained."

"The question is withdrawn. nuViel, if D'Arc had been brought to trial on your own world for the crimes she committed there, what would have been the result?"

"She would have been found guilty of murder and executed. But that was why we—"

"Thank you. That will be all. No more questions." The Prosecution sat.

Sheridan glanced at the Defense. "Your witness."

The Defense stood. "nuViel, is it true that your people do not sleep?"

The Prosecution stood. "Objection. The question is irrelevant."

Sheridan considered. "Overruled. nuViel, please answer the question."

"Yes. We do not sleep."

"Why?"

"I do not understand the question."

"Excuse me, Your Honor, I'll rephrase the question. nuViel, what happens to a Tuchanq if they sleep?"

"Our Songs of Being and Journey are broken."

"nuViel, could you explain that in terms my learned friend, the Prosecution, and the members of the press would understand?"

"We die. Not physically, but in our minds, we die. Then we are born again. Like all newborn we have the sensibilities and manners of children."

"And all this happens if you sleep? If you lose consciousness in any way, for any reason?"

"Yes."

"What if only one Song is broken?"

The Prosecution stood. "Objection!"

Sheridan did not hesitate. "Overruled. The Defense may continue. But be aware that this court will allow no indulgences."

The Defense nodded. "I am leading up to something, Your Honor. nuViel, if you would answer the question."

"In such a case the individual is considered insane until the ceremony of birthing can take place."

"I see. And in your experience has loss of consciousness occurred to any of your delegation?"

"Yes."

"Since you arrived in-station?"

"Yes."

"And when was this?"

"Shortly after we arrived. There was a fight. Some Narn and humans—"

"I don't think we need bother with the details. In short, there was a fight."

"Yes."

"And then?"

"The Susan—that is, Commander Ivanova—shot all those participating in the fight."

"She stunned them? Rendered than unconscious?"

"Yes."

"Everyone that was involved in the fight?"

"Yes."

"Including the members of your own delegation?"

"Yes."

"And what happened then?"

"We held the birthing ceremonies and the members who were rendered unconscious were reborn."

"All of them?"

"No."

"How many were not reborn?"

"One."

"And is that person here in court today?"

"Yes."

"And who is this person?"

"It is D'Arc."

"And bearing in mind what you have already said regarding the disposition of one of your people who has been rendered unconscious but not been reborn, how would you describe D'Arc's condition at the time of the murder?"

"In your terms her behavior would be considered psychotic."

"Can you expand that statement for the court?"

"Yes. In almost all cases where loss of consciousness occurs but only one Song is broken, the Tuchanq in question awakes with an overwhelming desire to replace the Song that is broken."

"And how can this be accomplished?"

"There is only one way." nuViel seemed unwilling to continue.

After a moment Sheridan prompted her. "Please answer the question, nuViel."

nuViel said, slowly, "The only way to take another's Song is to kill the singer."

The Defense came closer to the stand. Her voice softened. "And in your opinion is that behavior befitting a sane being?"

"No. As I have said, D'Arc is not sane."

The Defense nodded. "To use your own words then, being psychotic, D'Arc's overwhelming desire would have been to take another's Song and thus save herself from both madness and—in your terms—death."

"Yes."

"So she would have killed another Tuchanq?"

"No."

"Oh? Why not?"

"Because Babylon 5 is not the—our—Land. We are the aliens

here. You—all of you—are the People. D'Arc would have needed to take a Song of Being, it is true, but the Song she would have needed would have had to come from someone of this Land.''

''A human?''

''Not necessarily. I will try to explain. This Land is inhabited by many different People. Different *species*. All of whom are part of it. D'Arc would have needed Songs from all the different species here. But no one can sing more than one Song of Being. So D'Arc would have been instinctively drawn to the one whose Song intertwined with as many other species as possible. In your terms . . . the person who had the most intimate experiences of as many life forms as possible. You would say . . . a *representative* of the many Peoples of the Land.''

''I see. Someone such as Captain Sheridan or Commanda Ivanova? Perhaps a member of the medical staff?''

''No. If that were the case, then one of the people you have named would have been attacked.''

''I see. So in other words, because of his liaisons with aliens, Brian Grond seemed to D'Arc, in her madness, the most suitable person from whom to take a Song of Being?''

''Yes.''

''And thus kill.''

''Yes.''

''And she would not have done this if she were sane?''

''No.''

''Thank you, nuViel. No more questions.''

Sheridan nodded. ''You may stand down.'' nuViel returned to her seat. Jacintha saw that she was trembling as she walked.

Sheridan asked if either Prosecution or Defense wished to call further witnesses.

The Prosecution declined.

The Defense stood. ''The Defense calls Dr. Stephen Franklin.''

Jacintha watched him take the stand. Tall, slightly unsteady, he seemed overtired—exhausted might have been a better word. His voice was slurred as he was sworn in.

''Dr. Franklin. Would you please describe for the court the current mental condition of the defendant.''

''She has brain damage.''

"Can you be more specific?"

"She has suffered oxygen deprivation resulting in a significant loss of function to the areas of her brain which deal with behavior, with self-perception, and with memory."

"Is this function recoverable?"

"No."

"And how would you place her mental age?"

"In human terms? A child. No more than five or six years old."

"Thank you. No more questions."

The Prosecution stood to cross-examine. "Dr. Franklin, is it true this brain damage occurred as a direct result of the attack made on Brian Grond?"

"Objection! Prosecution is leading the witness."

"Sustained."

The Prosecution reconsidered. "It is your stated medical opinion that oxygen deprivation caused this brain damage."

"Yes."

"And you have no doubts about this? Are you sure the damage might not have been caused by a blow to the skull? Or a disease? I understand that the Tuchanq were fed members of their own population during the war. If there is a possibility that one of the reprocessed individuals had a transmissible degenerative disease such as Wadel's Syndrome, then the disease could have been contracted by eating the reprocessed body."

"Definitely not. There is no medical evidence to suggest either of these as possible causes for the damage. And as for your suggestion—it is so remote that it might as well be considered fiction—and poor fiction at that."

"So in other words there is no doubt in your mind that the brain damage the defendant suffered was caused by oxygen deprivation."

"None whatsoever."

"Thank you. No more questions."

Sheridan told Franklin he could stand down, then asked the Prosecution and Defense to sum up.

The Defense stood. "Your Honor, the accident that rendered D'Arc insane happened before the attack on the businessman

Brian Grond. It is the Defense's contention that at the time the murder was committed, the defendant was, in the words of her own people, psychopathic. It is clear that the defendant cannot be held responsible for the crime she is supposed to have committed.

"Further, taking into account Dr. Franklin's medical evidence, it is clear that the defendant cannot be expected to understand any punishment which this court may see fit to impose upon her, and that to punish her would not only be futile in terms of a deterrent to future criminals but would also be the height of moral injustice. I therefore move that this case be dismissed on grounds of insanity, and that the defendant be returned permanently to the care of her own people."

The Defense sat.

The Prosecution thought for a moment, then stood. "My learned friend's determination of insanity is based upon a philosophy that is alien, and thus not recognized in this—a terrestrial—court. We are not here to determine whether D'Arc is morally responsible but *actually* responsible. Whatever the philosophy of her people, the evidence points unavoidably to the premeditated nature of her crime. D'Arc needed to replace her Song of Being. To do this she needed to murder Brian Grond. And only Brian Grond. It has been shown that D'Arc has previously been responsible for more than forty other murders. The premeditated nature of this case is clear. It is the contention of the Prosecution that D'Arc fully intended to murder Brian Grond for personal gain; indeed that she carefully planned the murder and carried it out without thought of mercy. As such we must demand the most severe punishment the law can provide. Your Honor, the crime is murder. The punishment must be death."

The Prosecution sat.

"If both parties rest then I declare a recess for one hour, at which time court will reconvene and sentence will be passed."

The gavel crashed against the block.

Jacintha saw D'Arc jerk against her restraints at the sound of the gavel, felt the sound as if it were a blow to her own face, was assailed by a sudden, complete identification with the Tuchanq female, an empathy so strong it made her dizzy. And suddenly Jacintha saw the truth: that it didn't matter if D'Arc was guilty of murder. It didn't matter what she had been like before. Only what she was like *now*. And Jacintha had a sudden awareness that D'Arc was no more capable of committing violence than . . . well, than Jacintha's own children.

Whatever her crime might have been, she had already been punished enough.

The hour passed slowly for Jacintha as it passed for the others in the public gallery. Her back and legs were now in some pain. The press of bodies in the gallery was becoming claustrophobic. Once again she found herself questioning her motivation in attending the trial.

She was still searching for an answer when court was reconvened, an hour later.

The cameras swung to cover Sheridan as he stood to announce the verdict.

"D'Arc of the Tuchanq, I find you guilty on the counts of damage to Earthforce property and injury to Earthforce personnel. On the count of murder I also find you guilty."

There was a moment of shocked silence in which the only sound was the whirring of cameras. Jacintha felt the mood of the crowd begin to change. Shock to outrage to anger. Then a man in the middle front row of the public gallery stood and yelled, "It's a travesty! A damn travesty of justice, that's what it is!"

A moment of shocked silence and then pandemonium erupted in the courtroom.

A burst of sound erupted from the gallery: outrage, dismay, anger, the voice of the people crying out at this perceived injustice.

Sheridan was banging his gavel and calling for order.

The cameras whirred, swung from side to side, their operators eagerly jostling for the best angles.

Someone jumped over the barrier dividing the gallery from the courtroom. Cameras swung to cover the movement. The man was waving something, yelling.

"This is a petition! This is a—let me speak! This is a petition signed by—"

Security grabbed the man and tried to hustle him away. Immediately a dozen more people leapt the barrier into the courtroom. A fight started. And now the public gallery was emptying like a top-pled jug into the court. More than a hundred furious onlookers, out-raged and offended, screaming for *justice, not murder*.

The security men went down under the sheer weight of num-bers.

Sheridan banged his gavel.

Cameras whirred.

Jacintha was swept forward, felt herself topple over the barrier, landed on a news cameraman and tumbled to the floor in a tangle of arms and legs.

Dimly she was aware of the thud of shocksticks, the cries of those stunned or trodden on.

Then a heartrending screech that cut through the general melee. D'Arc.

The sound brought a lull in the pandemonium.

Panting breaths and small moans of pain, groans from those shocked into unconsciousness. Shuffling as they were dragged away.

And a voice spoke out firmly. "This is a petition signed by more than a thousand people, including the wife of the murder victim, Jacintha Grond, demanding the release of the prisoner. This verdict would not have been brought against a human! Pro-tect innocence! Free D'Arc!"

A cry of approval from the crowd. The cameras whirred, pan-ning to capture the moment of appeal.

All for nothing.

Sheridan was on his feet, gavel crashing loudly. His voice rang out into the courtroom. "Order in court! *I will have order in this court!*"

His voice held the crowd, not because of his authority over them—it was very clear to Jacintha that as far as these people were concerned he had none—but because his was the voice that would pass sentence.

Silence grew then. Gradually a calm settled over the restless court.

The cameras whirred.

Sheridan waited until he had the attention of everyone present, then spoke.

"D'Arc of the Tuchanq. You have been found guilty of the crime of murder. It is my duty to pass upon you the only sentence the law can pass for such a crime. You will be taken immediately from this place via a public route to a place of execution where you will suffer death by decompression. And may whatever gods you believe in have mercy upon your soul. Take her down."

If Jacintha had thought that previous outcry was pandemonium, it was nothing compared to the shout that went up as the sentence was announced. The cry held more emotion than she had ever heard. Terror, rage, incomprehension, a primal scream of outrage and denial echoed by the Tuchanq delegation and by D'Arc herself as she was dragged from the court.

Then, like the eye of a hurricane, a moment of utter calm among the barrage of voices—and Jacintha realized there was a camera pointed directly at her face. Close by a businesslike voice was saying, "—for Channel 57 News in the courtroom with Jacintha Grond, wife of the murdered businessman Brian Grond. Mrs. Grond, is it true that you signed the petition demanding the release of your husband's killer?"

Jacintha bit her lip. "Yes. It's true."

"And how do you feel now that she has been condemned to death? Are you pleased? Has your husband's death been avenged? Has justice been served?"

Silence.

No one spoke.

No one moved.

The cameras whirred.

"Mrs. Grond, can you answer the question? Has justice been served here today?"

And suddenly she knew why she had come here, to the trial. She had not come to witness the judgment of a killer but to celebrate her own freedom as a person, as a woman. Freedom from her husband.

Freedom D'Arc had made possible.

Summoning a strength she was little aware that she possessed, Jacintha looked directly at the cameras and through them to the galaxy. "Even if she is guilty of a crime, D'Arc has already been punished enough. However long it may be, the rest of her life will be determined by the injury she sustained through her attack on my husband.'' She paused. Silence. They were hanging on her every word. ''The decision to execute her is a moral travesty of justice. The petition should be presented to the Senate immediately and a request made for mercy in this case.'' Something leapt in her heart then, just opened like a flower and leapt into space, as if the words had been an anchor and saying them aloud had been the trigger to release herself from their grasp. ''The law is supposed to protect the innocent.'' She stared across the crowd, to Sheridan, the security men and women, Devereau, hanging on her every word, and then looked back to the camera. ''Protect innocence.'' The words became a chant. ''Protect innocence! Free D'Arc!'

The chant was taken up by the remnants of the people around her, quickly became a collective shout.

''*Protect innocence! Free D'Arc!*''

Jacintha stumbled then, her strength failing. Her back and legs ached, and she struggled to draw breath. She had to get out of here. Now. Get out and sit down, before she fell down.

The cameras panned to take in the chanting people, the wrecked courtroom, and Jacintha backed away into the crowd.

CHAPTER 10

As Franklin watched, D'Arc was brought into Medlab in restraints. Surrounding the alien were a group of security officers, Garibaldi at their head. About a dozen or so reporters and camera operators from various news channels accompanied the group, shooting vid footage and rattling off a barrage of questions to anyone who came within earshot. More guards kept the crowd of prolife protestors that had formed outside from pushing their way into Medlab.

D'Arc was awake, held upright by the guards. Franklin could see she was trying to get down onto all fours, perhaps because that configuration of her body was more comfortable—or comforting. Her spines rippled around her head; darting, agitated, frightened movements that mirrored her own very obvious emotional state.

Franklin told the guards to take D'Arc to the iso-lab. The alien was placed whining onto a medical gurney and wheeled away, followed by the camera-happy news crews and a new contingent of medical staff. As the group vanished into the heart of Medlab, Franklin felt his heart catch. D'Arc's whine was that of a battered animal, uncomprehending, afraid, in pain.

He turned as Sheridan pushed through the crowd and entered Medlab. Sheridan said nothing as he made his way over to Franklin. For his own part Franklin thought silence a good idea. Right now he was very much afraid that if he spoke at all, he would merely tell Sheridan exactly what he thought of the whole outrageous situation. He knew why Security had brought D'Arc here.

Followed by the press, they headed through the hospital facility toward the iso-lab. They passed by the room where Londo Mollari lay, pale, drawn, one step closer to death. Sheridan nodded toward the dying Ambassador. "No donors yet?"

Franklin just kept walking. "What do you think?"

Arriving in the iso-lab, Franklin confronted Sheridan. "You better be here to tell me you want me to try to alleviate D'Arc's suffering. Putting her on trial like that was outrageous."

Sheridan wasted no time on niceties. "Doctor, I'm sorry that the situation has come to this. We all know what we think of the situation. But the law is the law and must be upheld."

"At what cost?"

Sheridan sighed. "I don't have the luxury of being able to argue the case any longer. The sentence was quite specific. Unless it is overturned by the Senate after they have considered the petition, D'Arc is to be executed two hours from now by decompression. In light of her debilitated state and her potential violence I ask that she be sedated from now until the moment of execution."

Franklin felt a surge of anger rise up to choke him. "What

you're doing is immoral. A political expediency. You're a puppet for the very government you're invest—''

Sheridan glared at Franklin. So did the cameras. Franklin shut up then. It was useless. He had lost. So had the Tuchanq. So had D'Arc.

So had Sheridan for that matter. But that wasn't something that could be paraded before the press.

Franklin was aware that reporters were directing questions at him. He ignored them for as long as he could. Finally he shook his head. ''Garibaldi. I want them out. All of them. Now. This is a hospital not a circus.''

Garibaldi looked at Sheridan, who shook his head slightly. ''I had granted members of the press full access to all aspects of the execution—including the sedation.''

''Is that so?'' Franklin's voice was icy cold. ''Well, let me tell you something. The day you qualify for a medical residency is the day you can give orders about what does or doesn't happen in my damn hospital.''

There was a moment of quiet in which the only sound was a faint whine as D'Arc picked up on the emotions running high in the room. She began to shake, first trembling, then jerking hard against her restraints. Convulsions. She could be having a heart attack, a stroke, anything. And they wanted to kill her!

The cameras swung to cover the new movement. Questions still rattled around the iso-lab, a distant background mush of noise swamped by Franklin's anger—his *rage*.

A nurse brought him a sterile tray on which lay a loaded syringe. His anger and amazement increased again. ''Who ordered this?''

The nurse looked away.

''Nurse.'' Franklin's voice was like ice. ''I said who ordered this hypo prepared?''

The nurse shivered. ''Captain Sheridan asked me to—''

''That's enough! You're relieved. Captain Sheridan; this is my facility. You want something done you go through me. Is that clear?''

Garibaldi touched Franklin on the shoulder, seemed about to offer support or advice. Franklin shook off the hand.

Sheridan said, in a dangerously quiet voice, "Sentence will be carried out, Doctor."

Franklin grabbed the hypo and thrust it into Sheridan's hands. "Then why don't you do it yourself!"

The cameras swung again. Sheridan. Franklin. Back to Sheridan. He held up the hypo and stared at the liquid sloshing inside it.

The questions stopped.

After a moment Sheridan moved forward toward D'Arc. Her spines angled toward his and she began to tremble. Her whine rose to a series of meaningless barks.

The guards took hold of D'Arc, held her tightly so she couldn't move.

Sheridan placed the hypo against D'Arc's neck.

The cameras swung, focused, whirred.

With a cry of disgust, Franklin grabbed the hypo and pushed Sheridan aside. "Give me that." His voice was heavy with bitterness. "You'll inject into a muscle or put air in a vein. You wouldn't want D'Arc to die of an embolism before sentence was carried out, would you?"

Sheridan allowed himself to be pushed aside.

Franklin administered the injection, placed the hypo on a nearby tray. He stared at Sheridan, said as sarcastically as he could manage, "If there's anything else I can help you with I'll be in my office."

Franklin turned to leave the iso-lab but Sheridan stopped him with a gesture. "Thank you." His voice was an apologetic whisper.

Franklin uttered a short, humorless laugh. "Give my regards to your friend the President."

As Franklin left the iso-lab he was shaking with anger, his teeth grinding painfully. His vision was blurred and grainy. He needed sleep badly. *Very* badly.

Instead he slapped on another stim, tried to get himself ready for what was undoubtedly to be one of the worst days of his career.

CHAPTER 11

Garibaldi oversaw moving D'Arc into the corridor outside Medlab, then dropped back, allowing Allen to take over crowd control. He lounged against the wall, waited for the group to move away toward Blue Sector Plaza. The crowd moved past, following D'Arc, chanting, singing, in some cases, screaming.

Garibaldi watched the group until it vanished. Only then did he relax. But not for long. There was something else he had to do. Something vitally important.

He activated his link. "Control, Garibaldi. Can you give me a position on Jacintha Grond?"

The answer came back in a moment. Jacintha Grond was currently booking cargo space for her husband's cryotube in the liner *D'Alembert* due to depart for Mars in less than six hours. Garibaldi thanked Control and cut the link.

He turned, began to walk back to Medlab. As he walked, he couldn't help thinking of Londo, strapped into a cryo-unit in intensive care, dying by inches. How long before his brain shut down or his heart gave out? How long before the person Garibaldi had seen happy as a space-rat and high as a comsat became a two-meter chunk of meat with a funny haircut, cooling slowly in the morgue?

Garibaldi didn't bother with the obvious questions. Who had attacked Londo and why? They would be answered eventually. For the moment he could do nothing about them.

Anyway, he had something more important to do.

He reached Medlab, entered, moved slowly through the hospital complex, halted the first familiar face he saw. "Dr. Mendez. Could you help me, I'm looking for—"

He stopped. Out of the corner of his eye: a movement. Slow, relaxed. Someone walking casually out of the corridor which led to intensive care. A movement as out of place in Medlab as a cat in a spacesuit. He turned.

It was Morden.

The man saw Garibaldi, smiled, walked on, lost himself in the bustle of Medlab.

Garibaldi felt something cold grab the inside of his head and squeeze.

Londo.

At that moment a life-support sign flashed red above the entrance to IC.

Londo.

He ran for the ward, Mendez trailing him. He ran fast, dodging medics, nurses, patients, slapped a hand over the corridor access, waited impatiently as the hatch cycled, ran through, room after room, locked or empty, until there was only one left to check and that was Londo's and he was sure that—

Morden had come from Londo's room.

Garibaldi pushed open the door to Londo's room and dashed inside. Mendez followed quickly, took one look around, stuck her head back out into the corridor and bellowed, ''Charge Nurse! I need some help in here!''

Garibaldi found himself staring in amazement.

Londo Mollari was sitting up inside the deactivated cryotube, rubbing his eyes tiredly. He looked weak, shaken, but very much alive. Londo stared at him with rheumy, bloodshot eyes. ''Mr. Garibaldi, must you shout quite so loudly? I am a sick man, you know.'' As Garibaldi watched, Londo seemed to become fixated on the flat line of a now-deactivated brain activity monitor. ''Apparently, terminally sick.''

Medical staff came in then, stood stock-still in befuddled amazement, staring at their patient, one which until two minutes ago had been dying without hope of reprieve.

Londo returned their looks with a kind of hung-over dignity, said in a cracked and tired voice, ''If, as these instruments suggest, I am dead, there will be no harm in my having a drink, will there?''

Londo's feeble grin reminded Garibaldi of Morden's smile as he had left the isolation ward. He shivered, suddenly cold beyond the residual chill caused by the cryotube.

''What's going on here? Who brought this unit in here?'' Garibaldi turned at the sound of Mendez's voice. The doctor was staring at a trolley tucked away in the corner of the room. A trolley containing a familiar swirl of alien technology. A machine that had saved Garibaldi's own life less than a year before.

The *life giver*.

Mendez turned to face the medical staff surrounding and checking Londo. "This is supposed to be kept in the research lab. Who brought it here? Who authorized its use?"

There was no answer from the medical staff. Just a kind of muddled silence.

Garibaldi wasn't muddled. He didn't need an answer. He knew who had brought the machine here, who had used it to save Londo.

Morden.

Except that was impossible, of course. Because as Franklin had said, it would have taken life energy from a dozen people to save the dying Centauri.

Garibaldi shook his head slowly. Either the best medical practitioner in the quadrant was stone-cold wrong or—

Morden had saved Londo on his own.

And walked away smiling afterward.

The medical staff resumed work on Londo. They seemed, quite naturally, obsessed with the question: How had he been saved?

More important to Garibaldi was the question: *why*?

Garibaldi left the intensive care unit then, turned quietly and slipped away unnoticed by anyone. That was good. He still had work to do. Work which, although distasteful and somewhat immoral in its own right, was not half as frightening as the impossible resurrection he had apparently just witnessed.

CHAPTER 12

G'Kar entered his quarters. The dim red light, the steamy air, the heat: a tiny piece of home. Maybe the only piece of Homeworld he would ever see again.

His mind firm, G'Kar moved into the altar room, lit the candles, began to burn the ritual incense.

Shadows were coming fast now, he could feel them. Perhaps just moments away.

He unwrapped the dagger, laid it on the altar. It was covered in Londo Mollari's blood. He scraped drops of the blood into the incense burner. His fate and Mollari's. Joined forever.

He opened the Book of J'Quan, read from the appropriate passage; the rituals brought no comfort. He made them for the sake of form.

G'Kar opened his ceremonial robe, peeled the bandages painfully from his chest to reveal the healing wound there.

Placed the point of the dagger directly over his heart.

Father, forgive me for running from my responsibilities.

He gripped the dagger tightly.

Breathed the incense, felt it spark inside his head.

Father, forgive me for running from the future.

G'Kar felt the point of the dagger against his skin, focused on the pain, focused, breathed the incense.

Blood. Bruises. Contusions. Bitten lips. Staring eyes. Burst capillaries. Limbs contorted within metal retraints. Ruffs of blood at wrists and ankles, mouth and ears.

G'Kar's father slumped in death.

The past.

Blood. Bruises. Staring eyes. The insane laughter of Londo Mollari. Laughter and screaming shadows beckoning him to a terrible destiny.

The future.

Unable to bear the approaching darkness any longer, G'Kar

uttered an earsplitting howl and pushed the dagger harder against his chest. He felt the point pierce his skin, felt the warmth of a single drop of blood emerge from his skin, trickle from the blade, begin the long, slow fall to the distant floor.

The ritual incense was running his veins, coursing through his mind like a milky fire. He felt connected to the past, the future, saw himself as one link in the chain of history leading from his distant ancestors to his own children.

No. He had no children. Would have no children. There was no future and without a future the past had no meaning. He had no meaning.

Unless he remained alive to create the future he wanted.

The future his father, his family would have wanted. That his children would have wanted.

The future that Mollari would *not* want.

The drop of blood reached the floor, splashed in a silent concussion of sound.

G'Kar lowered the dagger from his chest.

He knew the truth then.

He was simply too afraid of the future to die.

G'Kar let out another moan then. He sagged to the floor, breathing deeply. After a while he rebandaged his chest. Then he stood, dressed in his finest robes of office. He sheathed and buckled on his ritual dagger.

He left his quarters. The time for fear was over. Now it was time for courage. G'Kar felt his back straighten and his weariness tumble away as he strode from his quarters.

I go to shape the future.

CHAPTER 13

He was gone. Brian was gone. This was ridiculous. No. It was outrageous, one more indignity to add to the insults she had already been subjected to.

Jacintha Grond left the chapel, reentered Medlab and grabbed hold of the most important-looking person she could see, a Charge Nurse wearing a name tag that read McCabe. "I want my husband. I have waited to take him home. Not through choice, mind you, but I have waited nonetheless. Now the trial is over and passage is booked and what do I find? Brian is gone. Missing. Not in the chapel, not in Medlab. So where is he? Answer me that!" She attempted to shake McCabe for emphasis.

McCabe broke free easily. "Mrs. Grond. I don't know where your husband's body is. It might be . . . being packed for shipping."

"And how do I find out?" Her voice was cold, angry.

"I'm afraid you'll have to ask at the admin desk."

"I've been there. They don't know."

"Then perhaps Dr. Franklin could—"

She scowled. "Oh yes. Of course. Dr. Franklin. I've only been trying to find him for an hour. Perhaps *you* know where he is?"

The nurse sighed. "As far as I know he's with Captain Sheridan. You know . . . the procession."

"The execution procession?"

"That's right."

"Well, where are they?"

"In the Park."

She found the procession in Green Seven by the simple expedient of following the crowd.

In truth Jacintha knew where D'Arc was long before she saw the first protestor, before she even left the monorail terminal and walked into the Park proper. It was the noise. It was incredible. It filled the Park. It echoed from the buildings, from the concrete abutments to the sun windows, from the walls of the Mosque. It seemed to shake the trees. It made her dizzy.

It was the voices of more than ten thousand people raised in protest, in anger, in outrage, in despair. It was a shout. An unending roar. It seemed to go on and on until her head swam with it. It battered at her, crashed around her as if she were huddled inside a lone habitat dome in the middle of a Martian sandstorm.

She moved out in the Park.

The noise swelled, broke over her like a wave.

She squinted in the daylight.

People lined the paths and filled the fields. Humans, Drazi, Centauri, Narn, Minbari, Cauralline, Xoth, Pak'ma'ra, Sh'lassa. There were hi-gravs and lo-gravs, mammals and reptiles, a scattering of aquatics in gleaming encounter suits. Some were sitting, some were standing, some running, some fighting. Security patrols coped gamely with the scattered violence.

There were placard wavers and passive protestors. There were prolifers and Home Guard. There were reporters waving cameras and audio recorders at anyone and anything that moved. The crowd wrapped around ten or fifteen degrees of arc, more people than she had ever seen in one place in her entire life. Somewhere in the middle of it all was the man who could tell her where her husband's body was.

There was no way she was going to find him.

She turned to leave, found herself facing a vid camera. Turned away to find herself in the middle of a screamed argument between a Home Guard and a prolifer. Turned back to find the reporter coming at her with a determined expression and a handheld microphone.

The crowd was everywhere.

There was nowhere to go.

The monorail terminal was fifty meters away; it might as well have been in a different star system.

The fight grew suddenly violent. Screams were lost in the roar of the crowd. Someone produced a knife. There was blood. Someone fell. Someone trod on them. A crack of broken bone. More blood. Lots more blood. It was madness. She had to get out, get out now before—

Someone banged her in the shoulder, knocked her sprawling into the mess of people. Her throat ached and she realized she was screaming. She couldn't hear herself above the crowd. She was hit on the head. Felt more punches. Blacked out for a moment. Realized she was no longer in the crowd. A Drazi female in security gray left her in the middle of a tiny patch of trampled grass and ran off without a word, shockstick drawn.

Jacintha tried to catch her breath. She had to get out. Get to her room. Get out of the crowd. She'd worry about Brian later. She could book passage on another—

As suddenly as *that* the voice of the crowd was stilled.

A concussive silence filled her ears.

She stopped trying to get to her feet, instead let herself fall back to the ground. It was solid. No one was going to yank that out from underneath her. She grabbed two handfuls of grass and held on for dear life. People shuffled around her. Miraculously, she wasn't trodden on.

Then more security guards came through the crowd, pushing people back. She felt herself lifted and pressed back into a wall of bodies. Her head spinning, she tried to draw breath; thick cloying air caught in her throat.

Hot bodies pressed against her.

But quiet. So quiet. She could hear the crowd breathe. A convulsive gulp of air, held, released with a collective sigh.

A sigh that formed a word. A name.

D'Arc.

And then into the hush came the clanking and clattering of caterpillar treads. A flatbed loader.

D'Arc.

She was here, right here, she was—

And the loader rumbled past, slow and near enough for Jacintha to reach out and touch it, close enough to smell the oil lubricating the treads and hear the rough scrape of badly maintained gears.

D'Arc was on the loader, shackled to an upright metal pole. The Tuchanq was on all fours, head down and whimpering. A contingent of security guards marched in close order around the loader. Sheridan, Franklin, Ivanova, and the other members of the Tuchanq delegation stood on a platform at the rear of the loader.

Reporters swarmed beside the loader. Cameras whirred, recorders hummed. Reporters screamed questions into the fragile silence.

Someone cried out, "Protect innocence! Free D'Arc!'

A harsh voice responded, "Burn, slag, burn!'

The sound of a punch was followed quickly by the explosive discharge of a PPG and a scream.

D'Arc threw back her head and howled, a heartrending scream that scraped at Jacintha's nerve endings, ripped into her mind, for a split second turned her inside out—and suddenly it was *her* on that loader and it was *her* being recorded and it was *her* being pelted with stale food and stones and questions, it was *her* being taken away to die it was *her* it was all happening to *her* and

the Tuchanq began to sing; their voices raised in a heartbreaking lament and

D'Arc howled, wrenched pitifully at her shackles and

the crowd roared again and she couldn't tell if it was outrage or approval and the sound smashed into her, pushed her back and hands grabbed her and pulled her and she was being crushed, mashed into a press of hot bodies, sweating bodies, howling, screaming, kicking bodies, and there were fists and screaming faces and staring eyes

and blood

and pain

and fear

and a joy more terrible than the fear

and there was *no air*

and she *couldn't breathe*

and there was a *camera in her face* and a *microphone*, and someone's elbow in her chest and someone else's foot crashing against her shin and it hurt, it hurt so much, and she couldn't stand up, in fact she was beginning to think it would be a lot simpler just to lie down, just to lie down and let it all wash over her, yes, just wash over her like water, like a river or lake to soothe away the pain, like the oceans she had never seen, just wash over her and carry her away to a distant, pain-free, quiet shore where there were no questions

or cameras

or punches

or blood

or Brian because they'd taken him away and she couldn't find him because someone had moved his body and what was she going to tell the children and why wasn't Brian here and where was he and *where's my husband what have you done with him why can't I take him home now you promised me I could take him home*!

Jacintha realized she was screaming the words aloud when a news camera swung to point at her.

Among ten thousand people it was the only thing to note her words.

CHAPTER 14

DeBora Devereau ducked to avoid a stone, swung her minicam to catch the spray of blood as the makeshift weapon cut into D'Arc's flank. The Tuchanq let out an earsplitting howl of pain, which rose to join the angry voice of the crowd.

The parade seemed to have been going on for hours—she made a quick check of the time and was surprised to find it had actually been less than thirty minutes since Sheridan had invited her onto the loader platform to record the procession.

Devereau felt the flatbed rock beneath her as Dr. Franklin moved forward to treat D'Arc's latest wound.

Keying the near-field mike, Devereau asked, "Dr. Franklin, I thought D'Arc was supposed to be sedated. Can you comment on the . . . humanity of this barbaric ritual'?'

Franklin didn't even turn his head from his work. "Can you comment on the humanity of *recording* this 'barbaric ritual'? "

Smartass. She was just doing her damn job. The people had a right to know what was happening here. The loader lurched again. The sound of the crowd was a cataclysmic roar. There were gunshots. Screams. Fights were breaking out all over Green Sector. The violence was escalating. Someone had sprayed *Burn Slag Burn*! over the baseball bleachers in ten-meter-high letters and set fire to the paint. Smoke billowed and flames licked hungrily at the bleachers; if the fire crews couldn't get through the crowd to extinguish the flames they were looking at serious potential damage and a definite strain on the Park life-support systems.

Devereau turned, determined to corner Sheridan. He was the voice of EarthGov here. His words were of paramount importance to the people. To the future.

"Captain Sheridan, could you comment on your choice of such a barbaric ritual to precede what can only be described as the most horrific form of execution that can be administered in this day and age?"

Sheridan turned away. Devereau caught a second or two of Ivanova's intense expression, zoomed in for a full close-up when it looked as if she might have something to say, then panned back to Sheridan when it became clear she didn't.

"Captain Sheridan, will you please answer the question?"

He swung to face her then, rage suffusing his face, but Ivanova stepped forward before he could say anything. "During the past year we've seen violence escalate throughout most of the major governments. The Narn-Centauri war is a prime example. Maybe if there *was* some kind of ultimate punishment, a deterrent, then life-threatening violence like that wouldn't happen." For a moment Ivanova looked as if she was going to say more—then stepped back instead, allowing Devereau to refocus on Sheridan.

"Captain Sheridan, you've heard in the words of your own station administrator how important it is to try to reduce violence in our society. A view that I'm sure you would not disagree with?"

"Well, no, of course not, but—"

"Could you then explain why such a huge gathering of people has been allowed here today? Tell me, Captain, aren't the public in danger from themselves here? Why not use anesthetic gas to disperse or subdue the crowd?"

Sheridan scowled. "Morph gas only works on certain human or very near-human metabolisms. If we gas the crowd, only about half the people would be rendered unconscious—and given the state of the violence here, I wouldn't rate their chances very high among those left awake.'' Sheridan anticipated her next question by adding, ''Any gas capable of anesthetizing the remaining rioters would kill those already unconscious. If we used gas, we'd just increase the casualty rate.''

Devereau wasn't about to let Sheridan go that easily. ''You haven't said why you allowed the crowd to gather in the first place.''

She could see Sheridan struggling to control his anger. ''There are a quarter million civilians on Babylon 5 and only seven hundred security guards. It's a simple equation. You work it out.''

Devereau ignored the anger in Sheridan's voice. There were a multitude of questions the people needed answers to. She was on the verge of framing the first when Sheridan's link bleeped. It bleeped for a long time before he heard it above the noise of the crowd.

''Sheridan.''

''Deitrich, C&C, Commander. I've got a Centauri heavy cruiser coming out of the jump gate. They are laying claim to the Narn freighter which the Tuchanq arrived in. They want to board her under the terms of the Narn surrender. The problem is, there's some contention as to who actually owns the freighter. The Tuchanq are claiming it is sovereign ground on behalf of their world. The Centauri haven't threatened violence, but they are awfully close to the station. It's a big ship, sir, with a lot of guns. And you know the Centauri.''

''I do. Tell the Centauri Commander I'll speak to him as soon as I can. Meanwhile . . . be ready. For anything.''

nuViel Roon leaned closer to Sheridan then. Devereau had to really stretch the near-field mike to catch her words. ''Captain, do not make any hasty or violent moves on our behalf. It is true that the Narn freighter technically belongs to the Centauri now. We will do nothing to compromise any help that may be offered to us . . . by either yourself or the Centauri.''

Devereau felt her heart race. Here was the real news. She flipped the camera around to shoot a CU of herself for CGI to map onto the riot footage in preproduction.

"You heard that conversation live from the heart of the procession to the execution chamber. If a stay of execution is not granted by EarthGov, it is in all likelihood a possibility that the Tuchanq will withdraw their request for help from Earth and represent it to the Centauri. It seems the situation here today may well have repercussions that will spread far beyond the Earth Alliance."

Devereau ignored Sheridan's angry glare at her listening in to his conversation, widened the angle to a 2-shot of herself and D'Arc, and reestablished her original line of commentary.

"With the procession here into its second hour and the violence showing no sign of abating, one is put in mind of nineteenth-century England and the march of the condemned from Newgate Prison to the gibbet at Tyburn. Although no actual footage of that time period exists, it is easy to imagine the parallels. The abuse, the thrown food and stones, the humilation, the pain and terror of the victim.

"Spectacle, ladies and gentlemen, that is the order of the day. And it seems the *spectacle* of D'Arc's execution is more important than the morality of her sentence, to EarthGov at least."

Devereau ducked again to avoid another thrown missile, tilted the minicam back up and tightened the shot to an ECU of D'Arc.

"I think I can safely say that the people here today want what is right and just, not what is merely the law. The feeling here must be that the judicial system itself is now on trial. And it will be guilty indeed if it does not grant a reprieve before the execution time set for just over an hour from now."

CHAPTER 15

G'Kar moved through the crowd, eventually drew near the rumbling procession. He faced the Tuchanq delegation, ensconced upon the rear of the loader, saw in them his future, in them and in the pitiful figure of D'Arc chained to the front of the loader.

Defying the human guards to stop him, G'Kar moved around the procession, through the crowd, and planted himself directly in the path of the slowly moving loader.

It was time.

He placed his hand on the hilt of his ceremonial dagger.

It was time to shape the future.

The loader rumbled to a halt. Security guards converged on him from all sides. He stood firm, hand on dagger. Let them come. The first moment of his destiny was upon him and *no one* could argue with that.

And they didn't. Something in his eyes, or his stance, held them at bay. Just for a moment. That was all—but it was all he needed.

Just a single moment.

His raised his voice in a cry and such was the force of it that it cut through the clamor of the crowd.

"nuViel Roon! I am G'Kar! Conqueror of Tuchanq! Destroyer of the Land and the People and the Songs!"

nuViel came forward, edged past D'Arc until she was standing at the front of the loader.

Cameras tracked her every movement. Others swung to cover G'Kar's.

G'Kar pulled out his dagger.

He raised it in a salute.

"I have come to ask forgiveness and make amends for my crimes!'

He fell to his knees. Placed the dagger on the ground, hilt toward nuViel. He hoped the implication would be clear enough.

It was.

She leapt to the ground, swung toward him, took the dagger from the ground, and in a second held it at his throat.

The crowd surged around them, still agitated, becoming more violent with each passing moment. Someone began to climb onto the loader, screaming obscenities and waving a Home Guard banner. A guard stunned him. Someone threw a stone at the guard. It bounced off her helmet, rocking her momentarily.

G'Kar felt the dagger against his neck, felt the moment lengthen toward the future, stretching out and beckoning it to come *here*, to *now*, to *this* moment.

And it came.

nuViel lowered the dagger.

When she spoke, she looked not at G'Kar but at Sheridan, staring helplessly from the loader. "On behalf of my people I accept your apology, G'Kar. I forgive your crimes. You are released from all obligation. Your Songs may continue."

G'Kar stood. For the first time in many months, he felt the edges of a smile touch his lips.

Too soon.

"*D'Arc is an animal! Let the animal die! She killed forty of our people! Forty Narn!*"

G'Kar swung, voice raised in hopeless protest.

Too late.

"*They killed J'Rod! They killed my brother in the Customs terminal and they hadn't even been here an hour!*"

So the deaths began. As they had always begun: with revenge.

He saw Narn in the crowd edging forward. Hundreds of them. Now they attacked, pushing through the guards and clambering onto the loader. Their target was the Tuchanq delegation.

nuViel turned to face him then, and he felt the accusation coming from her in hot waves. That and betrayal.

No! I didn't want this!

nuViel handed G'Kar his dagger. He took it numbly and turned to face the crowd. The violence. The hatred.

The future he had been unable to shape.

CHAPTER 16

Devereau had never seen anything like this. Oh, she'd seen riots before, on Mars or Europa. She'd seen bombings and the aftermath of accidents that had left people dismembered and dying.

None of that compared to the sheer hysterical, gut-wrenching frenzy that was happening here. It was almost religious in its ferocity.

The Narn were attacking the Tuchanq. The Tuchanq were fighting back.

The Centauri were attacking the Narn, attempting to defend the Tuchanq.

And then a Centauri staggered in front of the loader, carrying a limp bundle. He laid the bundle down directly in the loader's path, and she could see it was a body. The Centauri's voice rose above the crowd. "*Here is our brother! Our brother the Lord Askari! Killed by a Narn dagger! Murdered by a vicious coward! I say, kill the Narn!*"

And the violence stepped up another notch from the merely impossible to the almost inconceivable. Now Narn and Centauri fought viciously as the crowd surged against the loader, broke around it like a great sea of hatred.

Human against human, human against alien, alien against alien, Home Guard against prolifer, friend against friend—and all of them against the Earthforce security guards.

Devereau swung her minicam almost randomly across the crowd. Anywhere it stopped there was an example of insane violence.

She panned to a gang of humans screaming obscenities and smashing clenched fists into a group of aliens.

Zoomed in on a Drazi kicking a fallen human.

Refocused on a human ripping off a security guard's helmet and battering her face repeatedly with a stone.

Tilted as thrown projectiles smashed into the loader, tilted again as she was hit, lost her balance, toppled off the loader and into the crowd, struck out with the camera, saw a human fall and be trampled underfoot, turned again, and saw the SPNA cameraman being beaten to death with his own minicam, turned again and saw a guard shooting a Cauralline in the face, saw the guard buried under a swarm of mixed aliens, turned again and saw a Narn in ambassadorial robes being carried off by paramedics, turned again and saw Narn killing Tuchanq, killing Narn, killing Centauri, killing Narn, killing human, killing Drazi, killing human, killing Cauralline, killing Pak'ma'ra, killing Sh'lassa; killing each other, killing themselves in a blood-drenched fury of self-destruction. And at the center of it all the shackled figure of D'Arc, head jerked back, howling like a terrified child as fighters clambered onto the loader, all thought of action for or against D'Arc lost now in their fight to gain a meter of space in which to try to save their own lives.

Only when Sheridan gave the order and the first gas shells began to explode over the crowd did the violence show signs of abating. Humans, Centauri, and Cauralline succumbed within minutes. The Narn and Xoth rioters staggered. Some fell. Others, not affected so badly, continued to fight with ever slower and clumsier movements.

Devereau grabbed a breather mask from a supply that Franklin had ready for the Tuchanq to use and pulled it over her face. She aimed the minicam out over the crowd.

"Ten meters away I can see security guards dragging the dead Centauri to one side. Now the procession can move again, forging a path through the slowly ebbing violence toward a more sanitized, ritualistic violence. The death of D'Arc herself."

It was time for the execution.

CHAPTER 17

A short while later John Sheridan faced the huge circular air lock opening onto Cargo Bay Seven and wondered if he was about to become a murderer. In the eyes of those left injured or dying in Green Sector, he had little doubt what the judgment would be.

With Sheridan was a small group of people consisting of Delenn, Susan Ivanova, Stephen Franklin, and nuViel Roon. Various members of the press were also present with minicams and sound recorders.

And there was D'Arc, of course, still shackled to the loader.

The Tuchanq seemed drowsy as Franklin's medication finally ran its course through her system. She was curled around the upright pole to which she was shackled, whining gently and snuffling to herself. Unable to avoid thrown missiles, she had suffered many wounds in the riot, none of them life threatening, thankfully. Franklin was still tending her wounds. To Sheridan she was a wretched figure who deserved nothing but pity, not the excruciating death which it was his duty to administer.

At the moment Devereau and other members of the press were directing their cameras into the air lock, at the chair, which had been placed there to hold D'Arc while the lock was depressurized.

Devereau said, "You've seen the trial, you've witnessed the appalling violence that was the inevitable consequence of the verdict. Now . . . the execution chamber, empty except for a couple of tool lockers and the chair. This simple chair has been the icon of execution since the twentieth century. In just a moment we will see the defendant strapped into it while the air is removed from the chamber." She turned, brought the minicam out and aimed it at Sheridan. "But first let's meet the Executioner. Earthforce Captain John Sheridan, Commander of Babylon 5. Captain Sheridan, any final words before sentence—a sentance you determined—is carried out?"

Sheridan shook his head. "No." He hesitated. "Actually yes."

He paused again and then continued. "Death—this kind of death—it's an unreal thing. Oh, casualties of war or disease are one thing, certainly, but this . . . this is different. You have to convince yourself it's really happening. That you're really going to strap someone into that chair and deliberately and methodically . . . kill them." Another pause. Devereau waited patiently, camera whirring. Behind them, D'Arc snuffled uneasily as two security guards unshackled her and took her through into the air lock. "I think . . . no. That's it. That's all I really want to . . ." He shook his head. "That's all."

Devereau swung her minicam to catch the last straps being fastened around D'Arc. A hood was present, fixed loosely to the chair. It wouldn't fit the Tuchanq because of her ruff of spines.

The fixings secure, Sheridan ordered the air lock cleared and sealed.

The door clanked shut, sealed with a pneumatic hiss.

Sheridan realized that a circle of empty space had appeared as if by magic around the lock controls. Even Devereau seemed unwilling or unable to enter it.

Her voice was a whisper as he stepped forward. "Captain John Sheridan is now preparing to decompress the air lock. But first he has requested a moment's silence in respect of the being who will die here today."

Sheridan lowered his eyes. He began to say the Lord's Prayer.

Beside him nuViel Roon began to hum. A quiet, understated melody.

A moment passed.

Prayer over, Sheridan stepped forward. He reached for the lever, felt himself grabbed from behind, whirled. An angry face was thrust into his.

Franklin.

"You can't do this. It's immoral and you know it. At least wait for the Senate to respond to the petition."

Sheridan glared at Franklin.

Minicams whirred quietly.

Franklin turned away with a disgusted expression. He didn't have to move to be perfectly framed against the air lock. "You want some last thoughts? Here. Have mine. This is the twenty-

third century. We don't rape rapists. We don't burn arsonists. We
don't cut the hands off thieves. There are a lot of things we find
objectionable about the law.'' Franklin's jaw clenched. Was that
his teeth Sheridan could hear grinding? ''Not the least of which
is that someone with the mentality of a child can be executed, for
what amounts to no more than political expediency!''

Franklin fell silent.

The cameras whirred, turned abruptly to Sheridan.

''Captain, we've heard the moral viewpoint here. Some might
counter this by quoting your own administrator, Commander Ivanova, when she suggested not an hour ago that the imposition of
an ultimate punishment might deter criminals from committing
life-threatening violence. As Judge, jury, and Executioner in this
case, would you care to respond to the doctor's words? Something
simple for our viewers before the execution takes place. Captain
Sheridan, how do you view your own part in these proceedings
here today? And how do you think posterity will view your decisions and actions in, say, another hundred years?''

Sheridan made a disgusted noise, said nothing.

The cameras whirred, panned to catch Franklin as he stepped
away from the air lock's controls.

Wasting no more time, Sheridan entered his ID code. Hit the
decompress control.

Designed for cargo transfer, the lock cycled quickly.

A minute passed in silence.

Another.

From the lock systems a faint clanking of pressure hoses transferring load.

Another minute.

A stifled sound. A sob?

Devereau swung the minicam. ''Ambassador Delenn. Have you
any comment for Channel 57 viewers?''

Delenn made an odd expression, equal parts humility, disgust,
irony. ''Yes, I have a comment for you and your viewers.'' Delenn seemed on the point of tears, managed to hold them back
with an effort. ''This event has left in my mind an extraordinary
feeling of terror and shame. It seems to me I have been witness
to—and indeed, party to—an act of . . . of shameful violence per-

petrated by intelligent beings''—here she caught Sheridan's eye
and he had to look away—''against one of their fellows. No matter what anyone might say, violence will never prevent violence.''
Delenn fell silent. The camera whirred but she had nothing more
to say. Sheridan was grateful for that at least.

They waited ten more minutes in silence.

Sheridan recycled the lock.

He opened the door.

CHAPTER 18

Blood. Bruises. Contusions. Bitten lips. Staring eyes. Burst capillaries. Limbs contorted within metal restraints. Ruffs of blood
at wrists and ankles, mouth and ears.

D'Arc's body slumped in death.

The press recorded it all.

As they backed slowly from the lock, Sheridan's link bleeped.

''Sheridan. What is it?''

''Deitrich, C&C. We've got a Gold Channel Ultraviolet Priority
message from EarthGov here coded for your eyes only.''

Sheridan laughed, felt the Cyclopean eye of the press upon him
again. ''We'll take that message here, Lieutenant. I don't think it
matters who hears it now.''

Deitrich routed the message to Sheridan's link.

''Captain Sheridan? Senator Sho Lin. The Senate have received
your transmission containing the petition to free D'Arc. After
careful consideration it has been decided that a show of clemency
in this case would weaken Earth's position within the Alliance. I
am sure you understand it is not Earth's policy to make rules only
to have them changed again at the slightest excuse.''

''I understand, Senator.'' Sheridan was aware of a feeling of bitter irony as Sho Lin muttered some entirely inappropriate pleasantries and cut the link.

He became aware he was still being recorded.

He stared directly at the cameras. ''In the last few hours I had come to hope that my combat experience in the Earth/Minbari war would be sufficient preparation for the notion of execution. But . . . my God . . . there's nothing that can prepare you for this. Absolutely nothing.'' He sighed. He had to get out of here. There was a drink waiting in his office and he was long overdue for it. He pushed past the cameras, to the door to the access corridor, turned for the last time to face the open air lock and the blood-soaked corpse within.

''There *has* to be a better way to handle our worst problems.''

CHAPTER 19

Security continued to disperse the crowd with morph gas. Medics tended the wounded as they could, left the sleeping where they fell.

Two hours passed.

The riot left two hundred and fifty-seven wounded, more than a hundred seriously. There were fifty-three deaths, including one miscarried pregnancy.

The cameras recorded it all.

Faithfully. Emotionlessly.

For the people.

CHAPTER 20

Sheridan entered his office in a state of numb emotionlessness. He felt drained. Used. He sat at his desk, cradled his head in his hands. God what he wouldn't give for an orange. Just one orange. A tangerine even. And some decent sleep.

The communicator bleeped.

Gold level communication from Earthdome.

From the President.

Sheridan studied the face on the screen as the transmission decrypted. Was this the face of the Earth Alliance? On the surface everyone's friend, while inside . . . just a dark pit of hatred and paranoia?

Clark greeted Sheridan with a genuine enough smile. "Captain Sheridan. How good to speak to you face-to-face at last."

"Mr. President."

"Captain, I'll keep this brief. If the reports are anything to go by, you've got a lot of work to do."

Sheridan nodded.

"Well then, I'll just say this: I wanted to relay my congratulations to you on your performance during recent events."

Recent events? Someone's murder, you mean. "Thank you, Mr. President."

"No, Captain, thank you. Although we here at EarthGov were a little surprised at the . . . rawness of the footage, we feel that the execution itself was well handled and we would like to congratulate you on the matter."

Sheridan nodded. "The Senate is very generous."

Clark smiled. "I also wish to add my personal thanks for a job well done. As you can imagine, in my position I rarely get to meet the people to whom I am responsible, the citizens of the Alliance who have voted me into office. It is good to know that there are men such as yourself in Earthforce who share my feelings and my responsibility to both the people of Earth and to the future of the Alliance, and who can act as a conduit between myself and them when the need arises.''

Sheridan suddenly felt a savage bout of indigestion coming on. He licked his lips, managed to make his hesitation seem due to embarrassment rather than disgust at Clark's implication of similarity between them. ''Mr. President, there really is no need to heap such praise on a man who, after all, is simply doing his duty.''

''I know. But nonetheless you have my thanks. I will not forget this difficult time, Captain, you may be sure of that. Once again, I thank you.''

The transmission ended.

Sheridan sat at his desk. Steepled his fingers. Sighed. The old bastard. The sneaky, political old bastard. So he was supposed to consider himself the President's friend now, was he?

He wondered briefly whether he should feel amused or frightened.

Ah, the hell with it. Time enough for that another day. For now he wanted a shower. He wanted a drink. And he wanted to hit the sack for eight straight hours of dreamless sleep.

He also wanted very much to see Anna. Just once would be enough. She would know if he'd done the right thing. If winning the game had been worth the price of so many lives.

But Anna wasn't here.

And he didn't have the answers he so badly needed.

CHAPTER 21

Two hours later Susan Ivanova watched as nuViel Roon led her Chorus through the docking bay toward the shuttle that would take them out-station to the Centauri cruiser waiting beyond. nuViel looked drained. Her back was slumped; she didn't walk so much as *limp*, a clumsy, painful shuffle, somewhere between biped and quadruped. Her spines waved listlessly.

Fifty meters away the station hull curved beneath the Centauri shuttle, swinging upward until it slipped behind the roof. Cargo loaders gonged and clashed. Hose jockeys laughed and yelled instructions to each other.

The walk to the shuttle was by no means a short one, but despite repeated efforts, Ivanova could simply find nothing to say. The sight of D'Arc's dead body swollen and bloody within the cargo lock was inpressed on her mind as it surely must be upon nuViel's, stealing from her all possibility of conversation.

Swollen, bloody. An emblem of Terran justice. An icon of the future.

nuViel stopped then, turned to face Ivanova.

Ivanova hadn't thought until now how comforting the lack of eyes on a person could be.

Nearby an arc-welder flashed silver fire into the gloom. nuViel was momentarily transformed into a white-outlined silhouette, a shadow of her former self, with no depth or substance.

The moment passed, the flash faded. nuViel became real again.

Ivanova said, "You don't have to do this. The Centauri . . . well . . . you have to get to know them . . . I think—"

"Susan," nuViel's voice was soft, a whisper that barely carried above the clank and grind of cargo loaders. "You think we are wrong to accept the Republic's offer of help. How can it be wrong to accept that which saves the Land and the Song?"

Ivanova wriggled on that one. "It's not as simple as that."

"Things are never simple with humans. D'Arc learned this and now so too have I. Your Songs are complex, many-layered. But I have found the best Songs are always the simple ones."

Ivanova tried to find some words of comfort, something that would let her get a hold on nuViel, pull her back from the edge of what she felt sure in her gut was going to be a cataclysmic mistake.

There were no words, of course. How could there be? The Tuchanq had come here to beg assistance. Instead a tragedy had played itself out in the corridors of Babylon 5.

"nuViel . . . it's not too late to reverse your decision."

"I know."

"Captain Sheridan did the best he could to help."

"I know."

Ivanova sighed. "Then . . . all I can do is wish you luck. May your Songs remain strong."

nuViel tipped her head in acknowledgment of Ivanova's words. "I would be very happy if they would simply *remain*."

And with that she turned and, continuing the Song of Journey, led her Chorus toward the shuttle.

CHAPTER 22

The door to Sheridan's office bleeped.

He sighed, put down the photograph of Anna. "Come in."

Franklin. And Garibaldi. Had they spoken yet?

The medic's furious expression told him instantly they had not. "Captain, I have come here to lodge a formal protest about the way in which this entire case was handled. D'Arc's execution is a travesty of justice, both immoral and insupportable. Now I have something here in writing which I'd like you to see before I transmit it to Earthdome . . . '' Franklin stopped.

Beside him, Garibaldi was shaking his head and clucking his tongue.

"What?" Franklin demanded. "You agree with all this, I suppose?"

"I really don't think you want to be sending that report, Doc." Garibaldi said with a little grin.

"Oh really? Then I guess you support EarthGov in this matter? Or perhaps you're just 'remaining neutral,'—I certainly didn't see you at the execution, now did I?"

Garibaldi rubbed his eye sheepishly. "That's because I was busy switching D'Arc for Brian Grond's body and reprogram-

ming the Changeling Net taken from the lurker who attacked
G'Kar, so it looked to the cameras as if D'Arc was the one who
had been executed.''

Franklin blinked. "What?" He frowned. "Are you telling me
D'Arc's not dead?"

Sheridan stood up. "Doctor, I must apologize for the deception."

"Deception?" Franklin's expression seemed composed of
equal measures of stupefaction and anger. "Why didn't you tell
me? Needed a genuine reaction for the news team, did we? Well,
I gave you that, didn't I?"

"You weren't the only one." Sheridan sighed. "Garibaldi and
I were simply worried that if too many people knew about the
switch then it would leak to the press and the whole thing would
be ruined. I really am sorry. I should have confided in you, but
there simply wasn't an opportunity. I'm sorry."

Franklin was silent for a moment. Sheridan could almost hear
his teeth grinding in frustration and annoyance. "So in other
words the riot, the deaths, all that was simply to maintain the
deception?"

Sheridan lowered his eyes, unable to meet Franklin's gaze.
What price justice indeed?

There was a long silence. Then Franklin spoke again. "So let
me get this straight. If D'Arc isn't dead, then where is she?"

Garibaldi said quietly, "While the Captain here was reading
the Lord's Prayer I put her in a spacesuit, took her on a little
spacewalk around to maintenance lock fifteen. She's with the
other Tuchanq now, safely aboard the Centauri cruiser that's taking them home." Garibaldi glanced sideways at Sheridan. "By
the way, about the prayer. You could have read it a little slower,
stuck in an extra verse, something. You've no idea how fine I cut
it, getting out of that tool locker and suiting her up before the
lock decompressed."

Franklin interrupted. "Wait a minute. The Centauri are taking
the Tuchanq delegation home? I thought *we* were going to—"

"No." Sheridan pursed his lips. "It's true we saved D'Arc's
life, but the Tuchanq delegation were so distressed by the whole
matter that they decided they'd rather ask for help from the Cen-

tauri. Apparently they have the virtue of being 'more straightforward' than we humans."

Franklin's face fell. "I see." It was obvious he understood the ramifications of the Centauri offer of help. "And there's nothing we can do to change their minds?"

"Believe me I've tried, Ivanova's tried . . . they've made their decision." Sheridan shook his head. "The only thing even vaguely comforting about this whole affair is the knowledge that Clark was only doing this to gain votes. When the voters see the news footage, the parade, the riot, the violence, the sheer immorality of executing someone as . . . *innocent* as D'Arc was . . . well, they won't exactly be lining up at the polling stations to renew their support for him."

Franklin gave a humorless laugh. "Bearing in mind those injured or killed in the riot, I wonder which of you was actually the more immoral and manipulative."

Garibaldi said firmly, "Fortunately that's a question we'll never have to answer."

"Well." Franklin hefted his written report, folded it, tucked it into his pocket. "I guess we've all got work to do." He turned and left the office. leaving Garibaldi and Sheridan staring at each other across a mountain of paperwork.

"Michael . . . thank you."

"All in a day's work." Garibaldi fished something out of his pocket and flipped it to Sheridan. "Souvenir." He followed Franklin from the office.

Sheridan looked at the object nestling in his hand. Brian Grond's data crystal, the recording of his liaison with Belladonna. His moment of fulfillment.

Sheridan stared at the crystal, trying to imagine the scenes depicted in its record. Trying to imagine the life that had ended, the aftermath of that life. Jacintha Grond would be leaving in a few hours to take her husband's body back home and bury it. Perhaps the crystal ought to be buried as well.

Yes. Sheridan tipped the crystal into the recycler chute and went back to his desk. He was beginning to get a headache. And his indigestion was acting up something awful.

CHAPTER 23

The starliner *D'Alembert* emerged from the slowly rotating bulk of Babylon 5 and moved toward the jump gate.

From the second-class lounge, Jacintha Grond watched a screen showing the receding station and tried to work out how she felt about the events which had occurred there. Impossible. She was still too confused. All she could really say for sure was that her life had changed. Maybe for the better, maybe not. But it had definitely changed.

For the last six years, Jacintha had known nothing but a life of certainty. The certainty that her husband provided, imposed upon her. That she let him impose upon her. Now that certainty was gone. And yet instead of the insecurity which she might have expected to find within herself, she was surprised by an unlooked-for set of more positive feelings. A sense of freedom. Of pleasure. Of anticipation of all the things she had yet to experience—things she knew she would have experienced anyway but which somehow seemed to have a fresh sparkle to them, a keener edge.

But beyond all this, the most important thing she felt now that she was leaving Babylon 5 was a slowly building confidence in the future.

Her future, and that of her children.

At that moment, the jump gate sequence activated, obscuring the station and replacing it with silence and murky amber darkness.

In that moment, she realized the simple truth: The only certainty in her life now was uncertainty. The only constant, change.

She smiled. A tiny movement of the facial muscles of a single human woman among hundreds in a starship the universe might easily have overlooked in its vastness.

No movement is ever unimportant; no person either.

Jacintha Grond was taking her husband home.

The first step in a life that was now truly her own.

CHAPTER 24

When Garibaldi arrived at Medlab there was a party going on and Londo Mollari was right at the middle of it. The Centauri Ambassador was sitting up in bed surrounded by Vir, Lord Refa, several aides, two Centauri nurses, several bouquets of flowers, and rather more than several bottles of wine—most of them empty.

Mollari was laughing, sharing a joke with one of Refa's aides. The other aides were fawning. The nurses were plumping his pillows and giggling at the humorous nonsense he was spouting.

Garibaldi found the whole scene somewhat disturbing. Mollari should be dead. He should be *dead*.

Then again so should Garibaldi.

Under different circumstances, Garibaldi would have grinned his butt off. But things were different now. Now the whole idea that a guy whom he had once considered a friend was not going to die after all held overtones he really didn't want to think about too closely. No way. It was just too creepy.

That guy Morden now. What the hell was he on? How had he done what it was he must have done to save Mollari? For Jack's sake, he'd seen the damn wounds Mollari had suffered. Three of them, one at least puncturing vital organs. There was no doubt about it: Mollari had been heading for the morgue—big-time. It should have taken all of Morden's life energy to save Mollari— but not only was the guy still alive, he was still *smiling*.

So what gave?

Garibaldi's thoughts were interrupted as Mollari caught sight of him. ''Mr. Garibaldi!'' He waved a bottle of wine to attract Garibaldi's attention—in the process slopping some of it over the uniform of the nearest aide. ''My good and dear friend Garibaldi! You have stopped by to wish me well, have you not? Come over here! I don't believe you have met my friend Lord Refa.''

Garibaldi nodded and smiled uneasily. Hands thrust in pockets, he wandered casually over to Mollari. "Yeah. Hi. How's it going, Londo?"

Mollari beamed expansively. "Oh very well, Mr. Garibaldi. Very well indeed, under the circumstances." He shrugged. "Oh, I could have wished for more flowers—but then there is a limit. After all we do live in a space station, do we not?" He dug the nearest person in the ribs—it happened to be Vir. The aides and the nurses laughed but Garibaldi noticed that Vir's smile seemed forced. Refa maintained a cool air of aloofness.

He shrugged. "That we do, Londo."

Mollari allowed his expansive beam to melt seamlessly into a drunken grin. "Have you brought me a get-well present, Mr. Garibaldi?"

Garibaldi raised his eyebrows. "Sorry."

Mollari shrugged, glanced cheekily at the nurses. "No matter. I have all that I need here. Wine, flowers, my friends"—Garibaldi counted seven people at the most—"and of course, my good friend Mr. Garibaldi! What more could a man want, eh?"

Garibaldi didn't know what to say. Mollari was either five quarters drunk or so high on some drug you could hang a comsat from his hairdo. Maybe it was just the idea of being alive that did it for him. That wouldn't be too surprising. "Look, ah, Londo . . .I just dropped by to say . . . " Why was Refa *staring* at him like that? "Well, just to say get well soon, I guess." He shrugged. "Look, I gotta go. Catch ya on the flipside."

"Wait! Mr. Garibaldi, wait!" Mollari took a deep slug of wine from the bottle. "Lord Refa was just inviting me to a celebration when I'm better. You're my friend. Why don't you come as well?"

Garibaldi glanced quickly at Refa. The Centauri official did not look as if he was in the mood to party.

"I really don't think that would be advisable under the circumstances." Refa's voice was quiet. Garibaldi could tell he was hiding something. Impatience? Irritation? Annoyance?

"Nonsense!" Londo waved the wine bottle around some more to emphasize the importance of his words. "Mr. Garibaldi is my good and dear friend! Of course he will come. The planet in question is—"

Garibaldi managed a smile. "Look, Londo, I really gotta go. Um . . . about the party . . . why don't you see me about it later? When you're up and about?"

"'Up and about'?" Mollari drained his bottle. "Why, how could I be more 'up and about' than I already—" He stopped. His face twisted into a kind of surprised frown. "Than I already . . ." His eyes rolled upward and he crashed drunkenly back onto the bed, to the accompaniment of another round of laughter from everyone except Vir and Refa.

Garibaldi shook his head, nodded to Vir, and turned to leave. Franklin was waiting at the entrance to Medlab.

Garibaldi jerked a thumb back over his shoulder at the Centauri. "Ever felt like you should have gone into the entertainment business?"

Franklin pursed his lips. "Tell me about it. I leave Medlab for a couple of hours and come back to find a patient who was dying demanding to know what was for dinner and why it wasn't Oolian Bloodworm and why it wasn't brought on time—and by a pretty nurse at that."

Garibaldi raised his eyebrows in sympathy. He felt Franklin's eyes on him. "What?"

Franklin pinched the bridge of his nose thoughtfully. "Why did you come here, Garibaldi?"

Garibaldi frowned. *Good question.* He rubbed his chin. *The truth is, I'm feeling something I haven't felt for a while. I'm feeling scared. Londo is Londo, and I'm me. We're total opposites. But Morden saved us both. And that thought scares me to death.*

"Would you believe heartburn?"

Franklin shook his head. "No way."

Garibaldi shrugged, a little *Sorry I can't help you* gesture. "Ah well."

Before Franklin could say anything else Garibaldi left Medlab. He walked fast. Because the truth was somewhere back there. And the truth was that Morden thought he and Londo were both worth saving. In his mind they were the same. And Garibaldi had enough smarts to realize pursuing that line of thought would drop him so far back into the bottle they'd need a submarine to find him.

CHAPTER 25

John Sheridan placed one hand against the window of his office. His fingers, so tiny by comparison with the real size of the objects in view, were able to blot out vast tracts of the landscape beyond. A twitch of his ring finger and the Mosque was obliterated. A movement of his thumb and and the park surrounding the sports fields vanished.

Perspective. Sometimes it's so hard just to keep things in perspective.

D'Arc. The Tuchanq. They'd lost it all—he'd lost it all for them. By carrying out the masquerade, by doing the moral thing, the right thing and saving D'Arc, he had made a very different future for her species.

He was damn sure it wasn't the best future he could have offered them.

And he hated that thought. Hated and feared his own weakness, what he had learned about himself. That no one was perfect. That everyone got scared and did things they weren't proud of. That there were no-win scenarios and in those scenarios, quite simply, you *lost*.

He rested his forehead on the windowpane.

Perspective.

The door bleeped.

"Come in."

He turned as Kosh entered the room. The encounter suit glimmered softly. A quiet musical hum seem to emanate from within it. Kosh glided around until he was standing in front of Sheridan's desk. He waited.

Sheridan felt simultaneously drawn to the encounter suit and repelled by it. He very much wanted to touch it, whatever life was within it—but somehow felt he was already touching it—or it him.

Kosh said nothing. Quite obviously he was waiting for Sheridan to speak first. Sheridan blew out his cheeks and half shrugged. He looked questioningly at the Vorlon.

Kosh said nothing. He remained still, reflecting all Sheridan's curiousity, frustration, anger back at him like a mirror.

Like a *mirror*.

Fear is a mirror.

And suddenly it made sense. The whole lot. Look at it from Kosh's point of view. From a Vorlon's *perspective*.

Sheridan nodded, smiled, felt tension drain out of him. "Fear is a mirror. You said that to me the day before yesterday."

Kosh said nothing.

It didn't matter. He *knew*. "I understand now. Because I was scared I became devious. I took advantage of people and events to accomplish my own ends. I didn't like the behavior in the President and I don't like it in myself." Sheridan paused. Sometimes the truth was hard to acknowledge. "My fear has enabled me to understand myself a little more clearly."

Kosh said nothing.

"That was what you wanted, wasn't it? That was the lesson. *Fear is a mirror*."

Kosh spoke then, made no acknowledgment of Sheridan's supposition, instead said something that brought all the fear and anger boiling back up to the surface as if to an open wound.

"You are the light, yet the hope of all darkness."

Sheridan felt something tear loose inside him, felt it carried away on a wind of madness. "I don't . . . " He nearly laughed, it was such a familiar line. "I don't understand."

"You are touched by Shadows."

Without waiting for a response, Kosh turned and glided from the office. Sheridan watched him go, then turned back to the window. He saw his own reflection mapped onto the landscape.

Touched by Shadows?

What the hell does that mean?

Do I really look that old?

And he knew then what he had only guessed at before. His life was not his own anymore. His destiny was not his own. His career, his friends, the station, Anna, everything and everyone he had ever known was as predestined as if he were a character in a novel.

Sheridan stared out of his window at the trees and fields and grass and flowers and worms. And he wondered for how much longer they would exist. If the saplings would grow into trees, if the fields would know the touch of lovers and the lovers know the cries of children.

He wondered if everything he had ever taken for granted was coming to an end. If the thousands of years during which mankind had wrenched itself out of the mud and leapt into the heavens would ever, ultimately, have any meaning beyond the simple drive of life to exist and continue at any cost.

Good questions to which he would probably never have answers.

In that moment of ruthless self-honesty John Sheridan, Earthforce Captain, husband to Anna, brother to Elizabeth, son to Jacob and Miranda, knew his life would end as it had begun: with awe and wonder, pain and terror.

And Shadows.

Always with Shadows.

Epilogue

Truth

Legal scholars will be debating all year whether the Senate did or did not today flatly and irrevocably rule to end Capital Punishment. The answer for all practical purposes seems to be it did. Confusion occurs because two of the five-man majority said that the state can never take a life. The key votes were those of Senators Sho Lin and Voudreau, both of whom indicated they might reverse their decision if anyone could ever show them a case where the Death Penalty can be morally justified.

—DeBora Devereau, Channel 57 News,
evening edition. December 20th, 2259.

What do you mean EarthGov are subpoenaing the B5 footage? They can't do that. It's a breach of the public information act! Dammit, the public have a right to know what their President is up to in his spare time, cooking up one law for humans and one for the aliens. It's racism I tell you, plain and simple! They've only voted against the Death Penalty now to cover up the scandal.

—DeBora Devereau, Channel 57 News.
Ten minutes prior to the evening edition.
December 20th, 2259.

Morgan Eugene Clark looked out from the Senate Chamber across the city once known as Geneva. The setting sun cast the city in gold and pale bronze. Shafts of light slipped across the mountains, through the atmosphere shield, through the window. He saw dust glimmer in the beams that shot through the Senate chamber.

From dust we are born, to dust we return.

And when we are gone, what then? Do we simply vanish? Our souls, our experiences, everything that we are, gone along with our bodies? Or do we leave something of ourselves behind? A legacy. Words and actions the future may judge us by? Words and actions such as his own this afternoon, following the vote of confidence in which he had been called back into office by a narrow margin.

Dust in sunlight. It's all we ever are.

Refusing, though he could not say why, to watch the sun slip beyond the distant hills, Clark turned his back on the light. He watched as the beams of sunlight glided slowly across the chamber, illuminating, just as the decorators had intended, one Presidential portrait after another until it reached the end of the line, the spaces which awaited his own visage and those of Presidents who would follow him into office.

He moved; for an instant saw his shadow cast directly into the wall space where his own portrait would one day hang.

Dust in sunlight. Discernible only by our shadows.

And Clark knew then a truth both awesome and terrible: that his words and actions of today would shape the lives of millions; that not only would he be *remembered* by the future, he would *define* it.

Life, death, the fundamental condition of existence.

The shadow of his actions would touch it all.

To wound the Land is to wound yourself, and if others wound the Land they are wounding you. Those that heal the Land heal themselves, and if others heal the Land they become brothers. People of Tuchanq: the Narn wounded your Land. We, the Centauri, have come to heal it. We are your brothers.

—Centauri Emperor Narleeth Jarn in a
public speech immediately prior to
the "Greening of Tuchanq" program carried
out by Republic Navy terraformers.
December 22nd, 2259.

What people forget when they think of the Centauri as aggressors is the role of the carnivore in shaping our character and heritage.

—Centauri Emperor Narleeth Jarn
in a personal aside to Ambassador Londo Mollari
during the "Greening of Tuchanq" program.
December 22nd, 2259. *(Attr.)*

The Song of Freedom lifted above the Capital City of Ellaenn.

nuViel Roon galloped up the hill overlooking the city and stopped at the very top. She stood very still, then crouched onto all fours. She began to sing. She sang her Journey and her Being and that of the People. She sang life and death. She sang D'Arc, alone now with the Centauri, transferred to another ship on the way home, at the request of a human named Morden, for her own protection.

"After all," he'd said, "She is a murderer. We wouldn't want her to get hurt after everything Captain Sheridan did to save her."

nuViel sang D'Arc until her throat ached, and then joined in with the last refrain of her own Song of Freedom.

When at last the Song was ended, nuViel straightened, tasted the air with mixed feelings. The air was sick. The Centauri made it sick with their machinery, their very presence. But that machinery, their presence, was healing the Land. And that was good, wasn't it?

The question was replaced by another: Was the good that came of evil intrinsically good, or would it eventually sour and turn to evil itself?

nuViel knew that the ability to judge these matters came with age. Her Song of Being was old, but it had never encompassed this kind of dilemma. Her job had been simple: to ensure that the Land was healed. That job had been accomplished. Songs would be sung of her now; it was because of her that Songs could be sung at all.

But somewhere deep in her heart nuViel knew fear: the Song of Freedom had begun again, but it was no longer the Song of Tuchanq. It was the Song of the Centauri.

No. Even that was wrong: because the Centauri were the mouthpiece for a greater power, invisible except for the shadows they cast over those whom they touched.

nuViel Roon tasted fear and sickness in the air and suddenly, instinctively, she *knew* the truth that was to define the People and the Land, far into the future.

The Song of Tuchanq had become the Song of the Shadows.

Twelve hundred years ago Western man was paralyzed by the same set of fears being put about by bigots who pass for statesmen. The phrase "Mundus senescit, the world grows old," reflected a dire intellectual pessimism as well as a "religious" conviction that the world was a living body which, having passed the peak of its maturity, was doomed, suddenly, to die.

Henri Focillon's *L'An mil* quoted by
Bruce Chatwin in *The Songlines*. 1st pub:
Jonathan Cape Ltd., 1987. 21st ed. pub:
Pan Information Services, Datanet. 2201.

They came out of the gulf beyond the rim like ghosts: huge ships, more art than technology. By comparison the Wells Fargo jump gate–layer *Eratosthenes* was little more than a clutch of battered tin boxes bolted rather haphazardly around a less than optimal frame.

Earthforce Captain Johannes Varese had only seconds to register the presence of the aliens. It was more than enough. The alien ships were one-hundred-percent efficient. They were also utterly terrifying.

Because they *screamed*.

They screamed in his head.

They screamed as they attacked.

A knife edge of light; *Eratosthenes* shivered and fell apart at the midsection. The knives moved on, carving, almost casual. Metal vaporized, cabins depressurized, crew and passengers screamed and died, engines began a slow detonation.

Varese thumped a fist down onto the log recorder control, screamed aloud the truth that was to define the coming war in which the number of deaths would simply be too great to calculate.

"Mayday! Jump gate–layer *Eratosthenes* on rim survey Sector 913! We're under attack! Ships I've never seen before! We're under attack—and *they fired first!*"

Johannes Varese was never to know if his log recorder would be recovered. In the last seconds of his life, as the control deck opened to the vacuum of space and pain, and silence settled over his mind, a vagrant memory came back to him: a peculiar sense of déjà vu.

I've said that bef—

He never finished the thought. Everything he was, everything he had ever been or could ever be, emptied into the dark gulf between galaxies along with the rest of his ship and crew, was ultimately reduced to its component molecules and scattered throughout the void.

It was Christmas Eve, 2259: the dawn of the Third Age of Mankind.

The Shadows were coming.

Acknowledgments

Normally I write a little something here to personalize the whole experience for anyone that has the mixed fortune to know me . . . but it's eight-thirty Saturday morning and I just finished the damn book and I'm three weeks late on delivery and I gotta go three miles to print it, then three miles to post it, and then I gotta go a mile to talk to a bunch of small furry mammals about building a recording studio and then I gotta go another two miles to the music shop to check out some gear and . . . well, basically I'm just too knackered. Sorry.

Before I do set out upon the above odyssey there are some people I gotta tip my hat to.

Paul Hinder is one. The man is an absolute *engine* of damage limitation skill. (Listen you can hear the gears clanking—judging by the blue shift he's currently approaching Epsilon Eridani at two thirds C.) He told me the book was finished before I actually realized it was. And he was right too.

Robert Kirby is another. He's the geezer who utilized lashings and lashings of legendary legerdemain to sell the thing in the first place. So if anyone out there wants to know if it's worth turning a five-page synopsis into an eighty-K-word novel with no intermediary steps in seven weeks—Rob's yer man.

Andrew Dymond is yet another. I can't tell you what he did but it was as sound as a pound (and in these days of rapidly spiraling financial pigheadedness that's saying something.) Apparently I am allowed to say "Hi!" to Elisabeth, though. "Hi! Liz! Sorry we missed the flicks, but what the hell, you'd have been too busy groping yer bloke to chat anyway, right? And quite rightly so in my opinion."

Allan Adams is a fourth. Together with his mate Alan Robbins, Allan supplied me with more skanking background info about B5 from the Net than anyone could have a right to scoop. (And he makes damn fine music to boot.) Bottom line: This book couldn't have been written without Allan.

Rod Summers is a fourth. He too supplied bodacious amounts of neatly packaged infodump—together with a most excellent canal boating trip which I had to miss because of all the bodacious infodump.

Jeanne Cavelos is a fourth too. She put the icing on the cake (so if you like edible novels, she's your editor.)

Kurt Farmer is yet another fourth. Kurt is a diamond geezer. Kurt maintains airplanes and cleans kitchens and gets guilty cycling downhill. The man is GOD. His contribution to this novel was keeping my kitchen free of botulism while I wrote it. (Hey, look, I don't love ya or anything, baby. *I JUST WANT YER BODY!*) (Hey—private joke, so all you homophobes out there can just get a commonsense enema, okay?)

Before I naff off to the printers, I just gotta mention the following peeps: Mum and Dad, Jo and Andrea, Jo and Steve, all the various members of me family; Jo, Lizzie, and Lynne; Jon and Alison (congratulations); the furry mammals: Huw, Nacula, Martin, Martin, Ollie, Esther, Michelle, Mel; Sara and Simon, Andy and Helen, Lee, Alan and Alis, Thomas and Gizmo, Joe and Jacob for approving the storyline, Kathy for negotiating the contract, Nige and Debs, Sue, Sam and Benjamin and Dandu (Watch out fer them thar bicycles, Danny boy—the average Raleigh Sport ain't built ter withstand a direct hit from yer frontal lobes!).

Last but not last, I have to own up to the source material I used during the writing of this novel: The piping-hot Channel Four Lethal Justice season, including: *When the State Kills, Fourteen Days in May*, and *Let Him Have It* enabled me to balance out the moral issues. Bruce Chatwin's *The Songlines* provided a useful stomping ground for the Tuchanq. *Lord of the Rings* (a prize for anyone who can find the one, and only one, reference) just because it's a damn fine book to get moody with.

PS

I used to write on an Amstrad PCW 8256. One disk drive. Basic software. I wrote five novels on that and then decided to upgrade. This novel was the second written on an Amstrad PCW 8512 (yahoo!!! TWO disk drives!!) which I bought off my friend Jo Ensum whom I love dearly and miss beyond words for the price of six months' road tax. So who needs PCs anyway?

Sheesh, is that the time? Gonna miss the post!
Catch you on the flip side!
Jimbo